Brother Rabbit

The Road to Constantinople

Book I in the Chronicle of the First Crusade

Brenna Pearce

Brother Rabbit: The Road to Constantinople
by Brenna Pearce

Library and Archives Canada Cataloguing in Publication Pearce,
Brenna, 1959–

Brother Rabbit: the road to Constantinople
by Brenna Pearce.

ISBN: 0-9810701-1-6
ISBN-13: 9780981070117

I. Title. II. Title: Road to Constantinople.
PS8631.E23B76 2008a C813'.6 C2008-905535-7

Important Disclaimer:
This is a work of fiction. Any resemblance to any persons, either
living or dead, is purely coincidental.

Expositio

My name shall be Frater Cuniculus. That means only 'Brother Rabbit' in our tongue, of course. It is not my true name but rather a nickname in the Roman language used by all learned men, given to me by a great Italian lord many years ago. I believe he meant the naming in an affectionate way but it caused me embarrassment and inconvenience on many occasions during our diverse adventures together.

I am an old man now but in those days of my youth I was naive and perhaps simple in the ways of the world; far too trusting and gullible I would even say. Now, I prepare my own way to Heaven to be with our Saviour, and, as the time approaches to leave this world and enter that on the far side of the river of life, I find that before I cross the final bridge I would like to leave something of myself behind. I have no heirs since I have faithfully served the Lord most of my life. Unlike many servants of the Church, in grave error and to the imperilment of their souls, I took neither wife nor concubine; though once I did love a woman, more, I thought, than my God.

I must confess to you now that some of the following passages I write from my memories of those days. I had not yet developed the habit of dutifully recording events as I lived them. For the most part, I did not diligently begin this practice until I became the guest of King Coloman of Hungary before ever I met my lord. However, that is another tale to which I will come in time.

For the rest, I shall try to be true to those days and not exaggerate or embellish details that are contrary to fact. However, memory is faulty at times. Please forgive an old man his errors if the facts set down do not coincide with what you have heard from others or have read elsewhere about the events. I mean no disrespect to any authority on the subjects or to any other person in my interpretation and recounting of the Deeds of those former times.

As I mentioned, in my youth I met a gallant cnicht, a great man of Italia, a Southern Norman, with whom I shared many wonderful days and wondrous deeds. At his request I kept a chronicle of his exploits and those of others while I travelled with him and even when we were separated, as happened on numerous occasions, I noted all that occurred around me and made mention of his own acts whenever he or others had occasion to bring them to my attention. That chronicle I kept in the lingua litterati, Latin. Now I have decided to translate that journal into our own tongue that you might read it and learn from it and perhaps, just a little, enjoy the stories of events long past in a country far away across the sea. That which follows is the account of my adventures in the Holy Land with Bohemond, Lord of Taranto and Prince of Antioch.

Pars Prima

Carmina qui quondam studio florente peregi, flebilis heu maestos cogor inire modos.

Ecce mihi lacerae dictant scribenda Camenae et ueris elegi fletibus ora rigant.

Has saltem nullus potuit peruincere terror, ne nostrum comites prosequerentur iter.

Gloria felicis olim uiridisque iuuentae, solantur maesti nunc mea fata senis.

Uenit enim properata malis inopina senectus et dolor aetatem iussit inesse suam.

—Boethius, Consolatio Philosophiae

Who wrought my studious numbers smoothly once in happier days,

Now perforce in tears and sadness learn a mournful strain to raise.

Lo, the Muses, grief-dishevelled, guide my pen and voice my woe;

Down their cheeks unfeigned the teardrops to my sad complainings flow.

These alone in danger's hour faithful found, have dared attend

On the footsteps of the exile to his lonely journey's end.

These that were the pride and pleasure of my youth and high estate

Still remain the only solace of the old man's mournful fate.

(Translation by H.R. James, 1897)

Mainz

In which I relate my early life; in which I learn about the Council of Clermont and the call of Pope Urban to rescue the Byzantines from the Infidel; in which madness seemingly invades the minds of good men at Mainz; in which I encounter Godfroi de Bouillon and his brother, Baudoin, and travel with them to Constantinople to meet the Emperor.

Caput Unus

My father was a prosperous London wool merchant, and our family had excelled in the wool trade since my grandfather's time. My grandsire, who started the family enterprise, came to Aengelond from Normandy with the great Guillaume, he who has since been called 'The Conqueror' when Guillaume called for any adventurer who might be willing to serve in the war against Harold Godwinson. My grandfather, the son of a wool dyer, answered the call and fought with the great king at Hastings.

After the war was won, the new King of Aengelond himself granted my grandfather a yearly pension for saving the life of Guillaume's nephew.

My grandfather often told the story of how he had slipped accidentally into a muddy depression and tripped over the king's nephew who had fallen from his horse. Laughing, he would relate how the royal kinsman had knelt in the slop of the field with his eyes squeezed tightly shut waiting for a Seisun deathblow to fall. Grandfather had pitched forward when he tripped into the hole with his arms flung out for balance, spear in one hand. The butt of his weapon caught in the sticky mire just as the Seisun pedite charged forward, langsweord raised, ready to hack off the head of the king's relative.

Unable to check his momentum in time, the Seisun impaled himself on the rusty spearhead. The old, borrowed spear-shaft broke and the whole collection then fell atop the young cnicht with Grandfather sandwiched between the dead man and the live. When Grandfather rolled the corpse away from him and himself from atop the royal kinsman, the latter, so grateful to be alive, hugged and kissed my grandsire repeatedly, promising him lands and wealth aplenty.

I have always found that fraternity and generosity are much stronger in the immediate shadow of death, especially in war, than in the glare of sober reflection produced when the looming threat has fallen away. So Grandfather found it to be. For, in the months following the king's victory, when the king's nephew discovered that his saviour was a lowly commoner from Bruges in Flanders, his promise of lands and title dried up like the blood of the dead forgotten on the battlefield, no more than a stain of its former essence.

Instead of estates and money my grandsire received a yearly pension, generous enough so to admit, but nonetheless nominal. Still, Grandfather gratefully accepted the sum granted and purchased a quantity of wool that he then sold in Bruges to a cloth maker he knew there. This successful trading in wool carried on until, by the time of my own birth, my father, an only son with four sisters, had turned the family business a small fortune through investments in the wool and later the wine trade.

Unfortunately for me, my father produced several sons. Since I was the last of these and certainly the least, I could never inherit the family enterprise. Luckily, as my life experiences showed later, my father believed that all his sons should be educated.

We were taught to read and write and calculate with mathematics the necessary formulae for record-keeping, taxation, inventory and so all those things required to keep the family wool franchise smoothly operating. We were an unusual family in that respect since such an education was a difficult thing for most people to afford. However, there are always available itinerant, impoverished clerics eager and grateful for employment of any kind, willing to sell their services at almost any price, and my father took advantage of that fact on his sons' behalf. A constant procession of such generally unreliable and often intoxicated teachers paraded through my life, never staying long but passing on a variety of knowledge to my open mind.

Unlike my brothers, who chafed at every moment spent in study, never truly mastering their Latin, I excelled in academic pursuits. My eyes devoured every text I could lay my hands on and I searched for more. I read about far away lands, strange peoples, great cities with wondrous buildings; vicarious experiences that made my own life in my father's wool warehouse, where I counted inventory and prepared shipping lists, seem petty and mundane.

I learned about the Greeks and Alexander the Great, their unconquerable king, who created a vast empire; of the Greek war against the city of Troy, and how, out of that city's destruction, the founders of Rome and Britain fled across the Middle Sea. I learned much about those Romans who brought civilisation and who brought, eventually, the True Faith to Europe. In addition to all of this, I revelled in reading astronomical texts, medicine, geography, philosophy and, of course, the Bible.

This new knowledge left me with the conviction that I could never be satisfied in the London wool trade as my father's or brothers' clerk. At fourteen, I began to prevail upon my sire with discontented pleading and complaining about furthering my education. Eventually he capitulated.

My father agreed to let me go to Bruges where a kinsman, a beneficed clergyman, would help me further my learning. My father wrote to Bruges, and unknown to me, instructed our kinsman to begin to prepare me for the priesthood. My father was convinced that I would never take any real interest in the family business—which was true—and reasoned that I might best serve my family by serving the Church. So, in the spring of my sixteenth year, I sailed with a cargo of my father's wool for Flanders.

I spent the next three years in Bruges, where my father's cousin became my tutor and benefactor. He was a man about my father's age, Fromond by name. Fromond was a parish priest and ran a small clerical school in which I was one of a half dozen students present at any given time. We studied classical works approved by my cousin and also theology, philosophy, hagiographic works and the like. I particularly enjoyed the writings of St. Augustine whom I must say I came later to resemble somewhat. Not that I compare myself to the Holy Patriarch in his divinely illuminated state but rather to that young nobleman in his regretfully secular early years.

That tale, however, told by my younger, foolish self, must wait until later in this account.

I need tell little about my three years in Bruges. A few times each year my father visited with me while calling on his customers in Bruges. On these occasions, I spent my evenings with him in dining, drinking, and talking of the wool trade. My father's interests were fairly limited in scope and my attempts to engage him in any sort of philosophical discussions were generally abortive. Nonetheless, I found our time together pleasant enough.

As time passed at Bruges, I began to notice how old my father had become. Each year he seemed to grow thinner, his skin slacker, and his eyes mistier. He had been nearly forty years old when I was born; now, he was closer to sixty. My last year at Bruges, the year I reached eighteen years of age, was the last I saw my father alive. Thus I am grateful for the time we spent together, just we two—something that would not have been possible in our busy London household—during his annual week-long excursions to promote his commercial interests.

I came to realise during our visits that he cared about what happened to me. Whatever else I chose to do with my life, I was his son; despite being least among his other heirs, I was of his flesh and blood and bone. I was his youngest son and thus stood no chance to inherit the family business, but since I had inherited from him almost no interest in the wool trade that fact did not bother me. He did not understand that about me but he recognised that my future lay elsewhere and told me so more than once. He wrote often to me in the years after I left Bruges and I to him but I had no chance to return to London for many years. When I did at last return, he was long dead.

If I may presume to say, perhaps my close personal and professional relationship with the Lord Bohemond was predicated, on my part at least, upon my own feelings of guilt regarding my father. I worked diligently for the Prince of Antioch in all things, using all my skills and knowledge to their best effect in his service and I know that he was generally well pleased with my efforts.

Perhaps I tried overmuch to please that master because I had been unable to please my own father with respect to the family trade. If I had been able to settle down into my father's tiny world of commerce, as I believed such a sphere of activity to be, I know he would have been gratified. He knew that I had been blessed with excellent mathematical abilities that he could have put to good purpose.

I do not attempt to aggrandise myself by writing of this since, as we are all well aware, such modest skills as we all possess are given to us by God and we serve Him well by putting our abilities to their best uses possible. Perhaps I should have done, honouring the Lord by honouring the hopes of my parents, but I began to think, during my years at Bruges that I might best honour God by serving Him directly. Thus in a way, however unknowingly, I fulfilled to some degree my father's wishes for me by entering the service of the Church.

As if to validate such thoughts as I had in those days, Fromond in fact encouraged me to become a priest. Indeed, he took such an interest as to arrange for me a position with the Archbishop of Mainz, Lord Rothard. So it was that in the summer of 1095 I left Flanders for the Alemaigne lands.

Once again my father's business connections served me well if unexpectedly. Fromond contacted one of my father's customers, a textile maker whose name, I am sorry to say, now escapes me, and found a place for me in a merchant baggage train bound for Köln. This city was nearly halfway to my ultimate destination in Franconia.

These travel arrangements had their advantages. The country through which I passed, through Lower Lotharingia by the Liege road and thence into Franconia, while settled, was in places isolated and wild. Great tracts of dense primeval forest stretched for leagues along our route, though we generally travelled on good roads. In those days, as indeed today in that same country, a lone traveller always faced the dangers of thieves, marauding bands of lawless cnichts and wild animals such as wolves and bears attacking and killing him. Thus, few travelled alone.

However, we met no bandits or wild creatures to impede us. We came without much hardship to Köln. There, I parted company with my merchant friends.

Perhaps I should describe Köln before writing of the rest of my trip, since it is a most noteworthy place. The large and bustling city owes its size and activity to its position along the major trade route that runs from Bruges to the west to Genoa on the Middle Sea in the south and eventually on to Egypt, and ultimately, I suppose, to parts east beyond the Holy Land. But of course, no Christian has ever gone beyond the Holy Land.

Köln benefits greatly from trade between the North and the Middle Seas and all manner of goods and people pass through its gates. I myself saw in those days huge tuns of wine from Italia and the Frankish kingdoms, various metal goods and raw ingots of iron and other ores, and a stack, almost like logs, of a strange whitish bone-like material. This, I was told, came from far beyond Egyptian Alexandria in a land wholly unknown to Christians.

This substance is ivory, of course, and apparently comes from the horns of the elephantus, or oliphant. This large beast was the mount preferred by Hannibal and the Carthaginians when they tried foolishly to conquer the unconquerable Romans more than one thousand years ago. The story is related how Hannibal drove his army of oliphants across the Alpine Mountains from Iberia into Italia and created havoc in the lands controlled by Rome until eventually defeated by the great Roman general, Scipio Africanus. Many years later, I had the opportunity to see the animal itself while in the service of my Lord Bohemond.

But I digress, as old men tend to do.

The people of Köln were as varied as the products in which they trafficked. The native inhabitants were much the same as those in any other town in the North. Few stood out as unusual except perhaps those cursed by God and condemned to living in misshapen or dwarfish bodies. I saw many Jews in Köln, too; a race I had been taught to believe were also cursed by God because they had betrayed and caused to be executed His Son.

Among the natives and Jews of Köln circulated Iberians and Italians and occasional Greeks. One Greek I saw there, a very wealthy merchant judging by the tastelessly rich silks and linens he wore in gaudy particolour, had with him a man-servant or slave whose skin was as dark and shiny as a well-made leather scabbard. Such people come from the same country from whence comes the ivory-horned *elephantus*.

These folk live in a very hot, sun-baked region near the uninhabitable Torrid Zone far to the south. They wear almost no clothes when in their native haunts, even their women going about shamefully bare-breasted, owing to the heat. They live there in dark forests, huddling under the shade of the leafy boughs because of the sun's blasting rays.

My early life in London and my cloistered education in the clerical arts at Bruges had ill-prepared me to absorb the diversity and complexity of Köln. I found myself frightened of the strangeness of the place and its people, though for no rational reason. I had never thought of myself as particularly xenophobic so I had never sought to examine the reasons behind such paranoid feelings. I think, though, that this initial exposure at Köln readied me in some small manner for the future. In lands across the Middle Sea I would find people and cultures that were far stranger than any I had experienced in London or Köln or indeed anywhere else to which I had travelled.

However, I was writing of the journey.

The textile maker I mentioned earlier provided me with an introduction to one of his customers, Werner by name, whom he thought might possibly provide me passage to Mainz along the Rhine River. This prospect turned out to be a good one. Werner indeed found me a place on his vessel.

Fortune smiled upon me and by God's grace I boarded a large knorr out of Köln bound for Mainz. This craft had both sail and oars and was admirably suited for plying its trade along the Rhine. Broad of beam and with a deep keel, it could hold an abundance of trade goods, all open to the elements, tucked in among the oarsmen and paraphernalia of the marine métier: ropes, anchor, canvas and such. I spent the majority of the journey on this fore deck, leaning against the wale, watching the Lotharingian country drift by.

Journeys are strange events. They have always seemed to me in some ways like dreams. In one sense we are part of the event but in another removed from it. What we see and experience in a dream seems real at the moment, but when we awake we know that such places and the people who inhabit those places, while they may exist in reality, never were part of the experiential venue our dreaming selves placed them in. In a god-like sense we form that reality extant in our dreams. Indeed, it is probably proper to say that God Himself places these things into our somnolent universe. Perhaps we visit an alternate world that the Lord has prepared for us for tutelary purposes. Just so we are subtly removed, during our actual, physical journeys across the lands and waters of the Earth, from the world around us. We are not part of the day-to-day reality of those who inhabit the country through which we pass, but only transitory figures who are gone in moments, hours, or days.

So, on the journey to Mainz we passed a variety of folk engaged in various activities and never did I do more than casually acknowledge with limited sensibility their varied existences. Even so, we were all people who inhabited at that time the same place on earth, however briefly; all different but all the same, all the children of God. Thus, in this context, the events that were later to unfold at Mainz in the year that followed seemed completely inexplicable to me. I can only say that I must have inhabited one of those strangely surreal dream universes and my own reality concurrently. Luckily, I had no precognition of those events that lay so dreadfully near.

When we arrived at Mainz, I departed unceremoniously from my travelling companions and my captain-host. Indeed, most of the sailors barely noticed my departure. I thanked the captain who merely grunted and I wondered if I had been a burden to him in some way during the two-day voyage.

I shouldered the pack containing my few worldly possessions and stepped on to the streets of Mainz. Though I did not know the town since I had not been there before, the cathedral and the palace of the Archbishop were clearly visible above the rooftops of the tightly clustered dwellings on the banks of the river and its complex was, indeed, quite close to the southerly riverbank. I made straightaway to my new home.

Mainz, even in those days, was a large town, walled like most big centres of strategic importance. Moreover, like most areas where people pack closely together to live, at least in most Christian lands I have been in, it was filthy. Night soil and other filth clogged the streets, running in rivulets of stench or pooling in acrid puddles here and there.

Most people thought nothing of these repulsive conditions. Wealthy citizens rode horses or were carried in litters raised above all care and exposure to corruption. They never endured nor even acknowledged the conditions experienced by the mass of people. To me this seems symptomatic of the disease that gnaws at our Christian society, our Christian world. Though founded on ideals of charity and love of one's neighbour, we fail to acknowledge the miserable conditions endured by the greater part of our fellow Christians.

None of these thoughts actually crossed my mind that day, as I recall, except in the most cursory way; though I looked upon the urban scene with distaste, I saw nothing to which I was not accustomed when living in London or Bruges. Mainz was worse than Bruges, worse even than Köln, which, with its cosmopolitan nature, was bad enough. I have since had occasion to reflect upon these issues with the enlightenment produced by exposure to other cultures, non-Christian and Christian alike, which place considerably more value on cleanliness and neighbourly charity and I have found us wanting in many ways.

At last I reached the cathedral. It was a commanding structure, not least for its size. I marvelled at the expertise and time-consuming effort evident in its construction. It must have taken decade upon decade to complete. I imagined that from the upper clerestory windows one might look down upon the town below as the angels looked down upon the earth from Heaven. Only the hills surrounding the town stood higher. Truly, I thought, these people must be pious indeed to erect such an imposing edifice to the glory of God.

I saw that a high wall adjoined the church proper and enclosed a freestanding palatial dwelling. This house, as I took it to be, was built of alternate layers of stone and timber. It rose to nearly half the height of the adjacent sacred edifice. I knew instantly that this would be the palace of Archbishop Rothard.

The entrance to the bishop's home was not a door or doors like those of the cathedral. Rather, a portcullis gate of flat iron bands woven together and riveted at their intersections blocked the arched gateway. Its construction reminded me of similar doors I had seen in secular fortification walls. I wondered if this gate served a like purpose; namely, to prevent access to violent intruders.

At that thought, a chill like icy water trickled unnaturally upward from the base of my spine to benumb my scalp. An inexplicable sense of foreboding fell over me. I could not fathom why this feeling crept across my soul, especially in this holy place.

I tried to shake off the dread by loudly ringing the brass gate bell but the clamour failed to drive away the demon rustling its leathern wings upon my shoulder. Thus Satan attempts to strike fear into the hearts of those who doubt their own self-worth and who question their own resolve when undertaking projects in good faith. I whispered a prayer to St. Thomas who was relieved of his own doubt by the Christ's Wounds, hoping that the Lord would do the same for me through the saint's intercession on my behalf. Yet, the saint failed me somewhat, for a sense of foreboding lingered in me for a time thereafter.

This feeling was in no way dispelled by the man who answered the bell.

For your benefit, my patient reader, I shall now try to reconstruct that conversation and those with other people subsequent to it lest you grow disdainful of over-lengthy descriptive passages. Of course, you must try to remember the difficulty in bringing to life both those events now long past and the many participants long dead.

"This is the home of my lord Rothard, Archbishop of Mainz, you young fool. How dare you disturb his peace with this clamorous riot," he snapped through pinched, white lips from which I saw slight movement.

I thought him an ugly little man in that first meeting, in body as in spirit, impatient and truculent and I had no occasion thereafter to revise my opinion of him. He was short of stature and long of nose. This elongated organ was covered in vivid red lumps making it look like an inflamed cucumber. The rest of his face was no better. His green watery eyes resembled nothing so much as two withered grapes embedded in globes of yellow grease. His chin, hair-less but for a few dozen thread-like wisps dangling precariously here and there, thrust backward under his lower lip, the antithesis of the usual human mandible. His gibbous back twisted him forward and to the side. His posture always caused me to think of a blind shrew, sniffing, searching always with his long nose; searching, usually, for fault in others.

"What do you want," he snapped at me as though snapping at a defenceless bug.

Of course I was intimidated, being young and unsure of myself. I managed to stammer in the Alemaigni tongue, "I...I...am the new clerical student from Bruges. I would like to see the Archbishop, if you please."

His laugh came out as a vicious growl. There lived a wolf under the rodent's skin, I thought. Nonetheless, he reached into a pocket of his worn, dirty robe and drew forth a heavy-looking iron key with which he unlocked a smaller grate within the large portcullis gate. I stepped through warily, giving the unlikely Cerberus a wide berth. He glared at me and impatiently gestured for me to follow.

The gatekeeper strode briskly ahead of me so that I struggled to match his pace. We hastened along a flagstone path that led toward the palace, as I had begun to think of the Archbishop's home. My guide never once slackened his pace, so that I had no time to really look about me. However, some details did impress themselves upon me. On either side of the path grew apple trees heavily laden with unripe fruit, though some were already beginning to show the violent red colour associated with the full harvest.

There were birds everywhere, pigeons, sparrows, robins, all pecking and scrabbling industriously near the walls and in the trees. Suddenly, a black raven swept in like a wolf among sheep and scattered the little birds. An unfortunate sparrow dashed itself against the wall and fell thrashing as it died on the steps of the great house. I thought, 'Our Lord's hand will be there, since He sees even the smallest sparrow fall. None of His creatures is the least, none so inconspicuous as to escape His attention.'

This thought, and the next, that God watches even me, lightened my spirits somewhat as we left the warm, sunlit garden of Archbishop Rothard and entered the relative cool and darkness of his palace.

The gatekeeper ushered me immediately through a low wooden door almost hidden in one wall of a long hallway, a passage that led into the great hall in the central part of the palace. I glanced over my shoulder to the end of that passage to see two large heavy wooden doors that stood closed. I wondered why we were not headed for the Archbishop's audience chamber but then shrugged and followed my taciturn guide.

In my youthful pride I had assumed my arrival important enough to warrant immediate introduction to the master of this house, though, as it turned out, several weeks would pass before I met the great man. Instead, we wormed our way through a narrow passageway which skirted the outside wall—for I could see the wood, mortar, and stones of the wall's construction on one side of the tunnel—and on and on until I knew we must be at the rear of the building. At last, the scent of wood smoke and cooked food began to pervade the close air of the passage and I thought we must be near to the kitchen.

This conjecture proved to be truth. Moments later, we left the tunnel and entered the kitchen. I was amazed at its size. It looked nearly the size of my father's entire house back in London. A great fireplace formed the farther wall and in it whole trees blazed forth their heat and light and smoke. From the arches of its hearth hung all manner of cooking pots, kettles, hooks, and other iron gadgets and devices, all in various states of use, some hanging empty and unused, others steaming and bubbling or jammed in next to the bright red-orange embers.

Like a beehive the place buzzed with the activity of its workers: men, boys and adolescents. There were no women here, an absence of whom was proper in a house consecrated to the service of the Lord. They dashed back and forth carrying foodstuffs, utensils and dishes, or split wood for the smaller ovens scattered here and there around the kitchen.

Quite vocally, egged on by the promising odours of delicious foods, my innards began to remind me of just how very hungry I was.

Salivating, I reluctantly pursued my guide as he dodged artfully through the bustling kitchen workers. I, less skilful in my navigation through the sea of culinary staff, followed awkwardly in his wake, continually floundering in wave after wave of dashing cooks. Or perhaps they, like the waters of the Red Sea, simply parted before my guide with his Moses-like powers of penetration, leaving me to drown Pharaoically behind him.

To my surprise and disappointment, having departed the kitchen and all of its blissful aromas, we exited the main building through a door behind one of the great fireplaces. Presumably, with the mountainous stacks of dry firewood piled just without the door, this particular ingress the servants used mainly for re-supplying the kitchen's fuel stocks. We continued across a large open courtyard to the stables. I knew where we were headed almost immediately when the yeasty pungency of the bake-ovens was replaced by the musty, earthy odour of partially digested hay. An Olympian heap of horse excrement seemed to support one wall of the wooden structure housing the Archbishop's equine assets.

"This is where you will live from now on," said the gate-keeper blandly and jerked his chin at the dank depths within the barn.

I, used to the comfort of both the school at Bruges and before that my father's well-kept apartments in London, expressed my incredulity with a youthfully tactless verbal explosion in my own tongue, a mix of Aenglisch and the Frankish dialect of Normandy.

"Are you mad? This is for horses! I cannot live here!"

I could see that he did not understand my words but their meaning must have been translated through my tone and facial expressions. Indeed, despite the gulfs separating isolated islands of culture and religion, I have often found tone and certain gestures to possess a kind of universality of meaning.

Thus made subliminally aware of my intent, he snarled at me in Alemaigni, "If you will stay here in the Archbishop's compound then you will sleep in the stables, boy. Or perhaps you think that my Lord Rothard should move his quarters here so that you might have his bed?"

Since I did not believe the Archbishop should put my own comfort before his own, I meekly shook my head. The man sniffed haughtily at me and, looking down his long shrew's nose, snapped, "Then find Ulfrid within and he will find a place for you." At which he turned without another word and stalked back into the main house. I stood dumbfounded for a moment gazing after him. Then I entered the mouldering bowels of the stables.

◆

I was completely blind in my new surroundings. All around me I heard shuffling and stomping and the occasional clop of hooves. I might have been in the deepest pit of Hell with cloven-hoofed devils dancing around me, closing in to bind me and torment me and throw me into pools of burning sulphur. Except that I doubted whether Hell was this dark or reeked of manure.

As my eyes adjusted to the relative gloom of the barn's interior I began to make out the rounded rumps and the tails of its equine inmates. The relatively clean dirt floor had been recently swept and raked for I could see the marks made by the passing of the required implements over its surface. Cautiously, I stepped forward, not wanting to embarrass my only pair of shoes in a pile of clandestine dung disguised as shadow. I made my way to the farther end of the stables.

The light level increased to near brilliance once more as I found myself suddenly in a long, narrow chamber set apart from the main stable space by a solid stone wall. The floor likewise was built of stone, as was the stone wall opposite the door frame through which I had entered. The wall was pierced by several large windows, their shutters thrown back to invite in the bright sunshine.

Like the stables this chamber looked clean and neat. Various kinds of leather harness hung on wooden pegs along the walls. There were implements for grooming and other tools made of metal and wood at whose functions I could only guess. In one corner lay a pile of old sackcloth, its disarray in contrast to the order of the rest of the room. I looked the room over completely then poked my head out one of the windows, wondering where Ulfrid could be. I saw no sign of the man.

Then I heard a soft burr of air, something akin to a bee trapped in a bottle as it buzzes about trying to escape. I cocked my head like a hunting hound, listening. The sound seemed to come from the pile of cloth in the corner. I cautiously approached it with outstretched foot and toed it experimentally. I nudged with more force. Suddenly, as if propelled by a trebuchet, an older man shot out of the pile, scattering the sacks and landing upright as though he were an arrow fired straight into the air that had dropped back to earth. His expression of terror, I am sure mirroring my own, changed quickly to relief then evolved visibly into irritation.

"I thought you were Caesar. Scared my soul to Hades and back, you nearly did. What d'you want?"

His thick Alemaigni accent in an odd dialect made him difficult to understand as accustomed as I was to a more formal mode of speech. Nonetheless we were able to communicate. I decided not to answer his question right away. Rather, in order to satisfy my immediate curiosity, I asked, "Caesar? Do you mean the Roman general? Why would you expect him?"

He eyed me for a moment with a look better used to sight down the length of a cocked arrow. Then, apparently deciding that I was not a spy of some sort nor appeared any threat to his dignity, he chuckled and said in his peasant accents, "Oh, we just call him that around here. The Archbishop's major-domo, Julius."

He frowned and I saw his tongue roll under his upper lip across his teeth. Then he bent over and searched the floor until he found a bit of straw, which he picked up, straightening with a grunt of satisfaction or maybe back pain. Next he took a step backward to rest an elbow on the windowsill and began picking his teeth. I waited for him to continue, self-consciously shifting my weight from one foot to the other as he scrutinized me.

He pulled his toothpick from his mouth and pointed it accusingly at me. "You'd be the new cleric from Bruges," he stated.

I smiled tentatively. "Um…clerical student, yes."

"Well, then, you'll have met Caesar, lad. He'd be the one let you through the front gate like."

"Oh. I thought his name must be Cerberus," I said and explained quickly at his puzzled look, "The three-headed dog which guarded the gates of Hades and slain by Hercules? No? Nasty creature."

"Well, I known't about the three heads but the 'nasty' bit fits. Come to think on it, he does act like he gots six eyes sometimes, four of them in the back of his head. And he does slaver some when he gets pissed off at someone."

He grinned conspiratorially at me and we both laughed. "Eh?" He asked rhetorically with the verbal equivalent of a poke in the ribs with an elbow. "Eh?"

I liked Ulfrid immediately. He was of a height with me though many years my senior. He himself did not know how old he was, though he claimed that as a very young boy he heard about the coronation of the Henri the Seisun king on the death of the old king, Conrad. This Henri was the father of Henri, the aforementioned Emperor. Conrad died nearly sixty years earlier so I guessed that Ulfrid had to be a little more than that in years.

Ulfrid's hair grew only behind his ears, creeping low and stealthily around the back of his head to meet in a cowlick at the back of his neck. As a result, his forehead seemed abnormally large. This tended to bring his sparkling blue eyes into prominence and his perpetual good humour shone in those orbits for as long as I knew him.

A shadow passed over Ulfrid as he stood in the block of sunlight by the window. He shivered and looked out at the cloud blocking the sun.

Then he shrugged, "You'll be wanting to know where you'll sleep. C'mon."

He turned and went out through a side door, which I had taken to be part of the chamber wall.

Behind the stables, on the far side of a wide courtyard of packed earth, stood yet another building constructed entirely of stone. I marvelled at the size of the cathedral compound; so many buildings, so many people and all here to serve God. This latest outbuilding, as it came to pass, was a barracks that housed all the lesser servants of Lord Rothard. Here lived many of the kitchen staff, cleaning staff and stable hands, at least those who had no lodgings in the city. All the young clerics and clerical students, I among them now, lived here, too.

Often, visiting clergymen stayed in the barracks as well; usually those of lesser status, many of whom attended on their great lords, bishops, for example, who came to commune with the Archbishop about great spiritual matters or temporal matters of interest to the Church. Likewise, lay lords came with their trains of retainers and servants, the latter also accommodated in the barracks when necessary. Infrequently, my fellow students and I were put out of our warm beds to sleep in the stables when a visiting troupe was large enough and of sufficient importance to warrant better accommodations than we were allowed on those occasions. We all hated the inconvenience but dutifully obeyed our master and his major-domo.

Ulfrid took me to an empty cell on the second floor of the barracks. This cubiculum was bare of furnishing except for a straw mattress in one corner and a low cabinet opposite it. On the cabinet sat an earthenware ewer and a shallow krater for washing. The room had no window, no other opening but for the door.

"I thought I was to sleep in the stables. That is what Julius told me."

"He was just havin' you on, he was. Well, it's not the stable and it ain't the Archbishop's chambers," grinned Ulfrid, "but it's better'n nothing."

I laughed and nodded in agreement and bid him farewell as he left the room. A moment later he stuck his head back through the doorway.

"Meet me at the stable later and I'll take you to Mass." He winked and disappeared once more. I chuckled, congratulating myself on having made a new friend already, and threw my bag into a corner.

◆

I met Ulfrid in his chamber at the rear of the stables about an hour before Vespers. This I determined by the angle of the sun in the sky, of course. Any good student knew enough astronomy to do this, even without a quadrant or other instrument. The horse-master was far busier than the last time I had seen him. He vigorously directed half a dozen or so men in the maintenance of his animal dependants. His helpers carried water, fodder and grains to the horses, brushed their coats and combed manes and tails. I stood to one side of the stable door trying to stay out of the way of the busy caretakers.

Eventually, Ulfrid noticed me standing there and came over.

"Aye, young master, you've come a bit early for Vespers. But we can maybe stop at the kitchens first, eh?" Again he gave the wink that I began to see as a trait characteristic of the man.

I followed him into the kitchens.

As I later discovered, the Archbishop's kitchens provided not only the meals for the household but produced a variety of victuals, such as bread, pastries and meat pies for sale in the city of Mainz. This side-industry provided a lucrative source of income, along with the rents and profits from sales of agricultural produce from a myriad of landholdings in the province, for the Archbishop. Though such financial matters are beyond my field of interest and care, I know from experience in my father's business that the Lord Rothard must have been possessed of a very successful enterprise given the opulence of his home and the number of men in his employ.

Of course such a man, so highly placed in the Church, required an immense income. This must match his great status and responsibility in order for him to perform equally great tasks for the Pope and for Christianity in the name of the Blessed Lord Jesus. How else but through the coercion of wealth and its attendant political power could the savage nature of men be reined in and brought to the bit of morality? Secular rulers—kings, dukes, earls, counts and even emperors—in their vast military pride often balked at the many restraints Christian duty placed upon them. Without the tempering influence of God's Word, though, Christendom would fly apart like a badly braced mill wheel, torn asunder by conflicting powers exerting opposing forces from many directions.

Just a few years before my birth, for example, the Emperor Henri almost succeeded in destroying the papacy of Pope Grégoire. Henri took exception to statements regarding the powers of the Church made by the Pope. In the synod at Rome in the year of Our Lord, 1075, Grégoire effected many new decrees which threatened the secular powers of kings and emperors.

These doctrines emphasised the pope's position as a direct descendent of the first pope of Rome, Saint Peter himself and thus, as Saint Peter's divinely ordained successor, the Roman Bishop, that is the Pope, has the same powers to 'bind and loose' given to Saint Peter by Christ Himself. This doctrine is evident to anyone who chooses to read Holy Scripture: "Whatsoever shall be bound and loosed on earth shall also be so in Heaven." Thus, the Pope has the right to depose emperors, if he is inclined to do so, and indeed, as Grégoire did when he excommunicated Emperor Henri.

Thus did that most arrogant of kings, who foolishly tried to install a false anti-pope when he disagreed with the true pope's policies, discover the oft latent but God-given power of the True Church and its earthly ruler, the Lord's own terrestrial chamberlain. Eventually, the barefoot imperial penitent knelt in the snow before Grégoire, humble as a pilgrim, at Canossa, where he was most charitably and lovingly forgiven and welcomed back into God's grace by His Holiness the Pope.

Of course, no thoughts about these weighty religious and political matters entered my mind on that warm summer day in the year of our Lord 1095. Only after years of sober reflection upon the state of Christendom and my many experiences with foreign cultures have I considered these ideas. That particular day, in that pleasingly pungent kitchen, I thought only of the persistent growls and grumbles of my indignant stomach, which had endured the privation of fasting since the previous evening.

We found a couple of bowls and helped ourselves to some stew simmering on the hearth, and then a loaf of bread and went back outside to sit in the evening sun to eat. We sat in silence, each alone in our respective thoughts, chewing and swallowing. The stew was very tasty, as I remember, with bits of beef and cabbage and tangy spices. The cooks of Mainz cathedral were unsurpassed in their ability to turn out choice comestibles.

As the meal filled my belly, a warm sense of well being descended on me or perhaps I should say rose up from within, for I do not think that God sends His Grace down upon us simply because we enjoy a fine meal. That is to say, the inner peace I felt was rather more physiological than spiritual, dependant more upon the mechanics of the bodily functions than on any catabolism of the soul. On the other hand, though, all of our senses are God's gifts given us so that we might enjoy the Universe that He created for us in only six days. So, then, the feeling of comfort both descended upon me and rose up within me simultaneously, precisely as He intended for it to do, I imagine.

I practically wolfed my food down since I had not eaten anything since the evening before as I have previously mentioned. I set the wooden bowl on the ground between my flexed legs when I finished eating and leaned back against the cool stone wall, closing my eyes. As a contented fog settled upon my senses the bustling noise of the kitchen, the clatter and occasional laughter from the stables, the buzz and whine of busy insects, all faded away and my thoughts soared into the future.

Mainz would be a starting point for me, merely a stopping place on my journey to success. The cathedral school, as renowned throughout Northern Europe as was Bologna in the South, turned out graduates who had been called to Rome itself, who served popes and emperors. I hoped that if I succeeded here the Archbishop might find a place for me on his own staff. From there I could make my own contacts throughout the empire, throughout Christendom come to that. The world of the Church, far more political than my father's merchant sphere, offered astronomical possibilities for even a low-born man to become an influential power broker; perhaps even I might become an archbishop someday. The thought of such power thrilled me and, I regret now, filled me with an intense pride.

Of course that was merely a flight of fancy, that ambition of mine. For to believe the alternative, to believe that God later struck me down because of that species of hubris, is unthinkable. Still, as Nebuchadnezzar discovered to his peril, ours is a vengeful God. Anyway, all that came later.

Ulfrid nudged me back into the world and we got up to return our bowls to the kitchen and proceeded to Mass in the cathedral.

◆

If I had expected Archbishop Rothard to conduct the service, he disappointed me. He attended but sat to one side. The Mass itself was officiated by a visiting bishop, he of Meissen, Benno. On this occasion he had come to discuss with Rothard the weighty notion of recanting an act of submission he had made to the Alemaigni anti-pope, Guibert, who was also known as Clement III, installed by the Emperor Henri, and then declaring himself loyal to the true pope, Urban II. This particular dilemma had its roots in the aforementioned conflict between Pope Grégoire and the Emperor.

I, at that time, was not a party to such important discussions or their antecedent political conflicts. I only found out the reason for Benno's stay at the palace months later. On that first day I simply experienced disappointment at not seeing the Archbishop perform our most important daily Christian ritual.

I stood near the doors to the cathedral well back from the main tableaux. To be truthful I could barely see the Archbishop let alone make out his features. And so I contented myself in the ritual of the mass, losing myself in the worship of Christ and the contemplation of God's Grace; certainly a more admirable act than gawking around the Lord's House in an attempt to view His venerable steward. My meeting with Lord Rothard waited for another day. In the meantime, I breathed in, assimilated, savoured, the atmosphere of the vast cathedral. I knew I would be happy here.

◆

Gradually I fell into the rhythm of life at Mainz cathedral. Of course, mornings always began with mass. The Archbishop did not always attend and I learned that he often observed mass in his private quarters attended by his personal staff and occasionally acolytes from the cathedral school. People from the city attended the cathedral's masses and the thought went that if the folk did not know when Lord Rothard would officiate they would attend the church more often on the hope of seeing the Archbishop and being personally blessed by him.

Generally, I have found that throughout Christendom the common people are somewhat lax in their devotions and must needs be motivated and, often, coerced into attending church services. They cite the fact that their lives are busy, their time continually taken up by their efforts to eke out their livings. As often as not though such folk can be found at taverns and inns of a Sunday, on the commons wrestling or boxing or spectating at martial events held by equally lax lay lords who themselves should set a pious example.

In the cathedral, mass was conducted at prime, sext and again at vespers on a daily basis. This ensured the piety of acolytes since only those most dedicated to Christ could commit their efforts so rigorously, though I knew at that time, and certainly know now, that monasteries practised their devotions far more intensely and numerously.

The morning meal followed mass. This essentially communal event included clerical staff, clergy and students who gathered together at six tremendous wooden trestle tables and benches for the meal. Probably half a hundred men and boys sat down to break their fast together each morning. Seating was ranked in a strict hierarchy much as people in churches are ranked according to their social status: the least of all sat furthest from the front where the Archbishop's table stood, perpendicular to the other tables and so on down to the central chair of the man himself.

I, of course, sat at the end of a table in the back of the hall. Again as at cathedral mass, Rothard did not always attend breakfast and when he was absent his great, ornate, high-backed chair sat alone, no one daring to sit upon that throne. His place at table was perpetually made ready whether or not he attended. Indeed, more often than not, he did not join our little community for breakfast.

Despite the Archbishop's frequent absence, the first time I met him was at breakfast on the first Friday of my stay at his palace. We were all seated in our proper places. Our food was laid out on platters before us: apples, pears, cheeses of different kinds, loaves of fresh hot bread, butter, cream, eggs and freshly caught fish. Yet no one ate because we awaited the blessing of the food by the Archbishop's senior assistant and personal secretary, Father Benedict. Then, quite suddenly, the great main doors at my back opened and a hush fell over the hall, which moments before had buzzed with eager chatter. I turned to look over my shoulder, curious at the sudden silence, to find myself staring directly up at the Archbishop himself. I will never forget that first meeting with Lord Rothard.

I have always been fascinated by the fact that so many great men are extremely tall and prepossessing. The papal legate Adhemar of Puy, whom I met later, Bohemond of Taranto the Prince of Antioch, and Archbishop Rothard of Mainz were such imposing men. Rothard paused in front of me for a few moments and spoke to me.

As I have expressed, the most distinctive aspect that one immediately grasped about him was his great height. He stood a hand or perhaps two above those attending him. His eyes smiled dark and warmly beneath bushy white eyebrows. He seemed to invite me into his good grace. Beneath the eyes swept a noble Roman nose and under it his lips and chin hid beneath a long, flowing, snow-pale beard with none of the yellowish streaks usually seen in such facial adornments. In his flowing white robes, even devoid of his archbishop's regalia, he made the very picture of nobility and holiness together, as though he himself provided the nexus of the mundane and divine, an angel come to earth.

He looked down at me and spoke in flawless Frankish. "Well, I see we have a new face among us. Welcome, young man. I hope you will find your stay with us at Mainz as fruitful as that at Bruges."

For a moment I froze, awed by his powerful authoritative aura. Somehow his gaze seemed to penetrate to the truthful heart. Had he seen there in the centre of my being through the channel leading from my eyes my earlier daydream of ambition and advancement? Had he judged me unworthy and was his politeness merely a shadow of his intention to eliminate me from his see as soon as convenient? Then courtesy prevailed and foolish apprehension flew out of my mind as I hastened to humble myself before my lord. I kicked my immediate neighbour at table in my haste to kneel before the Archbishop.

I managed to fall on to the floor with one leg bent dangerously backward, the other at a right angle with my foot resting properly on the floor. I must have looked very much the youthful fool, clumsy and careless, unable to conduct himself in the presence of nobility. Surely I showed myself to be a commoner hopelessly out of his depth and station.

I kissed the Archbishop's ring and bent my head in obeisance. I felt his hand on my head, surprisingly strong and warm. A tingle ran through me, a touch of His Grace channelled through one among the greatest of His servants. Rothard chuckled and left me kneeling by the table, my eyes closed, trembling with awe-struck nervousness. After a few moments, having collected my strength and injected it back into my limp limbs, I stood up feeling foolishly exposed and returned to my seat.

The blessing had begun.

◆

My schooling took a new and, to me, exciting turn a few weeks after that incident. In Bruges, as I have mentioned, my education included literature, astronomy and mathematics among its principal subjects. Now I found an intense pleasure in the newest discipline to present itself for study: medicine.

Among its many services to the city of Mainz the cathedral's most charitable enterprise was its hospital. As a consequence of this service to noble and commoner, rich and poor alike, two clerics learned in medical lore lived at the palace. One was a barber-surgeon, the other a pharmaceutical herbalist and a doctor proper.

The doctor, a Benedictine monk imported by Archbishop Rothard, came from a monastery in northern Italy. He was garrulous, plump and short. He lived very simply in his personal habits although he obviously did not belong in the strict world of the Order of St. Benedict; I'm sure the Archbishop had little trouble persuading him to abandon the monastery in favour of the cathedral.

He always wore his Benedictine habit, though, a long, heavy black gown with its cowl flung back. He continually had to push up the flowing sleeves of the gown from his wrists as he worked for they continually fell inconveniently over his hands. A thick braided rope girdled his waist with two long ends dangling low from his midriff like two questing tentacles. He often walked barefoot, sometimes in well-worn leather shoes that buckled at the ankle, often, as he walked, tripping on the dangling ends of his belt.

And always he carried in his pocket, its tip protruding a finger's length, a small flute. I believe that to this instrument, which we often heard trilling in the hospital, its high, sweetly sighing strains soothing and cheering the infirm there, that he received his name. I am certain Brother Piccolo was not his real name though this is how he was always called.

Brother Piccolo, whose name means 'little flute,' took me under his wing from the moment we met, which event occurred one afternoon not long after my arrival. We took an instant liking to each other. My lessons done for the day, I had an hour to spare before supper in the great hall so I went to visit my friend Ulfrid in the stables and see if he might need any help around the stalls. But Ulfrid was not to be found. I assumed he had gone out into the city on some errand.

The afternoon was warm and humid and the room at the end of the stables with its stone walls and floor was relatively cool. I propped myself in one of the windows and leaned back against the cool stone. I felt guilty about this moment of leisure when I knew so many of the palace inhabitants were busy preparing meals or readying the cathedral for worship or engaged in study or intellectual discussion. However, I had yet met few of my fellow clerical students and none that I did know had invited me to their casual study and debating sessions. And certainly I was of no use in either kitchen or cathedral.

I suppressed my guilt by thinking about the busy days I had been spending attending various lectures, reading, writing, calculating, drawing, running errands for cathedral staff and racing to hall for meals and wolfing those down in order to attend the next lecture in the quarters of one of my teachers with my clerical colleagues. Gloriously, though still somewhat guiltily, satisfied with this rare opportunity for introspective inactivity I sat quietly soaking up the damp cold from the stones. I felt the chill flow slowly up my back and arms and through my legs like invisible rivers newly sprung from their fountainheads.

The thought brought to mind the story of Hagar, the consort of Abraham, and her son, Ishmael, when God granted mercy and caused the barren, searing sands of the desert Beer-Sheba, into which they had been cast out, to spurt forth with life-giving water. The coolness of the stones offered a like renewing, slaking freshness and I felt so comfortable I almost dozed off. In this state of torpor Brother Piccolo found me.

"'I went by the field of the slothful, and by the vineyard of the man void of understanding,' " he said, so quietly that at first I did not respond, thinking that I had imagined the sound of a human voice quoting the Proverbs as I drifted dreamily in the lazy warmth. I opened one eye.

"Oh ho!" he exclaimed, "Lazarus lives again!"

That startled me upright.

"I beg your pardon most humbly, sir," I said sheepishly. "I didn't hear you enter. I thought that I had dreamed a voice."

"Well, I'm not God and you're certainly not Abraham, Noah or Moses, to hear His voice," he chuckled.

I sat somewhat taken aback by such deliberate irreverence from a man so obviously recognisable as a monk of the Order of Saint Benedict.

"No, sir," I said lamely not really sure how to respond.

"Oh, you can stop calling me 'sir'. Most people call me Brother Piccolo. So you may call me. You are the new student, no?"

I replied in the positive. Word of my arrival seemed to have spread quickly throughout the cathedral community. I supposed that was normal. In such a relatively tiny, closed society the arrival of any newcomer would be news. Almost everyone would be curious as to what the stranger was like, where he came from, what rumours or gossip he had to share. For a short time I was much the novelty for the Mainz cathedral folk.

"Um…I was looking for Ulfrid, actually. Have you seen him, lad?"

"I'm sorry, no, Brother Piccolo." I shook my head. "I sought him myself but he was not here when I arrived. I assume he has gone out to the city."

Suddenly and disconcertingly he rapped violently on his forehead with the middle knuckles of his right hand. This action left a row of red spots on the skin for several minutes thereafter.

"That's right!" he exploded in sudden realisation. "Today is Wednesday. He's gone to visit with his wife and son in Wiesbaden, the village across the river."

I was surprised at this news. "Ulfrid has a wife? I thought he was…was…" I stopped. I really did not know what Ulfrid's position was here; other than his role as magister equi, master of horses, I had not known him to take any part in cathedral life. Though, of course, generally he participated in the evening mass.

"A cleric? A monk like me? The Archbishop's secretary, perhaps?" Brother Piccolo asked, amused.

"No. He, like many others here, is a lay member of the community. Not everyone has devoted his life totally to the service of the Church. Nor does everyone need to do. We each serve God according to our strengths and abilities. Mine are in the practice of medicine and so I aspire to ease the suffering of the sick. In this way I emulate, though admittedly in a very limited way, Our Lord Jesus who made the lame walk and helped the blind see. And you will serve God in your special way, whatever way that might be."

"I'm not really sure what special talents I have with which to serve Our Lord. If any…" I shrugged self-consciously.

Brother Piccolo had made me aware suddenly that I had no special skills that I had turned to the service of either God or my fellow Christians. Until now, all my efforts had been turned to the pursuit of knowledge and directed toward my own self-improvement. Worse yet, all this improvement I had stockpiled I intended to spend purchasing a place for myself somewhere in the hierarchy of the Church. The contrast of my own selfishness to Brother Piccolo's bald humanitarianism rendered me speechless with shame. I think Brother Piccolo sensed something of this in my manner or saw it in my face—always I found him extremely astute in reading people, delving deep into the animus, the spirit or soul, through the window of the eyes—because he quickly offered consolation.

"Well, then, perhaps God has directed me to you today for a purpose. Maybe you are a medicus like me, only you want the knowledge. How would you like to come by the infirmary tomorrow and see what it is that I do to serve God?"

I thanked him for his kind offer and we arranged a time to meet on the morrow. He left. I, or rather my stomach, decided that supper-time had arrived and, knowing now that my friend Ulfrid would not return today, proceeded to the great hall. On my way, I passed through the kitchen to see what was being served. I greeted Williborg, the cook.

"Good afternoon, master of the kitchens," I called with good nature and a wave. "What ambrosial comestibles are you preparing this day?" I asked with mock gravity.

"Snail livers and beetle tongues for you, I am afraid. They're all I have left," he said with counterfeit compassion.

He finished with deep, feigned solicitude, "And besides they were all I could catch being so old." Then he brightened and said, beaming widely, "The Archbishop, on the other hand, will be dining on roast beef tonight."

"Maybe I should taste his food for him just to be sure it is of sufficient quality for the august gentleman."

"What!" he exclaimed, picking up a meat cleaver. "Do you suggest that I cannot pick out the best meats in the city?" His eyes narrowed, "Or perhaps you're impugning my culinary skills…?"

"Never, master cook," I said gravely. "Even now your fame is spreading to the farthest reaches of Christendom, to the ear of the emperor of Byzantium himself."

He raised one eyebrow at me, shook his head and went back to stirring one of his delicious sauces. I chuckled and left for the hall, whistling quietly. I was very happy that day. I was beginning to make many new friends in Mainz and tomorrow I would be introduced to an entirely new sphere of knowledge. Perhaps my true path in service to humanity lay, like that of my new Benedictine friend, in the medical profession.

Caput Secundus

I began to spend a lot of time at the cathedral hospital. This facility adjoined the main palace building but could be entered from within the cathedral only through a separate external gate. Unlike the palace gate that depended upon the good will of Julius, the Archbishop's steward, for entry, this gate was left open throughout the day and was only closed up at night for the sake of the privacy and safety of the patients forced by their infirmities to dwell within until recovery or death took them away.

Even then the gate was not locked. Brother Piccolo believed that among the foremost aids to recovery for his patients were the good wishes occasioned by the visits of loved ones. Therefore, the presence of well-wishers and loved ones at any time of day or night might cheer somebody temporarily resident in the hospital.

The Benedictine himself slept in the hospital annex in order to be available for any sudden emergency whether occasioned by the arrival of a new patient or the relapse into sickness of a present patient. He had his own quarters there where he enjoyed some slight solitude. However, the door to his private chamber almost never closed. I am sure he seldom slept and listened intently even through his slumbers for the slightest sound of discomfort or pain from one of his charges. Gradually, I began to see something of how the monk viewed the world of medicine and his role in its practice and how seriously he took his responsibilities for easing the suffering of each of his patients.

This illumination was made possible by the fact that every free moment I had I spent with the Benedictine.

He made me a special student. I became a protégé, he my patron, demonstrating his art firsthand as he consulted with patients, giving me books to read and then testing my knowledge, drawing diagrams and writing out prescriptions for me to manufacture for him.

Over the course of the next half-year we saw many patients and I learned a vast amount of medical lore involving ethical practice of the *medicus*, medical theory, and pharmaceutical lore as well as various surgical techniques I gathered from both Brother Piccolo and the other resident practitioner, Brother Ambrose, the barber-surgeon.

Many of the complaints were simple in cause and as simple in remedy. Others were not.

Children's ailments were among the most numerous of cases. We treated a variety of fractures, sprains, cuts, and other minor infirmities. Setting a broken bone was relatively simple, as I discovered. Since the procedure was quite painful for the young patient, or even for older patients for that matter, a tincture of opium or deadly nightshade or even a goodly dose of wine if nothing else was available was given to control the trauma. I remember a couple of cases clearly.

Once, a young woman came to the infirmary complaining that she had been unable to sleep for several nights because her baby would not stop crying. She could not have been more than sixteen years of age. Her husband, an elderly man of some forty years of age, a smith by trade, waited for her on the street and would not come in, she told us. He had become quite angry, she told us tearfully, and blamed her for the baby's restlessness. In fact, he had taken to sleeping in his smithy the previous two nights because he could not bear the sound of the baby's cries and could obtain no rest in his own house. He understood, however, that the baby itself was blameless. The mother was responsible for its care and had failed somehow to provide for it properly. So the smith had brought her here, dragged her nearly as the girl told it, knowing of the hospital and its doctors. The girl had been in Mainz with her husband for less than a year and so had no female relatives here with whom to consult since she had come here from a village a week's travel from the city. She had failed also to acquaint herself with any of her neighbours because her husband was a solitary, taciturn man who had lived many years alone and had little use or time for socialising with his neighbours. She had prayed to the Blessed Mother of God for assistance, for it is She who cares for all women in distress and particularly mothers, to no avail. Clearly, she thought, she had offended the Virgin in some fashion and was beyond her care. Could Brother Piccolo help her then?

I recall that the monk laughed gently at this presumption. "Surely," he said, "if you were truly beyond the Blessed Virgin's care you would not have found me…I myself can do nothing without the intervention of God. Perhaps it is that She has sent you to me in answer to your prayer?"

The girl smiled at that, teary-eyed and reassured, and handed the baby to the Benedictine. Immediately, the baby, which had until that time, despite its mother's reports to the contrary, been silent, set up such a wail and hue and cry that I felt my ears would fold in upon themselves in agony. The monk seemed not to notice this at all but proceeded to inspect the infant after first unwrapping it from its swaddling. He then examined its face, the nose, mouth and eyes. He wiggled its various appendages, squeezing and pulling lightly on fingers, toes, joints. He poked and prodded under its arms, in the groin, in the belly, in its mouth and under its tiny mandible. Each time his fingers began their explorations in a new area of the baby's anatomy it began a new call of distress each seemingly louder than the one before. Then, his examination complete, Brother Piccolo rewrapped the infant and handed it back to the mother.

"Take your child home," He said. "Return this afternoon and I will have a potion prepared that should help to quiet your baby. Then you and your husband may rest, finally." He smiled at the girl. She smiled broadly in return and thanking the monk several times she left evidently greatly relieved despite the wailing baby in her arms.

"Now, young man," he said, turning to me, "What do you make of that?"

"Do you mean that noisy cub? Or the young woman and her husband?" I asked bemused.

He laughed at that. "Noisy cub, indeed. The thought often crosses my mind when I see a restless infant like that one that Our Lord Jesus was once a baby, too. Do you think that He might have kept the Blessed Virgin up nights with such cries?"

Naturally aghast at this near-blasphemy I burst out, "That is impossible, Brother Piccolo! Surely, the infant Jesus was the perfect child! How can you even think such a thing let alone say it?"

He raised his eyebrows at me, then slapped his thigh and emitted a loud snorting laugh. He looked at me, his eyes twinkling. "But as we all know, my young novice, Our Lord was also a man and thus, by definition, once a babe, as well. Do you not think that there is a possibility that He occasionally might have given His Blessed Mother a moment or two of trouble?"

"No. I do not," I replied indignantly. "The Divine Nature within Him would have prevented that eventuality. Human illnesses and bodily complaints would not have affected the Baby Jesus, Brother Piccolo. That is just not conceivable."

He chuckled again. "I do believe you are right, my boy. I was foolish to even suggest such a thing. But you must admit the Lord Jesus would have been the ideal patient: one who never grows sick."

I had to admit this was so but also remarked that with Our Lord in our midst we would have no need of physicians such as Brother Piccolo. He ignored that and spoke again of the girl and her infant.

"What did you observe in this case? Hmmm? Anything of note?"

"I definitely noted the baby's obvious discomfort, evident in his cries."

"Anyone could have observed that. I meant, did you notice anything out of the way that babies normally look and act?"

"No," I replied cautiously. "There seemed the usual sort of malodorous vapours, which in themselves are not considered harmful, as I have read. And the phlegmatic discharges seemed of the normal sort, probably induced by the baby's gluttony. As we all know, babies do not know when to stop eating because they have not yet learned during the course of their brief lives of the sins of greed and gluttony though they commit them constantly. When they are able to understand speech through God's Grace they may then change their habits and stop vomiting upon themselves so frequently."

The Benedictine was silent for a moment gazing at me. Then he said, "Now *that* is a unique analysis. I'm not sure I have ever heard such a thing before. Have you spoken to the Archbishop yet about your theological interpretations on the habits of babies?" With his deadpan tone I found difficulty guessing whether he was pleased, displeased or just sarcastic. I said nothing but waited for him to continue.

"Yes. Well." He cleared his throat and said, "Notwithstanding these again obvious manifestations of infantile behaviour, there are certain other clues that might indicate the kind of illness present. First, by testing the joints one might perceive a certain stiffness there that might indicate some serious infection at work. Next, by prodding gently in the various areas where the appendages come together and under the chin and jaw, one might detect the presence of swellings that are obvious indicators of a major upset in the balance of the humours and have various and unique remedies. And indeed, the eyes, too, betray signs of infection: redness, rheumy discharges, discolorations that might indicate the presence of excess yellow bile. I detected none of these positive indicators of disease in that infant. Of course, I had no opportunity to inspect the urine...but nonetheless, I'm fairly certain of the problem."

I waited, rapt, as he paused. This was what I had come to learn. The real guts, if I may make so bold, of medicine.

He continued, "The babe is most likely choleric."

"What is that?" I asked breathlessly, when he seemed not prepared to continue. Surely, this was a weighty medical problem that would take all his skills to combat.

"It means the infant is irritable," he said dryly.

Taken aback, I simply looked at him. I knew what the word meant. I just thought that in medical parlance it would be more significant in its application. I blurted, "That's all? Just 'irritable'?"

"The girl has probably allowed the child to overeat, as you suggested. Or perhaps something in her breast milk, present because of something she herself has eaten, has caused a slight disorder of the infant's bowels. Or something in the air has caused a small humoural imbalance in the babe or its mother. Who knows?" He shrugged for emphasis. "Whatever the cause, the effect is of little consequence. Even without my help, the child will be as healthy as before within a day or two. Unless, of course, some other as yet undiscovered symptoms make themselves evident. We shall see."

"What must be done, then, Brother Piccolo?"

"We shall concoct a tincture of sweet violet, cowslip and honey and mix it with wine. This will simply make the child drowsy when required and," he chuckled then, "that will soothe both mother and father as well as the babe."

We set about preparing this mixture. When the mother returned later, with the baby still squalling in her arms, Brother Piccolo administered a small dose to the infant's mouth and within a short time the child was fast asleep. The young mother began to sob quietly in relief. She bent her knees in humility, kneeling before the Benedictine and kissing his hand. The monk raised her gently to her feet and said a short blessing over her and then mother and quiescent baby departed.

I do not really know why I remember that episode so clearly these many years later. It was after all, a rather ordinary event. I suppose what impressed upon me most was the fact that this mother, in such misery over something that the physician could so easily remedy with a few simple herbs, had had her happiness restored and, presumably, the peace in her household restored at the same time. Her happiness was in itself a reward for the action undertaken by the medical practitioner, a reflection of God's Grace. I was struck by the notion that the world was filled with elements provided by God that could make human existence bearable even in the most trying of times. We had but to find them. If I may make so bold to write, perhaps after the expulsion of Adam and Eve from the Garden of Eden, that place was scattered throughout the world in tiny pieces so that God might provide His children with the necessary sustenance found originally in Eden and they had only to find and learn to use them. But that idea is only literary license on my part, for there is nothing in scripture to support this notion and I do not endorse it except as a flight of my own imagination.

Despite Brother Piccolo's years of training in the *ars medicinae,* despite his compassion and dedication, despite his versatility and practicality in matters chirurgic, even he found himself at a loss sometimes when presented with certain kinds of cases. Thus, I must relate another episode that I wish that I might forget but one that illustrates these very qualities I have mentioned and one that, in the end, had a profound effect on the course of my own life. You may judge for yourself whether our actions were correct as Christian men, as men of medicine, as human beings.

I remember the day quite clearly. On that dread occasion, several months after I began my studies with the Benedictine, the relative quiet and peace of the infirmary suddenly shattered into a thousand thousand tiny pieces. The air itself suddenly seemed to writhe in panic as havoc broke in upon us.

I sat at a desk poring over a medical text; probably Dioscorides or Galen or Celsus or perhaps Isadore of Seville, since they were the authorities I found most interesting at the time. The infirmary was nearly empty and, except for the occasional cough or moan or rustle of discomforted movement, generally quiet. Outside, the autumn air had begun to slow and cool. Grey soupy clouds, stirred by the winds, bubbled across the sky. Only an occasional window stood ajar to let in the fresh air and the zephyr thus allowed entrance was often spurred into gusts by the cold air that caused it to canter like a skittish stallion about the room, nuzzling the backs of our necks and our arms into gooseflesh. And then we suddenly knew that on the back of that cold, grey horse rode disaster…

The first hint of this came in the form of a clamour out in the street. The noise gradually increased in volume and intensity until as suddenly and unexpectedly as lightning and thunder the doors burst open and a small crowd crashed in among us like a tree instantly toppled by the force of a storm, landing there in the room like a pile of broken branches. Many of the crowd fell to their knees wailing and crying, others stood there howling like fiends from Hell while some just stood poised dumbly, uncertainty mingled with shock and horror on all their faces.

The object of this intensely emotional behaviour was a young boy carried on a makeshift litter made from a blanket who had been set on the floor by four men. I felt the shock and horror rise into my own face to mingle with theirs, darkening my clarity of thought as mud suddenly stirred up in a clear-running stream clouds its crystalline purity. And with it panic began to flow.

The boy can only be described as…broken; broken almost to the point of no longer being recognisable as human, each limb twisted at odd angles even from the individual joints whose positions no longer suggested for which natural movements they might be employed. His feet were crushed and beginning to swell like the bladders of sheep used to carry liquids. Indeed, those feet did look as though they contained not flesh and bone but some kind of fluid. Every joint and digit in his hands seemed flexed and splayed in unnatural ways.

And his face. Even now, the horror of that image brings bile to my throat and tears of pity to my eyes. His crushed face looked like an overripe melon that had been thrown against a wall. His eyes were invisible beneath a mass of bruised and cut flesh; the flesh protruding as though there were walnuts lodged painfully below it. His nose was unrecognisable as anything but a squashed gel of tissue and blood. His mouth bled profusely, as did his ears, and indeed everywhere he oozed his bodily fluids that had already begun to congeal and blacken even as fresh red liquor poured forth from his many wounds. I could only stare in shock and terror at this vision, frozen and immobile as Lot's wife, as if

I myself had been turned into a pillar of salt, unable to assist, unable even to think.

To his immense credit, Brother Piccolo showed no such confusion. I have striven ever after to emulate him in his calm courage and total confidence in the face of disaster. I do not think I have ever equalled his competence on that day.

He called to me but I could not respond. His voice reached me as across a vast distance, from so far away that it lacked interest because of its incomprehensibility. I felt myself shaken at the shoulders. I blinked and found myself staring into the monk's face. Dimly, awareness came to me again and I comprehended the noises and figures of the disaster.

"Can you not help me, brother?" asked the Benedictine, shaking me again.

"Wha…what shall I do?" I asked him in a whisper.

"Get these people out of here but for a few to raise him to my examination pallet," he commanded me. I was his soldier and he my lord. I obeyed immediately now that I came aware of myself again. I tried not to look at the broken boy as I passed. I opened the door that the wind had flung shut moments before.

Raising my voice, I implored the little crowd, "Please, good folk, you must wait outside and let the physician do his work. Please! Go!"

Some turned to me, their eyes betraying their lack of immediate comprehension, others glaring with indignation. I gestured to the door and they began to shuffle forward like a flock of sheep obeying the yips and snaps of the shepherd's dog. I found that if I circled the crowd, embodying that sheepdog analogy, they could be herded toward the portal, as if being escorted out of the fold and into the pastures. Several yet remained behind and I quickly realised that these were a few volunteers who had stayed to assist in lifting the boy and indeed, who had carried him to this place, and his parents.

Brother Piccolo directed the litter bearers to his examination table and the shattered little bundle was placed upon it.

"What is the boy's name?" he inquired of the parents.

"Isaac," spoke the father, quietly, his voice nearly a whisper.

With a start, I just then became aware that these people were not Christians at all but Jews, though I should have known at once from their appearance and would have but for the shock of the boy's physical aspect. The Benedictine had never paused a moment to consider rejecting their plea for his assistance. Indeed, I might say that they had not pled his help but simply assumed it would be given. I had little time to reflect upon that fact at that moment. Later, I would question the Brother on the issue. Now, there was much to do.

"Isaac," said Brother Piccolo into the boy's ear. "Can you hear me, Isaac?" The boy moaned quietly and then was silent. I assumed that Isaac had understood someone had called his name but I was not sure.

"Rest easy, my son," soothed the monk's voice sweetly and confidently. "We shall do whatever we can to help you and with God's assistance, all will be well."

He turned to the others, the boy's parents. "I'm sorry, but I must ask you now also to leave. The examination and procedures that will follow will be most distressing for you.

Leave my assistant and me to our work. It will be better for the boy if there are no distractions for us."

The bearers immediately stepped back and shuffled for the door. The boy's father gathered in his wife and virtually carried her away as she could barely walk by herself. She looked as though she might collapse at any moment.

When they had gone, Brother Piccolo issued instructions as rapidly as a Scythian bowman issues arrows from horseback, one upon another. Even as he spoke he prodded and tested the boy's limbs, assessing the damage.

"Bring me the flask in the box on the shelf above my window. Be careful you don't drop it. I have no other supply of that medicine. Then go to the kitchen and order hot water brought here. Next, find me as many splints of various sizes as you can find. Also, find Brother Ambrose. I shall need his help in setting the bones. Then go and find clean bandages and wraps for the wounds and to tie the splints."

I waited for more instructions to fly forth.

"Go," he urged. "The flask first."

I sped to his room and found the box containing the flask. I did not wish to risk dropping the medicine bottle itself so I carried the entire box, with the vial in its protective wrappings, back to the physician. I deposited it gently on a table as if it contained some expensive and precious crystal goblet.

"Open the box and hand me the flask. Uncork it first, that's right."

I unstopped the bottle and handed it over to him.

"Now help me hold his mouth open so that I may pour a few drops into his throat."

Gingerly, I pried open the swollen lips, trying not to cause the child any pain, as if it were possible to inflict any more injury upon him. His jaw seemed quite stiff and I found it difficult to hold his mouth open while Brother Piccolo deposited the liquid into it, about a spoonful of the medicine. He must have expected the stiffness and I was filled with admiration at his knowledgeable skill.

"Good," he said. "Off with you, then."

I did as he bid me to do. I rushed off without a backward glance. As it happened, I found Brother Ambrose almost immediately I had left the infirmary, as he had already heard about the arrival of this most recent patient and was hurrying to assist.

"The infirmary?" I asked. He nodded in mutual understanding of the truncated query. I hurried on.

When I had done all that Brother Piccolo had bid me do, I returned to the infirmary. There, the Brothers had begun the work of trying to undo the severe damage done to the young Jew. Clearly, the lad was unconscious for he moved not at all even though the surgeon and the physician were taking great liberties with the mechanics of his various joints. They had already reset the major limbs: legs and arms, each of which had been either broken or the bones thrown out of their sockets. Now they worked on the minor bones in the digits of the boy's hands, setting, applying splints and wrapping each joint quickly and skilfully. I stood watching, uncertain how I could assist.

Shortly, the hot water and bandages arrived, borne by a servant from the kitchen. He struggled through the door and I went to hold it open for him. I directed him to set the scalding pot of liquid next to the low examination table and took the bandages from him. He left, a look of horror on his face as he stared back over his shoulder. I forgot about him in a moment as Brother Piccolo, without looking up from his work, directed me to a new task.

"Find the box in the pharmacopoeia labelled 'black nightshade.' Take a couple of the leaves out of the box and crumble them in the boiling water. Take care that you use the pincers to remove them from the box, as they are quite deadly if handled improperly. Then soak the bandages in the water. I'll tell you when I'm ready for them." He went back to his work and did not speak again except to murmur occasionally to Brother Ambrose over some point or other as together they straightened out the boy's bones.

I did as he bade me, carefully removing the leaves with pincers and crumbling them in a piece of cloth so they did not make contact with my skin. Then I tore the bandages into varying sized strips and dumped them into the pot, stirring them around with a large spoon we used for such purposes.

Black nightshade is one of many medicines of dual nature. If used sparingly and correctly the leaves may be used quite effectively in medicinal treatments, for example, as a sudorific to help release excess heat in the body during fever or as a soporific to ease bodily pain and headache. However, the medicinal properties vary from season to season and place to place, as is common with many of the medicinal herbs used by physicians, and is therefore often unreliable in its application. When used improperly by incapable medical practitioners the herb can kill. In fact, I was somewhat surprised by my teaching master's use of the plant in this instance for I had read of its dangerous properties. I would later seek out an explanation from him on this subject and other inconsistencies in his treatment of the young Jew but at the moment I was too busy to think of these things.

For a full three hours the surgeon and the physician laboured over the boy. When they had finished, every joint had its splint and every splint was swathed in bandages that had been dipped and rinsed in the black nightshade solution.

Additionally, any large open cuts had been stitched and all the wounds washed with a cleansing solution of vinegar mixed with a portion of the nightshade tincture. After their constant work the two monks were exhausted and looked it. Brother Piccolo ran his fingers over his pate again and again and rubbed his eyes frequently. Ambrose looked thoroughly depleted. The two medical men stood over the boy looking at him for some time. Ambrose murmured to Brother Piccolo that he was going to sleep on his pallet in his cell back in the cathedral barracks and the latter merely nodded. Then Ambrose left, smiling wanly at me and patting my shoulder as he passed.

I stood beside the Benedictine, gazing down at the young Jew. The boy's breathing sounded rather laboured and bubbly to me. His breath came short and gasping through his mouth rather than his nose and I wondered if perhaps he might be conscious. I asked this of Brother Piccolo.

He let out a long drawn-out sigh before answering. Then he said, quietly, "No. I don't think he's conscious. That draft

I administered to him earlier was pure extract of the opium poppy. Not the local variety but that from across the Middle Sea beyond the Holy Land. It is a very expensive remedy and one that I use only in extreme emergencies. No. He is asleep, free, I hope, from all pain. He deserves that, at least."

I wondered what that last cryptic comment meant and of course his statements about the opium generated a whole new set of questions in me. Somehow, I knew this was not the appropriate time to ask, though, and I curbed my natural curiosity. I stood with the monk in silence. He placed his hand on my shoulder, a warming gesture, and I felt very much a part of the place and the event, as though I, too, had contributed to the welfare of this battered young patient.

After a few moments he slapped me on the shoulder and said, "You should go eat and then try to sleep, boy."

At his suggestion, I became immediately aware of my hunger. My mouth watered even at the thought of a slice of bread. I had not eaten since the noon meal and it was past Vespers now.

"I think perhaps I will pay a visit to the kitchens," I replied. "Will you come with me?"

When he declined to accompany me I offered, "What can I bring you, then?"

"Nothing. I don't think that I could eat right now," he said, rubbing his eyes in exhaustion.

I left him there, still staring at his patient and left for the kitchens, resolved to bring him the best of whatever I found there.

◆

As I left the infirmary the boy's father and mother immediately accosted me. They looked as haggard and drawn as the physician I had just left standing over their son. They spoke rapidly to me in oddly accented Alemaigne and I had to listen closely to gather what they were asking, though I knew what they would be asking even if they had spoken in the Saracen tongue. I tried to reassure them that everything that could be done for the boy had been done.

"*Danke, Herr Doktor,*" the father repeated over and over.

I felt rather guilty though secretly delighted that I had been taken for a physician like Brother Piccolo, but I could not maintain a deception. I assured them that I was not a doctor, only a medical student. If they would thank anyone it must be the Benedictine and his brother surgeon, Ambrose. In their language I told them as much.

"But how can we? We have not been allowed to see our boy, or the learned man, either," replied the woman. "When can we see our son, master clerk?"

I rankled a bit at this reduction of my status in their eyes but it was true: I was a clerk. I hesitated. I wanted to eat but at the same time I felt that they should be able to see their son now that the emergency was over. What would Brother Piccolo do? Would he want them to see the patient or should the boy be left alone to recover his consciousness? After all, his parents could not communicate with their son or help in any way.

I decided after a moment's vacillation to consult Brother Piccolo. I asked them to wait and went back inside. Moments later the Benedictine ushered them through the door and I went on my way again to the kitchens for food for all of us.

When I returned a short time later with a square of cheese, some small meat pies, a loaf of dark bread and a pitcher of wine, the boy's mother and father stood in a visually powerful embrace, for it so impressed me as I looked upon them, at the head of their son's cot. She, squeezing shiny tears from liquid dark eyes, blinking occasionally, her lashes bending in defeat upon the stricken mask of her face; he, stolidly supporting her, armouring her with his strength, grieving as openly as a child.

They were children themselves, lost and alone except for each other, disenfranchised from the routine and security of the obligations of parenthood. Theirs was a child who could no longer respond to or be bound by them. His fate, as we understand the Boethian conception of preordination, ultimately known only to God, lay out of the realm of parental influence. He was already dead or would continue living according to how the Lord had determined the compass of his life. Nothing they did or felt or thought with respect to the boy could change that.

And so they stood, locked in their embrace like two stone statues, frozen in their mood and physical attitude by the Hand of the Sculptor who created them; an Artist whose technique was unfathomable, Whose chisel marks were ineluctable and Whose conception of the finished masterpiece was unknowable. Their tableau rests unaltered in my memory today, an event charged with God's presence, their tragedy forever carved into my recollection of their mutual suffering, indelibly hammered home by the blows of the pain they suffered.

I could not know how this event, singular in itself, would affect the outcome of my life. For, in the months that followed, my association with this family and their community would bring about a chain of events that would determine my future for half a lifetime. The Jews of Mainz would know fiery persecution that would lead to their utter destruction an event that would set me on a path for an entirely new unlooked-for destiny.

But that was for the future. At that time, I had no inkling of what lay ahead for me and for these grieving parents. For the moment, I was impressed by their love for their son and the emotional demonstrations they displayed on his behalf that were so like those of Christians. I had until then thought such a thing impossible.

I set the food on a table close to the boy's bed and broke off some bread and cheese, then poured myself a cup of wine. I mumbled that they might help themselves but I did not wish to disturb their grief. They ate nothing. Brother Piccolo silently rose from his stool by the bed, took some food himself and then sat down at his vigil again. I set my food down on the desk at which, earlier, I had been peacefully reading my medical text and then picked up a stool in each hand and set them down next to the Jews. Then I went back to my desk and sat nibbling my food, though I found that I had very little appetite after all. I leafed through the book trying to read but able only to gaze across the pages not concentrating enough to apprehend anything entering my eyes from the vellum.

The boy never regained consciousness. In the several months that followed, Isaac's parents returned again and again to his bedside, the mother every day, all day, the father occasionally, perhaps once every few days. They talked to the boy since Brother Piccolo encouraged them to do this.

They read to him from letters and books and from their own bible, that which they called the Torah. Listening to them sometimes, explaining the stories in Alemaigni to the boy, I gradually came to learn that their bible was very similar to our own Vulgate excluding of course the life and works of Our Lord Jesus, which the Jews, to their everlasting damnation do not include in theirs or, inexplicably, even believe. In the end, their prayers and efforts and Brother Piccolo's excellent medical care availed them nothing for their son never once opened his eyes.

Since the mother visited daily, I came to know her well. Her name was Ruth, just like the faithful and steadfast daughter-in-law of Naomi, and indeed she was equally faithful and steadfast with respect to her son. The boy, she told me, was named Isaac, though I had not forgotten that fact, and her husband, Yaakob. They had lived in Mainz their entire lives. This knowledge surprised me at that time since I had always assumed that all Jews came from somewhere outside Christendom and only lived for a time amongst Christians before travelling on. She laughed at this naiveté. No, her family and her husband's family had lived in Mainz for several generations. They knew no other homeland but Lower Lotharingia. Further, she informed me, this was true of most of the members of the Jewish community in the city.

Many of the Jews of Mainz, I discovered from Ruth, were merchants and bankers. The latter were quite necessary in Christian communities, since by Our Lord's injunction we are forbidden to loan money at interest because this encompasses the sin of usury, as we all know. I learned from her that many Christian men of wealth and position actually invested money with the Jewish community in order that they might realise a return on that investment from interest on loans granted to both Christian and Jew alike. This seemed to me barely outside the bounds of the injunction against usury, but I suppose that technically such Christians were sin-free, though perhaps not so free in good moral conscience. I began to see just how necessary were the Jews to our society and how ubiquitous. Personally, I thought nothing ill about the practise of banking since my father had upon occasion found the necessity of borrowing money for various projects of his own. Moneylenders were a necessary evil, that was all. So on this account at least I had nothing against the Jewish community. However, I did not understand why they could not accept Jesus Christ as the True Messiah and Son of God. There are so many passages in the ancient biblical writings, those that are a part of the Jewish canon as well as Christian, which indicate the coming of Our Lord Jesus to earth. Clearly, His life and works demonstrate that He was truly the Saviour looked for so long by all men, including Jews. But I would not convert Ruth despite my efforts to do so. She remained adamant that Jesus, while a good man, a prophet even, was not the Messiah. All Jews still awaited their true Messiah. In the end we agreed to disagree, though I could not respect her viewpoint.

Despite our theological differences, I saw her as a woman no different in other ways than, for example, my own mother. She evidently cared for Isaac, her stricken son. She came each day as I have mentioned and assisted Brother Piccolo in his ministrations. She held the funnel and hose with which the doctor force-fed his young catatonic patient a mixture of water, healthful herbs and mashed foods. She helped to change his bed linens and soiled clothes. Always she performed these deeds with perfect dignity and complete dedication. I came to admire deeply her quiet acceptance of the new reality and her calm, peaceful and steadfast manner. I found that, despite the fact that she was ostensibly an enemy of Christianity, I liked her very much.

Eventually, when the pain of remembering it had passed, Ruth told me what had happened to her son. He had been on his way to the home of Isaac ben Moses the boy's namesake and their rabbi, a religious teacher somewhat like our own Christian priests, when, walking up a hilly street in the Jewish quarter, he had stepped out into the cobbles to cross behind a large heavy wagon pulled by several oxen and carrying a load of wine tuns. These huge barrels were piled high on the wagon and not roped in. Suddenly the tongue of the wagon had snapped in two as the wagon master turned his team and its freight. The vehicle rolled backwards, gaining momentum quickly as its driver leaped to safety shouting out a warning. That warning came too late for Isaac. The wagon spun down and around and its load tumbled over its width with barrels flying into the air shattering and smashing themselves into pieces as they struck each other, the disintegrating wagon, the cobblestones of the street, and Isaac, trapped beneath it all with no opportunity to flee. When all had settled the boy was left as broken as the wagon and its cargo.

One day, a week or so before Advent, Ruth came to spend the day with her catatonic son. She finished her ministrations and helped Brother Piccolo feed and medicate him, washed and changed him, then sat for several hours talking quietly to him, reading to him, and holding his hand. Finally, near sunset, she rose and walked over to me where I was preparing a few prescriptions for the Benedictine's other patients and putting things away as I prepared to leave for Vespers. She laid a hand upon my shoulder. At first, I barely felt the touch, so light it was, but I started as I became aware of the weight of her hand on me. I turned around to face her.

I smiled and asked her, "Is anything wrong, Ruth?"

"No," she returned the smile, somewhat shyly. She hesitated then took my right hand in both of hers. "You have been so kind to me and to my son and husband, young master cleric," She said in her heavily accented Alemaigne. She stopped, her eyes filling with tears. She looked at the floor.

"Yes, Ruth?" I inquired solicitously. I felt my own eyes beginning to mist and swallowed hard, blinking.

She smiled again and looked up at me. "I would like to repay some of that kindness in some fashion."

As I began to protest that this was not necessary in any way, she cut me off. "I suppose that I am asking another favour of you. But it's a small thing that I ask of you. Would you come to our home for supper?"

I stood taken aback. I had not expected this. I did not, for a brief moment, know quite how I felt about entering a Jewish home but then prejudice fled in the face of rationality and common sense. I had come to know these people and they were good folk, not the devil's allies that our culture's stereotypical image would have them be. These were God's children, too. Our Vulgate says as much. Moses, Abraham, David and Jesus Himself had all been Jews. Jews lacked only knowledge of Christ's Love to bring them to the Kingdom of Heaven themselves. I thought, naively, in the back of my mind that perhaps I could bring Jesus into their lives myself. This might be a beginning to that end. Who knew? Besides, Yaakob and Ruth had shown themselves to be kindly and trustworthy people. That alone should have been enough to make me accept their offer.

I smiled after this moment's thought. "I would be delighted, Ruth. When?"

We set the date for Sunday, a few days hence, and then she squeezed my hand and departed.

I turned to see Brother Piccolo smiling at me, his eyes dancing with amusement.

"What is it, Brother?" I asked, a little annoyed by his amusement.

He raised his brows and smiled wider, spreading his hands before him, palms up. "Nothing, young master cleric," he said, using Ruth's formal address to me in an ironic tone. Then he sobered somewhat. "Well, maybe something."

"Was I wrong to accept her invitation to supper, *magister*?"

"Not wrong, no...," he dangled the final word. "But I would advise caution for two reasons. The first reason is the least in some ways. Remember that Ruth and Yaakob are Jews and even though all are welcome in our infirmary, whether Jew, Greek or Saracen, that is not the case out there." He gestured vaguely around the room meaning to indicate the larger world beyond its walls. "I would advise discretion on entering the house of our Jewish friends for not everyone is as open-minded as you are my boy. There are Christians who would resent your association with Jews as there are Jews who would also resent your association with them as a Christian."

I laughed outright at that.

"What do you find amusing?"

"Well," I replied naively. "How could a Jew resent a Christian among them? I would think they would be happy about it and even...honoured in a way. We are Christians." I smugly uttered the last word.

"Even so has it ever occurred to you that Jews have every reason to mistrust us Christians? We do make a practise of shunning them for the most part. They even have their own quarter in the city and are not allowed to live among us. Why should they trust you, let alone you them?"

"I trust Ruth and Yaakob, why shouldn't they trust me?"

"I am not talking about Ruth and Yaakob."

"But they are Jews and they trust me. Why would other Jews worry about whether I visited Ruth's family?"

"Probably for the same reason that other Christians would. Each mistrusts the other out of long-standing mutual fear. But do not let that stop your friendship with Ruth and Yaakob. I caution only that you be circumspect and discreet. Do not openly go there and do not tell others of your intention to break bread with them. For your safety as well as theirs. Will you do that?"

I could see the wisdom in his suggestion though I could not really understand the threat from the Jewish community. After all, we were the Christians. How could they hurt me? But I agreed to his suggestion to be cautious about my visit.

"What is the second thing?" I asked.

"Hmmm?" he murmured absently, mixing a few herbs in a stone mortar and crushing them with a pestle.

"You said there were two things," I said impatiently. Brother Piccolo could be so absent-minded sometimes. I assume that is because his mind was always racing from idea to idea and constantly busy working out some new problem with respect to medicine.

"Oh. Oh, yes." He nodded. "Well, the other is something you shall probably have to discover for yourself. You are aware by now of the many cautions advised when dealing personally with patients." I nodded. "Keep those in mind when you go there. I'm sure you have no ill intentions toward these people but you don't know what they have in mind."

As I started to protest at this paranoid, precautionary, and somewhat proprietary advice he waved me to silence.

"I'm not saying that they have any ill intention toward you. I'm only saying that they are caught up in the emotions that have grown out of seeing their son lying near to death and they may be substituting you for their missing son at this point. Please respect that notion. Their transferral of affection to you may be discomfiting for you. I have seen such things before. You must be respectful and yet distance yourself from their attentions at the same time."

I must admit that possibility had not occurred to me. I was a few years older than their son but near enough to his age to make me wonder if what the Benedictine said was, in fact, true. I thought of myself as an apprentice *medicus* but they might think of me as just a youth like their son. Certainly, they had not asked Brother Piccolo or Brother Ambrose to sup with them, both of whom probably would have declined anyway because of religious, ethical or bureaucratic restrictions specific to their order and place in the cathedral. On the other hand Our Lord Jesus said, when asked by the

Pharisees why He ate with publicans and sinners, "Those who are whole need not a physician, but those that are sick." This seemed doubly appropriate to this occasion.

I promised my mentor that I would be cautious.

Caput Tertius

I arrived at the house of Ruth and Yaakob in the late afternoon on that Sunday three days after I had been invited, the twenty-fifth day of November as we Christians count the time, for the Jewish calendar is vastly different from our own. Brother Piccolo had relieved me of my duties at the infirmary—which were light enough anyway since it was the Lord's Day—for the afternoon, with the injunction that I return in time for Compline an hour or so after darkness fell. Naturally, I had agreed. Ruth met me at the door of their shop, a warehouse for spice imports. The landscape inside was quite familiar to me as it was not altogether dissimilar from my father's warehouse in London though, of course, much smaller. Ruth led me through the shop and into a back room where a set of wooden steps led upward. We climbed the staircase to the upper floor of the building.

Upstairs, the apartment was open and roomy. I suppose it was like many such buildings in Mainz or any other European city or town in terms of construction and interior furniture. The hip roof was made of thatch and supported by large upside-down wishbone-shaped trusses with a huge centre pole running its length. The end walls were of split timbers and chinked with mud and ash mixed with straw.

The space was well furnished with tables and chairs of fancifully carved dark wood with a large trestle table and benches on either side dominating the middle of the room. A door on one end wall indicated another chamber beyond this main room that I took to be sleeping quarters. Near the door stood a charcoal brazier below an opening in the roof that allowed its smoke to escape. All about, candles were lit since there were no windows on this second storey of the house. On the trestle table, in its centre, stood a large candelabrum with nine branches, but containing no candles and I wondered, briefly, what purpose it served. Strange that it should have the capability to carry so many points of light on its limbs when one would do, but stranger that it stood unfilled with candles.

Yaakob had climbed the stairs to the main room immediately after us. The shop had been closed for the day, of course, since it was Sunday. Despite the fact that Jews did not observe the Sabbath on the same day as the followers of the True Faith, all members of their community respected the customs and observances of the Christian majority.

As Yaakob explained to me, this practice brought them far less trouble from the Christian authorities and indeed, the town's people, despite the fact that he was thus limited to a five day week for his business to be open, than if they only practised their own customs and remained open on the Sunday. However, he used the time to put his books in order and clean the warehouse to prepare for business on Monday.

Yaakob invited me to sit at the table on one of the benches. I sat down and Yaakob sat down opposite me. Ruth stood behind him. For an uncomfortable few moments they both stared and smiled at me without saying anything. Then as if suddenly awakening, Ruth started and offered me wine.

I thanked her and accepted the offer, wondering if perhaps she had seen Isaac sitting there instead of me. Moments later she returned with a small cask of wine which she set on the table. Yaakob pulled the bung and poured two glasses, one for himself and one for me. Apparently, Jews do not consider their women drinking with their men appropriate in certain social situations as we think also, particularly when a relative stranger enters the house. We sat sipping our drinks in silence for a moment. I considered mentioning Isaac's stable health but reconsidered, as I did not know if this line of conversation might upset my hostess. Instead, I blurted out a question about the candelabrum.

"So why does this candelabrum have nine holders and no candles?" I have ever been insatiably curious and often reckless and foolhardy with my tongue and its questions. I thought immediately that this was a tactless question. "I mean," I amended, "it would shed a lot of light if it were full and lit." What if they thought I was criticising the light level, that I thought the room was too dark? I tried over-hard not to offend them, but it looked as if offence was all I might succeed in. However, Yaakob eagerly answered my question.

"That is a special candelabrum called the 'menorah.' It is for very special Jewish holidays, which we start celebrating tonight. That is the reason we invited you." He smiled and behind him, Ruth beamed at me. "Today is the twenty-fifth day of Kislev, first day of our celebration called Hanukkah."

"What is Hanukkah?" I asked, pronouncing it badly, with the wrong inflection and accentuation. He seemed to spit the beginning of the word from the back of his throat and I was unable to reproduce the sound.

He chuckled. "Hanukkah," he said, pronouncing it slowly and properly, "is like your Christ Mass holy day. Only we don't celebrate birth of baby Jesus. We honour Maccabees. It is a long history story and...mmm... I shall tell it to you if you would like?"

Despite his rather thick accent, I liked the way he spoke. He had a deep, melodious manner of speech that I remember fondly and clearly.

"Yes, please," I said. I was ever the avid student where history was concerned.

"All right, then. Sit comfortable. For it is a long story." He drained his wineglass and held it out for his wife to refill. She topped up mine as well and then disappeared down the stairs.

"You have heard of Alexander of Macedonia?" My eyes must have lit up eagerly for I knew the name of Alexander the Great as well as I knew the names of any of the great men of the past. Yaakob nodded. "Yes. I see you have. Alexander conquered the Jewish homeland of Judea many centuries ago hundreds of years before your Jesus was born. Then many years later, long after Alexander was dead, a king called Antiochus took control of some of Alexander's empire. This new king tried to make Judea into a Hellenic country, like Hellas but not Hellas."

I interrupted him. "What is Hellas?" I asked, for I had not heard that name before.

"Same as Romans call Greece. Graeca. Graeca is Hellas. Mmm?" He nodded. "Hmm." He always made that little musing grunt. I remember that clearly, too.

"So Hellenes ...mmm...outlawed...that is the right word?" I nodded to assure him. "Hmm. So. Outlawed all Jewish practices and customs. No more Sabbath. Now Greek gods come into the temple. No more worship of the One God... Greeks burn pig sacrifices to false pagan gods in our synagogues. Some Jews like this but most do not. One who does not like this is Mattathias, a priest. He kills a fellow Jew who is about to obey the Greek order to kill a pig in the temple. Mattathias and five sons fight the Greeks then flee to the mountains and keep fighting them. Later, when Mattathias is dead, his son, Judah the Maccabee, is the new leader to fight the Greeks. Many die as martyrs in order to win freedom for all Jews because they refuse to be told how to live. Finally, Judah and his army win against the Greeks and drive them from Jerusalem. Afterwards, when they first go to worship in the temple on the twenty-fifth of Kislev—today—there is only one flask of oil found to burn in the temple menorah but it miraculously lasts for eight days, for the length of the festivities to celebrate Jerusalem's new-won freedom. To celebrate the victory of the Maccabees over the armies of Antiochus and of their heroism to rather die than accept his perverse decrees, and to celebrate the miracle of the oil, we have Hanukkah."

I sat in silence thinking about this story. This chapter of history of which I had not been previously aware fascinated me. I realised that in the days of the Maccabees, the Greeks were a false people as they are even to this day, as everyone knows. Further, I realised that Yaakob, in speaking of the 'worship of the One God' meant the same God I worshipped, the God of Abraham, Moses, Noah and King David. The God of Joshua, Daniel, Lot and Adam.

In some inexplicable fashion, we Christians were intertwined with those of the Hebrew faith but the connecting thread had unravelled when we accepted that Jesus is the Son of God while they, for some unfathomable reason, denied Christ's divinity. I would later learn why this essential difference developed but during that December of the Year of Our Lord, 1095, I knew little beyond the fact that Christians and Jews, while similar in beliefs in some respects, diverged widely from the essential locus, the Birth of Our Lord.

However, I did at that time respect and appreciate how hard the Maccabees had fought for their religious beliefs and for the right, a right which had been stripped from them without recourse, to worship God according to their beliefs and traditions, to serve their Lord as He expected them to serve Him. This seemed an admirable and legitimate cause for celebration. I felt, then, that I was fortunate to be able to share the holiday celebrations of Ruth and Yaakob, even if the occasion for my presence was as a surrogate for their own unfortunate son.

"Does this story make sense to you?" asked Yaakob. I realised that my host and hostess examined me with concern in their faces lest I had not understood. I assured them that the story made perfect sense and was rightly observed as a seminal moment in their history.

We sipped our wine in silence for a time while Ruth fussed about bringing dishes and spoons and knives to the table. Soon, she had brought everything necessary to outfit a small banquet. Then she whispered into Yaakob's ear and he gathered up the candelabrum, which I now knew to be called a menorah, and carried it to a table which he then placed by the stairs. He explained that the candelabrum was always placed by a door or window so that all would see it and take heart during the Hanukkah festivities. All Jews he meant, of course.

"What happened to Judah the Maccabee?" I asked.

"Ah...good question. He dies before the struggle for freedom from Antiochus is over. He dies in battle fighting for Jewish independence and he is remembered as a great martyr who would rather die than give away his Jewish culture and heritage."

Yaakob walked to the brazier and stuck a straw into the coals. As the straw burst into a tiny flicker of warm orange light he called to Ruth, who had since disappeared downstairs, in a tongue I had never before heard. I heard the outside door below open and close again and she called back to Yaakob in the same tongue. Then she hastened back up the stairs with a tray of small breads or cakes as they appeared to be to me. She set them down on the table in front of me.

"The stars have begun to appear," she said, smiling excitedly, then went to stand beside her husband.

Yaakob, still holding the straw as its flame licked slowly toward his fingers, crossed to the menorah. Then he inserted two beeswax candles into the holder: one on the extreme right and the other on the extreme left. The left-most candle sat in a raised holder above the level of the other sockets. He handed the burning straw to Ruth and she lit this candle. Then she began to chant a prayer or a song as it sounded to me. As she spoke in the Hebrew tongue, Yaakob translated for my benefit.

"Barukh atah Adonai...," began Ruth.

"Praised are You, O Lord, Our God, King of the Universe, Who sanctified us with His commandments and commanded us to kindle the Hanukkah lights," Yaakob translated the entire verse she spoke.

Yaakob had closed his eyes and thrown his head back and I sensed that a kind of religious ecstasy or fervour had overtaken him. Ruth's eyes had misted over and shimmered in the candlelight. A chill ran up and down my spine and a surge of awe welled up from within me and ran through my entire body. Surely, God had entered me and these good people in the midst of this ceremony.

Ruth continued a second verse, "Barukh atah Adonai..."

"Praised are You, O Lord, Our God, King of the universe, Who performed wondrous deeds for our fathers, in ancient days, at this season," whispered Yaakob.

A tear welled over from Ruth's eye and slid unnoticed by her down her cheek. Perhaps she thought of her poor son as she prayed. I closed my eyes, partly from respect for her and partly from the need to suppress my own tears which threatened to flood forth. I squeezed my eyelids tight to prevent this.

For some reason I was embarrassed that Ruth might see me weep. I believe that this was because I wanted to appear aloof from this un-Christian ceremony and not seem to be drawn into it as indeed I was. I do not think that I can be found at fault in this now or even then since they clearly worshipped God in this ceremony however lacking it was in the precepts of Our Saviour, Jesus Christ. They might not have everlasting life as Our Lord promised us but still their respect and fear of God was evident in their ceremony.

Ruth finished her chant with a third and final verse. "Barukh atah Adonai..."

"Praised are You, O Lord, Our God, King of the universe, Who has kept us in life, sustained us, and enabled us to reach this season," Yaakob translated and a sob caught in Ruth's throat though she tried to suppress it.

I think I knew what she felt at that moment for surely then she thought of her son lying in his unconscious state in the infirmary at the Archbishop's Palace. A difficult season it was for Ruth and Yaakob. I sensed their belief that God alone might sustain them through their grief and that He alone might save the life of their child. Surely this demonstration of faith reflected their intense belief in God's power and grace as it would have done in any Christian household.

Yaakob opened his eyes. He handed another straw to Ruth who gave life to the right-most candle from the essence of the first she had lit. Then he came and sat down with me again.

He explained that the candles must be lit after the stars first appeared in the sky and only one candle would be added to the menorah each night. The first candle, that which had been lit last, was a special candle since it signified the beginning of the Hanukkah festival and so a special prayer would be said and special songs would be sung. The first two songs would be sung each night as a new candle was lit and the last only on the first night of the festival. No work could be done by the light of the menorah so everything came to a halt after it was lit. As a consequence, the candles were made small apurpose so that they would only burn for a half hour or so into the night and then normal activity could resume.

Perhaps I have not interpreted everything he told me correctly but I report this to you with the best power of my recollection of those events which occurred in their home so many long years ago. I must confess that as he spoke I was growing somewhat distracted by the aroma of the warm little breads that Ruth had earlier set upon the table. Yaakob glanced quickly at the breads and then back at me with a smile.

"Now we recite special passages from Scripture. For every family the reading is different, I think. Ours has been spoken each Hanukkah since the time of my grandfathers' fathers, at least; from a time long before we came to Mainz. Now I recite this passage. Then we eat." He chuckled at that. I hastened to bow my head and close my eyes for the recitation of Scripture.

There was a moment of silence as Yaakob gathered himself. Then he drew in a long breath and began to speak, slowly, so slowly, as I extended my awareness past the darkness behind my eyes to catch and absorb every word that he spoke.

"'Their idols are silver and gold made by men,'" he quoted. "'They have eyes, but do not see; ears, but do not hear. They rebel against the light; they are strangers to its ways, and do not stay in its path. For the shadow of death is morning to all of them; for they are friends with the terrors of darkness.'"

I shuddered as he spoke. As I was drawn into the holy words concerning the evil in all men, shadows crept in upon me and I felt as though I was trapped within them. The forces of darkness are strong when they begin to invade a man's heart and mind. A moving blackness engulfed me, dappled by rosy flickers of warm light from the single candle in the menorah. Threatening shades seemed to rise up from the darkness, reaching out to clutch me in their grasp, black armour and swords, and I felt the presence of God flying away from me as I succumbed to the evil within.

I sank beneath its weight, deeper and deeper into a dark pit that seemed filled with a black fire burning my soul and seeking to scour away all goodness from me. The fire became thick, viscous oil, like the black tar used in Greek fire, and I gasped, trying to surface into lightness and air. It seemed to me that I swam forever upward against the corruption sucking at my arms and legs, a foulness which threatened to drown me and consume me as a rotten corpse melts into the earth. I drove the malevolence away and focused on the sound of Yaakob's voice and the warm friendly light of the candles, attempting to keep Jesus uppermost in my mind. Once more I heard in my ears Yaakob's strong voice speaking holy words.

"'They grope without light in the darkness; He makes them wander as if drunk.'"

I imagined for a moment that he spoke of me, for surely I had been wandering from place to place throughout my life seeking an unknowable future without any illumination from within or without, from the world around me or from Heaven. I resolved in that moment to worker harder to find a place for myself in the Church.

Yaakob continued. "'And I will banish them from the sound of mirth and gladness, the voice of bridegroom and bride, and the sound of the hand mill and the light of the lamp. All the lights that shine in the sky I will darken above you; and I will bring darkness upon your land declares the Lord God. Listen, you who are deaf; you blind ones; look up and see...'"

These are the words that Yaakob spoke. They come from various books of Scripture and, of course, he spoke them in his clipped accent, but I remember all that he recited and

I have translated the passages as they appear in our own Latin Scriptures and written them down for you here in our language. For Yaakob, as he informed me himself, the words spoke of not only the general tendency of men to do evil but of the particular form of evil that is practiced against Jews as a displaced people far from their homeland living in the countries of Christians.

Yaakob's people are often vilified and persecuted by us, not because of who they are as individuals but who they are as a people. I have found little tolerance or acceptance for Jews in the Christian countries I have visited in my lifetime, as I have noted before, and I think it sad that so much is lost between our peoples though we worship the same God; far better we should grow to know them and tolerate them and, hopefully, introduce them to the Truth through the teachings of Jesus and His promise of everlasting life in the Kingdom of Heaven. I know, though, that many would still, even to-day, find this opinion intolerable if not blasphemous.

Yaakob stopped talking. I opened my eyes to find him and Ruth kindly smiling at me. I felt exhausted and light-headed all at once, together.

Ruth offered the plate of breads to me. "Now we eat," she said.

I took a small loaf, thanking her, and bit into it. I still remember how delicious it was. Ruth informed me that these little breads were filled with cheese and sweetened with honey. They were fried in oil and together with the cheese remind Jews at Hanukkah of many of their past struggles. The oil represents the oil burned for eight days in the temple by the Maccabees and the cheese represents the cheese dishes served by Judith to Holofernes the Babylonian commander whom she beheaded, another story from their troubled history.

This latter event is part of their Torah and is a story told in the Greeks' canonical texts although it is not part of our own. Holofernes, a general whose liege lord was King Nebuchadnezzar, set siege to a Jewish town and the town nearly surrendered. A beautiful widow named Judith secretly entered the Babylonian camp and seduced the general in his tent. After he drank himself into unconsciousness, she cut off his head. This was the first occasion upon which I had ever heard the story of Judith and Holofernes, although in my studies of Greek literature I have read it on numerous occasions since then.

Well after dark, and probably very near to Compline I guiltily realised, I left the home of Yaakob and Ruth. They saw me to the door and wished me a happy Hanukkah. I replied in kind although I must confess I felt awkward at exchanging this sentiment with them since I felt that as a Christian I might be betraying some essential native religious tenet in embracing this foreign Jewish tradition. But as someone once wrote about visiting Rome: one should do as the Romans do. In any case, I do not feel that my soul ultimately suffered any negative effects through this momentary politeness or by participating in their celebration any more than any of us do by reading those scriptures which precede the birth of Our Lord Jesus.

As I prepared to leave, my host and hostess and opened the door to the night, Ruth leaned over and kissed me on the cheek. She had to reach up to do this as I was about a head taller than her. I flushed with embarrassment and self-consciousness, although I was at the same time delighted and moved by this show of emotion and familiarity. I kissed her back and smiled. Yaakob nodded, smiling in approval, his eyes closing for a moment. Then I departed.

I made my way back through the dark streets of the city. The first snows had not yet fallen, unusual for that time of year but it was cold and my breath fanned out around me like a fog. I realised with apprehension that perhaps I might have stayed out too late. In every city thieves and drunken bullies often prowl the dark allies or lie in wait for defenceless pedestrians. Too, I thought about Brother Piccolo's injunction about Jews resenting my presence in their quarter. I feared their attack as much as that of a thief or cut-throat, I am ashamed to say. My shoes flapped loudly on the beaten earth of the street and my long woollen robe did not allow for rapid flight should I be accosted. I felt that I must be baiting any would-be murderer with my obvious helplessness while hoping that my clerical garment would prevent an attack out of respect for the authority of the Church, though this was no guarantee against violence. Nonetheless, I came without incident to the gate of the Archbishop's Palace.

I tried the gate but of course it was locked as I suspected it would be. I walked around to the side gate which led into the infirmary. This gate, as always, was not locked. Brother Piccolo made himself available at all times to any emergency no matter what the hour. Although, to be honest, few patients or visitors ever arrived after dark. I opened the infirmary door and immediately I experienced a deep sense of shock.

Isaac, the son of my host and his wife, sat upright in his bed, his eyes wide open. Brother Piccolo sat by Isaac's bed, holding the boy's hand and murmuring softly in prayer.

He turned as I entered and nodded that I should bring a stool and sit next to him. I did so, elation filling me at the thought of the joy the boy's parents, my friends, would experience at this news. For this to happen on this night of nights, their own holy day. Impatiently, I waited for the Benedictine to finish his prayers. I had already sent a loud mental "hallelujah" Heavenward. Strangely, though, Brother Piccolo turned to face me with anguish in his eyes. And I knew that something was not as it appeared to be. Else why should he not be filled with elation as I was; or had been until he looked at me, for his glance killed the joy in me.

"What is happening, Brother?" I asked him in a whisper.

"I am not sure. He sat up by himself. I was mixing a draught for him and when I turned around to administer it, there he was, sitting up in bed and his eyes wide open staring. I spoke to him, called him by name, but there was no response from him. I have seen something similar in other comatose patients whose catatonia did not last this long but never did they sit up with their eyes open. Look into his eyes, brother."

I did as he directed, walking around to the other side of the bed. Isaac sat staring unblinking. His eyes looked gummy, for he did not blink nor did any tears wash his eyes after having them open for such a protracted period. His pupils were huge and round and black, nearly obliterating his irises. I knew that he was not aware of either Brother Piccolo or me or of his surroundings and yet a dissonance echoed within me at the sight of him staring, apparently conscious but showing no consciousness. He reminded me of a sleepwalker. But even a sleepwalker's eyes are alive. Not so Isaac's eyes.

I had an eerie sense that his soul had already left his body. I did not think that Ruth would want to see her son's face in this way with his dead eyes staring into the infinite. I looked blankly at Brother Piccolo.

He shrugged, helplessly. "As I said, I have seen others like this but they usually only sit up for a few moments and then they fall back limply. He has been this way since before Vespers. I wish I knew what it means..." He finished lamely and I thought it strange that he, never without an answer regarding things medical, sounded so puzzled and impotent. The fact chilled me.

"Have you tried to lay him back down, Brother Piccolo?" I asked.

He sighed. "That is an excellent suggestion, my boy. I am happy to see that you are confronting this case with the circumspection I have tried to instil in you." I was unsure from his tone whether he meant this in a laudatory or ironic way. "Yes, I have tried that. His body is so contracted that every muscle is stiff as a stone pillar and will not bend. And his eyes are unusual as I'm sure you observed. So empty and without life," he said echoing my own thoughts. "We can only submit ourselves to the will of God. The boy is in His hands."

I knew then that Isaac's case was hopeless. If Brother Piccolo had commended him into the hands of the Almighty then all worldly medical knowledge was useless. We could not know the boy's fate now, but a sudden foreboding told me that it would not be the one desired by all of us. I found myself staring at a plate of fruit, bread and cheese that had been left uneaten on the table next to the bed by, I assumed, my Benedictine preceptor. The cheese had dried into a tough, leathery block, the fruit where it had been cut to reveal its sweetness had withered brown, and the bread though it looked edible I knew would be stiff and hard. All I could see was the waste.

◆

I knelt on the floor in the cavernous darkness of the cathedral. The sun had not yet risen, so no heavenly light flooded through the narrow, arched windows surrounding the nave nor the clerestory windows high above, to illuminate the heart of the building. Huge candles, some on wrought iron holders, some hanging from multiple chandeliers, some in wall sconces, shed a fitful orange glow about the interior.

Darkness would not be denied even here, though. Shadows filled in the areas between the warm lighted spaces created by the candles' flames, behind and around columns, within niches in the walls, inside gaps and holes created by statuary and bas-relief carvings, like an insidious evil that by its very nature contorted goodness and transformed it into something less than luminous perfection, something frightful, threatening. Like the mind of a man, the cathedral contained essences of both light and darkness. From its apse to the double nave one could not see light without its symbiotic shadow. I knelt on the floor to one side of the central aisle near the main entrance, in the penumbra of a column as huge as a tree trunk, alone, for few attended the Matins service besides the regular clergy and clerical students indigenous to the cathedral compound. Even I hardly ever attended the early morning Mass, except on Sundays, in those days.

I stifled a yawn. This early hour, before cock-crow, normally would have found me abed. Yet I felt attending the dawn service a necessity because the evening before I had missed the Vespers service while I had been at the home of my Jewish friends and then, unforgivably, missed Compline because of my compunction to attend Brother Piccolo in his vigil with Isaac.

We sat awake all night watching our young patient. The boy had eventually sunk back into his bed and the stiffness left his body. Brother Piccolo took this to be a good portent until within the hour Isaac's body had withdrawn into a tight curl; the Benedictine called it the foetal position, an aspect affected by babies in the womb. The boy's body remained fixed in that arrangement thereafter, every limb drawn in close, neck and back arched, chin drawn into the chest, like an unborn infant in the womb. The monk then found himself totally at a loss, for this was quite without his experience. Hours later, when I left him so that I might attend the early-morning Mass, he sat on the end of Isaac's bed, piccolo in hand, softly keening a long, slow, lonely tune partly in meditation and partly in supplication. For as everyone knows music is an expression of the Divine, linked to God directly and derives ultimately from the soul of the individual who performs and creates it. That is why at each service in the cathedral a choir chanted various tunes to the glory of God.

I listened to the choir that morning, growing peaceful within myself, feeling the peace of God within me. I regret to say that so tranquil did I become that I began to nod off because of the lack of sleep from the night before. A pleasant torpor overcame me, my eyes closed and I almost entered a dreaming state.

A commotion behind me forced instant alertness upon me. I turned, blinking, trying to focus both my eyes and my attention, to see a large procession of churchmen crossing the floor of the main basilica and turning towards the nave. I was astonished to see the Archbishop himself among the crowd of about a dozen canons. As the group passed me, seemingly unaware of me, I saw Julius, the gatekeeper, in the rear. Strangely, I thought, he turned to glare at me as he passed, a sinister grimace on his greasy face and with his eyes narrowed to hostile slits. Then he faced the backs of his companions once again as they entered the east nave.

I shuddered and thought his behaviour odd at the time but attributed it to his naturally antagonistic temperament. I mused on his hostility until I noticed that I had already missed the *Introit* and its Psalm reading and the *Confiteor*, the confessions of unworthiness by the Archbishop and his attendants.

The group stood now before the wooden screen that skirted the transept, except for Archbishop Rothard who stood before the high altar. He kissed it and then began to recite the Kyrie Eleison and finished with the Christe. "*Kyrie eleison.* Lord, have mercy on us. *Christe eleison.* Christ, have mercy on us." Then he spoke the words of the *Gloria*. His voice boomed out in the hollow confines of the earthly edifice, resonating with divine harmonics. I never failed to thrill to the power of his speech.

"*Gloria in excelsis Deo.* Glory to God on high." His prayer resounded as though Moses himself exhorted the Canaanites to virtue. "*Et in terram pax hominibus bonae voluntatis.* And on earth peace to men of good will."

I, in my arrogant, self-centred youth, began to think not of Our Lord and what the words of the *Gloria* meant but rather of my own selfish opinions surrounding the anguish of my two Jewish friends. Instead of praising and glorifying God as I should have done during the Archbishop's recitation I questioned Him about why they should suffer at the hands of Christians for being unfortunate enough to have been born outside the Grace of Our Saviour. I wonder sometimes if I had offered more devotion to the Lord and less questioning of His will that morning my friends would have received better treatment than that which they ultimately received at our hands. Perhaps the Lord punished me for my conceited desires and punished my friends on that account.

Today, I pray to the Virgin Mary often to intercede on my behalf and to ask God's forgiveness for that morning's transgression, both for the sake of my soul and for the sake of the souls of Yaakob and Ruth and Isaac. I strive to perfect my meditations on God's Will and the imperatives attendant upon a true Christian Faith in His Omnipotence. But in those days my mind wandered easily enough to more worldly problems and I often lost sight of how, daily, Christ affected my life and effected His Will.

Those words, *"In terram pax hominibus bonae voluntatis,"* stuck in my mind like a chicken bone in the throat, as welcome lodged there. I mentally gagged at the phrase, clawing to allow its meaning through the constricted confines of beliefs long ago lodged there. Surely, I believed, Yaakob was, if nothing else, a man of good will. His wife could be a peer to any Christian woman for her kindness, steadfastness and charity. Yet they stood condemned by us for their unwillingness to accept, or for their ignorance of, the Blessings and Mercies of Jesus Christ, all in spite of their God-fearing piety. Even the Archbishop as he spoke now seemed to me to condemn them, unaware that he even did so.

With his back to everyone in the cathedral he pronounced the words: "*Domine Deus, Agnus Dei, Filius Patris, Qui tollis peccata mundi, miserere nobis.* Lord God, Lamb of God, Son of the Father, Who takes away the sins of the world, have mercy on us." Suddenly, as he said these words, I truly understood the awful accountability of Christian Faith: by refusing to accept that upon Christ stood the world's only chance for redemption of sins, non-Christians—Jews, Saracens, and other infidels—implicitly assisted in the perpetuation of evil, the condition begun by the first woman, Eve. The only hope for the world's people to overcome that inherent evil was to live with Jesus in their hearts and submit themselves to His Will, accept Him as Master.

Suddenly, the tallow-lit church in which I sat, for all its shadow, seemed very safe and warm. The world outside huddled in darkness, a place cold and unforgiving for those beyond the Light of Christ. Ultimately, I realised, we humans do not condemn or manumit the lives and souls of our fellow men, but rather God does that. Nevertheless, I prayed that night for the souls of Yaakob, Ruth and Isaac. Still, in my deepest heart, I knew they were doomed.

◆

December in that year of Our Lord 1095 was a most difficult month for me. In spite of the fact that this season is usually a joyous one because we celebrate the birth of the Baby Jesus, I would not fare well for at least two reasons. Early on, I discovered that my friendship with Yaakob and his family engendered consequences of a most vicious sort and from a largely unsuspected and unlooked-for source.

Little more than a week after my visit to the home of my Jewish friends, I was ordered into the presence of the

Archbishop. I had attended lectures in astronomy and music that morning—the second day immediately following the first Sunday of Advent—in one of several large halls attached to the cathedral complex, when one of Lord Rothard's personal staff came to find me. He offered no discretion but announced in a loud voice so that all could hear that I must attend immediately upon our master in the latter's chambers.

Of course, immediately, twenty eyes turned their curious gazes upon me. I slumped in embarrassment for a moment then self-consciously rose to my feet and tottered weakly after the messenger. I felt a lump of anxiety growing in my belly that seemed to cut off the flow of blood to my legs. I could barely walk as a result of my nervousness at the thought of an imminent private audience with Lord Archbishop Rothard. Why should he wish to see me? I had never even really met the Archbishop other than that single time in the dining hall, surely not a memorable occasion for him, though quite the contrary for me. I tried to swallow my nervousness and tailed along quietly behind the messenger.

We came to the entrance to the Archbishop's private quarters. The door into his chambers was simple in that there was no ornamentation attached to it and rather short so that a person entering must duck his head, as if in humility, in order to enter through it. My escort rapped twice with his knuckles.

The door immediately opened as if by itself. I saw no one there to open it until I had actually entered the room. I looked back to see if it had opened by some supernatural means but there stood a doorman shorter than the door he guarded and with a face as hard and rough as the wood of which it consisted. He directed his gaze straight ahead and did not seem to see the guests he had just allowed ingress. I ignored him thereafter as he ignored me.

I examined the chamber. This was a sort of lobby or foyer which funnelled into the main audience hall of the Archbishop's private chambers. Like the door, the foyer was devoid of any superfluous ornamentation other than a golden cross hanging above the entry into the main chamber representing Our Lord at the moment of His sacrificial death slung on the crucifix. Unlike the outer door, the inner one was of a regular size and had a small square panel cut into its surface about eye level. My escort crossed immediately to the inner door and again rapped upon it with his knuckles. After a moment the panel opened, revealing that it too was a small door but for the eyes only. A pair of eyes looked out upon us when the panel swung back. Then the panel snapped shut and the main door opened.

As he crossed its threshold my escort genuflected and made the sign of the cross, and so I, self-consciously, did likewise as I crossed over into the chamber beyond. I am not sure what I expected of the audience chamber but what I saw disappointed any expectations of grandeur I might have imagined. Again, simple adornment was the rule. No rich tapestries hung here as they would in the home of a wealthy noble or merchant. My father's home was more richly appointed in that respect. No gold or silver did I see other than a pair of silver candle holders and another golden crucifix embedded with jewels hanging above a wooden alter draped with plain white linen on one side of the room. The charcoal brazier was of simple wrought iron and not dissimilar to that in my own *cubiculum*. A chill in the air demonstrated its ineffectiveness in warming the air.

Since the room was all cut stone, large and open, a fireplace might have worked better. One window, slightly ajar to allow the smoke from the smouldering charcoal to escape, looked out over the courtyard outside the palace. As a concession, I suppose, to the comfort of supplicants appearing before the Archbishop, a heavy rug blanketed part of the floor in front of the Archbishop's chair. This chair, though large and heavy, could not be considered a throne like that of a magnate or king or emperor.

In the chair, looking just as regal as any other great ruler, sat the Archbishop in his neat robes of white wool. Ranged in front of Lord Rothard in two rows stood various church officials, some of whom I recognised and some of whom I did not. I looked at them and one or two nodded in recognition and greeting. The loathsome, ugly gatekeeper, Julius, was there, too, standing closest to me, his face twisted in a mocking smile. He did not nod. I already knew he was not my friend, and shortly he reconfirmed it.

The Archbishop looked up from a conversation with one of the priests in attendance. He smiled warmly. Then he waved me to approach and I nervously walked to his chair and knelt down before him with my head bowed. He offered his hand and I took it and kissed the official ring upon it. The hand withdrew.

"Welcome, my son," said Lord Rothard in his melodious voice. For just a moment I did indeed feel welcome at his greeting. "We regret that we have been forced to draw you away from your studies but a matter of some urgency has come before us concerning you."

I knew immediately that he spoke of my visit to the home of Yaakob and Ruth but could not imagine how the

Archbishop had come to know of it. Then I thought of Julius standing at the end of the line of attendants with his self-satisfied smirk and I knew how the information had arrived in Lord Rothard's ear. From the slobbering mouth of the gatekeeper, Julius. My friend Ulfrid, the stable master, had told me how Julius made it his business to know everything that went on in the palace, in the cathedral, and in the city. He apparently had spies everywhere whom he either paid off or blackmailed or otherwise coerced into his service. To what end he practised such deviousness I am not sure except perhaps it was that he expected to receive some sort of reward in position and confidence from his lord, the Archbishop. Or perhaps he just liked to make others more miserable that he was himself. He had never liked me, a fact which I neither understood nor particularly worried about. Until the Lord of Mainz spoke to me in his private chambers that day, that is.

"Brother Julius, step forward," Lord Rothard commanded. I thought that I detected a hint of distaste in his voice but perhaps I merely wished that such an emotion was there.

Julius stepped up behind me. I felt the hairs at the nape of my neck rise at the thought of him standing there at my back. I half-expected a knife to fall between my shoulder blades, but of course, none came.

"Brother Julius, will you relate to us the information which earlier you testified to Father Benedict?" He indicated his private secretary.

I heard Julius clear his throat phlegmatically behind me. Then he spoke in his oily, slippery voice.

"Yes, my lord. On the Sabbath last, this novice here was seen entering the home of Yaakob the spice merchant," he paused here briefly for effect and then continued, a sure triumph in the emphasis of his tone, "in the Jewish quarter of the city. And further, after I made certain enquiries I discovered that he attended Matins, but after his visit with the Jews did not attend Compline. I therefore accuse him of heresy and complicity against Christians by his association with the corrupt Jewish race."

The Archbishop smiled indulgently. "Thank you, Julius, for your vigour and perspicacity in the prosecution of your duty. However, the novice's actions can hardly be considered heresy since he has uttered not one word of heretical speech to my knowledge. As for complicity, I do not think that missing his devotional prayers constitutes an attack on the structure of Christian authority. As you yourself have earlier stated he attended Matins that day and on the very next morning and has been in attendance in the cathedral regularly thereafter. You are certainly aware, are you not, Brother Julius, that I myself often do not attend the Mass in the cathedral proper?" He dismissed Julius with a wave and the gatekeeper resumed his former place at the end of the line of attendants. Then Rothard looked down on me with a frown.

"However, young man, we are curious why you happened to be visiting these Jews on that particular day? You are surely aware that that day was Sunday, surely the holiest of the days of the week, and one on which all Christians, particularly a clerical student, should attend the Mass when it is offered and not at his convenience." This was a statement of fact, not a question to me. I was suitably abashed, I do not hesitate to mention. I was speechless with nervousness and confusion.

"Well, my son? Why were you at the home of this Jewish spice merchant?"

"Be...because he invited me, lord," I managed to stammer.

There was a ripple of laughter at my response and my face warmed with embarrassment. In Rothard I could see little amusement but perhaps I detected a bit of sparkle in his eyes, for he asked tractably, "And why were you invited by him?"

"His son, Isaac, is a patient in the infirmary, lord. In the past few months I have grown to know this man, Yaakob and his wife, Ruth. They are kind and they have suffered horribly at the injury done to their son." I spoke quickly and breathlessly for I heaved with spasms of nervous excitement.

"Ah, I see," said the Archbishop. "I have heard about the young Jew in the infirmary. Why has he not been moved to the parents' home?"

"Lord, Brother Piccolo thought it best that he remain with us. The boy is in a state of catatonia and shows no sign of waking from his coma. Brother Piccolo is confident that he can maintain the boy's health while he is in this state."

"I'm sure if anyone can, our dear Benedictine can," he responded and I could sense real pity and concern in his tone. "However, we must still ascertain why you visited the boy's parents and left off with your devotions for the rest of the day."

I knelt mutely, with my eyes downcast. My only explanation was that I was curious about Yaakob and Ruth and how they lived. I was not sure, however, that the Lord Archbishop would accept this rationalisation. I elected to elaborate in a different direction.

"Lord, I thought that I would return by Compline and thus miss only the evening Mass. I was wrong about being able to attend the late service but I was in the infirmary at the time. You may ask Brother Piccolo about this. I was with him." The reason for my lateness for Vespers, celebrating Hanukkah with Yaakob and Ruth, was something I was unsure of revealing but I knew that I could not live with the guilt of lying to the great man sitting before me in his authoritative seat. Surely he would see the goodness of religious expression, so near our own, inherent in the celebration?

"One thing further, Lord? If I may?"

He nodded.

"During that afternoon and evening, I took part in a holy day observance which Jews annually celebrate." A gasp of collective astonishment and horror huffed out of the attendants standing on the rug behind me. I hastened to add: "It is a holy day which glorifies God as we are taught to do. It is called Hanukkah."

"You see, my lord," shouted Julius. "He is tainted by Jewish blasphemy! He has participated in unholy acts with them! This young Jew should be expelled from our infirmary and his family with him so that we are not tainted further!" I turned to watch Julius's outburst.

Rothard sat in silence for a few moments staring at the gatekeeper and Julius was cowed to silence. Then quietly and with immense authority thereby the Archbishop said, "You are dismissed, Brother Julius. Thank you for attending upon us."

Julius's jaw dropped. He seemed about to speak and then thought better of it. He wheeled around and marched out of the room. The door closed quietly behind him.

There were a few snickers in the group of those observing.

Lord Rothard spoke again. "In fact, you are all dismissed."

I again bowed my head, dutifully. I must admit that a small smile of self-satisfied amusement flickered upon my face and then was quickly extinguished as I remembered my place. A rustle of flowing robes surging toward the door and a final thud as the portal closed behind me told me that they had all left the room. I kept my head bowed.

"Come and sit here beside me, my son."

Needless to say this invitation to familiarity astounded me. I moved not at all until the Archbishop spoke again. "Come. Don't kneel there like an abject peasant. Sit in this chair."

I obeyed and found myself seated next to the most powerful man in all of Mainz. However, I did not for a moment believe that this indicated any change in my status. I was still the son of a London merchant. I waited for the Archbishop to speak again.

"Your answer concerning why you missed the evening prayers neatly sidestepped the heart of the matter, young man. That is to say, why you were visiting these Jews in the first place. You seem comfortable in flaunting your visit with them, my son," he said at last.

"Flaunting, Lord?" I could not believe that he thought I took this thing so lightly as to brag about it as if I was a young nobleman who had just lost his virginity by raping a peasant farmer's daughter.

"You just told all the important men in this cathedral that you have enjoyed the company of our enemy, the Jews. Do you not think that a certain degree of discretion might be preferred?"

"I'm sorry, Lord, if I have offended you or anyone else here. I meant no disrespect."

"I'm sure that is true. And perhaps 'flaunt' is too harsh a term. But there are many here who would see your behaviour as tantamount to treason in the secular world. Do you see that this is so?"

I gulped and nodded. I certainly did realise the serious-ness of my actions, at least as those actions might be used as arrows in the bows of certain vengeful men, like Julius. I was also convinced of the rightness of my actions in a Chris-tian sense and at a baser level in a human sense. All men are brethren. The Blessed Saviour Jesus taught us that this is so. I told the Archbishop as much.

"I agree," he responded. "In fact, though, in terms of Biblical exegesis, there are as many ways to support that real-ity as there are to refute it. You must learn to recognise when you are in the company of men who would gladly support your view and when you are in the company of those who would condemn you for it."

"And whose company am I now in, Lord?" I asked, in-nocently enough.

He frowned for a moment, and I realized, too late, my hasty words might have offended. "Your tongue is as barbed as an arrow. But I will answer you. I am also one who believes that Our Lord Jesus requires us to seek out both the unbeliever and those unacquainted with the Truth of Our Saviour's teachings. Why else did He send His Apostles into the world to spread the Good News? Why else did he eat with publicans and bless prostitutes? But even then, in Our Lord's time, there were those angered by His attempts to bring the lost sheep into His Blessed Fold. They murdered Him for it. You must heed His lessons and act discreetly when you might endanger yourself by angering fellow Christians, particularly today, here in Mainz when you consort with Jews. You realise that many Christians see them as the ultimate enemy of Christianity? For they put Our Lord to death, as you know."

"I know this, Lord," I responded. "But Yaakob and Ruth and Isaac are not the Jews who put Our Lord to death. They are our neighbours and fellow citizens. Perhaps they might even become Christians themselves someday."

"Possibly. But unlikely. Few Jews can be convinced of the error of their religion."

"But Lord," I exclaimed, "they use the same Bible we do. Or almost. They pray to God. They talk about King David and Abraham and Noah, just as we do. The only thing missing is a knowledge of the Messiah."

"And that is the essential difference between our two peoples. Most Christians, that is to say most lay Christians," he amended, "which is just about everyone not ecclesiastic, know virtually nothing about the Hebrew religion and do not realise that its holy book is the foundation upon which our own Old and New Testaments are built. And in their minds, the only thing that matters is that the Christ was arrested and taken to His crucifixion by the Jews."

I thought of another penetrating reply, then. "Yes, but not all Jews crucified Our Saviour. Just those in power. And Yaakob and his family were not even born then, let alone able to decide the inevitable fate of Our Lord and Saviour. Besides, the Romans not the Jews actually placed Him on the cross."

That stopped the Archbishop for a moment. "Yes. That is true. But at the behest of the Hebrew authorities, if you remember, and rather hastily, too. In times after the death and resurrection of Our Lord His followers and apostles were persecuted and rejected oftentimes by the Jewish people, and not always those in power; commoners, too. Consider the story of the Blessed Saint Paul among the Iconians and Lycaonians, for example. In both those regions, Iconia and Lycaonia, the Saint and the Gospel that he preached were rejected by the Jews there and he was driven away by them. So in a sense, most Christians are only returning to the Jewish people the violence that early Christians and the Lamb of God Himself received at their hands." He raised his hand immediately as if to still any objection I might make. "I do not condone these similar modern actions but I think I understand them. We must all strive to be better neighbours and to love our enemies as the Christ commanded."

"I see, Lord," I said, quietly. "But that is what I was trying to do, I think. I do not condemn my Jewish friends for the past deeds of their race."

"That is commendable, and Christ-like in its intent, I have no doubt," he replied. "I advise, though, that you do not put your philosophy to the test in so public a fashion. Most authorities both within the Church and among the nobility," he seemed to choose his next word carefully, "condone the presence of Jews for a variety of reasons, not least of which is our own Christian injunction of usury, the immoral act of loaning money at interest contrary to the notion of *caritas*, charity. They are useful to secular interests and the Church hierarchy tends also to support those interests and to instil just the kind of tolerance that you evidently practice for your own reasons. Again, I commend you, for not many have your unprejudiced scope."

He smiled at me and I felt myself warming to him, all nervousness and fear of his authoritarian office abandoned.

"We are satisfied that you have not been corrupted by your exposure to these non-Christian elements in our society. Brother Piccolo, with whom this *curia* has already met, lauds your good character and informs us that you are an able and adept pupil and a good, faithful Christian. However, as you are young and impressionable, we must advise that you restrict your exposure to your Jewish friends to the bounds of this cathedral under the supervision of those older and wiser than yourself. As they visit, you may spend time in their company. Otherwise, you must not again go alone to their home or consort with them beyond the limitations we have imposed upon you. Do you accept this judgement?"

Until that moment I had not realised that I was on trial. I suppose that if I had thought about the circumstances more closely or examined the situation with my present experience, I would have noticed the similarity between what had transpired in the Archbishop's chambers and any ecclesiastical, secular or military *curia*. At the time, though, I had little experience with such solemn, formal matters. I had been judged and found not guilty. However, I found myself released from suspicion *ex fide bona*, on good faith, on the condition that I could be the friend of Yaakob and Ruth only so long as I was chaperoned by my Christian elders, despite being exonerated of Julius's charges. This rankled me. In the foolishness of my youth I could become quite indignant at the strictures unilaterally placed upon me by my elders in authority. At that moment in Lord Rothard's chambers, I concluded that I had been found guilty only of being a friend to Yaakob and Ruth. The penalty for that friendship seemed to me harsh and yet I would not fully experience the full consequences of that friendship or its most profound punishment until the next spring.

◆

As I have written, December was a most difficult month that year. The second event to which I earlier alluded was much more disturbing for me, personally, than the incident with Julius and also for everybody at the infirmary. For on The Christ Mass day, a day which should be filled with the Blessed Love of Our Lord and Saviour, when each soul should rejoice in the blessings of that most sacred holy day, we in the infirmary were stunned and saddened when Isaac died.

The cathedral community woke early that day of the Feast of the Nativity. For on this day, one of the most important observances of our calendar year as we all know, huge crowds of people from the city and beyond its environs turned out for the Christ Mass. Everyone wanted to demonstrate the depth of their piety on the Lord's birth day.

One of Julius's assistants, a pale-faced choleric lad about twelve years of age named Guernar , rudely kicked my sleeping mat well before cockcrow. I awoke but did not respond to him. He was, of course, a partisan of his master, the gatekeeper, and had no love for me. I prayed to the Lord to give me patience and withdrew my reflexive hasty prayer that scrofula invade the boy's scalp and make his life an itching misery. He kicked my feet next and I could not help lashing out with my heel at his shins. He yelped like the puppy he was and jumped back.

"Get up," he said, truculently. "They're waiting for you at the cathedral."

"Get out," I growled back. "Unless you want to eat my pillow for your breakfast."

The little cur yipped at me and scuttled out with his tail between his legs.

I groaned and forced myself to rise. After I had voided my bladder in the chamber pot and then emptied it out the window, I visited the kitchen and helped myself to a bowl of gruel under the baleful eye of my friend, Williborg, the Archbishop's master cook, busily overseeing his culinary kingdom. Williborg did not speak to me, for he was occupied with charring the body of a large boar in his great fireplace, smoke from the beast nearly filling the room, but after glaring at me in mock suspicion for a moment he merrily winked. I waggled my eyebrows up and down once in acknowledgement and hastened on to the cathedral.

I was fortunate to have easy ingress to the main church that day. Otherwise, I would not readily have found my way in, if at all. For when I entered the vestibule, a fellow student and friend, Arbogast, signalled that I should come over to the stairs which rose up into the arcade surrounding the upper part of the church and which allowed access to the windows high above the floor.

I was surprised by his invitation since many of my fellow clerics avoided me of late after my brief falling out of favour with the cathedral hierarchs. I assumed his generosity stemmed from feelings of brotherly love generated by the season. However, as he bade me do, I followed him up the stairs.

At the windows I was astonished by the spectacle outside of the building far below. The arcade was a fascinating vantage point from which to observe the folk of Mainz and its neighbouring towns arrayed below us in a seething mass of humanity. Giants we seemed and they small creatures of the field and forest. I remembered my arrival at the cathedral many months earlier and how I had admired these windows and conjectured about the view they must provide. I was not disappointed.

Though the candle of the sun had barely been lit and lifted to be hung in its vaulted cerulean ceiling, and though shadows still clung coldly to the cobbles like lizards soon to flee under the stones before the light and heat of the celestial fire, a writhing mass of people squirmed about, there in the square. Such fervent activity seemed more fitting to mounds of ants than to human beings.

Beyond the main steps of the cathedral there lay a long open piazza, as the Italians call such an open paved area, and people congregated en masse awaiting the opening of the great cathedral doors for the first mass of the day. The folk below gathered in knots here and there, breaking the homogeneity of the crowd. Within these circular knots almost always some entertaining spectacle, quite without the dignity of the occasion, was being played out. Jugglers, pipe-and-tabor players, mummers and a variety of other entertainers kept the crowd occupied while it waited for the cathedral doors to open and earned a few coins as they did so.

I was surprised at this huge turnout since the midnight mass the night before had also attracted a large crowd of the pious. However, I thought it fitting that people should generally express their piety on this of all holy days of the year. Surely the birth of Divine Majesty on earth in Jesus Christ was the occasion for such expression and probably the fact that Archbishop Rothard would administer the mass himself increased their interest. Arbogast and I left the arcade and found our places in the cathedral to wait for the mass.

Soon the doors opened and the folk of Mainz poured in like a sudden flood through a mill-race. As is appropriate to such a gathering the nobility entered first and took their places at the front or in the naves. Behind them came the common folk: burgers who sat on the city's council and the wealthier merchants following, various guildsmen and their families entered and took their places, standing, according to their importance in the city. Some of their women were shamefully dressed, I regret to say, in rather sumptuously appointed garments and I saw the head of more than one noblewoman wag back and forth with a frown on her face at this conspicuous display of wealth quite inappropriate to its attendant social status. Indeed, some of the merchants and their wives dressed more richly than many of the nobles present.

Behind the merchants stood the bulk of the common folk. A noisy rabble of common artisans, carpenters, masons, and peasants of varying description, beggars, cripples and a host of unnotable, unwashed, low-born villeins surged into the cathedral squabbling over spaces to stand to the general amusement of their higher-born brethren in the front of the church. In fact, the crowd was so large that it spilled into the piazza beyond and many of the lower folk could not even enter the church.

Shortly, the choir began to murmur and silence descended upon the crowd. The singing voices raised in crescendo as Lord Rothard arrived proceeded by a crowd of other priests who would assist in the ministration of the Christ Mass. He looked out over the audience, slowly moving his gaze over everyone there and it was as if he saw and recognised every single person. On his face a benign, peaceful smile welcomed all into the House of God. Then he turned and began the Introit.

The Archbishop's words seemed to echo within me as he proclaimed his unworthiness before God and asked the Lord, through the Blessed Virgin, through Saint John the Baptist, through the Archangel Michael, through Saint Peter and Saint Paul, to forgive his sins and make him worthy to administer the Mass. I thought of how unworthy I was, in so many ways, to do the work of Our Lord. My vanity, my pride which extolled me to make a name for myself in the Church and thus abandon my earthly father as I served, for my own selfish reasons, my Heavenly Father; my theological ignorance which provoked me into befriending an enemy of our Faith; my medical ignorance which prevented me from helping the child of my friends, Yaakob and Ruth; my confusion in not knowing how to deny them my friendship in the face of their kindness even with the evidence before me of their disbelief in the Son of God whose birth we celebrated there that Christ's Mass Day.

I closed my eyes tightly and prayed to Mary, Holy Mother of God, for some sign that would indicate the direction Our Lord wished me to take in my life. Perhaps I prayed too hard. For on that day I received not one sign but two. The problem was, I did not read those signs correctly at the time. Only in retrospect do I see what God's plan was for me in the days and months to follow.

The Archbishop came to the reading of the psalm. Strangely, I thought at the time, he read one of the militaristic psalms of King David, an unusual selection for this occasion.

"Blessed be the Lord my strength, who teaches my hands to war, and my fingers to fight: My goodness, and my fortress; my high tower, and my deliverer; my shield, and he in whom I trust; who subdues my people under me," he read. "Bow your heavens, O Lord, and come down: touch the mountains, and they shall smoke. Cast forth lightning, and scatter them: shoot out your arrows and destroy them." He continued until the psalm was finished and then he paused. He pulled himself up to his full height, turned to face his audience and once again slowly looked around the cathedral. People shifted uncomfortably under his gaze. Everyone waited, wondering what this psalm meant, why he had chosen it. I think that all were struck with its incongruity and Lord Rothard himself knew this.

He spoke loudly to the assembled people of Mainz.

"My friends and neighbours, Children of God, Flock of the Divine Shepherd, I have important news from His Holiness Pope Urban sent from Clermont in the South. As some of you might be aware, the Holy Father convened a council in Clermont in the kingdom of the Southern Franks recently to discuss many issues of importance to all Christians. I have here," he lifted a vellum scroll above his head that all might see it, "a letter from His Holiness which outlines the accomplishments of that Council. In it, the Holy Father has asked a special favour of all princes of Christendom and their Christian subjects. I shall read to you what he asks." He bent his head and began to read from the Pope's letter and I am sure that each ear in that cathedral had turned itself to hear every word that Lord Rothard uttered. What could this 'special favour' be?

"'A barbaric fury has overtaken the lands of the East which afflicts our neighbours there and also the Emperor of Byzantium and his subjects, laying waste to their lands and homes. Further, and most blasphemous of all, the Churches of the East have been brought to servitude and Christians there subjugated to the Infidel and as well the Holy Places where Our Lord Himself walked and ministered and suffered His passion and died for our sins, especially the Holy City of Jerusalem, has fallen to their unholy wrath. We enjoin you, therefore, all Christian princes, to free the Holy Places and thereby remit your own penance in the doing of this great and most worthy deed. We appoint, thereto, our servant, Adhemar, Bishop of Puy, to be our envoy with plenipotentiary powers and command that all who wish to participate shall submit to his loosing and binding inasmuch as they are appropriate to his office. If any of your people take this vow to assist in this endeavour then you shall inform them that he will set out with God's help on the day of the Assumption of the Blessed Mary and they may approach him and join with him.'"

The Archbishop carefully set the letter down and then looked up at his congregation. The people sat as if stunned by this news. Not one person moved. They all stared at the Archbishop and he at them. Then, as if a dam had burst, a general clamour broke out, a most unusual occurrence in the cathedral, with everyone talking at once, noble and common alike. I, myself, said nothing to my neighbours beside me; I stood in stunned silence still, unable to fathom what the news augured for me or anyone else at Mainz.

Then the Archbishop spoke again.

"My lords, brethren, everyone. Please! May I have silence?"

People continued to talk among themselves for a moment, then gradually they stopped as Lord Rothard's voice, admonishing silence, overrode them. Everyone waited expectantly for his next words.

"I know that this is a momentous request by the Holy Father and perhaps particularly confusing for those assembled here today since introduced so unexpectedly like this in the middle of Our Lord's Mass. I may have been hasty in launching all my missiles over the wall at once. However, given the nature of the Holy Father's epistle and the intent of his proposed mission to the Orient, to liberate the Holy Land from the Infidel and cancel all other penance for those pilgrims who make the journey, I believed that there could be no more appropriate place than the house of Our Lord for laying this table before you, during this blessed season." He paused, looking out over the crowd.

"Indeed," the Archbishop then continued, "His Holiness announced his plan for the armed pilgrimage to Jerusalem in a similar fashion. I have heard from His Holiness's emissary that the crowds were so vast at the announcement at Clermont that Pope Urban found himself in a field outside the city in order that all the audience of the faithful might be accommodated. The words the Holy Father spoke were greeted with immense enthusiasm and devotion. Almost everyone there swore to take up the cause and never, I believe, has a display of piety been equalled in all of Christendom as at Clermont one month gone." Then Rothard's eyes sparked and his face became even more animated as his voice rose, impassioned. "And do you know what the people there, these true, faithful Christians called out as their battle cry? I will tell you: 'Deus vult,' they shouted! 'Deus vult! God wills it!' Now who among you will take up the cause of Pope Urban and journey to the Holy Land to drive out the Infidel? Anyone?"

He stopped and looked at them and they stared back at the Archbishop, amazed. For many long moments the people of Mainz attending the cathedral that day were silent. Then suddenly a voice rang out, clear as a silver bell.

"Deus vult!" someone shouted in the front. Then someone else near the back of the cathedral echoed the cry. "Deus vult!" And soon everyone stood and took up the cry: "Deus Vult! God wills it! God wills it! God wills it!"

The very stones of the walls and floor seemed to tremble at the pious vociferation of the faithful there in Mainz that Christ Mass Day. Surely Heaven itself must have rung with the clamour. The Franks would not outdo the people of Mainz. The Alemaigni would not stand by and let the Franks take all the glory in driving the enemies of Christ from His Holy City of Jerusalem. Nor would they miss out on their heavenly rewards nor lose the opportunity to become pure as any saint by performing saintly deeds as warriors of God. The Pope wanted a Holy War against the Infidel? Well, he found many a willing warrior there on that holy day in Mainz.

During the rest of the Christ Mass, while the many priests of the cathedral staff administered the bread and wine to the faithful, my mind flew far away from Mainz Cathedral, and such was my fascination with this entirely new concept, this Holy War, that I regret to say I heard barely any of the Archbishop's or his assistant's words and prayers. Indeed, I wonder if anyone there did. I hope that God will forgive me this transgression in view of the disturbance of heart and mind created by this news of an opportunity to do His work directly. Any person might go on the pilgrimage, Lord Rothard had said. Anyone might participate in this great expedition.

I confess to you now that thoughts of journeying to Jerusalem consumed me. However, in view of the events that enveloped me in the months and years which followed—and I hope none will think ill of me for writing these words— I wish sometimes that Lord Rothard and his ecclesiastical peers throughout Lotharingia and the other Alemaigne lands had never transmitted Pope Urban's message inviting volunteers for the pilgrimage to Constantinople and on to the Holy Places. For none of us had any idea at that season, in that year of the great Council at Clermont, how very difficult the journey would be, how consumptive of money, of resources both military and domestic, and, above all, of human lives.

The cost for all of us would turn out to be very high indeed. For some lost their lives in glorious service to the Lord, never returning home though they gained everlasting life instead. Some of these never reached the Holy Lands. Others stayed on in the country of Our Lord Jesus's birth and became lords or comtes or burgers or sergeants or simple farmers. Others sold their souls to evil to gain earthly wealth and the sinful delights offered in such abundance in those regions of the world and, living thus, died to God even as earlier they had strove to please Him in destroying the unbelievers.

I believe that not one of us there at Mainz had any conception of what this pilgrimage involved. Certainly it sounded simple. Those who would journey to the East would meet with the party of Bishop Adhemar and join together with his company.

I had no idea where he would be except that he would leave Le Puy on the following Assumption Day in August. I had the vague notion that if I went— and I eagerly anticipated doing so if I received Lord Rothard's blessing—I would travel with a group of like-minded pilgrims of Mainz and travel south to the Kingdom of the Franks. I had absolutely no conception where in the Frankish lands Le Puy was located but surely someone would know the way there who would lead us as Moses led the Jews from Egypt into the land of Cana.

I thought we would then travel to Jerusalem, driving out or frightening away the Infidel along the way with the help and blessing of Almighty God who would strike the unbelievers down as though we carried a flaming sword before us. We would arrive and free Jerusalem in plenty of time for the next Christ's Mass at the Feast of the Nativity, perhaps celebrating at Bethlehem itself, and return home by Easter to celebrate the Passion, Crucifixion and Resurrection of Our Blessed Lord Jesus and to describe to our friends and families the journey and the wonders of the Holy Places where Christ Himself and His Apostles had walked the same soil.

As to my conception of what those places were like, again I was entirely naive and rather misinformed by what I had read about Jerusalem and the Holy Land.

They must be wondrous places, I imagined. Jerusalem, God's own city, would have streets paved with gold, it's buildings roofed of the same material. The land around it would be fertile and green and God would provide us with bountiful harvests for as long as Christians chose to live there. Every day would be spent in praising God. Every evening would be spent in theological reflection and study. Blissful music written to exalt Heaven would be sung and played continually. Each Christian, noble or common, would be happy and prosperous as citizens of the Kingdom of God on Earth.

While I had no intention of remaining in Jerusalem I knew it would be a glorious place to visit and I fully intended to stay on there, for a time at least, to experience the Biblical country and all its wonders. I resolved to request an audience with the Archbishop to petition his permission to go with Lord Adhemar and his armies. I regret to write that my ambition to become a *medicus* like Brother Piccolo evaporated on that morning like a morning dew rising to the heavens, replaced by an intense desire to make the pilgrimage to the Orient.

Guiltily, and with a heavy heart at the thought of informing my Benedictine teacher of my impetuous decision, I left the cathedral after the Christ Mass. I decided to leave by the main entrance to the cathedral which meant that I would have to walk all the way round the building to reach the infirmary gate. I suppose I chose that route to delay as long as possible the conversation I must have with Brother Piccolo.

Strangely, after the promise of a bright sky earlier, snow had begun to fall. The brilliant blue sky with which the day had started had now turned sombre, mournful and dark. Clouds seemed to press down to smother the city and the air was as cold as waiting death. I gasped for air through my mouth with my chin tucked down into my robes since to breathe through my nose was to allow tiny icy daggers to form inside my nostrils and thence to stab into my lungs. A pale shroud of snow had already formed on the steps and on the street and I picked my way carefully with my toes freezing nearly to rigour in the light shoes I wore as I kicked through the clinging pallid dust.

The weather did nothing to lighten my mood, and as I came to the infirmary gate a sense of foreboding pressed down upon me. I whispered a prayer to Saint Peter that Brother Piccolo should not see my impending departure as a betrayal of his personal interest and tutelage of me. I passed through the gates. The heavy door swung back with difficulty owing to the snow banked against it but I managed to pull it open and entered the infirmary.

As it turned out on that Holy Day, the Nativity of Our Lord Jesus Christ, Isaac was the only patient present in the infirmary. This of course owed to two circumstances. The first, aforementioned, reason was that Ruth and Yaakob trusted the Benedictine medicus's skill and knowledge implicitly. Thus they had left their son in his care despite the protestations of both Julius, the Archbishop's steward, and those of their friends in the Jewish community.

Ruth had told me that a certain doctor, Aaron ben Malachi, a most successful and wealthy doctor in his own sphere had insisted that Isaac be brought to him and placed in his care. Ben Malachi charged exorbitant rates and cared more for the health of his purse than that of his patients, she said. I assured her that there were many doctors of that nature in the Christian world as well. In Bruges as I remembered, the city council had hired a doctor to meet the medical needs of the community and that *medicus* had grown quite affluent harvesting his crop of afflicted townsfolk despite his reputation for rather mediocre care. But Ruth and Yaakob refused to bow to ben Malachi's demands even when their rabbi, who had power and influence similar to that of a bishop, urged them to comply. They had witnessed Brother Piccolo's dedication and devotion to his patients and knew him to be the best possible physician to care for their son.

The second circumstance which made Isaac the sole occupant of the infirmary was that those who were well enough to leave the infirmary wished to be at home with their families during the Feast of the Nativity. Everyone but the young Jew met that criterion even though Brother Piccolo found himself obliged to visit some of those discharged to their homes, since their illnesses or wounds demanded daily attention in the form of specially concocted pharmaceuticals or the changing of dressings or other similar contingencies which provoked concern in the Benedictine.

The fact that the window shutters were closed against the cold made the interior of the infirmary darkly sepulchral, especially since it was lit only by a single tallow candle. Despite the gloom of the day outside, my eyes took a moment to adjust to the gloomier interior. I stood for a time at the door until I could make out the room's features, looking for Brother Piccolo. At first I could not see him. Then, I did.

He sat on his stool next to the boy's pallet with his head down, resting on his clasped hands on the coverlet. I stared closely at him and then at the boy, though nothing in the patient's appearance indicated anything had changed in his condition. The monk murmured softly. Though I could not make out the words, I knew he was praying.

Brother Piccolo looked up. And I knew. His eyes were red-rimmed and watery. His expression was one of helplessness. I stared at the Benedictine. I looked at Isaac. The boy was dead.

Tears flooded from the well-springs of my eyes. I sank to the floor. I believe I felt no real grief for Isaac since I had never known him except as a comatose patient, though of course, I had always fervently prayed for the restoration of his health for his parents' sake. Instead, my thoughts were of those friends, Ruth and Yaakob, and the misery which would surely overwhelm them at this news. I knelt and wept for their pain, at the same time wondering why God had chosen to burden their lives with this awful tragedy. They had suffered so much since the moment that their boy had fallen into the path of that runaway wagon with its load of wine barrels.

I thought about Christ's promise of everlasting life and how Isaac would never know that bliss; perhaps as a child, though, his innocence would propel him into the Kingdom of Heaven, for did not Jesus say: "Suffer the little children to come unto me?" I prayed for the boy's soul. I implored all the Saints and especially the Holy Innocents, who represent all those children who die in a state of innocence, for their intercession on his behalf, despite his Jewish upbringing, that they might plead with Our Lord and Saviour for Isaac's everlasting life.

Immediately I had fallen to my knees Brother Piccolo rose and crossed around the end of the deathbed and came to comfort me. I think that in doing this he alleviated his own guilty suffering at his helplessness in the face of the young man's illness. The monk's mission in life was to help those in need and I must have appeared to be such a one to him at that moment. He knelt and grasped my hands and pulled me to my feet. Then he embraced me as a father would a suffering son, saying nothing. I clung to him and wept like a girl child. He held me for long and long, until finally, when I could sob no more, he released me, emptied of all strength and joy.

The pilgrimage to Jerusalem seemed meaningless to me then, I regret to write. I could only think about how I must inform Yaakob and Ruth of what had occurred. I did not know how I could bear to bring them this news and yet I knew I must tell them, only me. I owed them my compassion because I was their friend. I owed them my friendship because they had freely offered theirs to me. I knew then what Brother Piccolo had warned me about when I had accepted Ruth and Yaakob's invitation to dinner a month—so short a time gone?—earlier: emotional commitment to one's patient or patient's family entailed personal grief and suffering of soul for the *medicus*.

I had always viewed the Benedictine's dispassionate detachment as somewhat callous but now I saw that this was merely a defence on his part to prevent these moments of personal grief from developing. I saw a question in the Brother's eyes. I nodded in response. I would go to the home of Ruth and Yaakob. I would tell them. He closed his eyes and nodded in acknowledgement.

I scarcely remember the walk through the city to the Jewish quarter. I thought not at all about the kinds of threats that on a previous occasion left me cold with dread. I cared nothing for my personal safety. I had only to reach my friends. I felt neither the chill nor the fatigue of trudging for what seemed hours through the ever-deepening snow. The walls of the city whispered to me as I passed, and so quiet had the streets become I felt that the entire world mourned with me.

In the Christian parts of the city I passed through many people trudged through the snow, happy and busy, greeting me with the exclamatory phrase: "Christ is born!" I tried to smile and return the greeting but from the many puzzled glances I received from them I knew that my agony must be evident on my face and in my voice. Of course, they—and I—should have been rejoicing that day, the birth day of Our Saviour, but I, unlike them, felt only a deepening sadness, a sadness which accumulated in my heart like the snow falling down upon the city and deepening with every step I took closer to the home of Ruth and Yaakob; especially as I knew that the promise of the Nativity did not extend to my Jewish friends and their dead child.

In contrast to the Christian sections of Mainz, the Jewish quarter was nearly empty of people. Again, they respected our holy day and so businesses remained closed. For all I knew, they celebrated their own Jewish holy day concurrently with ours. Whatever the reason, the absence of people seemed to me a fitting response to this most recent death in their community. This certainly could not have been the case since no one here knew yet the tragic news that I bore. Still, I saw no people in the street as I approached the shop of the spice merchant and his wife.

I hesitated at the door of the shop. I started to knock but stopped. I reached for the cord of the small silvery bell to ring my arrival but stopped. I stared at my feet numbly for a time, wondering what I would say to them, how I would tell them my terrible news. As if in prescience, the door suddenly opened before me and Ruth stood there with a straw broom in her hand, a tiny pile of refuse at her feet ready to sweep into the street. She started as she saw me standing silently there. I did not greet her. She smiled and welcomed me and still I did not speak for I could not. Her smile slowly faded from her face like a memory from the mind. Now she knew why I had come.

I stood dumbly unable to speak as she suddenly wailed and fell to the floor in a limp heap, screaming and crying and tearing at her hair. A moment later, Yaakob rushed to the doorway and halted there seeing me, seeing his wife on the floor. Our eyes met and I saw in his a recognition of why I had come and why the mother of his son lay in the floor writhing in agony. His eyes died as his life and home shattered forever and crumbled down to mix with the tiny pile of dust on the floor beside his emotionally irretrievable woman.

He stooped and picked up Ruth, gone silent now, a limp bundle in his arms. Then he turned and walked away into the darkness of his house leaving me to stand there or follow or leave as I chose. Quietly closing the door, I left.

Slowly I returned to the cathedral through snow that threatened to intensify into a blizzard. The snow continued to fall that entire day and the next. So much snow that nobody could remember such a storm. So much snow that it eventually buried the city and all its inhabitants.

Caput Quartus

Sadness attended me for many long, dark, wintry weeks after the death of Isaac, as though winter's ice had invaded and shrivelled my heart. His parents, along with the Rabbi ben Moses and some few others of the Jewish community, had arrived on the day the blizzard ended to claim his body and remove it for storage until the time that the coming of warmer weather and the loosing of frost's iron grip on the earth allowed for burial; for the Jews bury their dead just as we do: another point of connection between our two cultures. That occasion was one of only two on which I saw Ruth and Yaakob after the death of their son.

Life proceeded in the city and at the cathedral. Patients came and went at the infirmary. I attended my lessons and lectures and studied my medical books and those of the prescribed canon of learned authorities. I continued to learn new medical techniques and pharmaceutical methods from Brother Piccolo. He began to teach me the Greek tongue so that I might further my medical education from the several texts in his possession in that language and, I think, because he thought the challenge of learning a new and difficult language would take my mind away from thoughts of Isaac and his parents. I learned quickly, as I have ever been adept at learning new languages. Months passed. Spring arrived, bringing with it the promise of renewed life, and with the greening of the trees came the greening of my heart once more.

In March we began to hear stories about a preacher who wandered the northern Frankish lands, and the adjacent Alemaigni territories of the Empire, seeking recruits for the armed pilgrimage to Jerusalem called by Pope Urban. This holy man, this hermit, for such he was called by all who related these stories to me, spoke vehemently against the enemies of Christ and exhorted all who would listen to follow him and to meet at Constantinople the armies of Christendom led by Bishop Adhemar. Toward that great metropolis, the capital city of the Greeks, the throne of their emperor, Alexius, he led his own now-sizeable army of followers.

Peter the Hermit, as he was called because of his habiliment and ascetic habits, soon arrived at the gates of Mainz. The gates of the city were open to him for, when he had departed from Köln, word had arrived ahead of him that he would pass through Mainz as his next stop along the route that would take him through Hungary and thence to the Greek regions beyond. We heard through palace rumour that Peter would not be received by the Archbishop but that the holy man was free to preach to the city's inhabitants. I wondered about that until I spoke with Brother Piccolo.

We sat on the young grass under a newly budding tree outside the infirmary gates, enjoying the fine spring day. The sun warmed us, pleasingly welcome. As is normal at that time of year, a slight chill in the occasionally gusty breeze counterbalanced the great orb's heat, forcing us to wear our heavier winter robes; I had rolled up my sleeves to bare my arms to the breeze because of the excessive heat of my clothing. The snowy pall of winter's corpse had long since melted away in tatters, though the emerging frost made the ground spongy and damp in places. We did not mind, though, since the mere fact of spending more time outdoors in the increasingly longer daylight was a blessing. A few songbirds flitted here and there among the trees surrounding the cathedral, their tunes merry and light, celebrating and renewing the season.

Brother Piccolo sat with his back against the trunk of the tree, his eyes closed. I thought perhaps that he had fallen asleep since he often napped during the day owing to the irregular and often long hours that he kept in the infirmary. Then he surprised me by speaking, still with his eyes closed.

"Has your head filled with the notion of the pilgrimage to the East, again, Brother? I mean, owing to the coming of this hermit?"

I did not immediately reply. In response to his question, I began to think about how I had been disappointed in my earlier request to join with those from Mainz who would journey to the Holy Land. In fact, I had not made my request for several weeks after the death of Isaac owing to my inability to rationalise my grief for Ruth and Yaakob's loss and my inability, because of the Archbishop's injunction to avoid their company, to speak with my friends about the event. Thus, unable to unburden my woe, I carried it about, heavily weighed down with sadness, miserable and alone. Finally, through the grace of Our Lord and after much prayer and meditation, I threw off its yoke and returned my mind to a more normal state, though I never did truly requite my sorrow. I felt as though some part of me had died with Isaac that day, a piece of my youthful innocence shrivelling away perhaps or perhaps better to say that an ugly lump of bitterness had lodged in my heart to sour its earlier sweetness.

Eventually I came to believe that better I should leave Mainz than stay and be constantly reminded of the unhappy event. What could be better than to serve Our Lord in the East in the very place sacred to Him and His Blessed Apostles and to all Christians: Jerusalem? Since the idea had solidified in me after many prayers sent heavenward I felt that

God Himself must have approved it and planted it there in my heart. Archbishop Rothard did not see my point.

I had requested an audience with the Lord of Mainz through his detestable servant, Julius, who sneered at me and told me that his master was too busy to entertain every petty request to visit with him. I informed him that I would make my request through Brother Piccolo instead and that the Benedictine must certainly mention that I had been unable to seek the Archbishop's presence because of the lack of co-operation of his steward. The gatekeeper had blanched. The Archbishop gave Brother Piccolo access almost whenever he wished. Lord Rothard had personally selected and brought the monk from his monastery in Italy years earlier. Their friendship extended backward for many years beyond that, and it was this fact that had persuaded Brother Piccolo to abandon his abbey at Rothard's request and travel to Mainz to become not only the cathedral *medicus* but the Lord Archbishop's personal physician. With his lips tightly pressed together and a fury in his eyes Julius agreed to transfer my request to Lord Rothard.

Thus it came to pass later the same day that I had stood before the Archbishop and asked permission to join the Holy Father's armed pilgrimage. The great lord had listened attentively to my plea then turned me down flat. His reasons were simple and, it seems to me now, eminently sensible.

I did not belong on the pilgrimage, he said, because I was neither an ordained cleric nor an armigerous warrior. As I had not attained holy orders I could not represent the Church and as the son of a merchant, who had never borne arms nor indeed even lifted a weapon of any description, nor owned so much as a stone-sling, my presence would be unnecessary on the journey. Still, I had argued, with the medical training I had achieved with Brother Piccolo and Brother Ambrose I might be helpful as a physician's assistant.

"Yet you are needed here in that capacity," Lord Rothard had replied with a kindly smile.

This response both pleased me and saddened me. The knowledge that one is useful to others is always uplifting; however, I would rather go on the pilgrimage. Perhaps I might never again have the opportunity to make such a journey to Jerusalem.

"This is not a simple pilgrimage to the Holy Places. We know that many pilgrims journey to Jerusalem despite the dangers inherent along the route. Those who travel by ship risk death according to God's divine judgement and mercy in violent sea-borne storms or at the hands of Saracen pirates sailing out of Sicily or North Africa. Those who travel overland risk bandits, wild animals and, once past the Greek lands, Saracens; these hate all Christians even though their rulers tolerate our presence in Jerusalem. Indeed, they have, in the recent past, ceased to tolerate us even there, increasing the danger. But this time the penitents are armed and moving quickly in massive numbers. Their aim is to destroy the power of the Infidel in the Holy Places and in the former Greek territories that the enemies of Christ have unjustly stolen. The danger is increased ten-fold therefore since the Infidel will send their armies against ours to prevent this; we cannot allow your exposure to this because of your own youthful enthusiasm. Further, your inexperience in war and in political matters affecting both Church and Crown is an impediment in this venture. Hence, regretfully, we must forbid you to go."

I had stood speechless before my lord. I knew the uselessness of argument, not to say that to continue in questioning his judgement would have been impertinent and discourteous. I nodded in acquiescence of his unilateral decision. Numbly, I had taken my leave of the Archbishop and resigned myself to remaining in Mainz at least until I had achieved holy orders; then I would make the pilgrimage to Jerusalem on my own even if I followed ignominiously after the initial wave of holy warriors.

Now, thinking about Brother Piccolo's question, I weighed my desire to follow Bishop Adhemar and the Army of Christ against my conviction to make the pilgrimage alone. The balance tipped heavily in favour of the former. Yes, I did wish still to accompany the armed pilgrimage but I did not admit that to the Benedictine.

"Who would not want to make the pilgrimage, Brother Piccolo?" I answered equivocally.

Of course, the Benedictine's barbs of inquiry were not so easily deflected.

"I believe I intended my question to elicit a response concerning your own desires not those of everyone else." He smiled and looked at me quizzically waiting for my response.

"Hmmm...," I mused. "I intend to obey the Archbishop, if that's what you mean."

"So you are still taken by the desire to go?"

"Of course," I exclaimed impatiently. "Of course I want to go."

"They say that Peter the Hermit is in the city at this moment. Have you listened to his sermons, yet?"

"No. I knew he was coming here but I have not seen him."

"He arrived last evening. In fact, he is within the cathedral complex although his followers are camped outside of the city," the Benedictine said nonchalantly.

"What," I nearly shouted. "Where? Have you seen him? Have you spoken with him?"

"I have not spoken with him but I have seen him. Yes. He is altogether a most disagreeable man in appearance and personal habits."

"What do you mean?" I had imagined a man similar to Archbishop Rothard, tall, stately and powerful in appearance.

"He is short and ugly. And he smells."

"What does that matter? He is a man of God." I defended the hermit indignantly though I do not know why since I had never met him. I suppose that I felt in some way that the holy man might yet be my salvation from the Archbishop's decision not to let me go with Adhemar. Thus, I already felt myself to be in his camp. Still, I paused for a few moments before making further inquiries lest my eagerness to learn more about the hermit give me away.

"Why? What does he look like?" I asked nonchalantly.

"You'll see."

"What do you mean by that, now?"

"Just that. You'll see." He grinned and then, slapping his palms on the tops of his thighs, pulled his feet under him and rose, hitching up his robes.

"Come. Let us see if the Holy Hermit has started his sermon outside the cathedral yet. I suppose that his odour will precede him and announce his arrival but let us check the courtyard, anyway."

I followed him as he walked around the cathedral toward the great piazza out front, wondering at his repeated references to Peter's smell. Most people emanate at least some personal vapours obvious to others. So what? As we rounded the immense stone wall that enclosed this quarter of the complex, I was surprised by what we saw: nothing. The Benedictine's words had made me suspect a gathering already under way that I was missing, but none were here. Not even the occasional beggar sitting on the steps waiting for alms from some noble lady passing by on her way to the chapels.

"People are certainly staying away in huge crowds, to-day," observed Brother Piccolo dryly.

I rolled my eyes heavenward and wondered if there was a patron saint for the obtuse.

"Perhaps the hour is too early for Peter to start his sermons," I suggested.

"No doubt. He's probably stuffing his face in the kitchens or dining hall."

I wondered at Brother Piccolo's sardonic attitude. Perhaps the reader has read elsewhere or heard about Peter the Hermit's exceeding piety and oratory skill. These facts, of course, are true. Else, how could he have amassed the huge army of common folk he eventually did? Of his other habits, however, few have written or spoken about to my knowledge. I met Peter and I hesitate to write that, as Brother Piccolo suggested, despite the hermit's saintliness, he was indeed a most distasteful individual with some rather objectionable personal habits. Perhaps this is simply the way of the holiest men in God's service who have little time for the graces, manners and habits of the more worldly, socially fastidious among us.

"Let us walk to the city walls and look for the great army of the hermit," Brother Piccolo suggested with, I thought, a larger measure of verbal irony than seemed appropriate. I still did not appreciate his objection to the holy man from the Frankish lands. He seemed to want to draw me away from any association with the hermit. Nonetheless, I followed him to the ramparts.

From the city walls we could look out across the river to the far bank where, in a large open field beyond the outskirts of the town which had grown up there, lay the encampment of Peter the Hermit's army. I was astounded by its size. A small city of tents had grown up overnight and now rivalled the suburb in area. The smoke from countless cooking fires drifted lazily in the breeze, snaking slowly across the meadow, in appearance like a military pennant; suggesting by its ethereal nature, perhaps, that these were God's troops.

"Quite a rabble," observed the Benedictine.

I cocked my head and stared at him, puzzled. "Why do you object so to this pious congregation, Brother Piccolo? Surely, Our Lord sanctifies this activity. I have heard that a Frankish bishop saw a shower of stars fall from the sky, half a year before Pope Urban called upon all Christians to help liberate the Holy Land, which presaged just such a great movement of peoples as this."

"That is just the problem, Brother. The Holy Father did not call upon all Christians to liberate the Holy Land. He called upon military men to assist the Greek Emperor to drive away the Saracens from his territories and those happened to include the Holy Places as well. Look out there at your so-called army. Tell me: what do you see?"

I gazed over the meadow. There were all manner of people there; poorly dressed peasants, a number of men in rusty old mail or leather armour, women, children. Accompanying them were donkeys and dogs and chickens, horses, oxen and mules, and a variety of other livestock probably outnumbering the people. I began to see what the monk meant. This army, most of whose members were not and never had been warriors, though sizeable enough was a ragged collection of inexperienced and incompetent people and their farm stock. How could the Golden City of Jerusalem be liberated by such as these?

"They do not really inspire confidence do they?" I admitted reluctantly.

"Then why do you think they have all come here if they are so ill-equipped to fight against the trained armies of the Infidel?" He answered the question himself. "Because they are desperate. Desperate for a new and better life. They are people who come from lands with poor barren soil or from lands owned by lords who refuse to cut down the woodlands to make new croplands, because they would rather hunt than allow their people to feed themselves so long as they produce enough food for their masters. Widespread famine has made these people desperately poor, hungry and almost devoid of hope. Peter has given them a new but probably false hope. Their faith in God, while admirable in itself though misdirected, along with their blind faith in the hermit, and their inexperience can only lead them to their destruction beneath the spears and arrows of Saracen armies."

"But Our Saviour promises that those who die for Him shall find everlasting life. If they vanquish the enemy, they live. If they perish at the hands of that same enemy, they gain everlasting life in Christ. What do these people have to fear, then, from the Infidel?"

"Clever argument; one that Peter has undoubtedly used," he said calmly, then continued in the same low, even tones. "How do we know that Christ, that God sanctions this endeavour? The movement provoked by Urban is holy and legitimate because he has the power of binding and loosing given to the Blessed Saint Peter by Christ Himself, a power passed on to each successor at Rome. But this travesty of Peire-Pierre's? This unruly court of the ridiculous that traipses along behind him? I doubt that God can do other than frown in His beard at this stupidity."

Seriously taken aback by this notion, I considered his words carefully. First, I wondered why he had applied the name "Peire-Pierre" to the hermit. He meant this clearly as a vile, deliberate derogative, for in the Frankish tongue "peire" means to break wind. That Brother Piccolo even knew such an insult surprised me. I had often heard people refer to the hermit as "Chtou-Peter", "Little Peter", a term also meant as a slight, but never by the name used by the Benedictine. Why did he so vehemently disapprove of the holy man? However, Brother Piccolo's suggestion that this movement of Peter's might indeed prove false in its assumptions and mistaken in its aims truly amazed me.

The Benedictine's argument made sense, though. The Holy Father Urban's initiative clearly was beyond reproach. Did Brother Piccolo mean to suggest, then, that Peter deceived his followers? Perhaps; perhaps unintentionally because of his own exceeding piety and intense belief in God's protection, or perhaps truly intentionally because the ill treatment he had received in the past at the hands of the Infidel in an earlier attempt to reach Jerusalem during his own private pilgrimage drove him to revenge himself upon his abusers. If the latter case held true then his followers were deceived indeed, for the man served only his own ends.

These thoughts flew from my mind as I turned at a sudden commotion behind me. Around the corner of the street opposite the rampart upon which we stood, a broad river of people surged between the building walls like a wave driven by a mad wind. I heard shouts of "Hallelujah!" and "Deus Vult!" and "Peter!" from the herd. As more and more people overflowed the corner I saw in their midst a man seated on a donkey. Obvious symbolism. I could not see him clearly from atop the wall but I knew that this must be Peter the Hermit making a circuit of the city to attract an audience.

"It's him," I cried excitedly, Brother Piccolo's accusations dissolving from my thoughts like grains of sand washed out to see on the tide. "It's Peter." I felt myself caught up in the excitement of seeing in the flesh for the first time an individual I had only heard about, whose fame had spread before him like an ocean surge spreading toward an unsuspecting shore. His celebrity seemed to gather in followers around him in the way that a fisherman's net brought in the catch to the cog. Indeed this seemed a perfectly apt metaphor to me at that time. The hermit followed in the footsteps of the Blessed Apostles, gathering people to the cause of the Holy

Father Urban as those whom Our Saviour made fishers of men brought people to the Word of Christ.

I clambered down a wooden ladder propped along the wall, not wanting to wait for the slower route by the stone steps that Brother Piccolo and I had used earlier. The monk used the stairs and thus was slow to follow. By the time that he reached the ground I had already caught up with the crowd and in moments it pulled me into it like so much aimless spume on the crest of that mighty, shouting wave.

I no longer saw the Benedictine. The crowd carried me along the streets, the people exclaiming and praying the while, until I found myself in front of the cathedral once again. The surge stopped. Now the pull and push of the crowd became uncomfortably vigorous as it thrust me first one way then another as everyone tried to catch some glimpse of the hermit. We did not wait long to see him. He, having dismounted from his donkey, appeared suddenly upon the topmost steps of the cathedral. Immediately he came into view there, the crowd became still as if in a soporific stupor. None moved. Each person waited silently for the holy man to speak.

I took that interval of silence and stillness to appraise Peter the Hermit. I saw now why so many people called him Little Peter. His attendants surrounding him easily topped the hermit by a head and more. Nor did his physical ugliness belie the Benedictine's assessment.

His hair, what little of it there was even in spite of its tonsure, stuck out in tufts in every direction like a grey-blonde stick nest deposited there by a confused stork. His chin jutted out and downward, covered with stubbly grey and white whiskers. There were bags under his eyes. Wrinkles, themselves scarred by deep pockmarks, carved heavy slashing diagonal lines across his cheeks from ears to lips. His mouth, a mere line barely as wide as one of his wrinkles, was filled with yellow crooked teeth that jutted out haphazardly in front on a different tangent entirely from the curve of his lower face. The most startling features of all, though, were his ears and bulbous red nose. These were so long and wide that he resembled less a man than the very donkey upon which he rode about the countryside.

He stood flanked by several of his sergeants, self-appointed guardians I discovered later who, in a bid for power over the army or out of concern for their master's safety had elected to follow and guard him closely. These attendants, with spears and drawn swords, prevented the crowd from mobbing the holy man they protected.

One of these was Walter Sans-Avoir, I later learned, whose cognomen means 'the Penniless,' whom I never had occasion to meet but who has since gained fame as one of Peter's most devoted and capable sergeants. Despite the praise since heaped upon him, Walter was a nobleman quite without means who joined the expedition to further his own ends and make his fortune in the Holy Land. This despicable motivation occurred in more than one person on both Peter's pilgrimage and on that led by Bishop Adhemar, just as there were such men of despicable motive in the crowd come to listen to Peter that day.

Peter prepared to address his flock, opening his mouth as if to speak. Instead, he staggered a bit on the wobbly spindles of his legs so that his flanking sergeants quickly reached out to steady him as the crowd looked on, wonderingly. The hermit hiked up his filthy robe—apparently spun from some type of coarse animal hair but really more a collection of shaggy rags held together by the rope at his waist—above his knobbly knees and then plopped himself unceremoniously down on the cathedral step. He motioned for the people to sit likewise. Astoundingly, the mob complied. Soon Peter was preaching to us in the much the same fashion as Our Lord spoke from the Mount to the assembled folk of Judea and of Galilee and of Syria. As Brother Piccolo sardonically called it later, Peter the Hermit's Sermon on the Steps...

"People of Mainz," Peter began in an unexpectedly quiet and rich baritone voice, unexpectedly because from a man of such loathsome appearance and seeming frailty. "People of Mainz, flock of our good and all-powerful shepherd, Jesus Christ: The Lord be with you today. Let us pray as Our Saviour taught us. '*Pater Nostrum, qui es in coelis...*'"he began in Latin and the crowd as one closed its eyes and bowed its head. Of course, the reader knows this prayer and I need not repeat it in its entirety here. The recitation of the prayer in this outdoor venue, though, had the effect of uniting the crowd as if it had been assembled within the cathedral. As a result of this unity, the people implicitly recognised and embraced Peter's authority to preach to them as any priest would have done within God's temple.

When he had finished The Lord's Prayer, the hermit continued his sermon without the usual attendant ecclesiastical ceremony but instead spoke directly from his heart.

"I bring you greetings and news from His Excellency the Most Pious and Blessed Holy Father Pope Urban. The Holy Father has sent his ministers throughout Christendom to testify these things in the churches and the towns. He wishes me to direct you to join with other Christians in a brave and pious journey to the East. Perhaps you have already heard about this movement of people and have wondered why it has begun. Perhaps you have wondered who shall go.

Perhaps you have wondered why you and you and you," at this he pointed with a bony, shaking finger to various individuals randomly throughout the crowd," why you should go away, leave your homes and familiar places to travel to places foreign to you, inhabited by others whom you do not know and to whom you may believe you have no allegiance and to whom you owe no service. But I say to you this day that you do owe allegiance and service to those Christians in the East." He paused and gazed over the people intensely and when his gaze passed over me, I felt that he looked directly at me and into me and beheld my fear and doubt.

"Why?"

Suddenly his voice rose in volume and depth, carrying mightily over those assembled there.

"I shall tell you all the 'whys' of these things: You are poor in spirit living here. Many faithful Christians die in our countries because of poor harvests and famine, or because of warfare and bloodshed, fighting amongst each other or at the hands of the very lords and the sons of those lords who should nurture and protect but instead destroy their own people out of greed and avarice and viciousness."

This speech echoed Brother Piccolo's earlier assessment of why people followed the hermit. The notion struck a chord with the citizens of Mainz, too, since there were many murmurs and nods of agreement among the crowd.

"If you are among those whose spirit is downtrodden in these ways I give you hope. The Lord has said: 'Blessed are the poor for theirs is the kingdom of heaven. Blessed are they that mourn for they shall be comforted. Blessed are they that hunger and thirst after righteousness for they shall be filled. Blessed are the pure of heart for they shall see God.' God's work is underway and you can be a part of it. Receive thereby the blessing of God and ensure your place in the kingdom of heaven!" he exclaimed.

"If you are pure of heart and hunger and thirst for righteousness in the name of Our Saviour, you must come with us to the East. You must help us and renew your spirit. For the name of God has been lost in the wilderness, echoing empty in places where once Jesus Himself walked and taught. Yes! I speak of Jerusalem! We will go to Jerusalem," he thundered. The crowd rose to its feet and cheered, I among them, moved to great passion by his words.

When we had subsided in our devotion Peter began again in a low, even voice.

"I have mentioned God's work beginning here and reaching its peak in the East. As you may know, this is the result of two initiatives. The first is the request by the Emperor of the Christians in the East, Alexius, who has asked the Holy Father Urban to provide him with an army to fight the Infidel who threatens to overrun the Empire of the Greeks. That we will do. We shall overcome the unbelievers there and perhaps restore his lands to the Emperor. But that initiative is incidental to the true motive of our expedition. The second initiative, that of the Blessed Urban, is far more important to all Christians. We must go to the East to free the Holy City from the yoke of the followers of Mahmet who have in their great pride and vile gall seized the lands which belong to all Christians equally. We must free Jerusalem!" He fairly shouted this last and once again a great cheer went up from the crowd, heavenward.

Almost secretively, the hermit continued in a low voice, his eyes afire. "The world is changing O Children of God. The millennium has passed. The time of Our Lord's coming draws near to hand. We must be ready. We must ensure that His Kingdom is prepared for Him, that His throne is in an inviolable state, free from the blasphemous presence of the Infidel. I have seen a vision of Jerusalem as it is meant to be, inhabited by the pure of heart and the righteous whom God welcomes into His Kingdom. The fall of Babylon is at hand," he finished vehemently spitting out the name of the enemy, his white eyebrows an ominous smoke above the blaze of his eyes.

"We will prepare the Holy City for the prince of the kings of the earth, the Alpha and the Omega, the beginning and the end, He who loved us and washed away our sins in His blood. He has given me a vision of Jerusalem. I have seen Our Lord dressed in brilliant white with sandals and girdle of gold, His eyes flaming with fire. In His right hand He carried seven stars and out of His mouth came a sharp two-edged sword, His countenance shining like the sun. And He held a book sealed with seven seals and when He opened the book, there was a sound of thunder as the beasts were released upon the world. And a pale horse came forth with a pale rider, whose name was Death, and Hell followed with him, and he killed with the sword and with hunger and with death and with the beasts of the earth. I saw the altar upon which the souls of those who had died for Christ's sake were stretched out and they looked on me and cried out to be revenged. There were earthquakes and the sun became as black as sackcloth and the moon red with blood. The stars fell from the heavens like apples falling from a wind-racked tree. The kings of the earth in that place, and great men and rich, and servants and villeins all hid themselves in the bowels of the earth for they feared the vengeance of the righteous, the vengeance of the Lamb of God which arrived with the coming of His faithful."

"God's army was vast. It numbered two hundred thousand thousand. The warriors who rode at the head of the army on their fiery steeds had breastplates of fire, and of jacinth and of brimstone and their horses were as mighty as lions. And at the head of that army there rode an angel clothed in cloud, his face flashing like the sun and a rainbow crowning his head. He roared like a lion and the army thrust in its sickle and reaped death and the unbelievers were cast down and their blood pressed out of them beneath the hooves of the Faithful! The faithless soon came to repent of their murders, their sorcery and their thefts. Thus Babylon fell and Jerusalem and all the Holy Places were freed and the invader driven out!" Again, Peter's voice had risen in a steady crescendo until it crashed thunderously on his last syllables and the people shouted and cheered in pious delirium.

Peter closed his eyes and raised his arms heavenward in a kind of ecstatic trance. I could see tears running down his cheeks and indeed down the cheeks of many in the crowd. I felt my own eyes welling with an emotional overflow as I heard these words spoken.

Then the holy man began to describe the object of this holy quest, Jerusalem itself.

"Jerusalem," he murmured. "Jerusalem." The crowd quieted immediately, each hushing his neighbours so that every word might be gleaned and hoarded away in the storehouse of individual memory.

"The Holy City prepared like a bride for her bridegroom. God dwelling with us there in His own tabernacle. Jerusalem has no need of sun or moon for it shines in the glory of God, lit by the Lamb of God, and there is no night. Its foundations and its walls and its gates are built of precious stones and gems and pearls. All the nations of the world do homage to it. No abominations, lies or evil are in it. A pure river runs through it and on its banks grow abundant fruit trees which bear their fruits every month and their leaves heal all the nations of Christendom. The Lord Jesus dwells there and wipes away our tears and releases us from pain." Peter was crying aloud now, openly weeping as if waiting for Our Saviour to wipe the tears and take away his pain as he had said Jesus would do. Many in the crowd were moved to loud, lachrymose expressions themselves.

"It is done," he said simply and dramatically, as if he saw clearly into the future at what would be. I felt a chill run through me, the hairs on my body and neck and head rising up in supernatural awe. Then Peter looked directly at the assemblage, his tears suddenly ceasing as if his eyes were dammed. He spoke again, almost scornfully, less ecclesiastical than demagogic.

"Do not fear this pilgrimage, my brethren. Do not ask yourselves: what shall we eat? What shall we drink? How shall we clothe and armour ourselves? For Jesus will provide a fountain of life-giving water for the thirsty in spirit. What does it matter if you eat or drink? Your soul is more important than your life. God will provide for you. Behold the fowls of the air, they neither sow nor reap yet the Lord provides for them. The lilies of the field neither toil nor spin and yet are arrayed more worthily than the richest of men. Clothe yourself, armour yourself in the glory and strength of God. Do not think about tomorrow for God will care for tomorrow."

He stood up, tremblingly, his attendants grasping his elbows to assist him to his feet. Together they helped their master descend the steps, Moses coming down from the mountain. He walked through the sea of people, the crowd parting like the Red Sea before him. His sergeants lifted the hermit onto his donkey and he rode slowly away, face pale, swaying, his servants still clutching his elbows to help him balance atop the beast.

Suddenly, the donkey stopped and Peter twisted his ugly little body around to face the crowd over its rump. Everyone immediately attended his words once more.

"One thing further: if you go and fight for the Lord, all your sins will be forgiven," he said simply and nonchalantly as if he mentioned a minor detail earlier neglected. A murmur rippled through the crowd as those who had not heard this detail inquired of their neighbours what had been said and what it meant.

Peter slumped around to face the donkey's neck again, with the appearance of a martyr being taken to his execution, and clopped away, to rejoin his army outside the city walls. The pale rider, I thought, and wondered, would Hell follow after him?

◆

The people there stood silently, watching the holy man as he disappeared across the open flat-cobbled plain of the cathedral plaza. The moment he vanished into the farthest streets, though, the crowd buzzed with excitement like a droning beehive preparing its honey. Many expressed the wish to go on the hermit's pilgrimage. Others wondered how they would afford to feed and clothe themselves contrary to Peter's last admonition. The idea that all sins would be forgiven for participation in the venture garnered widespread appreciation and interest.

I spoke to none about these things. Instead, I looked for Brother Piccolo, wondering if he had heard the hermit's stentorian *oratio*. I wished to discuss the speech with the Benedictine, whose logical insight quickly saw through all holes in any wall of words. However, I did not see him. I reckoned that he had returned to his infirmary since he assessed Peter as a rabble-rousing huckster and took little or at best pessimistic interest in the hermit's words and actions. I turned toward the infirmary gate to seek out the monk.

And nearly fell beneath a great black war-horse. I caught myself before falling under its hooves and regained my balance by placing one hand on its neck.

Immediately I had done that I felt a stinging pain as a leather crop sliced my hand open, drawing blood. I yelped and stuffed my knuckles into my mouth. My momentary flight of fear conquered, I looked up angrily at my assailant.

The rider snarled viciously at me as I looked up, "Keep your hands to yourself, priestling."

I jumped back lest he lash me again. I said nothing in reply since I had no wish to provoke the man into further acts of violence that might prove worse than a twitch of the horse whip. I merely stared at him and took in every feature of that cruel, cold face; for this was Emicho, Comte of Leisingen, though I did not at that time know his identity. However, I would have cause to regret ever laying eyes on that evil, black-hearted *cnicht*.

Emicho sat very tall in the saddle and I guessed his height greater than average, certainly greater than my own. His long hair flew freely about his broad shoulders, as thick and dark as his horse's mane. He looked perhaps thirty years of age. His face was long and leathery of skin. A white scar raced across his face from the left side of his forehead to his right jaw. And his nose. Where his nose should have been was a gaping hole and I knew that some dread weapon in some dread battle had caused that scar and taken his nose.

Of course, clinically, I could dispassionately observe this long-healed wound and indeed, I had seen other, similar wounds, though none so severe. Having a nose sliced open was simply an occupational hazard of the chronic fighting man. Usually the wound could be stitched up and the flesh and gristle returned to a semblance of its previous natural order. Obviously, this man had suffered such a severe blow as to sever completely his proboscis. I wondered what had become of the appendage. Perhaps, I thought idiotically in my fearful hysteria, a dog had dashed in between the duellers and snapped it up as quickly as it had fallen. If so, the animal had probably immediately died at this man's hands. The Comte seemed to literally exude a taut viciousness and cruelty.

I edged slowly backward away from him. He narrowed his eyes and watched me go, like a predator watching its prey, waiting for it to bolt, the signal for the killer to kill. When I felt that I was far enough away to safely turn my back I marched quickly toward the side street leading to the infirmary gate. I would not give the stranger the satisfaction of noting any backward glance executed on my part to espy his pursuit of me.

At any instant I knew I would hear the whistle of an arrow's flight, or the swish of a thrown knife or pounding horse's hooves as the black rider swept down upon me to hack off my head with his broadsword. Of course, none of these things happened, for which I give thanks to God. I believe that walking away from Emicho that day was one of the bravest and most dangerous things I have ever done in my life. For I met Emicho again and grew to know him better than I ever dreamt I might and certainly better than I would have cared to.

◆

I found Brother Piccolo not in the infirmary but in the barns talking with Ulfrid. At the infirmary, Brother Ambrose had directed me to where I might find the Benedictine. I thanked him and hurried off down the street and through a small postern gate to which all the clerical students and lay members of the palace staff had a key.

This gate led to a stone passage behind the student barracks and thence to the barns in the posterior courtyard of the Archbishop's palace. I brushed cobwebs from my face as I walked through the narrow passageway. No matter how often someone used this unofficial route, the spiders seemed immediately to cast their sticky nets as soon as he had passed. I swept through the avenue destroying their traps, leaving the creatures to reweave their shadowy strings behind me.

The two elder men greeted me as I entered the stables. They sat together on stools next to the door, sunning themselves, out of the breeze, as old men like to do. I returned their greeting and found a block of wood to sit upon.

"Well, lad, how d'you think on the holy hermit, then," asked Ulfrid in his clipped Alemaigni. "Think you t'join his army?"

I frowned and shook my head. "The Lord Archbishop has forbidden me to make the pilgrimage. Pope Urban's anyway. So I assume that same refusal applies to Peter's."

Both men nodded in agreement.

"You're probably right there, lad," observed Brother Piccolo. "Still, if you had permission, would you follow Peter the Hermit?"

"I'm not sure. Maybe you're right about him, Brother. He doesn't have much of a military force. His army is composed mostly of poorly-armed peasants. I don't see how they can battle a well-equipped Infidel army. Even a small one. But Peter is quite convincing."

The Benedictine chuckled wryly. "Oh, he is that, all right."

"Did you hear his sermon, Brother Piccolo? I lost you in the crowd, so I wasn't sure if you stayed or not."

"Yes. I heard it. Quite the plagiarist, our eremitic friend."

"Plagiarist?"

"Surely you recognised from where the bulk of his speech came? St. John? The Revelations? And thinly veiled at that."

I had been so caught up in the emotion of the event and Peter's dramatic delivery of his words that I had hardly noticed that but what Brother Piccolo said was true. I had shared Peter's vision of Jerusalem without question, though I had recognised his descriptions of the Army of God led by the Angel as coming from the Apocalyptic prophesies of the Blessed St. John and recognised other bits from St. Matthew's description of the Sermon on the Mount.

I wondered how someone with little real knowledge of Holy Scripture, an unlettered peasant, for example, might conceptualise the Hermit's description of the pilgrimage to Jerusalem and of the city itself. Would he truly believe that an Angel would lead them, always victorious, no matter what well-armed force arrayed itself against our Christians? Would he believe that that same Jerusalem, Peter's Jerusalem inhabited by God, awaited him at the end of his journey? I think I too expected that for a time until Brother Piccolo forced me to think about the origins of Peter's description. Small wonder then that so many simple folk followed the hermit when they thought that such a marvellous denouement awaited them in the Holy Land.

"I suppose that a lot of people will be disappointed when they arrive at Jerusalem and the Lord Jesus is not there to greet them?" I offered.

Both men chuckled wryly at that.

"This expedition of the people will not turn out happily. Peter sells hope to the gullible and they, misguided downtrodden souls, purchase it with their blood. He is no better than the landlords in the way that he exploits people without thought for their welfare," said Brother Piccolo.

"Aye. And he's to hope the Emperor don't catch him at it," Ulfrid observed.

"Why is that, Ulfrid," I asked.

"Because, Peter nayn't supposed to be here in Lotharingia."

"Really? Why not?"

Brother Piccolo answered. "You remember Peter mentioned that Pope Urban had instigated this particular venture on behalf of the Greek Emperor? Heinrich, the German Emperor, would not find that a valid excuse for his people to scurry off to Jerusalem."

"Oh," I exclaimed, suddenly aware of the political implications. "You mean Clement?"

"Yes. Guibert of Ravenna, Clement, the anti-pope. Though many of our bishops and archbishops here in the German lands hold no true allegiance to Guibert, they must, of necessity, pay lip-service to the Emperor's choice in order to maintain their benefices. That is why Bishop Benno of Meisen visited us, those many months ago. He wanted clandestinely to maintain his ties to Pope Urban through Archbishop Rothard. And that is why Pope Urban's emissaries are not altogether welcome here. Official emissaries, that is to say. Peter is not among those."

"Surely Peter acts on the Holy Father's authority," I exclaimed. After all, I thought, witness the hermit's following. He could not have amassed such an army without some kind of official recognition of his right to gather up people for the expedition. The mere fact that the rulers of the lands he passed through tolerated his ministry seemed to indicate an authorised acceptance of it.

"Not at all. If he did, then Lord Rothard probably would have welcomed him as the Pope's ambassador, even in the face of imperial disapproval. Pope Urban is still the head of a foreign power, however much in conflict with The Emperor, and many German prelates still feel they owe him their allegiance; Urban is the Bishop of Rome, after all. Only because the hermit does not have official sanction can the Archbishop turn a blind eye to Peter's activities. But I suppose the result is the same, with or without Urban's permission. I have seen the Pope's letter to Lord Rothard and you have heard it read in the cathedral at Christ's Mass just past. There is no mention of Peter the Hermit or any request for him to herd the common folk to Jerusalem like this. The letter only requests the assistance of the magnates, 'all Christian princes' and their liege men; in other words: armigerous participants only, please."

"Then you are saying that Peter is doubly disapproved of? On the one hand, since he is not approved by the Holy Father he is not here as an official of Rome; so he can more or less do as he pleases. On the other hand he still represents, essentially, the interests of Pope Urban rather than Clement, the anti-pope. So even if Pope Urban is not aware of Peter's efforts or at least does not recognise Peter as his deputy, The Emperor does not welcome him?"

"Yes. Pope Urban will not welcome Peter's success, if success it can be called. These were not results the Holy Father expected or desired, I suspect. And the Emperor will not like his people leaving their homes in the empire to become involved in an initiative of Pope Urban's, however inadvertently and inconveniently arisen from the populace without official sanction from either power."

The more I thought about Peter's pilgrimage the less legitimate it seemed. I feared that somehow, somewhere between Pope Urban and the Emperor Henry, trouble would develop. Surely God would punish someone, if not Peter himself, for this vanity. Then another thought struck me. How, if Peter did not have the Pope's blessing, the binding and loosing deputation given to Adhemar, could the hermit go around promising absolution of sins to those who took the cross? I inquired of this from the Benedictine.

"A valid observation, my boy. Once again, your insight impresses me. Yes, indeed. How does the hermit presume to offer such a heavenly reward for terrestrial deeds done when he is not empowered to do so? This is another point of departure from Pope Urban's initiative. You may remember that the Holy Father's letter offered the remittance of penance, not sin. In other words, the armed pilgrimage serves a penitential function which, because of its magnitude, replaces those acts of contrition imposed by ecclesiastical authorities to date for the individual. But it does not absolve one's sins. Peter has corrupted the Pope's words and indeed, the very idea of such an indulgence."

"Then his promise to the people as he left the cathedral is false? Their sins will not be nullified if they follow Peter to Jerusalem?"

"I would think not. Not without the Pope's support and sanction; not without a deputation from the Holy Father."

I realised at that point that Peter the Hermit's pilgrimage, the people's pilgrimage, was a fraud. His thousands of followers were deluded if they thought that they could achieve the salvation of their souls by participating in this venture. Perhaps they might still redeem themselves through piety or through good deeds done during the pilgrimage but no more than they might have otherwise, if they acted independently of Peter.

Many people have taken the journey to Jerusalem in the past, and indeed, continue to do so. The journey is much safer now, of course, since we Christians have restored the city and its access routes to our Faith. But even in those days before our soldiers took the Cross and drove the Saracens away, people braved the perils of the trip out of piety and the desire to do penance.

A pilgrimage to Jerusalem, and indeed to many other holy places, such as the shrine of St. James at Compostela, has been long recognised as a legitimate form of penance. Maybe some small legitimacy inadvertently attached itself to Peter's initiative, then. After all, if each individual involved made his own independent pilgrimage, despite being part of the crowd, he too, like pilgrims before him, did it out of piety and the desire to do penance. The fraudulent aspect of the whole thing was in the hermit's promises to the people. His was the guilt; his followers, most of them anyway, acted innocently and in good faith. Though their sins would not be absolved as Peter maintained they would be, they still received penitential benefits by travelling to the holiest of Christian cities. This thought comforted me, though Peter the Hermit, himself, still disturbed me.

I sat in silence while the talk of Brother Piccolo and Ulfrid turned to other matters. I paid little attention to their discussion about horse breeding and care, merely nodded my head occasionally to show that I still listened, although I did not really hear what they said. I thought more about Peter the Hermit.

What was it about the man that made even sensible people—for such I considered myself to be, then as now—want to give up their homes and follow him on his possibly mad quest? I had been completely drawn into his conception of Jerusalem and into his contention that the armies of the Infidel would fall dead at our feet as we travelled through their territories. Everything about the man suggested his extreme piety and holiness. His unusual style of dress, the hairy mantle, reminiscent as it was of the image of Saint John the Baptist who lived, dressed in camel skins, many years in the wilderness before baptising our Saviour, exemplified the ascetic. Peter's long beard and generally unkempt appearance evidenced that he eschewed the vanities of this world. He travelled on his donkey, an image suggestive of the Messiah's triumphant entry into Jerusalem before His Passion and Crucifixion.

Perhaps these living symbols of our Faith displayed by Peter, symbols generally well-known to all Christians and especially important to the unlettered masses, explained the hermit's popular following. Perhaps the simple, common folk conflated the Biblical images with the images of Peter's showmanship. Perhaps folk could not grasp the difference between them, dependent as the discernment was on an ability to conceptualise the time span between New Testament days and the present. But I could. I had no difficulty grasping the symbolism inherent in Peter's habits and dress. Why, then, did Peter compel *me*, also?

The holy man's demagoguery was very effective. His strong, deep voice carried into and around a crowd, soothed it, enveloped it, and then carried it closer to the divine. He seemed to create a bridge between heaven and earth. He spoke with precision and authority. He seemed to draw his justification directly from Heaven and the listener accepted his position of command.

That was the reason, I believe, that people seldom stopped to consider whether Peter had any legitimate, ecclesiastic authority. His authority was implicit, self-resident, obviated by the power of his words and the manner in which they were delivered. I have found that I am often confounded by those who can speak with such personal sureness. Certainly, the hermit was only among the first of those whose powers of erudition led me along particular pathways throughout my life. That day in Mainz, I was wholly convinced of the need to make the pilgrimage to Jerusalem until Brother Piccolo pointed out to me the contradictions in the hermit's presentation. However, others there that day did not have the benefit of the Benedictine's astute insight. Among these was the black *cnicht* I have mentioned. If Peter the Hermit was the pale rider, then Hell indeed did follow with him, in the form of Comte Emicho and his followers.

I started, realising that Brother Piccolo had just addressed me. Peter and Emicho vanished from my thoughts.

"I'm sorry, Brother," I said. "What did you say?"

"I had just noted that the day has become chilly. Shall we retire to the infirmary?"

I nodded. Following him back to the infirmary after we had taken our leave from Ulfrid, my head filled with the bleak realisation that I would not be a part of the armed pilgrimage to the East since I could neither disobey Lord Rothard nor will myself to accept Peter's vision as legitimate. A chill ran through me but whether from the cold air of the late afternoon or from some grim premonition of the future I do not know.

Caput Quintus

May is the season when all things live again. Flowers bloom, songbirds return in all their numbers and glorious melody, trees provide comfortable shade and shelter from sun and rain with their canopies of newly grown leaves. Game is plentiful. Gardens begin to blossom, hinting at an abundant harvest of fresh fruits and vegetables later in the season. Long hours of daylight cheer the heart and mind and spirit. May is usually a happy month. Not so in Mainz that year.

Early in the month, we heard news that there had been a terrible massacre. Reports came in that an army of Christian soldiers, well equipped and on their way to Constantinople to meet the forces of Adhemar, had murdered twelve people in the city of Speyer. Those murdered were all Jews. This news was of course quite distressing to me and I thought immediately of my friends Ruth and Yaakob, whom I had not seen since that awful winter day many months ago.

More disturbing still, at least from my present perspective, was the identity of he who executed this outrage. It was none other than Comte Emicho of Leisingen, the dread lord I had encountered the previous month when Peter the Hermit had been in the city. Soon the army of Hell would invade Mainz like a maniacal storm, a tempest called up so carelessly by the ugly little holy man. The madness had begun.

Not long after the atrocity at Speyer, we heard that Emicho had arrived in Worms, only a few days' travel from Mainz. By Ascension Day, we had learned of another massacre, this one worse than the first. The reports said that in Worms a Christian had been murdered by Jews and dumped into a well, whereupon the water from the well, now poisoned by the corpse of the dead Christian, was used to taint the wells of other Christians.

Because of these alleged acts of sabotage, the people rioted in the Jewish quarter, probably abetted by Emicho. When the Jews of Worms fled to the protection of the bishop, Emicho and his followers broke down the door of the bishop's palace and proceeded to slaughter every Jew they found. Some said the number of the dead exceeded five hundred. And by Saturday, we learned that Emicho's army was on its way to Mainz.

This fact seemed inexplicable to me, at the time. If Emicho planned to join Adhemar in Constantinople, he travelled in the wrong direction. Why did he travel north, farther into the Alemaigne lands? The explanation was simple, though, as I discovered later. He needed money to finance his expedition to the East. He undoubtedly hoped to kill the Jews, who are generally believed by our people to be immensely wealthy, though this is not always the case, and rob them of their possessions and money. His justification was that since they were the enemies of our Faith as much as the Saracens whom the armies of Adhemar were set to destroy, the Jews should likewise be destroyed and their possessions go to the victors, though I would say murderers, as spoils of war. However, these renegade *cnicht*s had the sanctioned support of neither the Church nor the Emperor who later vehemently expressed their disapproval of such activities.

On Sunday, Emicho arrived at the city walls. Lord Rothard responded to his arrival by ordering the gates of the city closed against him. He did not wish a massacre like those that had occurred in Speyer and Worms. Unlike the army of

Peter the Hermit, that of the Comte of Leisingen was highly trained, well armed and very dangerous.

On that Sunday few people attended mass. The cathedral sat virtually empty. As I looked around the church, I wondered at the fact that the only folk present appeared to be those who lived within the cathedral complex and a few I recognised from the neighbouring streets. Archbishop Rothard was not present, either. The ritual began and I lost myself within it, offering devotion to Our Lord, forgetting about the unusually poor attendance and the army outside our gates.

I suddenly became aware that someone was shaking me. Confused, I started from my devotions and looked up to find Brother Piccolo kneeling at my side.

"What is it, Brother?" I asked him in a rough whisper, astounded and not a little perturbed that he would interrupt the holy mass in this fashion.

"Hurry, come with me...there has been...an incident."

He seemed breathless, panting as though he had been running. I saw in his eyes the seriousness of the business he spoke about. I nodded. Making the sign of the cross with my hand I rose and with him walked out of the cathedral.

We ran through the streets. I had no trouble keeping pace with the older man. His robes flapped in the breeze so that he looked like some clumsy bird struggling to take flight. He led me through the maze of avenues and narrow alleyways until we emerged into the Jewish quarter. Of course, my thoughts flew immediately to my friends there. I felt a chill at thoughts of something terrible happening to them, with Emicho so near, especially since the incidents at Speyer and Worms.

Then I saw that something was indeed terribly wrong but not just for Yaakob and Ruth. The entire area we passed through was laid waste. Doors lay on the streets or hung crazily by their twisted hinges. Shutters were smashed and broken. Bits of cloth lay scattered about, along with occasional shoes and crushed objects without definable characteristics. Debris lay everywhere. What had happened here? The place looked as though a battle had been fought over and through it. I had no time to question the Benedictine, though, for he hastened on.

We came to an empty house whose doors and window shutters had been ripped off. Debris scattered about its walls bespoke the desolation recently visited upon it. Inside, furniture and other household articles lay smashed and strewn about. I wondered to whom the place belonged. However, those thoughts almost immediately fled my mind as I saw, lying in one corner, attended by our friends Ulfrid the stable master and Brother Ambrose, a wounded, possibly dying man. Perhaps he was already dead for certainly he did not evidence any signs of life.

I greeted Ulfrid who merely nodded. The strange circumstances hardly prompted me to wonder how he came to be here though I found out later he had accompanied Brother Ambrose on an errand of mercy early in the morning, setting a broken leg bone for an old man, a Christian, who had slipped in the street in the Jewish quarter. His friends had sent to the cathedral infirmary for assistance since the old man refused to be moved so much pain was he in. Then somehow the two, after treating the Christian and sending him on his way with friends, had become enmeshed in the riots against the Jews and Ambrose had sent someone to the infirmary for Brother Piccolo when more people were wounded and in need of assistance after the riots.

I knelt beside Ambrose who had already begun to work on the patient. I visually examined the man as Brother Piccolo had taught me to do before beginning any course of medical treatments. Certainly, the Benedictine had already begun his own examination and questioned Brother Ambrose as he did so.

Ambrose had tied a tourniquet over the man's upper right thigh. On that limb a large gash showed just above the knee joint from which he must surely have lost a great deal of blood. Indeed, this blood loss evidenced itself in the patient's pallor and by the fact that a large pool of the sanguine liquor had puddled beneath the man.

Aside from various scrapes, cuts and bruises, there was a major wound, an open rent in his abdomen, on the left side. Ambrose had already begun to stitch the gash. I could see through the threads the pink and blue of ropy intestines threatening to bulge out of the skin and spill onto the floor. Fighting my nausea, for I had never seen such a wound before, I stood up and began to look about for cloth to tear into bandage strips. All I could find was the man's own clothing, dirty and blood-soaked. These would hardly do.

"Shall I go to the infirmary for clean bandages, Brother Piccolo?"

"Save yourself the trouble, boy. That will not be necessary," he answered sombrely. "This patient has expired." He made the sign of the cross above the man and, as the Blessed St. James advised, muttered the extreme unction over him. Ambrose ceased his efforts and bowed his head.

Strangely, I felt none of the anguish or the sense of loss I had experienced at the death of Isaac. I did not know this man and therefore, I assume, I had no remorse or regrets at his loss. Perhaps I had even begun to develop some professional detachment in the face of death. Still, he was a human being and I felt that I should feel some kind of sympathy for him, some unconditional hope that he might attain the Kingdom of Heaven. I said a short prayer for his soul, asking the Blessed Virgin to intervene on his behalf that God might recognise his worthiness.

As I pondered this man's death, several people rushed into the house. Wild-eyed men they were. Their leader, a ham-handed fellow with a thinning shock of red hair, stood over the dead man and folded his arms threateningly.

"Well? Is he dead?" he demanded of Brother Ambrose.

"Yes," replied Ambrose simply.

"Good. Then what are you doing? Why bother with the Jew? You weren't trying to save his worthless life were you?"

Brother Piccolo stood up. I had always thought of him as a fairly short man but in that moment he seemed to rise above the larger man in stature and presence even though the other stood head and shoulders taller than the Benedictine.

"All men are worthy of medical attention when they are in need. Even Jews," he told the red-haired man, staring right into his eyes.

"No. Jews aren't men. They're vermin. So they deserve nothing from any Christian."

"You are wrong. All men are the children of God, Who creates all people. He gives some the knowledge and ability to prevent death, to ease suffering, to remove pain and to make those well who might otherwise perish. Those whose suffering is eased in this way do so by the grace of God. What right do you or anyone else have to prevent this?"

"I agree that that is true for Christians. But Comte Emicho says that all Jews must be put to death if they won't become Christians. This has been ordained by His Holiness Urban and by our noble emperor, Heinrich, may God preserve them both. Those of us who act in this way are a part of the army of God sent to destroy the infidels in the Holy Land and the places between here and there infested by unbelievers." Perhaps someone should have mentioned to the man that the Emperor Heinrich did not actually recognise the legitimacy of Urban's papacy.

As the two men argued, a general background clamour had developed. Now there were many people out in the streets. I could hear a name repeated over and over and wondered whose it might be: "Emicho, Emicho, Emicho," for I did not know that the crowd chanted the name of that dread black *cnicht* who had committed such base atrocities in Speyer and Worms and now would perpetrate his evil in Mainz. The folk with us in that dead man's house and out in the streets seemed determined to aid him in this ambition.

That is what this destruction and chaos was all about in the streets, in this house, throughout the Jewish quarter. Emicho had brought destruction to the Jews of Mainz. The children of darkness had come to the city. The light had extinguished itself in the wickedness of destruction brought by these friends of the terrors of the darkness, just as Yaakob had said in his Hanukkah prayer. A black whirlwind threatened to destroy all of us in its madness, sweeping us out of our calm lives and into a maelstrom of chaos.

"Take the body out into the street and burn it," ordered the red-haired man.

"No!" I shouted and jumped to my feet in front of the corpse. I would not see such an evil desecration done to the body of this innocent man, Jew though he was. I suppose that I saw in him Yaakob, for if they could treat this man thus, so they might my friend. I surprised myself and everyone there with my vociferation. I do not know what I expected to do on the nameless dead man's behalf. I only thought to prevent the followers of Emicho from defiling his body, just as Saul had asked his armour-bearer to kill him that he might not be tortured and befouled by his captors.

The red-haired man sneered at me and pushed me with such force that I flew backward, landing heavily against the wall. I sat there stunned, my breath completely gone, gasping. Ulfrid jumped to my aid and the three men who were with the red-haired leader immediately set upon him and dragged him into the street, he protesting loudly all the way. He punched and kicked at them trying to escape their grasp. To no avail. Beating and kicking him, they pulled Ulfrid with them.

I came to regret my rashness. I should not have stood up to the leader and so imperilled my friends. Ulfrid would not then have rushed to my aid and would not have suffered his ultimate fate.

I ran out into the street hoping to assist Ulfrid in some way but the crowd had swallowed him and his captors and

I found myself soon swept along by its progression through the streets of the Jewish quarter. I followed along behind the throng hoping to catch sight once more of Ulfrid and somehow help him escape this madness. I heard footsteps running along behind me and turned to look over my shoulder. Behind me came Brother Ambrose and Brother Piccolo already gasping from this unaccustomed effort. They waved me on, puffing and snorting like over-taxed horses. I nodded grimly and doubled my efforts to catch up with the mob.

We, that is, the mob, with me following, turned down into a side avenue I had not before travelled. Here, the houses stood untouched, the street clean and unlittered by the debris that now characterised the main streets of the neighbourhood. A chill swept over me as I realised that the mob meant to do to this street and its inhabitants as it had done to the rest of the quarter. More worrisome now, we were drawing dangerously near to the home of my friends, Ruth and Yaakob. The crowd slowed in its progress and then stopped. Ahead, I heard shouting and loud crashes and bangs. The riot had begun anew.

Suddenly I found myself in the midst of a hellish insanity. All around me madmen tore shutters from windows, threw rocks and any other projectiles upon which they could lay their hands, tossing them into the houses along the street. A firebrand appeared in one man's hand and a pile of thatch along the avenue was set alight.

The fools. How could they not see the danger to the entire city if such a fire grew beyond all control? It would eventually engulf their own homes.

Perhaps, I remember thinking, the mob came from outside the city and had no stake in its preservation anyway.

Then I recalled that the Archbishop had ordered the gates of the city closed against Comte Emicho so no one could have come in or left the city in the past day or so. The fools. What of their families, their houses? Soon anything flammable on the street had been set alight and the madmen danced in a frenzy of violence, casting sanity to the hot winds of flame, dancing as if amidst the damned along an avenue in Hell. Where was Ulfrid? Was he still alive? Or had these fiends in their frenzied darkness already murdered him? Then the tone of the mob changed from that of careless mayhem to murderous violence.

Rounding a corner a small troop of Jews came, maybe a dozen in all, curious perhaps, alarmed undoubtedly at the noise and the smell of smoke in their neighbourhood. To this day, I wonder what possessed them to brave the streets knowing that the mob had already targeted other areas in the quarter for their violent anti-Semitism. But they came and the crowd shouted triumphantly for now they had a corporeal target for their efforts instead of just empty buildings and inanimate objects upon which to vent their rage and frustration.

I could see the terror suddenly whiten the eyes of the newcomers. They huddled into one another like a flock of sheep grouping together for mutual protection against a pack of wolves. They should have acted more like deer and bounded away. Rocks flew through the air at them, several in the huddle receiving violent blows that drew blood. Then good sense seemed to overtake them and they began to edge back the way they had come.

The mob formed a wall like a line of foot soldiers arrayed for battle. They shouted and gestured obscenely and threw more debris and moved closer to outflank their enemy.

Then someone from the mob threw a firebrand into the huddle of Jews, some of whom scattered forward into the threatening battle line. Some among the mob must have believed the Jews had decided to attack for I saw Ulfrid thrust forward by some person right into the oncoming Jews. As this apparent threat in the person of the innocent Ulfrid flew at them one of the Jews grasped a fallen stone and swung it straight down onto the horse master's head. Ulfrid plummeted to earth like a bucket into a well. Then the mob ran forward screaming and the Jews scattered in all directions, soon escaping their tormentors. This, I suppose, owing to the fact that they knew their own territory better than their attackers did and were able to find alleys and to find doors opened to them through which they could escape but which the mob would find locked against them.

I rushed forward to help Ulfrid. None stopped me. I called out to the horse master but he did not respond. A slick of gore began to pool under his head, fed by the wellspring of his new-opened skull. Panic rose up in me as I pried open his eyelids. His eyes stared blankly without sight, without life. I moaned and felt for his heartbeat in the places that Brother Piccolo had taught me to look, under his ear, in his wrist, listening at his chest. Nothing. Helplessly I looked around for Brother Piccolo and Brother Ambrose hoping against hope that perhaps they could find life where I had not. After a few moments of kneeling in the street beside Ulfrid, attempting vainly to stop the blood flow from the sticky head wound, the Brothers arrived on the scene. Almost immediately Brother Piccolo confirmed my worst fears: Ulfrid had died under the massive blow of the stone.

Numbly, I sat there, unable to weep, unable to think. Then suddenly I leapt to my feet in a blind rage and raced down the street after the mob. Brother Piccolo and Brother Ambrose called after me to stop yet I did not heed their cries. Rage. Instinctively I felt only the need for revenge. I could only blame the leader of the mob, the red-haired man. I sought only him. Soon I found him.

He stood at the centre of an intersection of two streets where they came together to form a cross. This time I determined that I would not jump upon him as I had done earlier. I knew that this would only cause him to react immediately as he had when I attacked him earlier and I would undoubtedly be thrown across the street, tossed on my head or worse. Instead, I confronted him, walking up and standing directly in front of him. Then I screamed into his face.

"You killed Ulfrid!" I screamed at him. I think that I did this several times. And then he grabbed me by the collar and lifted me right off my feet. The cord that bound the neck of my robe tightened around my throat and began to strangle me.

"What are you talking about?" he growled the question.

"Ulfrid" I uttered a strangled moan.

"Who is Ulfrid?"

I managed only to choke and gasp for air. Seeing that I was unable to breathe he set me down. He asked again, "Who is Ulfrid?" By then, of course, I had collapsed to my knees owing to my breathlessness. A small group of the red-haired man's followers began to knot around us. "The man you dragged out of the house before; where the dead Jew was," I gasped, in answer to his question.

"Was he a Jew?"

I shook my head. "No. He is the stable master at the cathedral."

A collective intake of breath around me by those standing there indicated some astonishment at this news. I looked up at the leader. His face seemed to have grown paler but then, as I looked at him, his visage took on a coppery red hue. He flushed with a sudden choleric rage. A light flashed in his eyes as if something important had suddenly occurred to him.

"A Christian," he said. "A Christian. Did anyone see how this man, Ulfrid, did you say," this to me, "did anyone see how he died?"

A grimy-faced, greasy looking man in a dirty leather apron spoke up. "Yes. I saw him. The Jews stoned him to death."

This was true in essence, or so I believed then, but a patent exaggeration of the event. Only one man had wielded the stone that killed Ulfrid and he would not have done that except that he believed his life endangered by the mad anonymous mob into the midst of which he and his companions had stumbled. But this fact did not deter the red-haired leader who surely had himself witnessed the attack on the Jews from the front lines.

He shouted as though he shouted a battle cry, "A Christian! The Jews have killed a Christian!" And the cry went round that the Jews had killed a Christian. In moments, I found myself alone still kneeling in the street. The mob rushed away shouting the name of Emicho, bound for the city gates to let the Comte of Leisingen into the city as

I discovered later though in this they were not immediately successful.

I had accomplished nothing. Indeed, I had only made things worse by further fuelling their rage against the Jews. I am not sure what I hoped to achieve by confronting the man but I felt the need to blame someone, someone other than the nameless Jew who had performed the deed, for the death of Ulfrid.

The thought of the horse master's death seemed madness to me. The mob had kicked him and beat him merely for standing up to their leader in my defence, dragging him with them, still abusing him, as they looked for other victims of their angry, mindless violence. The fact that my friend had been killed by the blow on the head was incidental since the Jew had not purposely murdered Ulfrid, only defended himself against a faceless, nameless aggressor. I did not blame the Jew any more than I blamed the rock he wielded.

I found Brother Piccolo and Brother Ambrose still hovering over Ulfrid. When I arrived, the Benedictine grasped my hands in his and looked into my eyes with deep sadness and sympathy. He knew how close a friend Ulfrid had been to me. Indeed, the monk himself had been a good friend to the horse master so I am certain that he felt as badly about our friend's death as I did. As I looked into Brother Piccolo's eyes my own suddenly spilled onto my cheeks in quickening rivulets. This was the second tragedy I had endured in the six months past and only the second of my entire life. I felt I could never endure any other such anguish; but at that moment I had no idea what awaited all of us on the following day.

Brother Piccolo broke the moment of agony. "We should get Ulfrid back to the infirmary and notify his wife, though how we shall tell her with the gates closed and Emicho's army outside, I don't know."

I nodded weakly and we all bent to the task of lifting and carrying the dead man back to the cathedral.

As we struggled along with our burden Brother Piccolo said, breathlessly, "The blow on the head is not what killed our friend, little brother. That particular wound he suffered was not fatal."

"But...but I thought..." I stammered.

"No. The many bruises on his body and their coloration indicate that the blows he suffered at the hands of the rioters caused internal bleeding which ended his life. He was likely already near to dead before the final head wound came, which is probably why he was thrown out from the mob. Although I shall have to perform a more complete examination of the head wound and the bruises before I can say this with certainty."

"Then the Jew is innocent?"

"Yes. And the Christians are guilty of one of the most abominable transgressions against God and His Commandments."

I finished the thought for him: "They have killed."

I thought again of my experience of the Hanukkah celebration and of Yaakob's reading of scripture that night. These blind followers of Comte Emicho, the lord of blackness who had descended upon our city, truly groped without light in the darkness, the very embodiment of the words Yaakob had used. They had no understanding of the real essence of Urban's Holy War against the oppressors of

Christianity. They did not understand that the Jews of Mainz, of Speyer, of Worms, were not a threat to our Christian beliefs or our way of life. Certainly, I had never met among the Jews of Mainz any such demagogues as Peter the Hermit, or like Emicho who whipped people to aggressive and dangerous religious fervour. The Jews kept to themselves and offered no harm to their fellow citizens. Urban had never included the Jews of Lotharingia among the targets of his expedition against the enemies of Christ. The mission of Emicho represented opportunism at its worst.

Like the men portrayed in the scriptures from which Yaakob had read that night, the followers of Emicho had in their sight only gold and silver. They knew intrinsically that they had no rational justification for their attack on the Jews, an attack meant ultimately to make the attackers wealthy at their victims' expense. Further, as events eventually showed, these demagogues and the rabble that followed them never intended to join with the armies of Adhemar at Constantinople. The only real result of their initiative was to increase the size of their coffers and kill thousands of innocent, harmless, peace-loving people.

I wondered if somehow Yaakob had foreseen these events. Else, why would he have chosen those particular passages from scripture at Hanukkah? Had he been forewarned? If so, why had he not fled before the arrival of Emicho's army? Or did he realise at once, as I came to realise only later, that there was no place to which his people could flee? That much of Christendom rejected and reviled him and his co-religionists?

Certainly, the hatred aimed against the Jews by Comte Emicho was not specific to Mainz, or the other cities he attacked, but symptomatic of an abominable enterprise that spread like a plague in the wake of our red-cross-bearing armies. Yaakob must have known that with the release of Urban's Holy War against the Infidel something like this campaign of hatred had to arise. Yet, the announcement from the Holy Father had come after I had visited with my Jewish friends. Coincidence then?

Ultimately, I think, the truth is that Yaakob's people had suffered so often at the hands of Gentiles that his prayers that Hanukkah evening represented a response to the context of his existence as a Jew living in Christendom. The warnings expressed in the scripture were emblematic of the interaction of Christian and Jew at all times. I could never know the whole truth because thereafter I never had the opportunity to question Yaakob about it.

We returned to the infirmary with our friend's body, the whole time apprehensive because we heard the noise caused by the rioters in nearby streets. Once we had left the Jewish quarter, though, we saw only occasional runners, either heading for the Jewish quarter or leaving it in haste. None of those who passed us were themselves Jews. An armed force sent by the Archbishop tramped by, dressed in oiled leather armour and carrying small round bucklers and spears, on its way to attempt to quell the violence that had erupted in various spots throughout the Jewish part of the city now. I thought that they were far too few in number to do any real good for I am sure there were less than one hundred of them and far more rioters than that.

Once we reached the infirmary, we locked both the gate and the door of the infirmary. This was most irregular an occurrence for, as long as I had been associated with the little hospital and its doctors, I had never known either gate or door to be barred against those wishing to avail themselves of the infirmary's services. The unusual had quickly become the norm in Mainz that day.

When we laid Ulfrid's body down, Brother Piccolo began to examine the corpse. Soon, he declared his verdict. As he had surmised earlier the blow to the head had not been fatal. The Christian rioters, not the Jew who had defended himself from the mob's attack, had caused Ulfrid's death. I sat on a stool dumbly rigid, unable to mourn or grieve further for this latest death. I stared at the body, disbelieving the information my eyes gathered in to my heart. Thus, my heart would not respond.

"What now, Brother?" asked Brother Ambrose of the Benedictine.

"We should seek out the Archbishop and inform him of what we have seen, I suppose, although I am sure that he has already some idea of the events transpiring in the city."

Ambrose nodded. Silently, they rose and made for the door. I sat on my stool partially aware that they were leaving but somehow unable to care. Then I felt Brother Piccolo's touch on my shoulder and he took my wrists in his hands, raising me up.

"Come," he said.

I rose obediently, woodenly, and followed the monks out of the infirmary.

The main hall of the Archbishop's palace, when we arrived there, was filled to capacity with citizens of Mainz and cathedral staff, the hall ringing with their clamorous tumult.

The walk to the building from the infirmary in the brisk evening air and the excitement in the air had by now braced me awake so that I had thrown off the earlier torpor caused by my sadness at the death of Ulfrid. Perhaps the resilience of youthful emotion made me forget about my grief for the moment. The excitement of these new events could not but sweep me up and carry me along in its swift current.

There seemed to be no regulation to the unexpected gathering. No one took charge or attempted to quiet the crowd, and so chaos disordered the room. The Archbishop did not present himself to the people gathered there, nor did I see any sign of the senior priests who lived in the palace.

Then, on a balcony above the sea of chaos, I spotted Julius, the gatekeeper, who seemed to be waving at me. Unsure, I looked about me but nobody else seemed to notice the gesture from above. I turned to Brother Piccolo and indicated Julius. When the Benedictine looked up Julius began to nod vigorously and wave us toward him. Brother Piccolo snorted and, gesturing for Ambrose and I to follow, made for the stairs leading to the balconies above. Julius met us at the foot of the stairs.

"Quickly," he ordered peremptorily, "follow me. My Lord Rothard is waiting for you." He glanced sourly at me but said nothing to exclude my presence.

We followed him across the hall, jostled and accosted by many who wanted to hear any news of the awful events occurring beyond the palace walls. I ignored all who approached me. Brother Piccolo shook his head and waved them off as they surrounded him. Eventually we found our way to the entry to the Archbishop's private chambers.

Entering his audience room we found a gathering similar, though less chaotic, to that in the main hall. All the senior priests and advisors were present as well as some of the burghers from the town. I recognised Gerhard of Neuss the chief lay lord of the city, a wealthy though lesser nobleman whose main interest was in trade and commerce and the customs collections associated with them. He was known to be a greedy, acquisitive individual who cared more for personal material profit than for Christian values and virtues. He was a bald, corpulent man, no taller than Brother Piccolo and somewhat similar in features, pudgy and round, though with none of the Benedictine's jocular expressiveness.

"Let me speak!" he called out as we entered. "I say, let me speak. Quiet!" This last he bellowed and suddenly all was silence.

Gerhard looked around at the sea of faces, glaring, daring them to interrupt him. Despite his nasty reputation, he was respected because of his wealth and influence. Even the Archbishop often deferred to his wishes over weighty civic matters if they did not interfere with the prerogatives of the Church. One would be hard pressed to choose between the two powerful men for leadership of the city. Each had immense authority in his respective sphere of influence. Therefore, as a consequence of their respect for that power, none broke Gerhard's invocation for silence.

Still glaringly defiant, Gerhard spoke again.

"Now. We have a problem outside our city walls and we need to cool the fire in our hearts and heads and begin to address how best to eliminate the threat of Emicho's army. For my part, I believe his main aim is to slaughter as many of our

Jewish citizens as possible in order to fill his purse with any and all assets he can carry away with him. This must not be allowed to happen."

One of the priests snorted at this. "Yes, Lord Gerhard, I can see why you would think so. I'm sure a lot of your investments might suffer as a result."

Gerhard's bald head blushed purple and he snarled a caustic reply. "And so what of it, priest? Of course I do not wish to see the Comte of Leisingen carry away my family's inheritance. Would you? Oh, but I forgot, you holy men do not keep wives or lovers anymore since the Holy Father, Gregoire, banned such activities less suited to priests and more suited to the natural desires of other less perfect men. And so you have no heirs."

The heavy sarcasm caused the priest who had spoken to blanche and he spoke no more. I glanced at Lord Rothard, whose face showed a dour expression. I do not believe he rejoiced at Gerhard's opinions nor at the fact that he, the Archbishop, must suffer the lay lord's impudent harassment of priests in his own palace. However, he did not speak.

"Who is to say that Emicho will stop in the Jewish quarter?" Gerhard continued. "Why should he not attack Christian households as well and carry off *their* assets? Once within the city walls, he will act as he pleases and no one to stop him or say him nay. We hardly have the military resources within the city walls to fend off his attacks. Days will pass before we can send to our neighbours for assistance. And what guarantee have we that any of them will help us when they are probably expecting an attack from Emicho themselves any day?"

"We must keep the gates barred against him, then!" One of the burghers shouted.

"Of course, of course," said Gerhard with a dismissive wave and an expression on his face that suggested he thought the speaker stupid. Then he spread his arms wide, palms up in a pleading gesture. "But how long can we keep our gates closed? Our commerce will suffer when vessels cannot approach our docks, when caravans cannot approach our walls. How long will Emicho wait? A day? A week? A month? Will he lay siege to our city? Break down the gates? Scale our walls?"

Those gathered stood in silence, considering Gerhard's words.

"Then give him the Jews." Surprisingly this comment that broke the silence came from Julius.

"What?" asked Gerhard quietly, turning to face the Archbishop's steward, the expression on his face showing clearly that this was the conclusion he had hoped someone would come to.

"Give him the Jews. Give him that which he says publicly he wants. Gather them up and force them out of the city. Then he will not have their assets but he at least will have their heads, which is what he says he wants, anyway."

The gathering erupted in a loud vocal burst of both assent and dissent. Many agreed with this suggestion, particularly the merchant burghers, many of whom would benefit by the nullification of loans and other financial debts owed the non-Christian money-lenders and merchants. However, I observed that many protested against Julius' suggestion. Brother Piccolo was such a one, of course.

"If we do that we pass a sentence of death on all of them," he said calmly. "We have heard what was done in Speyer and at Worms. We know that Emicho and his people will kill them. If...no, I should say, *when* that happens we will all be accountable for their deaths and we abet him and his followers in a foul contradiction of the Commandments. We will be murderers, too, as much as Emicho's people. You have all heard of the terrible massacres at Worms and Speyer. Do you believe that Emicho's people will do any less to the Jewish folk of Mainz?"

"Do you believe, Brother Piccolo, that any of us care what becomes of the infidels in our midst?" asked Julius scornfully.

Brother Piccolo moved forward to face Julius, barely a nose length from the other man. He glared fiercely at the Archbishop's steward.

"Do you believe, Julius, that I will stand by idly while you send these people to their deaths? Think, man! They are human beings. Whatever else they are, they do not deserve to die in this fashion, at the hands of a brute mob. Anything you do to aid the mob you will be held accountable for, mark me well."

Julius glared at the monk furiously, his mouth twitching, his eyes abulge, his face glowing angrily. But he said nothing. He stepped back a pace and then said, quietly furious, "Beware, Benedictine, there are men in the city who think as I do. Powerful men." He let the sentence hang, an obvious warning. And an implicit threat. Julius glared at the Benedictine who merely adopted a bland expression and said nothing. The people witnessing this exchange shuffled and coughed nervously.

Then Lord Rothard spoke at last.

"No Jews will be given to the Comte of Leisingen. The gates of the city shall remain closed and none will enter or leave without my particular consent." Then he turned to Julius, his voice angry. "You, churl, best think very carefully where lie your loyalties. We are Christian men, churchmen, paradigms of virtue, examples to those striving to be devout, and as such, we must show charity to all men, especially those who might be brought to the True Faith. Remember that Our Lord spent time with publicans and sinners, to bring them to righteousness. Seek the one sheep that is lost in the wilderness, not the ninety-nine safe in the fold. Go, Julius, and consider your sinful heart which prevents charity from lodging there."

Thus chastised before all those assembled there, made an example to all, the steward gasped in his throat as though he would speak. But he seemed to reconsider this action and, swallowing hard, staggered a few steps backward before turning and slinking out of the crowd and through the doorway. If the Archbishop had known what actions his criticism had spurred in Julius surely he would have reconsidered and gone easier with him. However, only the Lord God has the power to see the future course of human affairs and only subsequent events proved to frail human sensibilities the folly of Lord Rothard's words to his steward.

A short time after Julius left, during which time discussion renewed over Emicho's intentions though not about the ultimate disposition of the Jews of Mainz, there came a knock on the door to the Archbishop's chambers. The door opened to reveal who stood there. Those present immediately fell silent.

Into the room strode a tall, thin, elderly man dressed completely in black. He wore an odd wide-brimmed hat whose peak towered above his head and from under it, on either temple, dangled a curl of snowy hair the length of his cheeks. This feature I had seen before. Yaakob also wore his hair in this fashion, a fashion that signified the devout Jew. This man wore his white beard long and carefully combed, also a symbol of devotion. That he was an important man in his community showed in his regal carriage and in his eyes. He was a man to be reckoned with in the company of Mainz Jews. This was Kalonymos, their chief rabbi.

Kalonymos bowed deeply before Archbishop Rothard. The Archbishop extended his hand, which the rabbi took in his own and kissed lightly. Then the Jewish leader straightened and looked the other man in the eye.

"My lord," he said, utterly dignified even in necessity, "you are aware of the violence that has erupted in the city because of the presence of the Lord of Leisingen beyond its walls. Our portion of the city has endured indignities never suffered in the past at the hands of our neighbours and fellow citizens. We fear that the trouble will grow worse if ever Comte Emicho is allowed within the walls. We therefore implore you to guard our welfare and safety. Please aid us, my lord."

"What would you have me do?" asked the Archbishop blandly.

"The people," and by this Kalonymos meant his own people, "the people have gathered at the synagogue for guidance in their terror at this violence directed against them. Space there is limited. We have not the resources to protect them against the mob. The temple itself is easily penetrable in the event of an attack and the safety of the people cannot be secured. The elders of the temple have therefore asked me to come to you and offer you a certain weight in silver as security against their safety."

"What weight do you offer?" Gerhard asked quickly.

Kalonymos turned his head sideways but did not face Gerhard directly nor look into the nobleman's eyes. He hesitated as if offended by Gerhard's question or as if reluctant to reveal the value of the ransom he offered to Lord Rothard with so many ears listening. Nonetheless, he responded to the question.

"We offer two hundred silver marks to my lord, the Archbishop," he said curtly.

I watched Lord Rothard's face as Kalonymos announced this sum. The Archbishop's visage never flinched nor did he give any outward sign that he had been affected by the offer of this great measure of the precious metal. Although I cannot be sure, and certainly my memory may be in fault owing to the time passed since that day, I thought I saw a momentary glint in his eyes as if he coveted the money offered by the rabbi. If such a twinkle had been there, I am certain that the thought of the good that the money would achieve for the city accounted for its presence.

Lord Rothard replied without emotion as was his custom in such encounters, "That sum will be acceptable to us, my lord Kalonymos. However, I am not certain that we can accommodate all your people in the palace here. How many did you say?"

"There are at least one thousand of my people seeking shelter, my lord."

"Hmmm...that is indeed a large number of folk. No, I do not believe we can accept all of them here; half of that number at most. Perhaps my lord Gerhard may be able to help...?" He let the sentence dangle as an invitation for the lay lord to step in.

Gerhard's face betrayed his acquisitiveness immediately. His eyes danced at the thought, I am certain, of profit at the expense of the hapless Jews; particularly as he had anticipated the expulsion of the Jews from the city and had seen the hope of confiscating their wealth vanish with the utterance of Lord Rothard's words. Now he saw that he could still increase his coffers though not by the amount he had expected. He smiled broadly and nodded his head, his vast neck and chin shaking like a stiff aspic.

"Indeed, my lord, that is possible. My own palace is of adequate size to shelter that same number of refugees," he said and added slyly, "For a similar financial consideration, of course." And then he smiled like Reynald the Fox after eating the barnyard rooster. I was astonished that Gerhard could so blithely profit from the misfortunes of others but then, profit had ever been his principal motivation.

Kalonymos seemed to consider Gerhard's offer for a moment. His mouth moved beneath his drooping moustache and then he nodded though he said nothing. After all, he had no choice in the matter of the fee if he would succour his people. His shoulders slumped. He bowed Lord Rothard and to Lord Gerhard in turn, though less deeply and swifter, then he backed away and, turning on his heel, left the room. Gerhard watched him go with a self-satisfied smile and clasped his hands expansively over his belly.

"Then the matter is settled, my lord Archbishop. The Jews will be safe with us in our vast charity. The only other matter is what to do about the Comte of Leisingen. Have you a suggestion as efficacious as that you have just made concerning the disposition of the Jews?"

Of course, everyone there knew that the Archbishop had not essentially proposed the idea of sheltering the Jews. The timely arrival of Kalonymos had offered a solution beneficial to all concerned. Thus, Gerhard implied that Lord Rothard had been incapable of arriving at the solution himself. The implication did not seem to bother the Archbishop for his next solution was in fact no solution at all.

"We will wait for a day or two and discover the Comte's purpose and intent. Meanwhile, we shall send messages to our neighbours and to the Duke for aid. And the gates will remain closed until we have word that aid is on its way. We shall notify you of any changes, my lord Gerhard. You may return to your counting-house."

Gerhard gaped at the Archbishop. Several times he blinked and made as if to say something but then stopped. Then his face flushed red with anger. He spun around like an oak tree in a tempest with its roots torn loose from its earthly foundation and whirled out of the room. The burghers drifted in his wake like so many dry leaves whipped loose from their branches to flutter aimlessly in the winds. With the dismissal of Gerhard and his followers, discussion turned immediately to where the Jews would be housed and maintained after their arrival. Some thought the stable would be appropriate, others the barracks where the novices and staff slept, others in the open courtyards within the palace compound walls. None suggested the cathedral or the palace. The Archbishop himself suggested the latter.

"Our Jewish friends will be housed here within the palace walls. This is the only space sufficient to hold them all under one roof. After all, we do not want them wandering all about the compound, particularly since we seem divided about the acceptability of their presence. And I fear for their safety in such a climate of distrust." He spoke to one of the clerics present. "Inform our servant and steward, Julius, to prepare the palace for the imminent arrival of our guests." The young and eager cleric instantly obeyed, dashing out of the room like a hound pursuing a deer.

Presently, Lord Rothard dismissed those gathered except for Brother Piccolo, Brother Ambrose and me. He gazed at us for a long moment. Then he spoke with a sigh.

"*Nos Deus defendeat*," he said. May God protect us. I understood then how dangerous the Archbishop thought the situation. "I wanted to confer with you, Brother," he said, addressing Brother Piccolo, who nodded his head deferentially. "There is great danger outside our walls, as we are all well aware. If that trouble comes into our city, matters will be much worse than the violence that has already disquieted our streets."

"While we are relatively safe behind our palace walls the casualties outside in the city proper will be numerous and grave. How will we attend those in need of our, your," Rothard corrected himself, "ministrations out there?"

"That will be difficult, my lord," replied the Benedictine. "Particularly so since the infirmary may easily be breached if the gate is broken down. I think it would be best if all medicaments and medical instruments were brought into the palace and a temporary infirmary set up inside its walls. As for those in the city, they must rely on lay physicians and surgeons for their care unless they can be brought to the palace for treatment, which I doubt is possible with Emicho's followers at the door. Most of those requiring medical attention doubtless will be those involved in the riots and those within the palace if he ever breaches the city walls. Hopefully, none of our citizens will be foolish enough to venture forth into the teeth of the animal mob. The situation has grown far too dangerous for any to wander the streets without armed escort."

The Archbishop nodded his agreement.

"Forgive my impertinence, my lord," interjected Brother Ambrose, "but we must report to you the death of one of your servants, Ulfrid, the stable-master."

The Archbishop looked at Ambrose with sympathy in his eyes. He sighed then spoke quietly, "How did he die? Was it a result of the violence in the streets?"

Ambrose nodded. "He was beaten severely by a group of rioters mistakenly acting according to the dictates of Emicho that all Jews must be punished for their perceived crimes against Our Lord. Then they threw his body into a group of Jews, one of whom thought he was being attacked and defended himself." He described how Ulfrid had died.

"A tragic and unnecessary death. Let us hope not the first of many such, in either community," commented the Archbishop. "We shall make every effort to bring his murderers to justice. And, of course, his wife must be informed at the earliest opportunity." Lord Rothard reached for a tiny silver bell and it rang out sweetly. "If you will excuse us now,

Brothers, we must compose letters to the lords of Wurzburg and Trier and to the Emperor to express our concern about Comte Emicho's aggressions and request their aid in quelling this uprising."

His secretary, Father Benedict, entered as we left. I wondered if any relieving force could possibly arrive in time from the Emperor or the cities nearby to prevent Comte Emicho's incursion into Mainz. Both Wurzburg and Trier were several days' journey away and the latter lay in the duchy of Upper Lotharingia not in our own duchy of Franconia. The Lotharingians might not take any interest in the troubles of a Franconian city. In the end, the letters either were not sent quickly enough, or, as I believe, not at all.

◆

Early on the second morning after the meeting with Lord Rothard, Tuesday, Emicho broke into the city. No one at the cathedral at first knew how he got in for the gates were closed and barred. Since he did not actually breach gate or wall, none could explain his inexplicable incursion.

However, something my friend, Arbogast, said to me illuminated the event. Arbogast had seen Julius outside the cathedral talking with a tall, red-haired man after nightfall by torch light and then the two had disappeared into the darkness together. I knew this must be the same man who had assaulted me in the Jewish quarter earlier. Later, I learned that, contrary to the Archbishop's explicit orders, someone from inside the city had opened the gates to allow Emicho and his army entry. I knew that this had to be Julius.

I imagined what he had done. In the early morning hours, shortly before prime, the sun just beginning to rise behind the distant hills, he had stolen out of the palace, secretly and furtively so that he would not be seen. He made his way quickly to the walls. Arriving at the gates he entered the guardhouse and spoke to the sergeant in charge. *The Archbishop*, he would have said, *orders that the gates be opened immediately. Why?* the sergeant would have asked. *He wishes Comte Emicho to enter the city and go to the cathedral palace for an interview*, Julius would have responded.

If the sergeant hesitated at all Julius, true to his character, would have flown into a rage and shouted, *Do not question me! I am the Archbishop's steward and messenger! Open these gates immediately!* And the sergeant would have had no choice but to obey for Julius certainly outranked him.

The sergeant could not have known that the steward did not act on Lord Rothard's authority but independently and deceitfully. He would have ordered his men to open the gates. Emicho's men would have been waiting right outside, already informed of the trick somehow, perhaps by a written message thrown over the walls by the red-haired man. Immediately the gates opened they poured inside and subdued the small garrison of guards of whom several were killed defending their position.

We at the palace became aware of the entry of Emicho's army shortly after sunrise. I awoke in my cell behind the palace to a shouting and clamour that would have rendered the Last Trump inaudible. Outside, in the inner courtyard below, people ran forth into the stables, carrying things in and then hurrying back into the palace empty-handed. I wondered what had happened to cause such a flurry of activity and thought that this was indeed strange behaviour. Why should these servants carry supplies into the stable as if in preparation for an impending journey?

Entering the palace, I made my way directly to the dining hall. My eyes beheld an amazing scene of activity. For the hall was filled to capacity with men, women, and children, nearly all Jews as I immediately recognised. So they had arrived; probably during the night, I realised. I saw my friend Arbogast at the foot of the balcony stairs. He called me over to him and though I wanted to look around to see if my friends, Yaakob and Ruth, were present among the refugees in the dining hall, I followed him up the stairs as I had done before on that Christ Mass Day only a few months before. We followed the balcony arcade around to the windows opening onto the plaza at the front of the cathedral palace.

Below, I beheld a sight that immediately caused the blood to run from my face and my heart to leap into my throat in terror. Ranged outside the palace in rank after rank of armed foot soldiers and armoured horsemen stood Emicho's army. Still, despite my fear, I was fascinated by the spectacle.

This was the first such army that I had ever seen. Of course, the palace had its guard, a force of about two hundred men, but they paled in comparison to those outside besieging the palace in their thousands. In armament our force was far inferior to that of Emicho. Our foot soldiers dressed in quilted leather jerkins and carried small, round bucklers and short swords and spears. The foot soldiers of Emicho's army dressed in thick leather breastplates over heavy quilted shirts with leather buskins covering their legs. They carried large heavy upside-down teardrop shaped shields and long pikes with wicked-looking double-bladed tips. Each wore a conical helmet with long nose guard and leather aventail suspended from the rim at back to protect the neck and carried a long sword at his side suspended from a belt and baldric. A deadly force to be sure.

The most potent component of the army of Emicho was the mounted warrior of which there stood possibly one hundred in the plaza. The *cnichts*, as we say in Aengelond or *chevaliers* as the Franks call them, horsemen, were armoured in chain mail from helm to *sabatons*, their mailed foot coverings. Their hauberks, the mail surcoats reaching to their thighs, glinted dully in the early morning sun. The *cnichts*, too, carried the large teardrop shield slung over their forearms. They sat astride their huge war horses, immobile and implacable.

Then I saw the leader of the stern horde and I realised that he was the same man I had encountered months since when Peter the Hermit had passed through our city. Emicho, sitting astride his black charger, came prancing up through the ranks of his assembled men, grimly making for the open space left for him before the palace gates. He reined in and looked up. I shrank back from the window feeling his eyes bore into me. I knew the fear was unfounded because he could not possibly have seen me from that distance. Yet, the man intimidated. He was strong and cruel and brutal and most who met him or suffered at his hands learned quickly to fear him.

Emicho motioned with his fingers and one of his men stepped forward. This unarmoured man, clearly not a *cnicht* but a cleric as he was dressed in a knee-length tunic of simple design, snapped up a parchment and unrolled it. Then he began to shout at the top of his lungs so that any listening in the cathedral or the palace might hear his voice.

"My Lord Rothard, by the Grace of God, Archbishop of Mainz, my Lord Emicho, Comte of Leisingen sends greetings. By the authority of His Holiness the Blessed Father Pope Urban this armed force proposes to carry out the mission instigated at the Council of Clermont in November past; that is, to 'go forth against the Infidels,' to wage bloody war against them to the Glory of God. My Lord Emicho is here to do the work of Our Lord; to destroy the Infidel in our midst as he has done in Speyer and Worms. He commands that the Jews of Mainz be given unto him that he may exact God's Vengeance in the name of Our Lord Jesus Christ."

The announcer rolled up the parchment and tucking it under his arm retreated once more into the ranks. Emicho sat his horse, one fist tucked into his hip, and the other wrapped tightly around the crossed hilt of the long Norse-style sword lying in his lap. Patiently he waited for an answer from within. And waited.

And waited.

When no answer came forth, he nodded to a mounted man near him. The man swung his horse around and began to shout orders. Shortly, a band of men shuffled up through the ranks carrying between them, suspended from hemp ropes that crossed over their shoulders, a stout log iron-capped at one end. They ran up the cathedral steps and rammed the log into the great oaken doors. This assuredly represented the weakest point of the cathedral complex's defence for only at this spot was it undefended by thick stone walls.

I knew that the doors must be barred from within but I was unsure how long those bars and the doors would withstand such an assault. Even from where I stood above the dining hall next to the cathedral, the steady reverberating thud of the battering ram was clearly audible. Below, in the dining hall, the effect must have been even more pronounced for as soon as the pounding began those inside began to scream and wail.

Startled, I left my vigil at the windows and raced down the stairs. I do not remember if I meant to help those below in some way, for I cannot now see how I might have done so, or if I meant simply to flee from the sight of that hideous armigerous force outside the walls. As I reached the floor, I knew immediately that I must find Brother Piccolo. He would know what to do.

Hurrying through the dining hall, I literally ran into Yaakob and Ruth who stood waiting to greet me. I had not seen them nor even known if they were present in the hall. I greeted them with mixed emotions for, while I exulted at the fact that they were safe within the walls without having suffered in the earlier riots, I acknowledged the thought that the danger to them had increased a hundredfold with the arrival of the Comte in the city. I expressed my delight at their presence and tried to keep my fears to myself. But I think that those fears were evident upon my face, written there in lines of oppression in Emicho's black, terrorizing ink.

"Will they get in?" asked Ruth, tears brimming around her eyes.

"I do not know," I replied, "I hope not. Perhaps help will arrive in time from Wurzburg or Trier or from the Emperor." I finished the sentence without much conviction. I did not hold out much hope for any sort of timely intervention on the part of the lords of those cities or the Emperor, Henry.

Ruth took my hands in hers and folded them to her breast. "Whatever happens today, thank you for all your kindness and thank you for your friendship."

I could say nothing in response to this for my emotions overwhelmed me. I could only nod, fighting back my own tears as I looked on the fear and helplessness in her eyes, a lump growing in my throat. I do not know if she guessed at the full extent of the danger to herself and Yaakob and the other refugees. I hope not.

In those last hours of her life, Ruth lived as bravely noble as any Christian of my acquaintance or indeed any person so tried by the vicissitudes of fate. Yaakob said nothing and I am sure that he fully appreciated the danger to them and had already resigned himself to the inevitability of their circumstances. He knew what had happened at Worms. He knew what Emicho was capable of. He threw his arms around Ruth and me and gathered us in, holding the embrace for a long time. I heard the sound of my own heartbeat and beyond it, lower in pitch and slower, steadier, the incessant pounding of Emicho's battering ram against the doors.

I believe that in that moment I first began to have doubts about my own faith in God's mercy. Would God not protect those within against the evil horde who threatened to violate the sanctity of His temple? Why, after all, did He allow this destruction of so many innocents? Why did He not protect them as Our Lord Jesus said He would do? Why did He not strike those down who pretended to act in His name but whose motivations emanated from blood-lust and material greed rather than piety and a true belief in the necessity of protecting the integrity and prerogatives of Christian faith?

These people, these Jews, did not threaten that faith or our Christian community. They worshipped the same God as we and in essence, though they did not accept Jesus as the Christ, they were as much God's Children as we. The Jews of Mainz trusted their Christian protectors to deliver them safely but ultimately were betrayed by those same hosts.

I suppose, in the end, that it was their resistance to Christian belief that killed them.

Was that the reason God allowed Emicho to wreak his will that day: the fact that the Jews did not believe? Many doubts and questions were raised in me on that day, doubts which plagued me for years afterward, questions that remained unanswered for half a lifetime. Ironic, I think, that my doubts were raised in the context of an expression of violent Christian religiosity against meek, indefensible non-Christians.

I withdrew from Yaakob and Ruth's embrace and apologised for leaving them but I had to find Brother Piccolo. They wished me well and I them. I told them to have faith that God would deliver them to safety this day. They nodded, I think indulgently, for doubtless they did not truly believe this would be the case. They had a unique perspective regarding the One God with respect to their role as His Chosen People and the necessity of constant trial and suffering that that position of primacy, that covenant with God, required of them. So, as a result, Yaakob and Ruth had already prepared themselves for death I am sure; they would have seen their deaths at Emicho's hands as a necessary condition that God had imposed upon them. How much better they might have felt had they the surety of life everlasting through the Grace imbued in all pious Christians by Our Lord Jesus Christ.

I did not think such things at that time, for I simply feared for the safety of us all. I still believed that all would be well in the end. Of course, at that time I had no idea what would be the true outcome of the day's events. Death. Much death.

◆

I found Brother Piccolo with Brother Ambrose in the temporary infirmary the Benedictine had set up deep within the palace in a room usually reserved for scholastic pursuits. I had spent many hours here listening to theological lectures from various learned members of the cathedral staff but now the space could hardly be recognised as anything other than a chamber reserved for the use of a *medicus*. The Benedictine had brought most of his herbal medicines, unguents, tinctures, potions and the like and various pots and jars and boxes littered the room.

Brother Ambrose had set up a couple of trestle tables for surgical use and his frightening instruments lay neatly arranged on the plank surfaces. I had seen these instruments in use many times and I recognised them by sight and understood their usage. For example, one of his devices was a pair of forceps that had spoon-like attachments on their tips. These attachments were sharpened so that they could be inserted directly into an arrow wound around the shaft of the arrow. Then, by rotating the instrument, the flesh around the arrow head could be cut away enabling the arrow shaft, head, and the flesh immediately around it to be removed cleanly from the wound without causing excessive tearing of the flesh and causing further infection. I doubted that this particular implement would be required if Emicho broke into the cathedral, more likely sword wounds and severed limbs would be the result, but Ambrose came prepared for anything.

"Ah, you are here," the Benedictine greeted me. "Here help me to strip this cloth into bandages. We shall need them if any of Emicho's men find their way over the city walls."

"Brother," I cried, exasperated. "Emicho is already in. His army is outside the palace beating down the doors at this very moment.

The pathetic look of shock that suffused his face startled me for I had never seen him look so unsure of himself. I had counted on him knowing what to do. Now I felt unsure that even the calm monk could offer any solace in the face of danger now presenting itself.

"What do you mean?" he asked.

"He is here," I replied simply. "Emicho is here."

"*Benedicite*," he whispered, nonplussed.

"In fact," I continued, "I do not think that we have too much more time before he is inside the cathedral. Has no one informed you of this?"

"No. I had no idea."

I could believe this because deep in the palace no sound of the battering ram at the doors could be detected. Further, I had begun to suspect that the Archbishop fully intended to flee the palace now that Emicho had arrived and seemed unstoppable in his resolve to invade the sanctum. Why else port all the baggage to the stables if not to load it onto horses for transportation elsewhere? I knew that Lord Rothard had a villa in Rudesheim to the west of Mainz along the Rhine and I believed that was where he was bound. This did turn out to be the case as I later discovered.

But what would be the fate of the Jewish refugees in the palace if its master fled? Surely, this would be an open admission to Emicho that his invasion was unopposed and his power greater than that of even the Archbishop. In fact this was true since, as I have mentioned, the Archbishop had no real military force to speak of. My lord indeed had no recourse but to flee, since if he stayed he was unprotected and vulnerable to Emicho's army.

Brother Piccolo's face changed suddenly. The apprehension I thought I detected disappeared, replaced by resolve. And anger perhaps.

"Come with me," he barked at me.

I followed him out of the room, wondering to where we were bound. Soon I realised that the monk was leading me to the Archbishop's chambers. We took an alternate route down a narrow corridor that enabled us to avoid the crowd of refugees in the palace's great hall. The Brother strode up to Lord Rothard's door and, not even bothering to knock or otherwise announce himself, threw it open. I was aghast at this breach of convention.

Inside, the audience chamber, which only the day before had been a veritable beehive of activity and voluble discussion, stood empty and completely deserted. The stone walls and floor echoed our footsteps hollowly. Even the Archbishop's chair was gone.

The Benedictine wheeled around so quickly that he nearly knocked me off my feet. His eyes flamed in anger.

"Gone," he said hoarsely, "without a word. Gone," and swept past me out of the chamber.

I think I understood his anger although the reasons for it were varied and complex. First of all he was upset by the fact that the Archbishop and his close retainers had abandoned not only the Jewish refugees but also those among the palace staff and its students who had not been privy to the plan to forsake the city, who were all now without a protector. Second, the Benedictine had not known about either Emicho's presence within the city walls or about the fact that Lord Rothard had fled.

Since the monk and the Archbishop had been friends for many years, this must have seemed double the betrayal to Brother Piccolo. After all, his friend and lord had not kept him informed about these important events but instead had left him to fend for himself; left him to die, probably. Why Lord Rothard left his friend alone and uninformed in that manner I did not discover that day. I believed perhaps he knew that the Benedictine, always a man of conscience and duty, would not have left the palace in any case even in the face of the danger posed by the vicious Lord of Leisingen. Or perhaps he felt that if he must abandon those left at the cathedral, those for whom there was no place in his train, out of guilt and charity he must leave the one person most fitted to aid those assaulted by Emicho's men.

For myself, I could only accept the monk as the nominal leader of those left within the palace. Even the Archbishop's steward, Julius, was nowhere to be found, nor indeed were any of the other of Lord Rothard's designated lieutenants, nor even those of his palace guard. Thus, in the event, we stood alone against the army of Emicho; a handful of clerics, students, and priests and half a thousand Jewish refugees, all of us non-armigerous participants in a violent confrontation in which we were ill-equipped to participate.

I followed Brother Piccolo into the great hall. There, a palpable mood of fear had swept over the refugees. They stood around in knotted groups, holding each other, wringing their hands, eyes white with dread. A constant moaning and sobbing echoed throughout the hall and the steady thud of the battering ram enveloped all the other sounds. The Benedictine took in the spectacle: the lack of guards, the presence of women and children, the abject fear of all those waiting for Emicho to violate the sanctuary of the cathedral. They had nowhere to flee to and no way to protect themselves. All knew that Emicho's entry was only a matter of time.

Suddenly a distant crash and the sound of splintering wood resounded throughout the hall. Instantly, all was silent. Then, just as suddenly again, a great howl went up round the room. The door's integrity had given way under the continued assault of the huge battering ram. More splintering noises. A thud. Curses. A sliding sound as of metal on metal. Another crash.

We stood transfixed, unable to react. Everyone in the room froze with fear and horror. So soon. So soon. I was sure that I was living the last moments of my life. I began the Pater Noster, whispering quietly to God and imploring the Blessed Virgin for the protection of all in the cathedral against the depredations that must surely follow the army's entry.

Then Brother Piccolo dashed away, headed for the foyer where the Comte's army must surely already be making their way in. As wood as if the moon controlled me, I ran after him. What maniacal impulse caused me to do so I have never understood except perhaps I sought to protect my mentor or at least to assist him in whatever madness he would invent.

In the foyer I saw what I expected to see. The great oaken doors had buckled, their metal bands twisted inward, the rivets bulging out here and there like black greasy eyeballs popped from their sockets and hanging crazily. The huge bar, carved from a single tree trunk and so heavy that a double handful of men could not lift it, was cracked and bent like a bow. The thick ropes which were used to lower it into place hung limply, unstrung from their block and tackle. The planks of the doors themselves looked like broken bones, their jagged edges testament to their inability to support the integrity of the main structure.

I could see Emicho's men milling about outside trying to breach the entry through the gaps now evident in our defences. Heavy iron pry-bars prised at the boards trying to loose them from the bands that girdled them. I heard a shout and suddenly a spear was launched through the opening between the two doors. I jumped aside and it clattered past me onto the flat stones of the floor.

Brother Piccolo shouted at the men outside to cease their activities, invoking the sacred nature of the dwelling place of the Lord. Those outside but laughed and jibed that the sanctity of the cathedral had been defiled already by the presence of the Jews within. Thus, the church no longer represented a sacred inviolate structure, they said, though probably not in so many words; I do not recall now. I knew, however, that in this conception they were mistaken. They were the unlawful interlopers here. Yet, I felt powerless to do anything to prevent the coming tragedy.

Then the same madness that had possessed me when Ulfrid was killed and that had caused me to confront the red-haired man entered me again. I wheeled round and snatched up the spear from the floor and turning hurled it directly at the hole in the doors. The men outside jerked back reflexively but the spear head only embedded itself in one of the broken boards of the door. Then a great peal of laughter sounded from the men as they ridiculed my impotent effort. In anger, I rushed to the door to dislodge the spear and once more to use it against them but as I came closer several barbs intruded and prevented me in this attempt. I felt hands on my shoulder and turned to see Brother Piccolo and my friend Arbogast, who had suddenly appeared in the foyer, pulling me away from the conflict. I struggled against them but their insistent efforts eventually made me relax and withdraw.

"Oh, Brother," I sobbed, "what will we do?"

Brother Piccolo patted my shoulder reassuringly. "We can only stand in their way and invoke the grace of God and the mercy of the Blessed Virgin against them. Pray, brother, pray."

Again, my lack of faith condemned my friends. I remember feeling doubtful that the Lord even cared what happened to us there in the Mainz cathedral. Surely he had abandoned us in our hour of need? Nonetheless, I prayed, albeit dubiously. Perhaps if I had embraced the effort with simplistic credulity the Lord would have answered our pleas but I know that my efforts were half-hearted at best. Still, faith or no, I stood that day with the Benedictine and Arbogast against the army of Emicho as they burst forth in a bristling flood of metal and leather through the shattered doors of the cathedral.

Caput Sextus

The metal bands of the doors parted from the wood with a snap and the great oaken bar which held the portals fast against the Leisingen horde groaned ominously and then cracked apart with a sound like thunder. The doors flew open with a bang, hanging crazily on their hinges, and a dozen or so men lurched into the foyer, tripping over the splintered wood generated by their destructive efforts. A trumpet sounded from somewhere outside. The soldiers of Emicho inside the doorway shrank back against the walls with their pike-tips pointed menacingly at Brother Piccolo and Arbogast and me. The soldiers outside on the steps parted and made an opening. A clatter of hooves resounded loudly as a horse and rider mounted the steps. Then Emicho rode triumphantly into the cathedral.

He rose in the saddle, as viciously awesome as ever. His black hair flowed out from under his metal basinet. His black, diabolical eyes peered out at us from behind a nose piece that restricted our sight of his visage, though I could make out that he wore some sort of metal prosthetic nose in the bone socket of his missing proboscis. The cheek pieces further reduced his aspect and yet the livid scar on his cheek was clearly visible beneath.

He was dressed in a chainmail hauberk, all of a piece with his gauntlets and his leather-greaved leggings. Over this he wore a black surcoat with a slashing, blood-red chevron design embroidered upon it. Over his left shoulder protruded the pommel and handle of his great-sword and in his left hand he brandished a long spear with a wickedly sharp double-edged point at its tip. He smiled a sinister, scornful snarl and chuckled deep in his throat.

"Is this all the defence of the great and powerful Lord Rothard? Two priestlings and an old man? Step aside, brothers," he accented the word with contempt, "or die."

We three of the cathedral instinctively had stepped back a pace upon Emicho's ingress on his great sable stallion. Now Brother Piccolo strode forward purposefully and stood directly in the warrior's path. The Lord of Leisingen looked on nonchalantly.

"Leave here. Now," growled the Benedictine in his deep, sonorous voice.

"Or?" asked Emicho in tolerant amusement.

"Or the wrath of the Lord will surely fall upon you. The eyes of the Lord are in every place beholding the evil and the good. The wrath of God is revealed from Heaven against all ungodliness and unrighteousness of men. Beware, Emicho. This is a holy place you attempt to defile."

"This place is already defiled," replied Emicho, "because of the presence of Christ-less Jews. And no quotations of scripture will make me fear God's wrath when I know that I serve my Liege Lord, Jesus Christ, and I will destroy His enemies as a dutiful *thegn* should do."

He swung the point of his spear down and levelled it at Brother Piccolo, standing a dozen paces away, menacingly.

"Now stand aside, monk. Or die."

The Benedictine responded by folding his arms across his chest indicating his resolve to not let the Black Lord pass lest through him. Emicho's mouth curled in a wry smile. He resolutely nodded his chin once and spurred his horse ahead quickly.

The next moments for me were a blur. In disbelief I observed the events transpire as if from a vast distance. Brother Piccolo stood his ground as Emicho set himself in the saddle to ride him down across the forty or so feet of floor separating them. The point of his deadly lance preceded him by about the length of his horse. Only a matter of a second or two waited the death of the tiny monk standing in the path of the huge war horse and its rider.

From the corner of my eye I saw Arbogast dash out ahead of the Benedictine, slowly, ever so slowly, as he attempted to deflect the spear head away from its target. This he managed to do and with sudden relief I observed the point pass safely to the right of my monkish mentor. Then relief turned to horror as I saw what Arbogast failed to see since he now faced away from the charging warrior.

Even as Arbogast stumbled after deflecting the spear, trying to regain his balance and remove himself from the path of the war-horse, I watched Emicho's right hand drop the lance and slide almost instantaneously across his body to his left shoulder to grip the handle of his great-sword. The weapon glinted brightly as it flashed, joyously humming, from the confinement of its scabbard and swept in a backhanded whistling arc like the beak of a hunting raptor circling through the air in search of prey. The sword's arcing flight ended as it sliced through Arbogast's neck.

I cannot describe the sick horror of observing my young friend's head, neck attached, flying through the air as if launched from a trebuchet, blood spurting both from neck and torso as each fell to the floor forevermore parted, on his frightful face an expression of stunned surprise, forever frozen into my memory, mouth open, turning, turning, tangled hair, thudding to the flagstones before me and then rolling into a corner like a forgotten ball of flaxen thread.

And then Emicho was upon me. The moment of horror gave way instantly to a reflex of self-preservation. I ducked down and threw myself to the horse's left side as the biting blade swung up once more, ready to steal my own head from my shoulders. However, so close was I that the *cnicht* could not use his sword to any advantage. I heard him curse as he kicked out at me but his stirrup prevented his mailed foot from doing more than grazing me. Still, I was knocked down by sheer momentum and came perilously close to being trampled to death under the heavy horse's iron-shod hooves. I rolled back out of harm's way. Emicho rode on in a thundering clatter of iron on stone not even turning to look back, as if disdaining us as a threat.

A victorious shout went up from the doorway. I looked up in alarm to see Emicho's soldiers springing forward to follow their master. They had awaited the outcome of our conflict with their lord and now believed we were fair game. I scrambled to my feet. Brother Piccolo, too, I saw had found his feet again after having been knocked down by the warhorse. Together we dashed ahead of the soldiery into the bowels of the cathedral.

We knew our way through the building where Emicho's men did not. As they hesitated at the door to the cathedral sanctum proper, perhaps out of a guilty piety or simply out of mere disorientation, Brother Piccolo and I were already through the door to the hallway at the end of the east nave leading to the great hall. Emicho, who had ridden his horse right down the main aisle of the cathedral to the altar itself, shouting like a hunter who suddenly sees the roe deer he has flushed out and spurring his horse after us, called his hounds to the chase.

We were quicker than he, though, and dashed through the door before he had even turned his horse awkwardly into the nave. I took the time to lodge a cast-iron candle holder between the door and the opposing wall in vain hopes that this might slow the progress of our pursuers. I could hear Emicho shouting angry orders to his men to break down the door even as we raced down the corridor.

We found the doors to the great hall closed against us. The pounding we made was echoed by the banging on the door down the hallway where the armed men behind it were trying to break it down. Apparently, my device of propping the candle holder delayed them as I had intended. We convinced those behind the door that we were friendly and finally they let us in; fortunately for us as it turned out since moments later we heard the crash of the other door as it gave way before the assault upon it by Emicho's men. However, immediately we had a new problem since they were soon at the doors to the great hall.

Inside, perhaps as a result of the increased urgency of the situation with the soldiers immediately without the hall, absolute chaos reigned. Women wailed, and children sobbed. Men moaned and cursed.

Many of the men had brought weapons of one sort or another. Many of them grasped knives, swords or clubs in their hands. Many of them shouted that they would rather kill their families and die themselves before they would succumb to Edomites. Others shouted that they should take what weapons they had in their possession and die fighting like men rather than timid mice cowering in a hole waiting for the cat's paw to sweep them out into its waiting maw.

This latter opinion prevailed. Men began to gather in knots throughout the hall. All the while, the howling and roaring and pounding continued on the far side of the doors.

One of the Jewish religious leaders, Rabbi ben Moses, he who had been at the infirmary with Yaakob and Ruth the day their dead son was removed, urged the men to reconsider and behave rather like Hananiah, Mishael, and Azariah. I think that by this he meant that they should accept their fate as God's will and trust in God to deliver them just as He did those named of His servants from Nebuchadnezzar's fiery furnace. However, few seemed to see the parallel between the two events and the Rabbi's injunction fell on deaf ears. The men of Israel had different thoughts about their salvation.

Yaakob approached me with several rather wild-eyed men. I sat crouched in a corner, breathless and with heart still pounding after our narrow escape, completely at a loss as to what to do to aid these people or how to defend even myself. I admit that I feared for my life that day. Even though I mouthed prayers to the Blessed Virgin and to St. Jude for some hint of salvation, I felt certain that I would fall, we all would fall, beneath the swords of Emicho's army. In my dejected state I barely acknowledged Yaakob's presence. He greeted me and asked a question of me nonetheless.

"We would like to know if there is a place here where we can fortify ourselves against Emicho. Do you know of such a place, Brother?" he asked.

I thought for a moment about all the places that might prove defensible although I wondered hopelessly at the same time what use there was in the attempt. Perhaps the gallery above the hall or the one above the foyer? No. Both had too many access routes, too many sets of stairs leading to them. The defenders would be easily outflanked. The infirmary? It had only the one doorway which might be barricaded successfully and its gate would be nearly impossible to breach but there was no way to get to it without going outside of the cathedral complex and into the street where Emicho's men waited. Besides, I was not sure if the gate or the door to the little hospital had been closed and locked. If not, then Emicho's men probably had already got in and might be there yet. I could think of no space other than the hall we now occupied that the army could be prevented access to. The only places left were the stables and the hostel next to it.

Then the thought occurred to me that the courtyard in which those two buildings sat itself might be a reasonably defensible space. If a force of men could occupy it then the only access to the courtyard for an invader would be through the kitchen. The only other way in was through either the huge gate at the rear of the complex or the iron postern gate which opened onto the street near the infirmary. Neither entry could easily be breached. If the kitchen doorway could be barricaded successfully then Emicho's men could be cut down by the Jewish defenders one by one as they tried to enter the courtyard. I explained this to Yaakob, my aspect growing somewhat cheerier.

He nodded his approval of the plan.

"Can you show us the way?" he asked me.

I agreed to guide them and with half a dozen men, including Yaakob, we set out.

The only logical way of reaching the courtyard now was through the kitchen itself, since Emicho's men had control of the rest of the complex. We did not know but that they were already in the kitchen too. Nonetheless we could reach the kitchen, I believed, through the Archbishop's quarters.

I reasoned that there must be a private hallway leading from the kitchen to Rothard's rooms since he often remained in his chamber for long periods and the kitchen staff must surely bring food directly to him on those occasions when the consideration of weighty matters kept him and his clerks and advisors contained for days at a time. So with this in mind I led our little exploratory party up the stairs to the Archbishop's audience chamber. Obviously, I knew the way to that place since I had visited it often in the past.

Once in the audience chamber I was unsure where to proceed. The room looked much the same as the first time I had visited although anything portable of any value had been removed. The tapestries were gone, as were the silver candle-holders and the golden crosses from the antechamber doorway and the altar; the altar itself remained although devoid of its linen drapery. As I looked around the room I noticed two doors at the furthest end which I had not descried on any of my previous visits. This was hardly surprising since generally my attention was focused more on the master of the cathedral and less on my surroundings.

I crossed to the nearest door thinking it as likely as either to be the passage to the kitchen. The door opened instead on to a small chapel. I assumed that it must be the Archbishop's private chapel to which few probably ever had access and

I felt a moment of guilt, which quickly passed in awe, at having breached its sanctity.

The room contained nothing of any value, but I found myself staring in fascination at the way in which the roof had been constructed. For instead of a conventional wooden vault with a plank overlay as was usual in such structures the roof had been cunningly contrived from slender wooden rafters and stained glass panels. I could see out through some of the panes.

The chapel appeared to be built in a vacant area formed when the palace had been built next to the cathedral at a point where a buttress intersected its wall. The designer had decided to leave the buttress in place rather than tie the wall of the palace in at that point creating a small gap in which the chapel had been built. The palace roof was visible on one side, and above, on the other side, the cathedral soared into the sky. I wondered how the glass roof could support the weight of snow laid down on it over the course of an often harsh Franconian winter. The vitreous canopy must have been thicker than the material generally used in windows built for ecclesiastical structures and for the houses of the very wealthy. I envied the Archbishop and those privy to the peace and sanctity of such beautiful surroundings in which to worship Our Lord.

I had little time to ponder the chapel, though. Almost immediately upon seeing that the chosen door did not lead to the kitchens, my companions had retreated to the other door. I followed them, somewhat put out by my loss of mastery of the expedition. Indeed, from the moment I had attempted to lead my friends out of the audience chamber any one of them knew as much as I about the spaces we must traverse. Not until we reached the kitchen would I be in familiar surroundings again.

The second door led down a short corridor to another doorway leading directly to Lord Rothard's private apartments as it turned out. Only a single window lit the vast interior spaces. His rooms were spacious and lavishly adorned with wooden carved panels, stone statuary and ornate masonry scroll-work.

The room boasted a huge fireplace which easily rivalled that in the kitchen in capacity though far exceeded it in decoration. For on either side of the hearth stone grape vines with a bounty of fruit hanging from them seemed to grow out of the floor and up to the top of the hearth. Above the soot-stained marble mantle block, a carved scene depicting the fall of Jericho, Joshua in the foreground blowing his ram's horn, spread out in three panels attached in some ingenious fashion to the stone walls built around the smoke flue.

As in the other rooms anything portable had been removed. Now, all that remained of furnishings or decoration not part of the walls or soot-stained ceiling were a huge, roofed, four-posted bed with its curtains missing, a heavy-looking dark wooden table, several writing desks of the kind used by scribes, and a small simple wooden footstool. Otherwise the room was bare.

I marvelled at how thoroughly the Archbishop's personal quarters had been stripped of their valuables for I had certainly expected far more lavish furnishings and accoutrements than we found. Truly, all the evidence suggested Lord Rothard had been prepared to flee upon Emicho's arrival in spite of his promise to Rabbi Kalonymos. I wondered also if he took his palace guard with him when he left for we saw no trace of them that day. Surely they must have accompanied him to Rudesheim to act as bodyguards along the way and as a result none remained to act in the defence of the people, Christian and Jew alike, who had counted on the Archbishop's protection.

Yaakob called to me as I stood gazing at the Jericho carving. Reluctantly, I pulled my eyes away from that marvellous scene of conquest and destruction. I followed him through a doorway which opened to another corridor leading, I hoped, to the kitchens.

The corridor ended at a landing where a set of steps led down and to the right. We clambered down the stairs and suddenly I knew where we were. The large hallway in which we found ourselves led from the kitchen directly to the dining hall. I had crossed this space many times on my way from the clerks' barracks to the dining hall. I stepped forward to tell Yaakob this news.

"Then this is where you must leave us and return to the safety of the great hall," he said.

"No," I replied softly, "I am in this thing, too. I am no safer than any of you. And I will not wait for the end of my life with the women when I can help defend all of us."

He smiled and nodded indulgently. "But you are not a warrior. You are a priest. It is not right that you should commit the sin of murder."

I interrupted him to say that defending one's self against the aggression of others was not murder; I did not bother to point out that I was yet only a lay clerk and not a priest.

"Of causing the death of another then," he amended. "Either way killing is not a business you are suited for."

Stubbornly refusing to leave I said, "Nonetheless, I am coming with you."

Yaakob sighed and bowed his head. Then he stiffened. He reached into his over-tunic and pulled out a long, gleaming knife. Slowly and carefully he placed it, pommel first, into my hand. "May God be with us, then," he whispered and turned away.

I must confess I felt a moment of exhilaration, of power, of unity of purpose with my comrades in arms, non-Christians though they were, at the sensation of the weight and form of the weapon within my grasp. This quickly faded. A sudden fear at the thought that I actually might be forced to kill someone and at the thought that I myself might be killed replaced it.

Of course, the latter fear was one that I had lived with since the moment that Emicho had entered the cathedral and taken the head of my friend, Arbogast, and I think that I was slowly growing accustomed to the pervasive sense of impending doom. I commended myself into the arms of Our Blessed Mother with a silent prayer I hoped She heard and walked to the door where Yaakob and his people stood waiting for me to catch up with them.

"I think that I should go first," I told them.

"No," said Yaakob. "It is too dangerous."

"I must be the one who goes first." I gestured at my robes and spoke quickly. "If Emicho's soldiers have found the kitchens and they see me in these clothes perhaps they will ignore me or at least refrain from attacking me. If they see a party of Jews they will at once fall upon you and kill you all. Then everything will be lost for they will use the passage through which we came to strike at the people left behind in the great hall. First we must set ourselves firmly in the courtyard so that they will be drawn out to us and ignore this door and passage and in order to do that we must know the lay of things and whether Emicho's soldiers already control the territory we seek."

This seemed to make sense to them for they allowed me to venture forth silently and cautiously through the doorway and into the kitchen.

I let the sleeve of my robe fall over the hand in which I carried the knife, turned so that its blade rested along my forearm. With the weapon concealed I hoped again to allay suspicion should I encounter any of Emicho's soldiers. This was no guarantee that they would not attack me anyway but at least I could give them less reason to do so out of hand.

As quietly and quickly as I could I reconnoitred the kitchen and the rear courtyard. There were only three access routes into the kitchen: through the passageway I had recently used, through the door from the rear courtyard and through the tight hallway that led from the main palace foyer through which I had first encountered the kitchens on the first day I had arrived at Mainz and its cathedral from Bruges. Apparently, the invaders had not yet discovered that particular passageway but had concentrated their efforts on the Great Hall and the cathedral proper. Certainly, I detected no sign that the army had been in the kitchens or the courtyard.

I looked cautiously around the courtyard, stealing along with my body pressed tightly to the exterior walls so as to be more difficult to see if I did happen to encounter anyone. I rushed over to the stables as quickly as my floppy sandals and heavy long robes would allow. Again I saw no sign that Emicho's men had been there.

I walked hurriedly through the empty stables, my thoughts turning briefly to my friend Ulfrid. I felt a sudden rush of grief at the lost peace and friendship I had known in that place. The earthy smell of dung and hay and old floor planking conjured up many memories of long, tranquil afternoons spent here with Ulfrid and Brother Piccolo chatting and laughing together. I swallowed and walked on, exiting the stables through the low door in the tack room.

I crossed from the stables to the student barracks. I assumed them to be empty, but nonetheless I entered in order to be sure they were. The lower floor's cells were barren of life as I suspected they would be.

I climbed the stairs to the upper floor. Unexpectedly, I heard shuffling and mutterings from an unknown source. I checked each cell in turn. In the very last cell I found a number of my fellow students, all of them my juniors, cowering on the floor, among them, Julius's pet, Guernar.

I thought about advising them to retreat into the Great Hall with the refugees there but then I realised that they would be far safer in the barracks as a group, obviously not Jewish, than with the others since they might fall victim to the hysteria or the blood-lust which I had heard often overcame soldiers in the heat of battle. I told them as much and advised them to remain in this cell no matter what else happened, saving the building being set ablaze, for their own safety. I told them what might happen, the carnage that might soon ensue but I believed they would be safe from both Jew and Christian soldier alike since they were essentially neutral with respect to the coming conflict but no sense tempting the blood lust of raging, armed men. They nodded submissively and huddled closer together. I left them there and continued my reconnaissance.

Leaving the barracks, I stole around its bulk to the wall that bordered the passage to the small postern gate. Cautiously, I peered around the corner, crouching low. I gave thanks to God for giving me sense enough to do so since at the gate I spied a knot of Emicho's men milling about and testing the bars trying to find entry.

The gate itself was virtually impossible to break down constructed as it was of heavy iron. Further, no space existed between its top and the wall above through which a man might climb over it. I felt that we were safe enough for now from this particular point of entry.

I turned and retraced my steps around the barracks and then the stables. The latter building blocked the view of the gate and thus that of me from the gate by the soldiers there. In moments I was safely inside the kitchen and back through the doorway where my companions awaited me.

I told them what I had seen and asked them to spread word that there huddled a small cluster of clerical refugees in the barracks who were not to be harmed. They agreed to this. I could only hope that Emicho's army would likewise leave them unharmed. We made our way back to the great hall without incident and immediately we arrived in the hall my companions scattered, heading off in separate directions to organise the planned resistance.

I stood alone near the bottom of the stairs leading back to the Archbishop's chambers, not a part of the planning process, not knowing in what direction to turn. I could overhear some of the Jewish men telling their women of the plan to fortify the courtyard and to try to attract Emicho's soldiers to their position. Most of the women were crying as they listened to their husbands tell them of their intent to confront the invaders and this of course set many of the children to crying as well. Hearing their plaintive cries, despair threatened to overwhelm me. How could any of us hope to survive even if, *especially if* I should say, we resisted?

Despite my limited involvement in their venture, as I contemplated the men's scheme I began to think it madness. What could they hope to accomplish but to die fighting a far superior force who outstripped them in both numbers and military capability? How would their deaths serve their women and children? For the wives and babies would be utterly defenceless here in the great hall with their men away in the courtyard trading blow for blow and death for death, if they did even that well, with their enemies. If the hall was attacked and Emicho's men gained access how would the women defend themselves?

Truly this was an irresolvable dilemma. Either way, Jewish lives would be lost and maybe all of them, not just those who fought back, would be killed. Maybe the outcome, the utter destruction of these Children of Abraham, was inevitable. I wondered what Pope Urban would think of all these innocent lives taken in his name. Would he have agreed with Emicho that the Jews were likewise the enemies of Christianity of a kind with the Infidel Saracens? He had not written anything of the kind in his letter to his bishops and somehow I doubted that this travesty, this prostitution of the conceptual basis of Urban's notion of a Holy War, was something he could have conceived when he wrote the letter or when he spoke on behalf of the Byzantine Emperor at Clermont.

I would never know the truth of that supposition. At that moment I cared only, indeed prayed despairingly to Our Saviour because of that care, that somehow someone would intervene and stop this barbaric farce and put Emicho to flight. My prayers, however, went unanswered.

Not all of the men marched off to the courtyard to fight. Necessity dictated that many must stay here to offer some small protection from or at least diversion to the armed pilgrims without the hall. If they did manage to break down the door the men left behind might hold them back until the women and children could flee to some other hiding place, perhaps Lord Rothard's private chambers. But most of the men filed up the stairs before long, retracing our earlier path to the kitchens and the courtyard beyond. When I moved to follow them, Yaakob intercepted me.

"No, young master. I have reconsidered. You may not accompany us," he growled at me. By way of emphasis he held his hand out palm up at right angles to his straightened arm forbidding me to pass.

"I must come. As I have said, this is my fight too," I replied, though I do not think that I sounded convincing even to myself. The truth is—and I do not hesitate to admit this now in my advanced years as I write to you, dear reader, about that terrible time—I was terrified. Terrified that I might be killed, terrified of seeing my fellow men slaughtered like defenceless deer in the forest, terrified of having to kill another human being, another Christian, in order to preserve my own life. My stomach rose into my mouth then and only the fact that I had not eaten in many hours prevented me from vomiting and shaming myself before all.

"This is not your fight. You are a Christian. We are Jews."

And that was the crux of the matter. We worshipped the same God but not in the same way. We, Christians, knew that the Messiah, the very Son of God, had once walked the earth in the lands across the Middle Sea. They, Jews, expected that the Messiah would arrive someday as the ancient prophets said he would but did not believe that Jesus the Christ had been the Saviour of Mankind, the fulfilment of those prophecies.

The pretext for the gathering of multitudes of armed Christian pilgrims was that we wanted the Holy Places preserved and occupied by our kind instead of by the enemies of our faith. In our paranoia, we saw those enemies at every turn, even living amongst us in our own cities. Never mind that they were our fellow citizens, business associates, sometime friends, who had never given us harm. Because they were not exactly like us, did not believe exactly what we believed, they were considered evil and inimical to us. The Army of Christ must be turned against that enemy or so many Christians believed.

Emicho was a Christian. I was a Christian. Therefore, from a philosophical perspective and in the eyes of my Jewish friends, I was in Emicho's camp; never mind that the Lord of Leisingen's soldiers would not see me that way. Whatever else I believed about these Jews with whom I shared the limited protection of the Archbishop's hall, I knew I truly could not be their ally because ideologically, theologically, I followed the same beliefs *in spirito* as the army assailing us.

The awful truth was that I was part of neither camp. I did not agree with the principles embedded in Emicho's initiative nor did I share the tenets of faith upon which his victims based the activities of their daily lives and their spirituality. I stood somewhere between in the gap that separated certainty from anticipation in the beliefs of the two combatants. Thus my fate alone, paradoxically, of all those there that day, was most uncertain.

In a way, Yaakob had taken from the me the difficult decision of whether or not I could or should take the lives of fellow Christians on behalf of the Jewish innocents. For that, at least, I was grateful. Nonetheless, I felt that I abandoned him in that hour of desperation and need.

Struggling to maintain my composure, for I could feel fiery tears welling up, I closed my eyes and nodded my head. *"Cum Deo agite...,"* I whispered to my friend, go with God, knowing with dread certainty that I would never see him alive again.

Without a word Yaakob embraced me, holding me to him for a long moment. And I knew in that moment that he blamed me neither for the tragic events unfolding nor for my inability to help in the defence of his people. Then he said, "Shalom," which in the language of the Hebrews means something like 'peace,' and was gone.

I suddenly became self-consciously aware that I stood alone in the centre of the room. Everyone had moved to the walls or sat huddled in small groups on the floor. As I looked around, many of those present stared blankly at me with nothing written in their hollow eyes but despair and disbelief. With the arrogant self-centredness of youth I believed that they thought all of this my fault in some way as if I stood as a symbol for all that they had suffered and would suffer at the hands of Christians. I know now that that was not so because certainly none offered me the least harm or reproof.

Still, I remember that I felt very uncomfortable amidst their misery.

I saw almost none there I knew other than Ruth, who smiled wanly at me when our eyes met. I wondered where Brother Piccolo and Brother Ambrose had gone and suspected that they must have returned to their *ad hoc* infirmary. Though I knew my proper place was with them acting as their assistant, I conjectured that what Emicho intended—based on my knowledge of what had occurred in Worms and Speyer the total annihilation of these people—rendered the Brothers' services not only wholly inadequate but horribly unnecessary as well.

I resolved to stay here in the great hall and defend myself and the women and children if I could. I might be able to make a difference in our fates with my long knife or at least make the attackers' lives more troublesome, their conquest more difficult. I believed that was more than Brother Piccolo could do with his herbs or Brother Ambrose with his saws and scalpels. And so I sat down on the bottom step of the stairs leading up to the Archbishop's chambers, the weapon weighing heavily inside my robes, to wait, perhaps, to die.

◆

I wonder now that I survived that evil day. You, my reader, will hardly credit what I am about to write since I, myself, who was there and witnessed all of the dreadful events, scarcely believe what I saw and heard and experienced. For I witnessed nothing less than the complete destruction of all those people in the great hall. Hardly less believable is the fact that most of those who died did so at their own hands or at the hands of their loved ones, those dearest and nearest to their hearts.

I sat for a time on the cold stone steps, my mind empty, my heart devoid of feeling or empathy, my eyes staring as blankly as those of the despairing people around me. Suddenly, the door above on the gallery burst open. A young man dashed down the stairs crying passionately that the enemy had breached the gates of the courtyard.

My blood ran as cold as January ice on the Main River at that pronouncement. I had thought the rear gate virtually impossible to break down. If Emicho's army was through the gate and in the courtyard then I had led them to their doom and all was lost. Only a miracle could save us.

Everyone in the room realised this fact. At this latest news the women and their children began to wail anew. My heart pounding, I waited for the bloodthirsty soldiers of the Lord of Leisingen to come crashing through the door above and swarm down upon us. My knife appeared in my hand without my consciously being aware of how it came to be there. I felt ready to burst into tears myself but I knew that I must die bravely for otherwise my family would find only shame in my actions when they learned of events here and I felt that I had disappointed my father enough for one lifetime. Then, before any horrors roared down on us from above, a horror, singular in its inconceivable and thoroughly unexpected barbarity, began to unfold in the great hall among the Jews themselves.

At first I was hardly aware of what was going on around me. I noted absently, for my mind and eyes were concentrated on the place from whence I thought the invaders would arrive, that some of the folk had gathered together in little family groups. Here a woman alone with her children, there a husband and wife, there a couple of women together with youngsters.

Then I happened to glance over at a young couple and their two children. Their children lay on the floor and I thought at first that they had fallen asleep for they lay still, face-down. Idly I noted a pool of dark liquid beneath them and thought at first that something had been spilled. As I looked more closely though, I saw that the liquid appeared far too dark and thick to be wine or water and I realised with shock that the spreading pool was one of blood; the blood of those two innocent infants. Stupefied, I watched as the young man thrust the long knife in his hand into the woman's breast, driving it into her heart. She fell to the floor without a sound. The man called to another nearby, who plunged the self-same dagger into the first man's chest. Stunned, I looked around to see if anyone else had witnessed the heinous villainy unfold. To my disbelieving horror, similar scenes were being enacted throughout the hall.

"No," I whispered, hardly able to catch a breath let alone cry out. Then the word repeated, louder, in a normal speaking tone, my words loud as a trumpet in my own ears. Finally, "No!" I shouted. "No! What are you doing! Stop!"

A few people looked up at me, those who apparently had not yet garnered the courage to imitate the ghastly deeds of their fellows, but most simply ignored me, already lost in an orgy of prayer, sacrifice and death.

I spied Ruth bent over with a young woman and her four children. I ran to her to prevent what I knew surely they intended to do.

"Ruth," I gasped and grasped her wrist.

In her hand she, too, held a dagger ready to cold-bloodedly murder the young woman; Ruth so gentle and kind, Ruth who had been so devastated at the loss of her own child but a few short months ago.

"Ruth," I implored her, "Do not do this thing. Please, for the sake of your immortal soul, do not."

Then I saw that she was not so unmoved by what she intended to do as I had thought. Tears brimmed in her eyes. Her voice shook, heavy and deep-throated with emotion as she spoke.

"This must be, my dear one. This is our way, our covenant with the Lord demands as much of us."

The woman with Ruth began to weep in great wracking sobs.

Ruth turned to her and threw her arms about her. "Hush, Rachel. Everything will be all right," she said.

But I did not believe, and I did not see how this Rachel or Ruth herself could possibly believe, that everything would be "all right" when she and her children would soon be dead at her friend's hand. However, Rachel closed her eyes and nodded in agreement, hugging her four children to her in a close-knit huddle. They clung to their mother, cold tears rolling from their eyes as if fed by springs from the River Styx. I trembled with empathetic agony seeing them thus.

Rachel moaned loudly. "Do not spare the children, Ruth. I will not see them brought up in the false religion of the Christians." And with those words she glared at me defiantly.

Taken aback by her words I was unable to respond. I should have urged her to turn from her own erroneous religion and seek the mercy of the Lord Jesus for the sake of her soul and those of her children if she must die at Emicho's hands. I should have told her that suicide is a faithless crime and more so murder since it violates the Commandment that states: "Thou shalt not kill." I should have told her that only God may take life by whatever instrument He chooses. But I could say nothing and only stood there in dumbfounded silence. I do not think that Rachel hated me personally but perhaps I was not mistaken in my belief that I was something of a symbol, for some of the Jews at least, of the religious oppression that had overtaken them in a most violent fashion.

In any case, I do not think that she was completely happy—as how could any human being be, at the prospect of murdering her own children?—about what must come next for, as Ruth raised the knife once more, she broke away from her children and staggered away a few feet, hauling Ruth with her.

Raising her friend's hands to her own cheeks Rachel spoke to her imploringly in a low voice. "Let us take Isaac aside. I do not wish for Aaron to see his brother die for he will be afraid."

Ruth nodded in assent. The two women took young Isaac's hands and led him away from his brother and sisters.

The lad looked up at me for a moment as he passed. To this day I cannot remove his face from my memory. He was a beautiful little child of perhaps four years. Dark curly hair hung down a little longer than his ears, framing a cherubic face. Huge, dark, expressive eyes shaded by long, wispy black

lashes. Tiny button nose. Cheeks as round and red as pom-
egranates. A tiny pink-lipped mouth. His eyes and cheeks
and mouth smiled at me in a face full of life and innocence
and beauty. I felt for an achingly brief moment as if a holy
fire had filled the boy's soul and manifested in his eyes and
smile as if to reassure me that God was present in spite of
all the evil that occurred.

Then I seemed to see everything unfold as from a
great distance and the reality of the event crashed down
around me when the boy, in quick, dwarfish steps, and his
escorts, moved on. I could only stand frozen, detached
from that time and place and from those incomprehen-
sible people who had such an awesome, terrible covenant
with God. The event, their plight, touched me not in the
slightest.

What had they done, I wondered in cold abstraction, to
have made God contract with them thus that He demanded
even their children as sacrifice to Him as He had of Abraham and his son, also named Isaac, so long ago? Was their
relationship with God a result of the fact that, as people like
Emicho insisted, they had crucified Christ? But as Yaakob
had told me at the feast of Hanukkah, even during the time
of the Maccabees before the coming of the Christ to earth,
the Jewish covenant demanded death before compromise of
belief. Were they cursed in advance of the coming of the
Lamb of God? The Blessed Augustine might be able to explain this terrifying paradox, but I could not.

The women knelt down with Isaac between them. The
boy faced his mother, whose back prevented her other children observing what transpired. Ruth, behind little Isaac,
leaned over him as if to hug the child, her arms enveloping

him, sleeves enfolding him like a pair of angel's wings, and with a swift, sure motion slit his throat.

The infant did not cry out. I am sure that even had he tried he could not have done so with his windpipe thus severed. He simply slumped forward into his mother's arms.

As the boy fell onto her bosom, Rachel spread wide her skirts and caught in its folds the red fluid pumping from his neck. Tenderly she stroked his hair as her breasts, which had at one time suckled the boy their nourishing life-giving milk, now became engorged with his dying blood. I heard her singing a song in her own language, her soft voice throaty and broken, but I cannot say if what she sang to him was a lullaby or a prayer or simply some favourite tune of her son.

When the boy's blood ceased to issue from the fatal wound, his mother laid him down on the floor and arranged the lifeless body in a pose suggesting sleep. She laid a hand gently on his little cheek, a cheek that still retained its round, babyish appearance but was now devoid of colour, looking more like a brittle, cold eggshell than the tender, plump fruit it earlier suggested. Rachel sighed. Her head tilted slightly, she considered her baby as if she had just successfully sent him off to sleep as she might have done so often in the past. Then she gathered her skirts tightly in front of her to hide the gory mess they contained and stood up. Ruth rose also.

Together these two angels of death advanced on Rachel's remaining children. The boy child, Aaron, arm in arm with one of his sisters, appeared quite beside himself with fright. I am sure that he knew what the two women were about, since he could see what was going on all around him and could see his younger sibling lying motionless on the floor. A puddle of clear fluid formed at the youngster's feet as he lost control of his bladder in his fear. Then suddenly he dashed away as does a boar before the hounds who are set to tear out its belly. He ran to a sideboard set against one wall and slithered beneath it as quickly as if he had been a lizard scuttling under a rock to escape the owl.

The women ignored the boy for the moment and turned their attention to the girls instead. Rachel's daughters stood in dignified silence with their arms wrapped about each other in mutual support. They were to be much admired, for they met and accepted their deaths with calm dignity.

Their mother gave them each a final hug as though bidding them farewell against a journey. The family slumped to their knees, not only in defeat but in resignation to the end of all things for them, and assumed an attitude, I would have thought if I had not known better, of prayer. Then, carefully, lovingly, Rachel pulled her daughters' long dark hair back away from their necks and spread their tunics open to expose bare skin. But this was too much for me to bear witness to.

I turned my head at the moment that I saw Ruth's hand plunging the dagger toward the fair skin of one of the girls. When I could bear to look again, both of the girls lay on the floor fallen over one another, looking like two shapeless heaps of discarded clothing. Blood seeped slowly out from under their shiny black tresses. They, too, had become sacrifices to the Jewish covenant with God: die rather than become Christians. I hardly need write that at the time I did not debate with myself the incongruity of that notion.

The child, Aaron, still lived. Crying, Rachel crawled across the stone slabs of the floor to where her eldest son shivered in fear beneath the sideboard. I heard her crooning softly in an attempt to cajole him from his hiding spot but the boy huddled closer into himself and refused to come out. His mother finally dragged him out by his feet unable to persuade him otherwise into her grasp. Aaron kicked and screamed but it availed him nothing. His mother managed, with Ruth's assistance, to pull him to her bosom, his back to her while she pinned his arms to his sides in a hideous parody of mother love. Ruth, with a strange blank expression on her face, plunged her dagger home one last time and all of Rachel's children lay dead.

After Aaron's struggles had ceased, Rachel picked him up and carried him to where her two daughters lay and set him down. Then she gathered up the beautiful, innocent, dead little Isaac and placed him beside his brother. She knelt down with the two girls on her left hand and the boys on her right and spread the voluminous sleeves of her gown over their faces as if to hide her awful crime and bent her head forward, weeping, her shoulders heaving with every silent sob.

Behind her, Ruth knelt and I saw her examine the dagger in her hand, studying it closely as if it was some wondrous thing she had never seen before. Whatever she planned to do with it next I did not discover at once for the shock of the multiple infanticides and hours without food or without surcease from stress overcame me and I lost consciousness. The last thing I remember before awareness faded was Ruth turning to stare at me, her eyes like two dead coals and I wondered dreamily if I would be her next victim.

◆

I awoke to feel my head snapping to one side accompanied by a burning sensation on my face. Another vicious slap sent my head whipping to the other side, as loose on my neck as I were a new-dead cadaver. Painfully, my eyes opened and

I looked up to see my tormentor. I did not know the man who stood over me but after a moment I recognised from the emblems on his costume that he was one of Emicho's men.

My thoughts seemed to tread through my mind as though mired in the muck of a bog. I remembered that the soldiers were not supposed to be in the great hall. So if they were not here or I was not there—I knew not which—where was I? No. That did not make sense. Had I been captured? And if so, how had Emicho's men taken me? Had I wandered away to the rear courtyard without realising that I had? Then further muddled speculation was cut off as the soldier clutched my collar and hauled me to my feet.

Throughout the great hall knots of Emicho's soldiers surrounded small groups of those Jews who remained alive. The soldiers held swords or pikes pointed threateningly at their captives but for the moment they seemed disinclined to harm the refugees. Rachel still knelt among her dead children, her robes yet covering their faces. The feet of the children poked out from under the material of her sleeves, the only evidence of the horror that lay beneath. Ruth lay behind her friend, quite still. I knew she must be dead.

I heard a tramping of booted feet and the jingling of war harness and looked up to the top of the stairs. I had expected to see Comte Emicho arriving but the man who led the company of warriors down the steps was unknown to me. With an unkempt moustache and equally dishevelled hair, he was shorter than the Lord of Leisingen and built like a wine barrel. From the appearance of his ugly, flushed face and the web of tiny veins etched haphazardly across his bulbous nose I suspected he probably easily contained the contents of such a barrel. I smiled at this internal witticism, then giggled in spite of my fear, unable to control myself, giddy with anxiety. Then I swallowed my laughter as Emicho's lieutenant turned to face me.

Pointing at me he commanded, "Bring that fool here to me!"

Two men dragged me to stand in front of him.

"Who are you?" he demanded.

"I am a clerical student here at the cathedral, my lord," I managed to stammer, though reluctant to give him my name.

"Well, cleric, tell me: What has happened here? Why are all these Jews dead? Have any of my soldiers been here?"

"No, my lord," I responded, looking at my feet. "Not until now, at least."

Realising that I had but answered his last question, he asked again, "Then what has happened here?"

"They preferred to die rather than..." I hesitated not wanting to admit to him the motivation behind the mass suicide.

"Rather than what boy? Answer!"

There was no help for it, I had to tell him. "Rather than become...Christian."

I assumed he would be aghast at this notion and at the very least become angry enough to strike me down. I was astonished therefore at his reaction to my revelation. He laughed.

When he had finished his laughter and wiped away a tear of mirth, he said, "And what gave these stinking heathens the idea that we would allow them to become Christians?"

That response also surprised me. What indeed? I had hoped for a brief time that because of what Rachel had said before she and Ruth destroyed her children, the *raison d'être* behind this assault on the Jews of Mainz had been not to destroy them outright because of their beliefs, as the women believed would happen, but to convert the Jews to Christianity.

It was a small hope. After all, the mission of Christians is to bring unbelievers into the body of Christ as the Lord Jesus commanded His disciples to do. Had this entire atrocity been promulgated in the name of greed alone? If nothing else I had thought that some good might come of the event if the Jews could become faithful Christians. That eventuality would have been best for everyone, especially for the Jews themselves since they would no longer be persecuted or reviled by their neighbours for their erroneous religious beliefs; not to mention they would also gain everlasting life and the salvation of their souls for doing so.

But I had never heard Comte Emicho claim that he had come here to save the Jews. No, he had come here by his own admission to wage bloody war and to destroy them in the name of vengeance for the Passion of Our Lord. I could not answer my interrogator for I had no answer. Instead, I asked him a question.

"My lord?" I began. "May I ask your name, my lord?"

He looked at me through narrowed eyes, appraising me. I looked down, not wishing to offend him, for of course he might easily order my death at any moment. Then, apparently deciding that I was no threat to him with the knowledge of his name, he answered.

"I am Drogo, Lord of Nesle." He puffed himself up to his full height which was somewhat less than my own. "And you are my prisoner."

◆

Immediately Drogo said this I was shoved aside and dragged to the wall where my hands were bound and my ankles hobbled with ropes as though I was a horse. I slumped down to the floor with my back to the stones. For the moment at least, I was safe. I did not know what Drogo planned do with me but he had not killed me outright. Indeed, he had named me a prisoner. I realised with a surge of nauseous surprise that I was afraid to die. Surely, I should have seen the prospect of my own death as a fulfilment of sorts, an opportunity to attain Heaven and the blessed afterlife promised by Our Lord. And yet sitting there with my heart thrumming and my innards twisting into visceral knots I thought only of how I might escape an almost certain death on the blade of one of Emicho's swords. In all things, however, no matter what any one individual man might personally think of the matter, the Hand of God works to construct and implement His own divine plan. I would not die that day.

Even so, the day's evil was not yet done. Although, certainly, enough blood had seeped out upon the stones of the Archbishop's Palace floor already, more would yet flow. I knew this with certitude as Drogo suddenly became very interested in Rachel's hunched form.

"You. Jew woman. What have you under your skirts? Hmmm?" He spoke in a loud voice and his soldiers all turned to observe him, nudging each other and pointing and laughing.

Drogo drew his sword from the scabbard slung across his back as he stepped forward to stand an arm's length from the young mother. The tip of the blade slipped under her chin and forced her to raise her face to him. But she kept her eyes closed and would not look at Emicho's lieutenant. This angered him immediately and he pulled the point of the sword out from under her chin and passed it across Rachel's cheek leaving a scratch that wept blood. She opened her eyes at that but I saw no fear there, only fierce defiance. The hatred in her countenance burned unmistakably.

"Pull back your sleeves that we may see the treasure you have hidden there," Drogo ordered.

"Treasure?" Rachel laughed sardonically, bitterly. "Treasure? You seek treasure? Yes there is a treasure without price beneath this cloth." Her voice, so cold, chilled my blood, for I knew what she would reveal. "But this treasure you shall never use, my lord. You will discard it unwanted on the garbage heaps of the city."

The lord of Nesle laughed, hollowly. "I do not think so, you Christ-killing bitch. Give me your gold or you will die."

Bravely, insolently, Rachel pursed her lips and spat at Drogo. "Here is my treasure then, great warrior."

She swept both of her sleeves back in one graceful rustle of material to reveal the bloodless faces of her children, the wounds on their necks dried and congealed into horrid smiles of bitter triumph, ghastly reflections of that of their mother.

Drogo's eyes bulged and his mouth dropped open for one frozen instant of surprise and horror. Then, angry, and obviously aware of the eyes of his men upon him, he roared deeply and loud in the pit of his belly. His sword tip arced back behind his right shoulder and the blade paused for an instant, quivering, at the top of its swing then whistled forth once again. It bit deeply into her neck and passed on through flesh and bone in one astonishingly brief motion. Rachel's head dropped to the floor and rolled a small distance until it came to rest face up, the bitter smile still in place. Drogo casually kicked the severed head aside as he strode past, the woman and her children apparently forgotten as he moved on to the next cluster of refugees. I sank to my knees in dry heaves at this new horror but was quickly kicked to my feet again by Drogo's men.

I could hear him speaking in loud, threatening tones to the Jews he confronted. He warned them that their fate would be the same as Rachel's if they did not immediately yield up what valuables they possessed. The refugees looked confused for the most part and I do not think that many of them, if any, possessed the sort of riches that Drogo demanded of them. I saw his sword raised again to murder another innocent Jew.

Remotely, distantly, I heard my own voice shouting, "Wait!"

Drogo turned to me with an angry scowl, pig eyes glaring. Stopped in mid-stroke, he appeared ridiculously unbalanced with his torso twisted against his hips and both arms in the air holding up the heavy broad-sword. I was surprised that he had halted his attack but I immediately took advantage of the pause, forging ahead, hardly knowing what I should say next.

"My lord Drogo," I said, raising my voice to carry across the floor of the great hall, "I believe that before these people are summarily executed they should be offered the chance to abjure their false religion. My lord Emicho offered as much at Speyer and Worms, did he not?"

In truth, I did not know if the Black Lord had indeed offered life in exchange for religious conformity or not but perhaps Drogo was unsure of that point as well. He seemed somewhat thick-headed to me, more a beast of war than a man of intellectual forethought. I could see that he was considering the possibility, at least. Silence followed for a time as he worked out the implications in his mind.

At last, he spoke. "Very well. Any of you who will become Christians will be spared the sword. If you do not become Christians then you will share the fate of that Christ-killing slut whose head I parted from her shoulders. May she burn forever in damnation for her crimes against her children and the Lord God." He spat on the floor as he finished the last sentence.

This last statement was rather ironic since I am certain that if those Jews who remained alive had not renounced their faith and taken up ours Drogo would have ordered all of them killed, men and women and children alike. Strange that he should condemn Rachel for a crime he himself would have committed without remorse if given the opportunity. As it was, though, all of the Jewish refugees left alive agreed to become Christians.

How this was to be accomplished I am not certain. Nor am I certain that Drogo knew, since no priest remained in the cathedral who might perform a mass of baptism for them. That issue turned out to be of little consequence in the event.

For the moment, Emicho's lieutenant required only that they all kneel before him and swear an oath of loyalty to the Emperor and one of faith and fealty to Our Lord Jesus Christ. Then the refugees were herded together like cattle and marched out the main doors of the great hall, through the cathedral and out into the piazza. I shuffled ignominiously along behind kept apart from them by my warders, still hobbled at the ankles and bound at the wrists, a pike at my back to urge me forward.

Emicho's army had begun to reassemble in the great square before the cathedral. They had not convened in any particular ordered formation but were ranged in groups around the centre of the plaza where a large number of the Jewish men who had survived the assault on the Archbishop's palace awaited their captors' pleasure. Whether that pleasure would be to render mercy or death I was not sure yet. Of course, my own fate was in Emicho's hands in just the same manner.

I searched the faces of the captured refugees for any I might know. Yes. There was Yaakob. He had survived, though he had a terrible gash over his left eye that had crusted over and a seeping slash in the muscle of his upper right arm.

I saw him searching the faces of the women who had been brought from the palace by Drogo, searching for Ruth. Then his eyes fell on me. A slight look of surprise froze his face for a moment. Perhaps he found it odd that I should also be a prisoner since I was a Christian or perhaps he believed that I had died in the great hall defending the women and children there. If the latter, I must have disappointed him terribly if he discovered that I had been no defence for them at all. At least he might seek me out as a source of information about his wife. I could prove useful for that, if nothing else. I could reveal her fate to him and the knowledge would be of no comfort. But what fate did he himself now await? Had he survived his wife only to join her in death, to be murdered in some horrible manner by the Lord of Leisingen?

As that thought crossed my mind, the Black Lord himself rode into the piazza. He had doffed his iron helm, carrying it on the saddle before him, and his thick black hair flew out wildly behind him like a pennant of victory. His bronze nose gleamed dully red in the late afternoon sun, a splash of blood in his otherwise bloodlessly white face. His wicked, black eyes sparkled with malice at the sight of so many captive heathens. He drove his steed into the centre of the standing Jews, a vicious smile on his face, and wheeled around sending many of them sprawling. Those of his men observing this laughed out loud.

I took advantage of the distraction to edge close to Yaakob. He had not been one of those thrown off balance by Emicho's horse, but had moved outward toward me with the momentum of the displaced crowd. This had helped bring us to within an arm's length of each other.

I could see that he had suffered terribly. Apart from the major wounds he bore, I could see that he was bruised and scratched on every part of his visible skin. His cheeks were drawn in exhaustion and his eyes hooded with defeat and despair. He looked at me askance and I shook my head slightly, indicating wordlessly that information he sought of me: his wife was dead. His chin sank low as he bowed his head in utter loss. Everyone in the world he had loved was gone, his people destroyed.

A sob welled up within me at his misery and I struggled to contain the sound of weakness within myself. If I succumbed to my own despair, I knew I would be lost completely. I was determined that I would die bravely. I would not give my captors the satisfaction of destroying my dignity and shaming me before them. They might take my body but my soul belonged to God. I saw myself, foolishly perhaps since I in no way altered the course of subsequent events or was even much involved actively in them, as a martyr to the cause of justice and righteousness, to the true spirit of Christ's words if not, strictly speaking, to the furtherance of our Christian faith. I would at least die willingly for my beliefs as my fellow captives would do for theirs, divergent though our beliefs were.

As we stood awaiting inevitable death, Emicho, a simulacrum of the Angel of Death on his iron black steed, spoke.

"Jews of Mainz," he bellowed, "The few handfuls of you I see before me are all that remain of your nest of vipers in our midst. Your fellow pagan Christ-killers are dead. Your wives. Your sons and daughters. Your fathers and mothers. They have all been put to the sword."

He paused a moment for that to settle into the minds of his prisoners. Nodding, he looked around the miserable mob of refugees, his gaze settling on each in turn, myself included. As he looked at me I thought that I detected a slight start of surprise, perhaps recognition, in his eyes, though I could have been mistaken. He smiled a smile not unlike that of the beast that lurks in the waters of the rivers of Aegypt, that evil, scaly, predatory monster known as the *crocodilus* that lurks beneath the surface waiting to suck its unsuspecting victims down to their doom.

He continued, "I give you now a chance to save yourselves and only one chance. You must recant your vile religion and take an oath to accept Jesus Christ as your new Lord and Master."

At this statement many of the Jews looked one to the other in consternation and apprehension. I could read in the faces of many that they were prepared to do as Emicho requested and I felt a surge of joy for them though I believe not many of them felt the same. At least if the Black Lord decided to kill them after they converted they would have the salvation promised all Christians by Our Saviour. Then Emicho added his proviso and my hopes dropped.

"But before you take this oath you must make a gift to Our Lord. You must renounce your wealth and surrender all your worldly possessions as Christ Himself commanded his sainted Apostles to do when they set out to bring His message to the *pagani*. I will personally act on behalf of my Lord and Master, Jesus Christ, to receive your gifts to Him. Then and only then, after you have cleansed yourselves of worldly greed, will you be shriven and accepted into His earthly flock."

The faces of the hopeful Jews then fell and I knew that even if they wished to convert and save themselves they had nothing to give as an offering to Emicho. They had already given everything to Lord Rothard or Gerhard of Neuss for their protection. In his desperation one of the refugees, one who had been present in the Archbishop's Palace not one who had fought in the rear courtyard, stepped out from among his fellows and, slowly, with great dignity, stripped off his robes and laid them at the feet of the Black Lord's war-horse. He stepped back and stood there, naked, waiting for Emicho's response.

In a sense, the Lord of Leisingen was cleverly trapped. Since the Jew had indeed turned over to him all his worldly possessions, Emicho was honour-bound to take the man's oath as a Christian convert. I did not think, however, that the Black Lord would be content with a ransom of heaps of clothing rather than of gold. If the rest of his prisoners followed this man's example, though, Emicho would be humiliated before his troops, outwitted by the Jews acting according to the terms of his own proposed contract.

Emicho's face did not change its expression; that crocodile smile remained on his lips. I knew that he had already decided that his captives would die this day but how now would he accomplish this aim without appearing to go back on his word? I am sure that he had not expected many of the Jews to take advantage of his offer and those who did would further enrich his coffers when they became Christians. He pointed to the naked man.

"Kneel to me and receive Christ's blessing."

The Jew complied and sank to his knees, head bowed.

"Not like that. Head to the ground in true humility, Jew. Have you no notion of Christian piety?" he snarled the question.

The Jew looked up at Emicho and blinked quickly, several times. He looked hesitant and near to shedding tears in his shame but he complied and bent forward to place his forehead to the paving stones of the plaza, his arms outstretched before him. He knelt there for a long time with the cheeks of his white bottom exposed to everyone. All were silent, waiting to see what would transpire next. Finally, Emicho spoke again.

"I have changed my mind. To appear truly contrite before Our Lord in Heaven who looks down upon us, and Who I am certain would wrinkle His Holy Nose at the sight of your heathen ass pointing up at Him, you will assume the posture of the true penitent."

Tremulously, from his abject position, the Jew said, "I do not know what that position is, my lord."

"Stupid Jewish ox," Emicho said in an ironic tone that suggested he was speaking patiently to an idiot. "Assume the posture of Christ on the cross there on the stones."

The Jew did as Emicho bid him, lying with arms stretched at right angles to his body, legs together, head turned to one side, his cheek pressed to the pavement. The Black Lord left him lying like that for a time. The other Jewish refugees shifted uncomfortably. Clearly, they did not relish this humiliation of their coreligionist. I wondered if any of those who had bethought themselves to embrace their own conversion now were having second thoughts. Just as clearly, Emicho was baiting the man and purposefully attempting to dissuade any others to follow his example. Again, Emicho sat thoughtfully smiling down at the object of his derision.

"No. No, that does not look right either," he said at length. "I do believe that Our Lord would be just as scandalised at the sight of your buttocks even in this position. On your back, then."

With a small sob the Jew again complied so that now, while still in the cruciform position he lay on his back, his face turned up to the sky. His eyes he kept tightly closed so that he did not have to look at those staring down at him in his humiliation.

"Och!" exclaimed Emicho. "Surely that is worse, neh? That hideous bald-headed *gallus* of yours must surely be an affront worse than your nether areas. Draw the cowl over its monk-headed pate, Jew."

Emicho referred, of course, to the Jew's male member which, unlike those of Christians, had its fleshy head circumcised. For among the Jews the *praeputium* is cut away soon after birth. Therefore, what the Lord of Leisingen demanded of his penitent was impossible and he knew it. This was but another attempt to humiliate the man and intimidate his fellows. Now the naked man did shed tears of abject mortification though he visibly tried not to do so. A thin rivulet of lachrymose fluid trickled down his cheek.

He stammered, "I...I cannot, my lord."

Emicho laughed aloud.

"He cannot. He cannot!" He shouted in mock surprise.

He threw up his arms and held them out as if to include all of his followers in his mirth. They, naturally, responded in kind. On all sides, Emicho's soldiers roared loudly in amusement at their lord's efforts to embarrass the Jew.

This laughter went on for a time until, suddenly, Yaakob, standing near me on the outskirts of the knot of prisoners, uttered a low guttural growl and then with a howl of despair attacked one of the soldiers standing behind him. He smashed the man's face with his fists and whisked away his sword not at all hampered by the wound in his arms for I am sure a kind of crazed blood-lust then consumed him. Instead of skewering the soldier, though, he raced immediately to the supine naked man and ran him through the heart. Immediately he had accomplished this act of murder he flung himself on the same sword driving it so far into his left breast that the point of the weapon emerged from beneath his shoulder blade as he collapsed onto the pavement, as dead as its stones.

A stunned silence followed this amazing sequence of events. Then all of the Jewish men were attacking Emicho's men attempting to wrest weapons away from them and destroy their owners. Obviously, they had decided to eschew the Black Lord's offer of conversion and those who had already accepted their new, though possibly invalid, Christian status from Drogo now recanted.

Needless to say, the Jews were easily defeated by Emicho's soldiers since even had its members been weaponless, the size of the army far exceeded that of its opponents and they could have brought them down by sheer weight of numbers even without weapons of any kind. In the meantime many of the Jewish women had followed Yaakob's example and thrown themselves upon swords and knives dropped by the Jewish men as they were killed and wounded, choosing to die rather than to be violated by Christian warriors after the battle.

I did not become embroiled in the conflict. Rather, as the fighting began I tried to make my way, still hobbled at the ankles thus making my progress slow, from the centre of the violence back toward the cathedral. However, I was halted in this attempt suddenly and unexpectedly when one of

Emicho's foot soldiers reared up in my path raising a heavy war club. I still see clearly his thick black beard, the stumps of his yellow teeth, the wild look in his blue eyes, and I can smell his fetid breath in my face. The last thing that I remember of the confrontation was an intense searing pain in my head and thinking that I was dead. Then all was blackness.

Caput Septimus

As it happened, I did not die, for God in His Infinite Mercy, for which I give thanks, kept me alive through all that followed. And of course, you who read this are witness to my continued existence. However, there were many times in the months afterward when I might have wished that I had died on that day in the plaza adjacent to the cathedral and its environs. The travails of the siege of Lord Rothard's palace were as the pleasant days of summer when compared to the icy winter of the staggering hardships I faced on the journey to the east.

Emicho fully intended, at least when he had finished his persecution of the Jews of L'Alemaigne, to travel on to the great capital city of the Eastern Empire, Constantinople, and thence to the Holy Land. He fully intended to join with the force led by Peter the Hermit whose evangelical mission had first inspired him and he fully intended to ravage the eastern lands occupied by the Saracen all the way to Jerusalem. But as the eminent authority, Boethius, states: "Wealth in it's own darkness clouds the thoughts," and thus Emicho's thoughts, clouded over with dark acquisitiveness, failed to rest securely on the supreme goal envisioned by the Blessed Father Urban at Clermont, that is, to free the Holy Places from the grasp of the Infidel. As he, and of course his following, enthusiastic or otherwise, journeyed eastward, the Black Lord became ever more confused about the true purpose of the armed pilgrimage to the orient. In the end he completely abandoned both the mission and his men; but of course all that comes later in this narrative. For we did not immediately make our way to the east.

When I at last awoke from the stupor caused by the blow to my head, I found myself bound hand and foot and lying in the bed of a rough-hewn narrow wooden cart drawn by an ox. The wooden wheels of the vehicle squealed and ground loudly, and the cart jounced about horridly. Neither phenomenon effected anything in the way of relief to the bright, fiery, searing pain in my head. I attempted to sit up to take stock of my surroundings but the nauseating agony of the simple motion sent me immediately back in sick suffering. I resolved to remain prone for the moment, barely able to endure the continual spasms and paroxysms induced throughout the shuddering length of the two-wheeled *plaustrum* by each pothole or branch or stone in the road but better able to bear that than the pounding pressure in my own head.

I lay like that for a time listening to the noises of people and animals moving all around the cart. I tried to pick out individual sounds in order that I might take my mind off the pain I felt. At first there was only a tumultuous, thick soup of human and animal voices but soon I realised that I had begun to hear bits and snatches of conversation, dogs barking, children laughing or wailing, shouts and curses and whistles, and of course, the ever-present protestations of the pegged wheels turning bitterly beneath me. At any rate, I decided that the riot of sound had to be the result of a vast number of individuals all travelling together.

When the wagon stopped abruptly, after what seemed to me an infinite time enduring its abusive cart bottom, I tried once more to raise the upper half of my body in order that I might see more than the knotty rough planks of the *plaustrum's* sides. This effort was made the more difficult because of the fact that I was bound at the wrists by a rope tied to a metal ring embedded in the cart bottom and so could not throw out my arms for balance. After two or three attempts I did manage to sit up and look about me. At first I did not believe the information my eyes transported to my thoughts as a variety of impressions struck me all at once.

My first reaction was one of amazement at the sheer numbers of the persons around me. In any direction I cared to look into the immediate and intermediate foreground I saw milling individuals dressed in all the colours of the rainbow. Mixed in among them I could see more ox-drawn carts, the occasional horse and rider, cows, dogs, a flapping chicken or duck or goose tethered about the neck or carried indignantly by its feet. There was too, most remarkable of all, a large, fat, black bear shuffling along paw over claw obediently tethered to its master's thick, hempen leash. Needless to say, that man and his charge walked through a broad avenue created by the wide berth given him by the pressing throng. I saw no soldiers evident but that was because they were far ahead of this rear vanguard of simple folk whose company of course they disdained. The overall impression I had was that this was not at all a dignified pilgrimage but rather a comical festival or holy day celebration or a spring fair.

In the distance beyond the crowd of commoners and their movable chattels I could make out a city. We had come to rest along a relatively low, flat plain that nonetheless rose above the *municipium*. Our elevation above it gave a rather good vantage point from which to see the place and its environs. Then my heart sank. I realised that I had been in this place once before as I recognised the walls and the age-old Roman fort; we had reached the city of Köln. This surprised me because that city, as I have mentioned, lies to the north and west of Mainz, that is to say, away from the direction one must travel in order to reach the Holy Land. I surmised, with a sense of dire inevitability, that Emicho desired to continue plaguing the Jews thereabouts and I was not mistaken in that assumption.

I hardly need write that I dreaded a repetition of those events at Mainz that had led to the death of so many innocent people, the many Jews, including my friends Yaakob and Ruth, Ulfrid the *magister equi*, and, for all I knew now, the gentle Brother Ambrose and my mentor, Brother Piccolo. I knew that Emicho's greed and his innate viciousness probably guaranteed a disastrous outcome for the Jews living in Köln and for any who stood forth to aid them or to try to prevent the Black Lord's predation. Thanks be to God that in the event I was proved wrong. The Jews of Köln did not suffer the same fate as those at Mainz.

This fact did not result from any change of heart on the part of Emicho or because his army had lost its taste for ravage and plunder. Nor did Emicho fail to inflict his vile temper on the city. But he did not kill any of its Jews because there were none to be found.

By this I do not mean that no Jews lived or had ever lived in that city. Like any other large or medium size city in Europe, Köln had its Jewish ghetto. We are all aware and I have made mention of the kinds of commercial enterprises in which Jews are involved and of the many financial services they provide for the larger Christian populations where they dwell. No exception to this circumstance, Köln likewise had its share of such financiers and entrepreneurs.

When we arrived at that city, though, they were absent. All of their shops were empty, their homes fled, their synagogues un-visited. The Black Lord's soldiers smashed in door after door of shop after shop in the Jewish quarter of the city but they plundered little or nothing and they found no one. They burned the synagogue but none arrived to rebuke or contest them for this act. They shouted in the streets for the Jews to show themselves but none appeared. Finally, in his last act of enraged desperation, Emicho, believing that the Jews had hidden themselves behind the robes of the Church as they had in Mainz, attacked the bishop's palace with the intent of smashing down its doors, too, and killing all whom they found. Unlike Archbishop Rothard, though, the Bishop of Köln had no fear of Emicho and his soldiers.

I heard the tale, though I did not see with my own eyes the event of which now I write, of how the Bishop accosted and berated the Black Lord and then sent him away with his tail tucked between his legs like a kicked cur. As in Mainz Emicho convened his army before the cathedral in a show of force meant to intimidate those within. He made essentially the same announcement concerning his mission that he had made in Mainz and then waited for the ecclesiastics inside to either open the doors or ignore him. Meanwhile, he made ready to break down the doors of the Bishop's palace should the latter eventuality develop. To Emicho's surprise, though, the Bishop himself immediately strode out upon the palace step and confronted the army.

In a loud and commanding voice, he rebuked the army and its leaders.

"Followers of Emicho, Lord of Leisingen! Hear me!" he shouted so that all might hear him. "Your liege lord has mis-led you and now precedes you into damnation. The writ of the Holy Father concerning the pilgrimage to the East is not meant as a charter by which to destroy our peace-loving and law-abiding Jewish neighbours here in the German states. Its purpose is to aid our fellow Christians in the Greek lands and in the Holy Land and to free the Holy Places for those pious pilgrims, lay and ecclesiastic, noble and poor alike, who would seek to journey there so that they might, in peace and security, visit the lands where Our Lord Jesus Christ lived and performed His miracles. You are not commanded to murder innocents in our own country but to purge the eastern lands of the abominable false religions whose practitioners aggressively seek to destroy and enslave the adherents of the True Faith. Depart from Köln, therefore, in peace. Strike no more discord among your Christian brethren, neither here in the German lands nor along the route to Jerusalem; neither abhor nor murder your Jewish countrymen. If you are truly pious and wish to serve Our Lord and Saviour in holy war against the Infidel leave this city in peace and take yourselves eastward to Constantinople, there to convene with the other armies of Christ as the Holy Father has commanded."

He stopped and regarded the crowd. Any of those upon whom his glance fell thought themselves accursed did they not follow his edict, such was the power of his gaze on them. The army milled about mumbling and whispering among themselves. But Emicho was not a man to give up easily in the face of the frustration of his own desires. He stood up on the rump of his horse—a truly admirable feat of balance as the horse continually shifted its feet under him—and addressed his soldiers, or more correctly, his lieutenants, in a loud voice.

"My lords and kinsmen, do not be swayed so easily by such charitable rhetoric and misplaced mercy. It is true that the Holy Father has commanded that we destroy those who threaten our Faith. It is true that we shall meet the Army of

Christ in the Greek capital. It is true that we must fight the God-cursed infidel. But we must battle the enemy wherever we find him and he is here in Köln as he was at Mainz!" With that last sentence his voice rose to a thunderous pitch and heads nodded in agreement at these words. He continued. "Here in Köln, as it was in Mainz, the accursed Christ-killers are sheltered behind hallowed walls," and his arm swept round to indicate the cathedral, "protected by the arms of Mother Church who should cast them out as the vile murderers of Our Lord and Master, Jesus Christ. Strike, I say, not with mercy and charity and benevolence but with fire and steel and anger." He rounded on the bishop, still flawlessly balanced astride his steed, and he was terrible to behold. He pointed his finger and his eyes glowed with evil fire. "Surrender them to us. Now!"

An ordinary man would have blanched in terror at his devil's aspect but not so the Bishop of Köln. He was old, I am given to understand. His beard was long and white and his hair equally long and equally white. Though not a tall, overbearing man, he calmly regarded the Lord of Leisingen. With strength and dignity evident in his face, I was informed, he rolled up the cuffs of his gilt-trimmed sleeves, each in turn, his piercing eyes blinking not once as he returned his opponent's gaze.

Then he lifted his hands, revealing powerful forearms, the arms of a fighting man. Surely this bishop had known battle himself at one time and perhaps the nobility evident in the face and fearless manner of the church man stemmed from that of the warrior lord he might once have been, for such often retire to the service of Mother Church when they weary of battle and bloodshed. Who better, then, than a former warlord to oppose the Black Lord in the matter?

Of course, the bishop's history is mere supposition on my part. I never met the man in person, nor did I ever learn much about him. However, the fact that he so easily stood against Emicho suggests to me that he may have been at one time a lay lord or a *cnicht*. At any rate, in the event, he raised his arms and coldly and directly spoke to Emicho, his voice insistent.

"Emicho, Lord of Leisingen, I command you now to leave this city and hasten to Constantinople. For the Holy Father himself has stated at Clermont that anyone who, having taken the cross in order to embark upon the pilgrimage to Jerusalem, then turns away from his duty shall be considered anathema. Therefore, turn from this place and carry out your vow. And if you attack these holy environs and threaten us with violence you shall suffer God's wrath. For Pope Urban has declared also that whosoever seizes a bishop shall be considered an outlaw and an excommunicate. Thus, in attacking us, you will be doubly cursed and all your followers with you, cast out in your sinfulness to darkness and damnation, bereft of God's Mercy. Renew your vow, then, and follow Christ and His army on the journey to Jerusalem or be condemned to Hell."

Many of the Black Lord's lieutenants heard this admonition, of course, spoken in a calm and reasonable manner without passion but with absolute assurance, and they began immediately to mutter among themselves. Shortly, some of them, casting suspicious, side-long glances at their leader, began to drift away, their thegns following them. None there had reckoned on the notion of becoming an excommunicate for his actions, the most heinous of punishments as we are all aware, though I am certain that Emicho's followers were undoubtedly prepared to defend themselves from any attempts at secular punishment. But how could they hope to defend against censure of a type that even within living memory had proved disastrous for the Emperor himself, surely the most powerful man in all secular Christendom, when he set himself stubbornly against the Blessed Pope Gregory; against censure of a magnitude that would set every devout lord against them, allowing anyone to attack and conquer them without recourse to any sort of justice, temporal or ecclesiastical?

At the moment that the Bishop of Köln pronounced the eventuality of excommunication, Emicho's advance against the Jews of that city effectively ended. He had no choice but to proceed to Constantinople. If he did not, his followers were set to abandon him and go forth on their own.

And so we left the Alemaigne lands and began the journey to the east.

◆

On the day we left Köln, the day following Emicho's confrontation with the Bishop, there was much confusion in the army's ranks. The Black Lord needed once more to gather his followers together and reassure them that he might still command them and lead them on the armed pilgrimage in spite of the Bishop's threats. Those nobles who, because of their rank and status, commanded the greatest number of retainers after the Lord of Leisingen himself compelled him by way of their own combined superiority of numbers to abandon any further notions of exploring the region around Köln in search of more Jewish communities to plunder. They stated that they would no longer risk excommunication by defying the terms of the papal edict. Emicho acquiesced in this, knowing, I believe, that without the support of his nobles and their armies, he had no hope of gaining anything in the way of the spoils of later conquests, either in the Holy Land or in the lands held by the Infidel in the vicinity of the Eastern Empire.

However, even in granting this accord to those lesser lords, he demanded from them their renewed oaths of loyalty to him within the context of enacting faithfully the Papal dictum concerning the implementation of the armed pilgrimage. Many of Emicho's lieutenants grumbled at this but eventually all those of importance and influence had taken the oath. Satisfied, the Black Lord ordered the withdrawal of his army from the city.

Some of the confusion attendant on the departure from Köln resulted not from the machinations of the great men but from the weather. As dawn broke, heavy, chill, grey rains began to fall and continued for the entire day. Even the most organised and disciplined of armies can be disorderly when camp is broken for the march. Emicho's pilgrim army, composed as it was of a huge force of what were essentially common camp followers totally lacking in military discipline, reassembled in an utterly chaotic fashion as it congregated on the road, ready to make the journey to the south and east.

The rains only compounded the chaos. The fields around the city, yesterday hard-packed by the passage of thousands of pairs of feet, today became rutted and sloppy with new-made mud. Most of the vegetation growing in the fields had long been trampled underfoot and so nothing remained but bare ground which quickly soaked up water and turned to slimy ruts and pits, trapping animals and humans alike and sapping their efforts at forward progress. Wagons, mired to their axles, became barriers in the road which must be detoured around, the detours into the meadows even sloppier and more treacherous than the road itself. As a result, forward progress was slow at first. I endured the delay and the weather stoically, however, despite my suffering.

I sat in my simple conveyance, hungry, cold, without protection from the elements, soaked to the skin, water running in rivulets off the tip of my nose, into my eyes and down the neck of my robe. My teeth chattered with the chill and I drew myself up into a miserable ball, uselessly trying to maintain some body heat. I ignored soldiers and commoners alike who must needs pass off the road and onto the muddy ground alongside, all the while cursing me and my transport as they passed. What could I do about their inconvenience? I was bound and completely without resources to affect anyone, including myself.

In my misery I tried to think of something other than my physical discomfort. At first I prayed and tried to take strength from that. However, I must confess, reluctantly, that after a time my thoughts wandered away from contemplation of God's Grace to that of my present situation.

Aside from the physical discomforts the main problem was, simply stated, I did not know why I was a part of Emicho's train. Why had I been kidnapped? Of what use was I to Emicho? If he wanted a hostage, either of the two Benedictines would have been far more valuable than I. And what of Brother Piccolo and Brother Ambrose? Dead, probably. But why them and not me? I put that line of thought away for the present. I had no certain knowledge of their deaths.

Instead I returned to the contemplation of the question, more immediately of concern to my own welfare, of why Emicho had taken me. Then the thought occurred to me suddenly that perhaps the Black Lord did not even know I was a prisoner now in the keeping of his army. As why should he, insignificant as I was?

Indeed, the idea was borne out by the fact that in all the time that I had been conscious, riding in the wagon, bound hand and foot, none had come to question me or to inquire as to my welfare, nor fed me nor gave me water. Needless to say, I was actually thankful for the rain at least in terms of slaking my thirst. As to food, earlier I had begged a crust of bread from the old woman who walked along at the side of the ox dragging my wagon forward and she had reluctantly tossed a dry hunk into the cart for me but other than that I had not been fed nor debriefed by anyone. Most of those who passed by simply ignored or avoided or cursed at me for I was evidently not a pilgrim in good standing, bound prisoner that I was, and even at best my status was uncertain. I could only conclude then that Emicho had no idea that I was his captive and I was here now for some reason quite apart from any design in the mind of the Lord of Leisingen.

But why had I not been killed along with the Jewish refugees that day? How long ago? Barely more than half a week. A few days and so much changed. So much destroyed. So many dead. Tears mingled with the cleansing waters from heaven and slid unfelt down my cheeks. The huge caravan, in its totality like some fantastic, mindless organism, writhed onward through the downpour as heedless of it or the countryside through which it passed, as implacable, as a plague of locusts.

◆

By the time we had reached Mainz once more, a couple of days later, I discovered the identity of my captor. The pilgrimage, if such I dare call that strange assemblage of folk, had halted a few leagues from my former home. As evening came upon us the sky at last cleared and the clouds shredded apart like old fabric, worn thread-bare by the expense of rain they had shed onto the earth, to reveal the inner surface of the crystalline azure sphere behind, its skin studded with the occasional, brilliant, gem-like star.

For a moment my heart lifted. In that glorious depth of darkness I sensed God's realm for an instant and felt His Grace touch me even to my very soul. Such hope as arose in me I cannot describe to you; I can only write that I knew this must be a sign of better days to come, as I felt myself coming alive again.

As I sat in my miniature, mobile prison, still bound and myself immobile, contemplating this gift of life, I was startled out of my abstraction by the approach of two armed men. I knew immediately I saw them they must be part of some noble's personal guard since they were dressed not at all like common soldiers. Instead of worn leather jerkins they wore chain-mail hauberks extending to the knee over their padded, woollen tunics. Their surcoats each held strips of red cloth sewn on in a cross design over the left breast, the sign that they had taken the cross on behalf of the Holy Father Urban. Their legs and boots were also sheathed in mail as were their arms. Each carried a great sword slung over his shoulder and a smaller short sword buckled on at the waist. Neither wore a helm nor carried a shield since these were not necessary to their purpose as the men were not intent on battle. Rather, I quickly realised, they had come to fetch me.

I was not unkindly, though roughly, handled. One of the soldiers severed my bonds with a knife he drew from his belt in back and then they essentially dragged me from the cart, heedless of my inability to walk owing to the stiffness and apathy of the unused muscles in my legs. Standing straight and erect I found difficult since my back had likewise suffered from being in a bent position for most of two days.

I must have looked a sorry sight indeed hobbling hastily along after the soldiers, led by a rope they had tethered around my waist, and bent forward like a withered old man. Gradually, though, the humours balanced themselves as my heart pumped their essences throughout my body once more— for it is this organ, both the seat of all emotion and the conveyor of life's substance and spirit through the body, that most suffers from inactivity and dullness of mind—and I found myself able to walk erect once more though still somewhat stiffly, yet weak from thirst and my long fast. As we wound our way through the encampment, its squalor and stench a reflection of the station in life of those who created it, I began to feel somewhat heartened even so, though apprehensive about our destination, for my guards would not tell me where we were bound and quite ignored my questions.

Finally, we came to a group of tents arranged in a square with a large, clean, open space in its centre. There we stopped. One of the men left us and disappeared into the largest tent. Shortly, he returned and they hustled me within.

For a few moments my eyes were dazzled by the brilliance within since they had adapted to the low light level of the evening twilight outside. But here the vast cloth-enclosed space was lit by dozens of beeswax candles which shed a bright, clear, white light throughout. I blinked, trying to focus on my surroundings. I could see that we were at the edge of the main focus of activity which was at the end of the space farthest from where I stood with my escorts. Then, once again, I was half-dragged through the little crowd, the guards elbowing their way in, me drifting along behind them like a hooked bait trolled in the wake of a fishing boat.

As I have written, the crowd was small and momentarily we were at its edge in an open space that had as its focus a low field chair of the Roman style. Sitting in it, already far along in drunkenness, sat Drogo of Nesle.

He was not alone in his drink. Around him crowded his lieutenants, some of whom I had already seen in the cathedral at Mainz, and some others of notable dress I had not and whom I assumed to be his noble peers. These latter folk sat in chairs similar to that occupied by the Lord of Nesle. Obviously men of some importance.

After a short time, Drogo happened to glance up. Immediately he saw me his eyebrows rose in surprise and recognition then he frowned at the two bodyguards who flanked me tightly and they stepped back at his subtle signal. Without their support I nearly fell to the dirt floor as my knees threatened to give way from my growing weakness at this unusual effort and from hunger and thirst. I wavered yet on my feet, though desperately attempting not to shame myself with frailty.

Clearly Drogo took notice of my unbalanced state for a simple, three-legged wooden stool appeared before me and I found a tankard of ale placed in my hand. I could barely hold it up so heavy did it seem to me in my weakened state. I let it sink to my lap as I sat there, feeling dizzy and sick in my stomach from hunger. Drogo, with a wave of his hand and a nod of his head, urged me to drink.

Given the circumstances of my captivity and the need for some refreshment I thought it best to comply with my captor's wishes. The ale was bitter and strong to my taste but settled into my stomach very comfortably. I felt its effects almost at once. The ale dizzied my mind at the same time that it filled my empty hunger and I began to feel vertiginously jovial. I heard Drogo speaking and I lifted my head trying to focus my eyes.

"This is the cleric I spoke about. He will record for me the deeds that transpire from here to the Holy Land. We shall write a great chronicle of Christian victories, our victories, against the Infidel!"

This announcement was news to me, of course, although the others stamped their feet in approval. I had not realised I would do that which he confided to his colleagues I would do. Clearly, though, he was excited about the possibility of having his accomplishments recorded in this fashion.

Puzzled, I looked at him through bleary eyes.

"Why do you not keep your own journal and record these things yourself?" I asked.

A stunned silence followed this query. I looked around at the circle of noble faces wondering what was amiss. Many of them frowned and looked uncomfortable. Drogo, a bit of meat dangling from one horn of his droopy, crescent-shaped moustache, set down his own tankard and leaned forward in his seat. Fixing upon me his pig-small eyes he spoke impatiently.

"Because I cannot read nor write. That is for such as you, weaklings who cannot fight."

"Oh," I said. This surprised me somewhat for I had thought until then that all nobles tutored their families in the written word. However, I have since learned that this is not the case. Indeed, most do not. The *ars grammaticae*, the grammatical arts, are not their weapon against the world but rather the *ars militarii*, the martial arts, and the martial campus, the field of war, their school. Now, Drogo would use my own well-developed tools to forge the chains that would imprison me in his purpose.

"Oh," I said again, puzzled, and lost consciousness.

◆

When I again awoke I found myself once more riding in a wagon. This particular conveyance, however, I found much more comfortable and to my liking than my previous mode of transport. Its walls were of wood and high, as tall as a man standing. The canvas roof that completely enclosed it from the elements stretched across an expanse as wide as two men lying down toe to head. Rather larger, as I could see when I opened my eyes, than the simple plaustrum which had carried me from Mainz to Köln and back again to Mainz, the wagon nonetheless, like its humbler counterpart, translated the obstacles and pitfalls it met in the road to its passengers within.

Still, the change in my condition was profound. I lay on the softest of cushions, unbound and luxuriating in the smoothest of furs which completely surrounded me, making the jouncing and bouncing of the wagon as it traversed the difficult road almost sufferable in the way it rocked me pacifically back and forth. Then I remembered where I was and why I was there.

I sat up with a start. I could see that the sun now shone, which indicated that I must have slept through the night. I surmised that we were again on the road to Constantinople, the pilgrimage once more on the march. By now, since the daylight was strong, suggesting that the sun was well risen, we must be several hours out of Mainz where we had camped the night before. So close I had been to my home and yet now that home was irretrievably lost to me. The wagon, even though better accoutred than the previous vehicle in which I had been restrained, was nonetheless as much a prison to me. I lay in an alcove at the rear of this space in one corner and I was alone within.

I struggled to my feet, weak as a new-born lamb, and shuffled across the shifting floor surface. My only thoughts as I rose were to satisfy my hunger. There was a table with benches set alongside, apparently anchored to the floor in some fashion, in the centre of the room, for so I thought of the space within the wagon, and beside it, affixed to the wall, there were several cabinets. I rummaged through these in search of such sustenance as might be available.

I was not disappointed for in one of the cabinets I found a block of cheese and a loaf of bread. And for liquid nourishment there also I found a jar of water and a cask of wine. I set these on the table, holding them close all the while against the unpredictable movements of the vehicle and sat down on the bench to satisfy my intense appetite.

I ate slowly and sparingly for I had heard from Brother Piccolo that one who has fasted long might not retain sustenance at first; this owing to an excess of phlegm and bile that develops without the balancing effects of food and liquids to sustain the blood and causes the body at first to reject the excess of quality substances required to regain its proper equilibrium. This is evidenced in the putrid bile that spews forth along with the jettisoned food stuffs. Since I followed the Benedictine's advice I did not experience the problems associated with this circumstance, although shortly after drinking the wine I began to feel drowsy whereupon I tottered back to my bed and fell dreamlessly asleep once more.

When I again awoke, this time to a gentle nudging, night had fallen and my conveyance had stopped. I found my feet at once in alarm as I saw that the wagon had taken on several more passengers. I backed away into my corner, defensively, although none of the men there offered any sort of threat. Still, my experiences so far had prepared me to expect the worst.

Drogo sat at the table, amusement evident in his face, with two others; a third stood a few feet from me.

"Perhaps the puppy has been kicked one too many times, neh?" the Lord of Nesle observed, looking me up and down as he would a new hound. His companions laughed with him, stopping when he did. He gestured to me, indicating that I should join him at the table. I obeyed, for what choice had I? His was the power here.

"You seem something recovered, whelp. Now you've drunk my wine and eaten my bread, are you ready to repay your debt?"

I refrained from pointing out the obvious facts that I had been abandoned and nearly starved in the generosity of his unlawful confinement of me, although some of the evidence in the remnant of my earlier meal sat on the table between us; the wine and water jars, though, had fallen to the floor and shattered for which I felt a twinge of guilt. Although I had nothing to gain from challenging the authority of one such as he still I thought that he owed the debt of my hunger to me not the other way round. I said nothing from where I sat, fearing that my mouth would undo me, but merely stared at the table. He took my silence as *in silentio consensus* and continued.

"So. Then you shall begin with the setting down of our victories over the enemies of Christ in the Alemaigne lands and an outline of my character and of those qualities which make me particularly suited to the Holy Mission to the East. I will narrate these facts to you and thereafter you shall keep a daily record of my deeds and set them down each evening when we have halted for the night. You will find writing materials and tools in the cabinet behind me. Be quick."

I found the materials and returned to my place at the table, kicking potsherds from the wine jar from under my feet, resenting the whole time his peremptory attitude, but resigned that there was nothing to be done about it. I was wholly in Drogo's power. No use jeopardising my very existence because I chafed at his hold over me.

Then began Drogo's account of his life and of his deeds done in the name of Our Saviour. A more vicious and vile accounting one would have difficulty imagining, although Drogo evidently thought himself the epitome of piety in those horrors most recently made in the Alemaigne cities he had attacked. I do not recount these things to you now because they are of little consequence in my own tale. Suffice to say that I was not overly impressed with either his early life, mainly spent in drunken depredation of the lands neighbouring those of his father's demesne, or with the past few weeks spent in rapine and murder among the Jews of Lower Lotharingia. I wrote quickly and glossed over as much as I could though keeping the thread of his narrative intact in the event that he asked me to read it back to him. After all, he could never read it himself.

After what seemed a space of several hours of scratching quickly and abbreviatedly on parchment in an attempt to keep pace with his dictation I began to feel cramped and sleepy. Drogo himself grew hoarse in speech and slurred with wine and his one remaining man, the others having slipped quietly away on one pretext or another, had by now nodded off in sleep. Mercifully, the Lord of Nesle sought his own rest at last and left me to mine. When he had gone with his remaining companion my head sank under its own motive sympathy to the table and there I spent the night, too tired even to seek my bed.

◆

During the next several weeks our journey continued with little interruption in the routine of travel, at least insofar as the movement of literally thousands of individuals and their movable possessions could be considered routine. The horde of Emicho's followers slowly wound its way through the valley of the Main River. We did not stop long at any town past which we must travel for always we found the gates closed against us, finding ourselves unwelcome and barred from entry. Word of Emicho's plundering surely had preceded us.

However, this general rebuff satisfied me since I had no wish to witness or be associated in any way with the kind of depredations Emicho had inflicted on the other towns through which he had swept with his host of murderers. Occasionally, though, when we camped, small raiding parties attempted to breach the defences of any proximate town but without success except in those unwalled villages where the inhabitants had already fled before our arrival. The Lord of Leisingen did not sanction these raids nor participate in them but neither did he discourage them. I believe that these excursions gained the participants little, execrable as was the endeavour, preying on the poor.

Thus, in the main uneventfully, we proceeded through the long, narrow valley, walled in—claustrophobically to my mind—by steep hills on either side. We turned up a tributary of the Main, passing by Nurnberg, then over the high hills and through the mountain pass behind Regensberg to the valley of the Danube. From there we made our way downward past Vienna and the other many villages whose names now escape me, until at last we reached the borders of the lands ruled by the Hungarian king, Coloman.

The boundary of Hungary represented for me, although I was unaware of the fact at that time, a dividing line of time as well as place. By this I mean that the course of my own future altered by being there with Emicho, sundered me from my past, and had I not been dragged along by Drogo as he straggled along to Hungary with the so-called pilgrimage, I might never have left Mainz at all, never experienced the life I afterward lived, a strange and wondrous life filled with adventure enough for a hundred such simple men as me. In a way, then, I suppose that I should be grateful to Drogo although I certainly felt no gratitude for my treatment at the time.

Very little of consequence occurred along the journey up the Main River Valley, as I have noted, and thus Drogo's visits to the wagon in which he had installed me were few. Nonetheless, he tendered the possibility that there might yet be events for me to chronicle for him. In the meantime, as I suspected he might, my captor had me read back to him his heady deeds, the admirable events of his life in which he took great pride. At least he thought them so. I reserved my own opinions to myself and sought only to preserve my own head by dutifully retelling his story to him. If I was ever to regain my freedom I must appease him through my literary efforts on his behalf. Thus far, he seemed satisfied.

By now, of course, we were sufficiently removed from the possibility of my escape back to Mainz, in terms of the time and distance that separated me from my old life there, that my captor allowed me free run of the encampment. I was certainly grateful for the opportunity to remove myself from the wagon and breathe fresh air and stretch my legs. No one bothered me as I wandered around the camp each evening when we stopped, although I was not allowed to leave the confines of Drogo's tented ghetto. This sort of segregation appeared normal in military bivouacs and I saw that all of the various factions within the loosely organised army kept to themselves in their own enclosures whenever we stopped to make camp. Thus the army was arranged when we eventually came to rest ourselves on the very edge of the lands of King Coloman.

I knew that we had reached some sort of impasse to our forward progress when the steady plodding of the oxen drawing my *plaustrum* along ceased and did not resume. Drogo's soldiers, when my curiosity and impatience to be moving finally compelled me to investigate, milled around ahead of the baggage train to which my wagon belonged. The foot soldiers stood in a compact group, hundreds of spear tips rising into the air, a pointed forest of branchless, leafless trees. The mounted cavalry ahead of them shuffled back and forth in the hundreds of tiny repetitious fine motions required to keep their mounts under control in a crowd of beasts and men confined to a tight space. Riders and runners went back and forth from the crowd to the unseen forward ranks where rode Drogo and his lieutenants and presumably beyond them to Emicho himself.

I assumed some sort of physical obstacle such as a rock slide or a washed out bridge or other such inconvenience had caused the delay. I settled myself in the doorway of the wagon. There I waited with a loaf of bread and a piece of cheese, enjoying the sunshine and fresh air.

Soon, there came a change in the motion of the sea of horses and men. Like ripples spreading out in waves from a stone thrown into a pond, the soldiers began to disperse from their compact position and it became apparent that the ritualistic routine of setting up camp was underway. This activity confused me for it was barely midday; the army always kept on the move until near dusk before preparing to stop for the night. Before long I learned the reason for the unexpected halt.

A mounted *cnicht* made his slow way through the hustle of camp routine. I watched him come and was surprised when he stopped in front of me. Without dismounting, he addressed me.

"The Lord Drogo requires that you attend him."

His formal and peremptory attitude irked me, I must admit, so that I was slow to respond even in spite of or perhaps because of resenting my powerlessness. The truth is I had grown somewhat complacent with my position in Drogo's following. Dangerously nonchalant, I returned the bread to the table, keeping the cheese, and sauntered back outside. The *cnicht* scowled at me and wheeled his horse around. I hastened to follow him. Worrying now that I would lose him in the press of the crowd of soldiers, I grasped the hairs of his horse's tail and hung on tightly. The crowd parted and I followed in his wake relatively easily, stealing a bite of the cheese from time to time. Presently, we reached his master's side.

Drogo glanced side-long at me, angrily, contemptuously. What had I done to offend? I was not sure at this point. His red-rimmed boar's eyes glared at me for a moment then he looked away.

"Get him a horse," he growled to one of his men.

Immediately I felt panic rise burning in my throat. I had never ridden a horse in my life. I was no soldier, schooled in equestrian skills. I supposed though that shaming myself with a lack of ability in that area was probably the least of my worries anyway. So what if Drogo and his men should laugh at me? Far better that than some horrible death riding into battle in another pointless raiding expedition. Was I to ride along with him then, to be an eyewitness to his military greatness and proficiency that I might more accurately chronicle it later? I hoped that that was not what he had planned for me.

The horse arrived and it was hugely awesome. I trembled at the thought of sitting atop it. I blanched when the groom handed over the reins to me for I had no idea even how to climb up onto it. Where was the ladder? Or the stool?

"Come, come," said Drogo, impatiently as I stood there stupidly staring at the saddle and wondering how I should arrive on its summit. "Mount, boy."

I must step into the stirrup in order to mount the horse, I knew that much. But which foot first? I calculated that I could thrust my right foot into the stirrup and then throw myself on my belly across the animal's back. To that effect I hiked up my robes and started to reach up with my right foot. But I was completely unbalanced by the height of the stirrup and on account of my legs becoming entangled in the hem of my robe. I fell flat on my back.

Amid loud guffaws Drogo, truly angry, screamed at one of his men to throw me into the saddle if need be. "*Just get him mounted*", he shouted, his droopy moustache flecked with spittle. As a consequence of his impatience I found myself lifted and hefted bodily atop the horse, facing backward. I cautiously turned myself around and hung on to the reins handed up to me by the smirking groom, hung on for my soul, and hoped the war-horse knew where it was going.

Apparently it did since it followed along obediently after the horses ahead of it.

Drogo led the company of about a dozen of his lieutenants and guards and myself. We rode around the bulk of the army, across a low flat area along the river bank and up a low, gorse-covered rise, away from the pilgrimage's main body. Ahead of us, over the rise, the landscape dropped once more to the water's edge. I saw from this vantage point that the river forked here. To the right was the Leyta River which converged on the Danube River further down-river. And on one branch of the fork, to the left, crossing the Danube, stood a wide stone bridge, overshadowed by a massive stone fortification blocking the way into the Hungarian lands. Emicho and various other lords in his train had gathered there for some kind of consultative meeting.

Drogo kicked his horse into a trot and hurried down the low hillside toward the group near the bridge before the fortress, not wanting, I supposed, to be left out. Sighing to myself, already weary and sore from the unaccustomed method of transport, I grimly kicked my own steed into motion. I thought my eyes would bounce out of my head and my backbone would be jarred to pieces by the hurried, awkward motion of the animal I perched upon, my comfort not in the least regarded by it, as it hurried mindlessly after its four-legged fellows, not wanting, I supposed, to be left out, either.

◆

The emissary had already arrived when I rode up with Drogo's party to where Emicho and the others had congregated. Earlier, some confusion apparently arose when no one within either the Hungarian or the Alemaigne parties who met at the bridge spoke the other's language. Needless to say, suspicion and defensiveness were high. However, the swarthy man, of dark complexion and tight-curled black hair, now speaking, used the Latin tongue.

I understood immediately why Drogo had called for me. Since he himself could not read, naturally he could not understand spoken Latin, either, and this was the only language seemingly common to both groups. Drogo did not wish for any of the other factions within Emicho's army to possess information firsthand that he also could not possess.

This of course would have left him at a disadvantage, not to mention feeling vastly insecure in his position among the others since they would know what was occurring while he did not. Drogo despised others who knew what he did not. Obviously, I was here to translate for him. He confirmed this when next he spoke to me as I sat listening to the conversation between the Hungarian envoy and the Black Lord's interpreter.

"What are they saying, boy?" he snapped at me.

"The dark man says that we are not permitted to cross the bridge into the lands of King Coloman," I replied, hesitantly, not certain if this information would send Drogo into one of his characteristic rages.

He merely snorted. Even if he could not understand the words, I am certain that even Drogo, not the most sensitive nor intelligent of men, clearly comprehended the dark man's arrogant disposition.

I continued translating the words of Coloman's emissary.

"He also says that this is a result of recent experiences with barbarians, that is the word he used, my lord," I added quickly, lest he blame me for the insult, "barbarians from the West following a disgusting, dirty, little priest; he must mean Peter," I appended, unnecessarily, receiving an impatient scowl from Drogo, then continued without further unappreciated commentary, "...and later a horde led by an Alemaigne *cnicht* that fell on innocent peasants and townspeople in a most rapacious and greedy fashion. Therefore, we are to return to our own lands or find some other way to Constantinople. He does not care how this might inconvenience us." This last statement by the emissary was a response to a protest by Emicho's own translator, a young, handsome nobleman dressed in chainmail, to the effect that we would have to back-track all the way to Italy to make the crossing from Brindisi into Byzantine territory. I had no idea how far this might be.

Emicho's translator then spoke his lord's mind.

"The Lord Emicho's man says that his liege lord harbours no ill will toward the people of Hungary but that he will not bear such an insult as to be turned away by the king when he, Emicho, has the sanction of the Blessed Father, Urban himself, to cross all of Christendom to wage Holy War against the Saracen."

Translating from Emicho's man, who was only a few horse lengths away from us, a relatively short distance, was necessary since we could not hear Emicho's own words to his translator. However, the Black Lord's interpreter spoke loudly, and was thus easier to hear, in order that the Hungarian, who sat astride his horse in the middle of the bridge, might hear over the greater distance separating the two.

"He warns the emissary of the consequences of denying us our crossing."

We waited for further words from the dark man who simply sat and stared at Emicho for a long moment. When at last he did speak, even I, though convinced of the folly and bitter hypocrisy of the Black Lord's pilgrimage, found his words insulting.

"You make it obvious that all Alemaigni are ignorant as peasants and as filthy and stupid. You are forbidden to pass. Return whence you came. This audience is concluded."

With those dire words he wheeled his horse around and clattered away through the crowd of mounted soldiers lining the track to the fortress behind him. I sat dumbfounded as the blood rose to my cheeks. Then I must have turned white with the realisation of the implications of the envoy's pronouncement.

"What has happened? Why is he leaving?" Drogo demanded.

"He says we cannot cross through his lord's lands and he does not wish to discuss the issue further," I translated, weakly.

"Well, Emicho will not stand for that. And neither will I," he stated vehemently.

And then with a smile of cruel joy he pushed his horse closer to his leader. Voices arose from the front line in indignation and rage, Drogo's vociferous among them. Emicho's face twisted into an evil, satisfied smirk, his black eyes glowing, apparently unmoved by the dark man's words. But I knew in my sinking heart that he had accepted the challenge. One way or another he would pay out his desire to cross that bridge; he would pay in coin minted in blood; he would pay in coin cast in the image of his own vicious revenge.

◆

Smoky flurries of motion. Blurring, burning colours. Noise. Shouting, in tandem with the clang of metal on metal, sword on sword, screams from both human and horse. The sound of wood splitting and cracking coming from a thousand spears breaking against bloodied ground, against stone, against bone. Bone breaking with the sound of splintering wood or with the sound of a stone smashing through thinly frozen water. All the horrifying, sickening, momentary impressions of battle heaving forth like vomit, raw and burning and poisonous in my memories of the event. I shudder to remember such things.

I waited in the camp over the hill beyond the bridge, of course. I was no soldier, had never raised arms against a foe or ridden a war horse over the broken body of an enemy. I was merely Drogo's clerk. A prisoner of no means and little value. I was stored away like a forgotten flagon of wine, to be taken out only when the celebrations of victory made me useful again. Drogo kept me waiting there in the camp for six weeks while June passed into August.

In the meantime, Emicho and his war host were not idle. In skirmish after skirmish at the stone bridge, the Hungarians kept the Alemaigni at bay, refusing them access to the farther bank though Emicho's men tried; nothing fought in the way of a serious pitched battle but Emicho's soldiers in their turn prohibited their foe from gaining ground against them, refusing to be driven away. About two furlongs from the stone bridge the army began construction of their own wooden bridge.

This became the objective for the Hungarians. Every few days they would sally forth in their hundreds from the castle of Wiesselburg, cross the river and through their own blockade to attempt to bring this activity to an end. However, the path to the bridge and that to our encampment were always well protected and the Hungarians gained little ground. They threw fire arrows at the new bridge, which of course was being built from timbers cut in the nearby forest but Emicho's men built the bridge components in sections and dragged them into place all at once, throwing up shields to protect the men and horses engaged in these efforts. Besides, they would have needed a thousand archers' burning arrows to set those logs alight, green and wet as they were.

So the Hungarians' efforts to impede the process were largely in vain; more a hindrance than a real impediment to progress. Within a month the new crossing was in place. Unable to defend both bridges at once, the Hungarians lost in their efforts to keep the Alemaigni on the far side of the river, falling back to the protection of their fortress.

During those several weeks of combat after our arrival at the river crossing, being indisposed to idleness, I kept myself as busy as I could. None now attempted to keep me within Drogo's compound since all were too busy with the little war against Hungary to bother with me. I found myself free to wander around the huge military encampment.

In truth, I needed something to keep me occupied in order that my mind did not dwell on the possibility of Emicho's defeat. I did not want to think about the consequences of that eventuality since I was sure that Drogo, if needs must, would abandon me without a thought. I hated to think that I was so utterly dependent on his good will and, yet, he had none toward me. I depended on his protection but I knew he would not safeguard me. As much as I wanted to see Emicho humiliated and defeated, may God forgive me the vanity of vengeance, I prayed for the success of his endeavour. And while he fought, I contributed to his efforts in my own small way.

I sought to employ the medical skills I had learned with the Benedictine in Mainz, and as I explored I found a camp chirurgeon working alone in one of the large tents close to the battlefield treating the broken bones, the stab wounds, the hacked-off body parts, the cuts and sprains, all the major and minor wounds of soldiers. To him I volunteered my services. He expressed joy and relief that I had found him for his burden was a heavy one and he had no assistant. And, indeed, I learned much from him about dressing wounds in the field and field surgery which served me in good stead later. Thus, the relationship was mutually beneficial.

Every few days, proportional to the frequency and length of battles, a dozen or so men were brought in or walked in under their own power, for treatment of a variety of wounds. In my first day assisting Waldebert, the chirurgeon, for example, we treated a score of men with arrow wounds in a variety of places on their bodies. They had been involved in the initial stages of the bridge-building and had been attacked from across the river by a company of Hungarian archers.

Waldebert used a technique I had not actually seen before since I had never assisted in treating wounds inflicted by arrows during my stay at Mainz. He explained to me that the important thing was to extract the arrow head without doing further damage to the flesh, that if the arrow was simply pulled out of its lodging it would rip and tear at the body and damage the victim even further. In order to extract the steel tip neatly and cleanly he used an instrument, nearly identical to that I had seen on Brother Ambrose's table in the cathedral on the day of Emicho's attack, like large scissors but with two sharpened spoons at the ends instead of the blades normally found in such an instrument.

He inserted the spoons on either side of the arrow head after first determining its aspect by pulling gently on the shaft and observing the lines of the skin, which clearly showed the outline of the flat cross-section of the end closest to the shaft. Then he gouged as quickly and as neatly as possible to cut the flesh around the arrow head and closed the spoons over it thus extracting it without tearing the body further. Finally, he cauterised and stitched up the hole produced by this operation.

I eagerly watched the chirurgeon's technique. Later, I made notes about what I had seen and drew sketches of the technique so that I would not forget what I learned that first day. In fact, I ended up repeating this operation so many times, though not always with the hoped-for success I must admit, that I became somewhat expert in its execution my-self. After overseeing a number of my arrow extractions Waldebert left me to carry them out alone while he busied himself with the many other patients who came to him for medical assistance during the bridge-building and, later, the siege of Wiesselburg.

Wiesselburg. That name, that place, I remember well. For Wiesselburg was Emicho's undoing. The first day's as-sault against the fortress marked the beginning of the end of Emicho's armed pilgrimage to the east, although, of course, no one knew that at the time. They all thought the plunder they would gain by taking the castle would finance their fur-ther progress to the East. Greedy fools. It is truly written that "the triumph of the wicked is short and the joy of the hypocrite but a moment."

At first the Black Lord's army made great progress. Within the week construction had begun on the wooden bridge that would eventually completely span the river. This work continued each day for some weeks despite the constant, bloody harassment from the Hungarians on the opposite bank and despite their many sorties from the fortress against the pilgrim army. Then, with an admirable and uncharacteristic display of co-operation, the disparate factions within the army co-ordinated their efforts and took the stone bridge away from the enemy.

I remember well the taking of the bridge that August morning.

In the grey light of early morning I rose from my cot near the doorway. I had taken to sleeping in the *infirmarium* tent since I seemed always to be there anyway and Drogo's wagon was lonely and boring and food deliveries sporadic at best; the Lord of Nesle gave little thought to my well-being. Indeed, he never once looked for me during that entire time spent along the shores of the Danube. The patients we tended, however, were more than generous with gifts of food and wine in their gratitude.

On that early morning in August the medical tent was still since all the previous day's wounded had been attended and had gone but for a few patients remaining with wounds more serious but who rested quietly. Outside, a dense fog spread over the ground and smothered the low hills around the encampment. The chilly air hung thick with moisture. In the distance I heard low bangs and thumps and realised that the final stages of the bridge-building must be underway. I had to admire the cunning initiative of placing the last portion of the bridge under cover of the fog. The enemy's archers would have extreme difficulty fixing a target through the dense blanket of airborne vapours.

I climbed to the top of one of the low hills overlooking the river, slipping and cursing the wet grass all the while. There was little to see at first. But then, through the mists below, ghostly figures moved, churning the white clouds into tortured motion, and were quickly consumed themselves as the hazy whorls and tattered strands congealed again into a cottony cloak of concealment. Snatches of conversation drifted up to me, no less fragmented than the men's appearance. Evidently, the soldiers below attempted to work as silently as possible so as not to alert the Hungarian garrison to their activities, although, to my mind, the fact that they would try to complete the final stage of the bridge crossing on this day seemed self-evident and thus impossible to hide since predictable.

Remarkably, though, the Hungarians seemed to have no idea that the final act of union was underway. The last pre-built section was rolled into the water with a scraping sound of wood on wood and a huge splash and then, only then, did the enemy garrison become aware that something was afoot. The entire performance would have been laughable were it not so tragic in its consequences.

I could see a commotion on the far side of the stone bridge. A flurry of black shapes disturbing the fog. A runner dispatched to Wiesselburg, lost to sight in a moment. A cluster of shapes congregating and moving toward the new bridge.

But all this took time, and by then the gap was closed. Emicho's soldiers ran across on foot from their hiding places crouched low on the river bank. Then the clash of metal on metal, shouts and curses flung freely, a familiar cacophony, the raucous melody of warfare. I could see the Hungarians tighten their defences at the stone bridge expecting a full-scale assault but only a score of Emicho's horsemen sat astride their mounts waiting on the moment of need. Meanwhile, men on foot continued to pour across the new bridge to the far side.

Shortly, the small force of Hungarians sent to block this progress lay dead on the riverbank. At least, they were no longer visible to me through the fog. Then the Alemaigne horde fell upon the defenders on the fortress side of the stone bridge, outflanking them. At the initiation of that attack, the horsemen launched themselves across the bridge.

Those defenders who did not bolt at all speed toward the castle died where they stood. Completely surrounded and outflanked, there was no defence. Foolishly they died, those who stayed and did their duty. Emicho took no prisoners.

The river and its crossings were ours. Much good it did us. We should have moved on but we remained. Emicho and his followers wanted their revenge and their plunder.

Wearily, I stood up from where I had been sitting in the damp grass and made my way down the hill, thinking that I should cross over and tend to any wounded needing medical attention on the opposite bank. I wondered at my reaction: weariness now rather than the revulsion I had earlier felt at such wholesale harvest of human life. Perhaps I was becoming inured to slaughter. I do not know. I only knew then a feeling of the inevitability of such suffering and the weariness stemmed, I think, from the repetitive nature of an activity, war and its butchery, that necessitated massive, ofttimes futile, intervention into the human body and its natural, God-given life processes. War held no dread for me now only weary resignation to the difficult work ahead. I had a fair idea what I would find on the other side of the river.

A week passed. A heavy rain set in, curtain upon curtain whipped by the wind. Sometimes I could barely see the castle on the rise between the rivers. The heavens wept down upon the folly of men while the constant downpour engendered a feeling of hopelessness and frustration in me. The rain was an ill omen for our endeavour.

The *infirmarium* tent roof leaked and I found myself forever moving my work table about within its enclosed space attempting to find a dry place to do my work, grinding herbs and preparing medicaments. Waldebert's supply of medicinal herbs dwindled and this forced us to ration them, much to the discomfort of our patients. The only good point about the situation, if it could be called good, was that the wounds of those who came to us for help were either of such a minor nature that they required only stitches or a field dressing or sling, or they were deadly and required little attention since our limited skills could not help the afflicted. In other words, our patients either went immediately back into their lords' service on the battlefield or they died. I grew very tired tending to the constant stream of suffering soldiers and my own exhaustion only added to my frustration and my resentment toward both Emicho and Drogo.

What did the lords hope to accomplish with this siege? Taking the castle would not speed our progress to Constantinople. Indeed, if anything, matters would be made worse since King Coloman could not stand idly by and let this marauding host traverse his kingdom unchallenged. Perhaps the Black Lord felt that he would instil such fear in the Hungarians that they would dare not challenge his right to pass. Only a madman would believe that, though I had doubted Emicho's sanity from the first day our paths had crossed. He spared no effort, whatever his motivations, in trying to take the fortress of Wiesselburg.

During the period in which the construction of the alternate bridge took place, construction also began on several siege engines. Hitherto unaware of this project, I learned from Waldebert, who was very attuned to the camp gossip, that a contingent of woodcutters had been sent into the forests on the hillsides above the valley floor to cut timber to this purpose. Then teams of horses and oxen dragged the logs below where the building of *onagers*, movable towers and battering rams commenced. These war machines now rolled heavily and noisily past the encampment, the men cursing the teams of oxen pulling them, cursing the thick mud and the sluggish progress of the equipment, across the stone bridge and into place below the castle walls.

The *onagers* truly represented a marvel of engineering, the more so since I had never before, though ofttimes since, seen them in operation. Much like those in use by armies generally, I suppose, they consisted of heavy timber frameworks with a large, padded wooden beam joining two uprights and a long pole ending in a large sling from which to hurl stones or other missiles or indeed anything one wished to hurl at an enemy. I have even seen the decapitated heads of enemy corpses flung over an opponent's defences, though that was not done at Wiesselburg. The pole was winched down flat with ropes and then released from its bonds to hurtle upward, slamming into the padded cross bar which checked its momentum. The load in the sling, unchecked, hurtled on to its destination, there to create havoc, hopefully, among the foe. The most difficult part of its operation lay in calculating the arc of the load's flight, how far it would travel and where to fling the load so that it would do the most damage.

The towers and battering rams, though much more simplistic, were the mainstay of any force attempting to breach fortified defences. One simply tried, with brute force and little elegance, to batter down the gates with the ram. Difficult and heavy work to be sure. The towers could be rolled near the walls and from them arrow fire launched within the fortifications or trundled in tight to the walls from where men attempted to run from the tower to the wall hoping the defenders did not cut them down as they did so. This was a very dangerous proposition since usually only one man might cross at a time and thus the first position, though considered an honour, was also the most hazardous. Scaling ladders usually complemented the tower which, in my experience, is often utilised as a mobile archery platform in defence of soldiers attempting to scale the walls in the more conventional fashion.

At Wiesselburg, Emicho had some difficulty with his siege machines. The ground approach to the walls was difficult since the earth had been hard packed for some time in the summer heat and now that the rains fell the surface had become slick and slippery. The heavy assault equipment bogged down in deep ruts, slowing progress. A ditch, about the depth of a man standing, also surrounded the castle on three sides, the fourth backing onto a swamp which provided natural defence from that direction, and this trench the soldiers must needs fill in to effect a crossing for the siege engines. The army lost a day or two simply moving the equipment close enough to the fortress to be effective while the defenders contented themselves with simply waiting for the assault to begin, occasionally harassing the Alemaigni with arrows or spears or verbal abuse the latter of which no one on our side of the walls understood anyway. Once in place, the Alemaigne attack was most energetic.

For several days the three onagers Emicho had built bombarded the defenders with rocks, flaming bundles of wood, and offal. The effects of these efforts, though, often were hard to judge since the damage they did behind the walls we could not see. From two siege towers set up near the walls archers continually fired arrows at the defenders inhibiting the latter's efforts with arrows of their own and rocks and boiling oil to counter the work of those manning the ram below in an attempt to batter down the gates. I found the depth and precision of Emicho's efforts to take the fortress quite amazing but while I admired his ability to unite and co-ordinate such an attack, at the same time I abhorred his principles and his purpose.

I am certain that, given time and soon, he would have successfully taken Wiesselburg. The defenders had no way out of his encircling assault, trapped as they were by the convergence of the two rivers behind them, no way to bring in supplies or get word out to plead relief from their king. Even without the siege machines, Emicho might simply have waited them out, starved them into surrender. I began to believe that he would take the castle for after a week of battering the walls with huge stones the fortifications began to crumble in places so that a definitive breach seemed imminent and inevitable.

Then the word came that King Coloman and his army were on their way and everything changed.

I am not sure to this day where that rumour, for such it was since the King did not come to Wiesselburg, began.

I believe that the story was in fact a clever ruse on the part of the defenders of the fortress. I remember that a small party of a half dozen merchants appeared one day along the eastern road claiming to be Viennese recently come from Buda-Pest. I myself did not speak with them but, as I noted, Waldebert was very well informed with respect to camp gossip and the explication was his.

I watched the merchants pass over the stone bridge and then cautiously, and I think wisely, give the camp itself a wide berth. I wondered, if they were indeed merchants as they claimed, why they had no armed escort. They felt very confident of the roadway it seemed to me. Apparently, some of the soldiers loitering along the bridge waiting for their turn at the ram or the tower, questioned the merchants and discovered the intimidating news concerning the imminent arrival of the King's army. Remarkably, Emicho's forces quite panicked at the report. That is probably what the fortress defenders hoped would happen when they sent their counterfeit merchants out unseen from some rear postern gate.

In the event I was in the *infirmarium* tent with Waldebert as I had been every day since the siege began, for the wounded never stopped coming. That day a foot soldier came in who required stitches to his thumb which he had laid open to the bone while sharpening his spear's head. As I examined the depth of the wound and applied pressure to staunch the flow of blood, the brave warrior whimpering all the while, we suddenly heard shouting and the pounding of horses' hooves through the little vale which led from the stone bridge through to the encampment between the rolling hills of the river valley. I quickly finished wrapping the soldier's thumb in a tight bandage and hurried to the tent's entrance.

A moment later my patient pushed me to one side and was gone. I turned to look at Waldebert who simply shrugged and carried on with his work pulling the several broken teeth of a man who had been in a drunken fist-fight with one of his fellow soldiers. He seemed not to feel the pain of Waldebert's pliers worrying the yellow stumps of his teeth.

Wondering what could be happening to cause this sudden flurry of activity, I climbed up the hillside in order to see down across the Leyta River and the Danube and on the farther shore, the fortress. To my surprise I saw that the army had abandoned the siege. A few men still clambered about the mobile towers though it appeared they attempted to abandon them as well. I watched as a man fell from one of the towers pierced by a spear thrown from the fortress wall.

Though I had heard by now the rumour that the King came with his army, there was no army in sight and, puzzled as to why this retreat was happening, I turned to look behind me at the camp. I gaped as I saw the compounds of the individual lords in chaos. Horsemen rode around and around in circles apparently trying to induce everyone to decamp, buffeting sluggards with their spears or whacking them over the backs and heads with the flats of their swords. After a few minutes they gave this up and just grabbed what they wanted from the tents or wagons or from peoples' arms and fled in small clumps of riders.

Not all the horsemen fled of course. Some, probably out of a sense of duty or perhaps even just out of simple humanity, stayed to protect those still preparing to flee. At that moment I could seriously see no cause for alarm since no enemy threatened. However, I suppose the looming danger presented by the King and his forces made them wary and provoked the decision to abandon the siege and find a more defensible position of their own. I did not know then that Emicho not only abandoned the siege and with it his war machines but indeed abandoned the pilgrimage entirely and fled for his home in Leisingen.

I looked for the Black Lord in his compound. At first I did not see him but shortly I saw him stride out of his huge tent and leap on to the back of his horse. Evidently he had not himself given the order to leave because I could hear him shouting in fury to those around him to rally to him and to ride to protect the bridge crossings. His own men, to their credit, did gather about him and they all rode in a group through the vale toward the river, those horsemen Emicho left behind in the camp already fleeing, only to be met by a mass of armed foot soldiers and horsemen from the fortress who had taken advantage of the disorder to charge out to attack the pilgrim army.

The clamour of battle reached my ears where I stood on my hilltop outpost as the two groups fell into one another. Then another group of riders emerged from the garrison across the river to circle behind their comrades toward Emicho's temporary wooden bridge. Seeing this, some of the Black Lord's men split off from the main group and attempted to protect the crossing. They were too late. By the time they reached the other bridge two furlongs away, the Hungarian defenders had already begun to pour across onto the near shore.

How ironic, I thought, that they should use Emicho's own flanking tactics against him now. Now his forces were split in two. Both parties of pilgrims were outnumbered by the respective groups of Hungarians against whom they fought.

Gradually, the two groups of Germans were forced back together again and into the vale. Then the Hungarian forces split into three, one holding the Alemaigni bottle-necked in the vale and the other two flanking them by riding up the hillsides on either side of it, some no more than a hundred yards from where I stood watching. From there they unslung bows from their saddles, a tactic I had not seen before—which is not odd since up to that time I had seen little of military activity beyond my recent experiences with Emicho—and began raining showers of arrows down into the massed pilgrims. Few actually died from this attack since their mail coats were proof against the arrows but the occasional arrow pierced a man here and there, in the eye or in an unprotected or weakened joint in the armour. Emicho gave a signal to retreat and his force wheeled back up the vale.

Straight into a mass of foot soldiers marching to their lord's aid. I had not seen them massing for the attack since I had been so preoccupied by the spectacle on the far end of the vale. Nor had any of the horsemen known they were coming for as they rode up through the vale toward the encampment the entire company was thrown into total chaos. Clearly, the footmen saw the panic among the riders approaching them and they themselves whirled and fled, many of them pitching heels over spearhead as the riders thundered through their ranks, not pausing for a moment, still fleeing before the Hungarian mounted archers. Emicho slashed and hacked with his sword at his own countrymen as he pounded by, his only intent to fly as quickly as possible from that place.

I watched, astounded, as he and all his followers galloped through the encampment and continued to gallop until they had disappeared beyond the rolling hills in the valley of the Danube, heading west, back, I learned later, toward their homes. Then the Hungarians poured into the encampment from the hills in a vengeful flood of pounding hooves and flashing swords, preceded by flights of whistling arrows, delivering red death everywhere into the midst of the chaos.

I heard hoof beats behind me and turned just in time to narrowly duck a spear thrust from a Hungarian horseman that would have taken me in the throat. As he rode past, failing to steal my life with his spear point, he whirled the shaft in a flying circle and its butt slammed into my face. I saw it coming, could not avoid it and knew in the moment of awareness that the horseman had me after all. That realisation is the last thing I remember before consciousness fell away from me like daylight before the night.

◆

In the night I awoke. My head felt as though it was on fire and blood had dried on my chin. I had bitten the inside of my lip for it was now swollen and it blazed as sullenly painful as my jaw. For a few moments I lay there in the wet grass, disoriented, gazing at a midnight black sky glinting with steel-bright stars, wondering why I was still alive. Surely the Hungarian horsemen should have returned to kill me? They must have forgotten me on that hilltop away from the main camp. I would need something for my pain and food to fill the emptiness of my belly so I stood and began to walk, somewhat less sure-footed than usual, down to the encampment or to what was left of it. I hoped something of it still remained.

A full moon hung in the black sky about three handspans above the hills to the southeast. I could see clearly the fortress of Wiesselburg bulking large and coldly hostile somewhat more to the east. The waters of the Leyta, wanly reflecting the moonlight, lay dull and torpid beneath the stone bridge. I walked away from both moon and bridge, intent on finding what remained of the *infirmarium* for there I might find medicine for my pain and, in what remained of Drogo's wagon, I hoped to find food.

I could see the *infirmarium* tent lying on the ground like the flayed carcass of some huge beast, its cloth tattered and muddied. And bloodied. Bodies lay everywhere, on the ground, on the grassy hillsides, atop the deflated tents, darkly staining the one-time shelters with their dearly spent blood. I made the Sign of the Cross and trembled in terror at the sight.

Most of the dead, lying far away from their homes, dead for no reason but Emicho's greedy purposes, most of the cold, lonely dead, were soldiers. Many of them had been stripped of their shoes or weapons or clothing, presumably by the Hungarians as spoils of war. I shuddered at the thought of moving bodies aside to search for medicine in the tattered folds of the *infirmarium*. I could not even begin to entertain the notion of walking further back into that field of murdered souls to hunt for food in Drogo's wagon. It is one thing to see the dead in daylight bereft of life and worldly care but quite another to walk among the dead at night where their tormented shades drifted, waiting to take the unsuspecting living into their realm.

What sight would meet my eyes where the women and children had been camped? I had no desire to see it. I stood there a long time unable to decide what I should do next. At last I was startled aware again by a clanging and then a scrabbling sound somewhere in the dark distance back along the way we had come, towards the West, towards L'Alemaigne. Then I heard the chilling, deathly howling of wolves not so far away as L'Alemaigne and I knew that the time had come to cross the bridge into Hungary.

I had heard that wolves will chase a man and pull him down if he runs away from them. Thus, I walked toward the bridge quickly, rather than running for it as I longed to do, looking over my shoulder constantly, waiting for the lightning-quick lunge and the blood-curdling snarl that would precede the beasts tearing out my belly. Neither came and no wolves followed me across the bridge.

I felt naked and exposed crossing the wide stone span across that flat river in bright silvery moonlight. But then, I reasoned, the fortress stood too far away from the bridge for an archer's arrow to reach me. However, I could not remain on the bridge. It was far too exposed to marauding wolves. I had to get to the castle.

As I crossed over to the east bank of the river and cleared a line of trees growing in a copse along its shores I could see a town in the distance; a town which the fortress of stone probably had been raised to protect. It was far too distant for me to feel comfortable walking there at midnight. Too many wolves.

Besides, I was certain the town guard would not admit me or welcome me at this late hour if they did not attack and kill me. No. Better to remain here and wait until morning. I hoped that I might linger until dawn and then slip away quietly and unseen to the town and perhaps look for a church and a kindly priest who might suggest some means for me to find my way safely home to Mainz.

The only safe place that presented itself to my eyes was up inside one of the siege towers standing forsaken near the walls. But what if there were more dead bodies in the towers? The image painted in my memory of the man with a spear through his guts falling from the lofty height of one of the towers returned and I balked at the thought of entering the tower. Just then a cloud shadowed the moon, all but killing its light, and a wolf howled in the distance and gave me the impetus I needed to climb the closest tower. I ran to it and hauled myself up into its scaffolding and up the ladder to the uppermost platform. Thankfully, there were no dead left guarding the tower.

The walled platform had a thick plank roof for protection from arrows and other projectiles and made an admirable shelter. I lay down on its rough-hewn timber floor, hungry and cold and in some pain, but alive and grateful for it. I vowed to myself that I would remain awake and steal away at the first fire of the dawn before the garrison awoke. But while my spirit was indeed willing to act according to this plan, my flesh was weak.

I awoke to the sun's rays slanting in through the wall boards and a Hungarian spear lightly jabbing me in my ribs. Startled, I shrank back violently and sat up with my hands raised in the air, palms outward.

"*Non ego miles sum*," I exclaimed. "*Non ego miles sum*! I am not a soldier!"

"*Siess! Na ne!*" the Hungarian shouted at me.

I sat silently cursing my weakness and stupidity for falling asleep.

"*Non ego miles sum,*" I said again, this time slowly, thinking that with careful repetition I could make him understand.

"*Gyerunk! Rajta!*" He jabbed me painfully in the ribs once more. "*Siess!*" He added for emphasis, which I did not understand though the gesture he made with his spear clearly illustrated his intent.

I slowly gained my feet. He backed warily into a corner, keeping the spearhead between us and indicating the ladder leading down to the ground.

"*Siess! Fekudj!*"

I saw his point, though I could not understand his language and, not relishing another jab in the ribs, clambered at once down the ladder.

Below, on the ground, more Hungarians waited, clearly curious about what was going on inside the tower. When they saw me emerge from the scaffolding they were surprised, looking me over carefully from toe to tippet. They were all dark men, swarthy of complexion, with slightly slanted brown eyes and dark wiry hair. All dressed similarly with leather breastplates and breeches and swords belted at their sides. None wore a helmet or carried any other weapons.

As I stepped from the platform, my robe caught on a splinter of wood and before I could check myself I had sprawled headlong into the muddy ground. Gales of laughter went round the knot of soldiers at my expense and as I stood up, my face and clothing wet with reddish mud, I insisted once again, "*Non ego miles sum.*" But they only shook their heads and laughed once more.

One of the men, huge and bearded, put his arm around my shoulder and squeezed the back of my neck vigorously. "*Siess*," he said firmly though not unkindly, as I believe, and led me into the castle of Wiesselburg.

As I have previously written, these are the memories I have of that time and those events and those places which I have described. I avow that they are true to the best of an old man's ability to recall such things long past. However, for the remainder of this narrative the reader may rely on a more faithful recounting of events and places, for it was there at Wiesselburg that I first began to chronicle the *res diurni*, the deeds of the day, for no other reason than that I was bored in my captivity. Therefore, read now the words and deeds, humble though they are, of my younger self and I pray that you judge me not too harshly nor vilify that foolish boy I was once.

Deo Gratia

Caput Octavus

VIII Idibus Augustus, MXCVI

The day has dawned bright and cheerful once again, for the third day in a row. My breakfast again, for the third day in a row, is spicy sausage, eggs, cheese and a spiced wine. Every morning I start the day off with a lead weight in my belly. This food.

Still, why should I complain? I am alive. That is something more than I can say for most of my fellow pilgrims.

Wiesselburg is not so bad, really; rather draughty and chilly at night, though they do not stint on the charcoal here and the brazier has so far been refilled each day. I am confined in what must be some kind of store room for there are barrels and pots and other junk piled in one corner and my straw sleeping pallet is in another. There is only a tiny window too small for a grown man to crawl through but which allows the smoke from the brazier to escape and the only entrance is a heavy door which is kept locked from the outside so that I cannot leave.

I have decided to write down what occurs here daily at Wiesselburg Castle for the days are long and I have little else to do. I am a prisoner here. I am not sure what my Hungarian jailers want of me but they treat me reasonably well. I find the fact interesting that since Drogo of Nesle took me from Mainz as his captive scribe my accommodations have become steadily better. First an open peasant wagon and days without food or water, then Drogo's own covered *plaustrum* with food and drink fairly reliable and now a room of my own with a charcoal brazier and two rich meals each day. Yet, notwithstanding the quality of my lodgings, I still have no freedom. I cannot leave the room unless somebody takes me from it.

They brought me here the day they found me asleep in one of Emicho's siege towers outside the garrison's walls, the day after Emicho's armed pilgrimage came to a bloody end. Curse me for a fool, I had thought to slip away unnoticed to the town beyond Wiesselburg and, once there, to arrange some means of getting home to Mainz. Instead, I fell asleep. I was so tired after the battle that drove away Emicho and the rest of his army. I walked out of the fight with only a few scratches, a bloody lip and a sore head but most were not so lucky. Many died there in our camp in the vale beyond the river. They found me in the tower and, rather than kill me, probably more out of curiosity than magnanimity, as I am obviously not a soldier, took me inside the fortress walls to meet the garrison commander.

His name is Scipio or so he says, but I think that is an affectation, naming himself after the famous Roman general, Scipio Africanus, who defeated the Carthaginians. He speaks the Roman tongue, though, so we can communicate at least. I understand nothing of the Hungarian language nor have I found that any of his people speak the languages with which I am familiar, Latin, Greek, Alemaigni, Frankish and Aenglisch, though possibly some do but will not, which makes communication between me and my captors difficult. It was the commander who gave me the sheets of parchment I asked for in order to begin this record. He thought that a noble idea and enthusiastically compared me to Boethius writing the *De Consolatione* as Theodoric's prisoner. Still, the parchment is rough and worm-holed, and barely suitable to the task. I shall just have to make do, though.

Scipio is unimposing for a commander of a garrison, though truly I have not met many commanders of garrisons. In fact, Scipio is the first. He is a short man, the top of his head reaching to about my own eye level and I am not tall, but whenever we talk he makes me sit on a stool so that I have to look up to him as he sits in his chair or paces about, which probably gives him the impression that he is greater in stature than I. In a sense, he is, I suppose, at least from an authoritative perspective.

He wears his hair in a short cut that suggests statues I have seen of Romans important enough to have had busts made of themselves. His hair is dark and springy like most of the Hungarians here and, like theirs, his eyes are brown. His face is clean-shaven, not even a moustache, which is so unlike the Alemaigni custom; Alemaigni, except for many priests, almost always wear long moustaches and beards. Also, he seems a very quick, energetic man, always pacing or drumming his fingers while sitting or with his leg bouncing up and down on his heel in a staccato rhythm. He seems a decent person. And he is very curious about the armed pilgrimage.

I did not meet him the first day of my captivity, for that was Sunday. Scipio is a pious man, so on Sunday he, with his wife and two sons, and a small escort of horsemen, rode into the nearby town for mass. While the town does not boast a cathedral as Mainz does, it does possess a very fine church or so Scipio tells me. A person as important to the town as Scipio is, owing to the fact that he is their protector, inevitably is invited to feast with the local dignitaries there, and they are especially grateful since he routed the Alemaigni; that is what he told me. Thus, he was absent from the fortress for most of the Sabbath Day, feasting with the burghers of the town. How fortunate for him that the siege did not last beyond Saturday or he might have missed a fine meal. As for my own soul, well, I say my prayers, though without benefit of Mass, and try to remember the offices of the Virgin. I am, after all, a prisoner.

Yesterday, the commander summoned me to his presence. A couple of soldiers came and escorted me to Scipio's quarters. These are in the same building where I am kept, although on an upper floor, while I am confined on the first floor near the kitchens. That was about terce, I think. A couple of hours past prime, anyway, for I had already eaten my breakfast of spicy sausage, eggs and cheese and washed it down with a cup of spiced wine. The novelty of the meal on the second day was starting to wear away and by today, well, I am ready for a piece of fruit. And some bread would be nice. Maybe I should ask Lord Scipio about the bread. I will if I remember. He has been very insistent I tell him everything I know about Emicho and his army and I have told him what I know so a little bread in exchange for information seems fair.

He bade me sit on a Roman-style camp stool much like the ones Drogo used. When I was seated, he looked down at me for a long moment then said, objectively, "You are not a soldier."

"No, lord," I replied, and did not volunteer anything further in my nervousness.

"Then you are a cleric or a priest," he stated with some assurance.

I did not want to mislead him and felt the truth would not hurt me so I replied honestly. "Lord, until a few weeks ago I was a clerical student in Mainz at the cathedral."

"Until you joined the army of Emicho," he growled.

"Yes. Well, no, I didn't join him exactly."

"But you are here," he observed dryly. "What do you mean you didn't join him exactly?"

"I was kidnapped, Lord."

"Why should..." he began to ask me, I am sure, what Emicho would want with a clerical student but he changed his mind, saying, "Never mind. Leave that for now. We have heard that an assemblage of armed pilgrims invaded several cities in Lotharingia and murdered the Jews there. Was this the army of Emicho?"

I nodded. Then I explained to him the atrocities committed by the pilgrim army near Mainz and at the city itself where I had witnessed all the horror of the Black Lord's initiative. Then I told him how I had come to be a prisoner of Drogo, Emicho's lieutenant, although I left out the details of the events within the cathedral itself. Even now, I do not like to think about those things that transpired there. Perhaps later I shall write of what occurred but I am deeply pained by the memories.

I tried to make clear to him how much the Jews of Mainz had suffered at the army's hands and how those who had agreed to convert to the True Faith had been humiliated before Emicho's men. I told him how, in the aftermath of the slaughter of the Jews, I had been struck unconscious and then 'borrowed' by Drogo so that I might chronicle the deeds of his life, both before and during the pilgrimage to the East.

That was an experience I could have lived without. Drogo is an abominable human being and so apt a companion for the evil Lord of Leisingen. Still, since Drogo cannot read,

I had no difficulty in abridging the reprehensible details he supplied concerning the things he has done. In the event someone ever reads those words I wrote, I do not want them thinking he is anything less than the foul, violent drunkard I know him to be. I suppose the narrative is lost now amid the ruins of the army left on the field of battle across the river. I don't care. The world is a better place without the knowledge; much comfort may that be to those whose lives Drogo has made a misery or taken away completely.

Scipio had said little during my retelling of my adventures. He only nodded from time to time and encouraged me to go on with my story. Then he spoke.

"So you had no wish to make the journey to the east?"

"I did, lord, but not as a part of that mob. I begged my Lord Rothard to let me go on the pilgrimage but not as a part of Emicho's army. He hadn't even arrived in the Main River valley then and we had not yet heard of him."

"How did you think you would find your way to the East, then? The journey there is long and filled with great hardship. Surely you did not think to travel alone?"

I assumed that Scipio had heard about the Holy Father Urban's request for soldiers to travel to Constantinople to aid the emperor in his fight against the faithless Saracens. I asked him. He had, he said. Had he also heard about the great popular movement led by Peter the Hermit?

"Indeed," he replied in the affirmative with a wry grimace.

I was puzzled by his reaction but I did not ask.

"I asked my Lord Rothard if I might join the pilgrimage of folk from Mainz who would journey to Constantinople to meet Bishop Adhemar but he refused me since I was neither a soldier nor an ordained cleric. He believed I might better serve in my existing capacity as an apprentice *medicus* at the cathedral with a Benedictine monk who was the Archbishop's personal physician. After that disappointing refusal I admit I was taken by the notion of disobeying his command and following Peter the Hermit, though I didn't in the end."

Scipio snorted loudly, looking down on me sitting on my stool. "And be glad you did not," he exclaimed. "What changed your mind about the Hermit?"

I hesitated for a moment, thinking. Peter was a man of God after all and believed vehemently in his own divine mission. I did not know what Scipio thought about that mission and I did not wish to offend him or his notions of piety. But I answered honestly.

"Although I believe that Peter is a very holy man I also think that he does not truly embody the wishes of the Holy Father Urban. He has unrealistic expectations and misleads his followers, who are mostly poor and ignorant people. Also, I believed in the duty I had sworn to my spiritual and temporal liege lord, the Archbishop Rothard; so I stayed." I must admit though that I remembered that my lord had fled the cathedral and abandoned, without a word or a warning, those he was obligated to protect.

The reply seemed to please Scipio. He smiled wryly and nodded.

"Yes, that is what I thought about Peter, too."

"You have met the Hermit, my lord?"

"No, I did not meet him myself but he passed through with his people some time ago. We here in Hungary had heard that armies from the West might come after Pope Urban's call to help the Greek Empire of the East but of course we expected actual fighting men not the pack of filthy peasants and masterless men Peter brought with him; although, to be fair, there were a few *equites* among them. No one of importance, I think."

"They were like a swarm of locusts, eating everything in their path. They passed across our country peaceably enough until they arrived at Semlin, which is on the border of the Greek Empire. They attacked the town and killed thousands for no reason other than their anger at being kept waiting by the Emperor, and all began because of an argument over the purchase of a pair of shoes I am told."

"Another rabble led by a man named Volkmar arrived at Nitra, a town north of here, and began to assault the Jews there but that lawless horde was destroyed and the survivors driven away. And then a third rabble arrived, passing across the same bridge you see before the castle now, that which your Emicho tried without success to cross. I allowed through these men, led by a priest named Gottschalk, on my King's orders but then they began to plunder and ravage so that the King's army was forced to destroy them. After these experiences, the King's reluctance to allow other armies of the West to pass is understandable, is it not? That is why your Emicho was halted at the bridge and refused passage across our land. I shudder to contemplate what horrors he might have attempted had he been allowed to enter."

I understand his feelings perfectly, for I do know, have seen firsthand, what horrors 'my' Emicho is capable of.

I asked Scipio what had become of Peter and his followers.

"They have since been taken under the protection of the Emperor at Constantinople and now await, I presume, the arrival of other armies from the West. They shall wait for the coming of Emicho for some time, I think. He will never be allowed passage through Hungary, that is certain."

I wonder if Emicho will now try some other route to the Greek capital city. There are none but the passage through Italy and taking ship from Brindisi across the strait to Dyrrhachium or Avlona or the journey down the coast of the Adriatic through Dalmatia and Bulgaria and the people of those lands might be no more inclined to grant passage than the Hungarians, especially if they hear about what happened at Wiesselburg or at Semlin. More likely, he will just abandon the pilgrimage altogether, for not much is left of the force he arrived here with and certainly he feels little of real piety or of belief in Urban's purpose. Yesterday, I saw the dead he left lying at the Hungarian border.

Scipio could not recognise Emicho since he had never seen him except from the distance separating the defenders on the walls of the fortress from the attackers on the ground. I am certain that the Black Lord never came close enough to the walls for anyone to truly see his grim, nose-less face or Scipio would have mentioned it. So the commander wished me to identify him among the dead if he could be found, for he intended to set Emicho's head on a pole at the bridge as a warning to others from the west who might arrive later. But I had seen Emicho ride off, abandoning the camp and all within it, after a sortie by the garrison routed his forces.

Still, Scipio had said, after the attack on the encampment by the garrison, the Hungarians had chased after the horsemen and cut more of them down. He wanted to be sure if Emicho was among the dead or had escaped. I really did not want to follow him through that field of death, but I had no choice except to accompany him.

So it was decided, and next day horses were readied and we mounted in the inner courtyard of the castle. I am not a good rider and that was only the second time I have ever ridden a horse. The first was with Drogo when we arrived at the river crossing here and had been turned back by the Hungarians. He had summoned me from the encampment to ride with him and serve as his interpreter. I did well enough then but I was nervous about this second outing on horseback although nothing untoward happened.

As we clattered out through the open gate, I could see where its wood was splintered and buckled from the effects of the battering ram used to try to force it open. As we rode out we avoided chunks of stone and broken blocks lying here and there throughout the courtyard, pieces of wall and missile, debris produced by the impacts of the projectiles hurled by Emicho's *onagers* against the walls. Oddly, I felt guilty somehow, as if in part I was responsible for this destruction.

We crossed the stone bridge, the horses' hooves clattering on the cobbles and then rode onto the soft turf on the farther shore, its surface still marred by the violence of a few days earlier. We rode back across the river over Emicho's bridge and on through the vale and into the field beyond where the remnant of the pilgrim camp lay in the litter and scattered chaos of its destruction. Already, people had been set to the task of dragging the bodies of the soldiers killed in the struggle into rows so that the corpses lined the vale like dead fish laid out for sale on a market table, their eyes staring just as lifelessly and cold.

I knew none of these dead.

Everywhere I could see the evidence of the consequences of Emicho's blundering bellicosity. He and his followers had lost almost everything. The Hungarians, however, profited in this. Scipio must have been very pleased for to him went the greater share of the profits in salvage from the Black Lord's failed venture. His people busied themselves with retrieving what they could out of the ruins of the pilgrimage, gathering up what might be saved for their own use or sale. The tents were folded and piled separately or piled with other rubbish if they were deemed useless, too ripped and tattered to be repaired. There were cooking pots and other kitchen utensils, cups and spoons, jugs of wine and ale and mead, and, wandering freely about, chickens and ducks and goats and cattle, all waiting to be rounded up by the victors.

To the victor went the spoils and to the victor also went the disposition of the dead, in this case at least. On both sides of the track leading to the vale bodies were now stacked two or three deep like firewood. The poor were left alone but the wealthier among the dead had been stripped of valuables, of clothes, of arms, armour, boots, weapons. These were piled near the centre of the camp beside the road.

Grief welled up in me when I saw the evidence of this great folly, this tragic endeavour disguised as holy purpose. I saw children piled up with the others, children who probably had had no understanding of the reasons they had been uprooted from their homes and dragged across countless miles, brought to this place only to die in innocence. Just as I had been unwillingly uprooted and now faced an uncertain future, a future that might hold only imminent death as well.

We rode on through the vale of death continuing to ride for several furlongs down the road. Occasionally dead soldiers and non-combatants lay along the track, as yet not unburdened of their valuables for the scavengers sent out from the fortress had not reached them. Scipio asked me several times if any of the dead might be identified but so far I had seen none I knew.

Then we reached a spot along the way in the midst of some trees where perhaps some of Emicho's men had thought they might turn and block the advance of their pursuers for the path was narrow and bounded by tightly growing vegetation on either side where one might not pass around the road except if he pushed his way forcefully and slowly through it. At least a dozen dead men lay on the ground there and several horses which had died under their masters. One of the mounts had the broken shaft of a spear protruding from its neck immediately below the lower jaw which, probably driven into its brain from underneath, had killed it. I could only imagine that the horse had reared up in panic and then taken the spear thrust from a soldier standing on the ground. All the dead I identified as Alemaigni by their dress and arms. And one I knew. I dismounted to look more closely at him.

One of Drogo's chief lieutenants, Odo, who had been in the tent the first night I met with Drogo. He lay where he had fallen, in the middle of the track, his guts spilling out all over the road. Somebody had sliced through his expansive belly under the too-tight leather breastplate he wore and opened his viscera to daylight. Now, the coils of his intestines had shrivelled and blackened and flies had begun to lay their eggs in the offal. His eyes held a look of surprise and horror, the expression he wore when he first realised his death had found him, the debt of his lifetime's deeds repaid to him at last. I certainly felt no regret at his death. I could not grieve for the man. Instead, my hatred and the pain of all the losses I had seen over the past few months because of his master welled up in me and I spat on his corpse. Spat again.

Then I knelt and pulled the broadsword from the stiff claws of his fingers and unbuckled the belt around his body with the sword's scabbard attached to it and tugged the belt from under his bloated corpse. These I kept to remind me of all that I had endured as a result of Emicho and his followers taking the cross. Lord Scipio watched but said nothing, nor did he object to me taking the sword.

I had not found my personal captor, but only one of his lieutenants; Drogo and the Black Lord himself were no-where among the dead. If any deserved to die here it had been the Lord of Leisingen and his miserable captain. But they escaped their deserved fates and that must be God's will. Not mentioning Drogo, I told Lord Scipio that Emicho was gone, probably even now slinking like a serpent back to L'Alemaigne. He grunted and wheeled his horse, then waited a few paces down the road while I remounted and joined him. We returned to the castle having failed in our mission to find the body of the Black Lord.

VI Idibus Augustus, MXCVI

Death. And smoke. And the odour of burning meat and hair. The dead are gathered in the vale. Piled on great wooden racks constructed to the purpose they have been set alight. The funeral pyres are enormous but this is the most efficient method of disposing of the thousands of corpses before sickness arises in the propinquity of their putrefaction. I watch from the battlements as thick, boiling, black clouds smoke up into the air from the biers as they are set ablaze; one by one the pyres greedily consume the gristle and grease and hair and bone that make up a human being, fire consuming all in a purifying blaze, flaming fingers reaching in supplication to heaven. Even on the fortress ramparts I hear the crackling laughter of the fires devouring everything they surround, happily feeding on the bodies of the dead, jumping from one to the other, at first delicately tasting and then gorging on flesh and bone, father and daughter, mother and son. Now, in my room, I whisper a prayer for these lost souls and send it aloft with the smoke. Does God hear my despairing words to Him? I weep. Alone.

Idibus Septembris MXCVI

I have not written a word since the day of the bale fires for the Alemaigni dead. Now the month of September is half gone. Have I been here so long? What is to become of me? I am no closer either to Constantinople or to returning to Mainz. Lord Scipio does not hold me responsible for any part of the assault on the fortress; still, he will not let me go. Indeed, he lauded my Christian generosity in trying to help the wounded among Emicho's soldiers, even though they were in a sense my enemies, they the wreckers of Mainz, the murderers of my friends; but that is my duty only. For a *medicus*, the duty to heal the sick and help the ailing is as much a liege bond to his profession as that of a *thegn* to his lord in war. There was no value judgement on my part either to offer or to withhold treatment to Emicho's wounded and

I would have done the same for the Hungarians. Brother Piccolo taught me that much, at least.

I think of the Benedictine often and wonder what became of him. Did he die at the hands of Emicho's soldiers, men whose suffering perhaps I eased here at Wiesselburg? That is an irony too bitter to consider. In any case, God's judgement reached them in the end.

I thought my *magister* a fool at the time of the attack on the cathedral for imagining that his medical skills could be of any use to the people trapped within, as he stayed and set up an *infirmarium* inside the besieged building, when I knew absolutely that we would all die that day. Now, I think I understand his reasoning better than I did then. He stayed true to his duty despite the sober certainty of his own death. He was as brave as any soldier on the field of battle defending the last patch of the killing grounds not yet taken by the enemy. For him, the human body was the highest ground to be protected.

Duty. Loyalty. Courage. They seem immutable concepts, and yet they are not unique to those whose glory and reputation comes from seeking out death and destruction in war. Perhaps anyone might be courageous beyond the norm if the circumstances warrant, even in the face of his own death. I pray to St. Luke, the patron of all faithful *medici* and *chirurgi*, that the Brother is well and enjoys continued good health or that if he is dead he is received into Heaven with honour and with praise, for he was a great man, and a pillar of his profession.

I hope he fares better than I, at least. I have never felt so completely alone. Lord Scipio has ordered a small cell in the main hall set aside for me so that I no longer sleep in the store room near the kitchen. This room is actually somewhat smaller than the other but there is a sizeable window from which I can observe the activity within the fortress courtyard.

Not that anything much occurs down there. The *pedites* train each morning in their *ars militarii*, forming shield walls and marching back and forth or forming up with cloth-wrapped swords and stabbing and hacking at each other until they are exhausted from banging on each other's shields. The exercise is rather dull after seeing it more than a few times and I think I have memorised the moves better than some of those involved. Few receive injuries requiring medical intervention so even though that might have offered itself for a diversion it has not materialised. Therefore, I try to occupy myself in other ways.

I am allowed to walk freely about the castle although I am not permitted beyond the walls. At first I received resentful stares from almost everybody but now they seem to ignore me as I take my exercise around the open spaces inside the fortress. There is little to see, though. I am sure that by now I know every weed in the paths and every crack in every stone in the walls.

Life here is made somewhat more bearable by the company of Lord Scipio. Only when I am with him am I able to make myself understood and to communicate with another human being. The Hungarians I have met find difficulty in trying to make out what I am saying to them and they wave me away impatiently so that I have been unable to learn more than a phrase or two of their tongue. And now the commander has been called away to a town to the south taking with him about half of the garrison. So I am left by myself to read the books he has loaned me and endure the loneliness and isolation of my circumstances. I pray to Saint Dismas, the Good Thief, to deliver me from my prison before I go mad with boredom.

Kalendis Octobris MXCVI

Some very heartening news today. Lord Scipio returned to the fortress and with him came not only his own squad of *equites* but a contingent of soldiers and workmen from the army of the Lord Duke Godfroi de Bouillon. I watched from my window as Lord Scipio rode in to the courtyard, at his side a tall, white-faced, dark-haired man. I thought him some other commander of the Hungarian armies perhaps sent to aid in the defence of the fortress should any other Western armies suddenly appear. In this I was mistaken.

Shortly after sext, midday, I was taken before Lord Scipio in his quarters. There, seated in a large, comfortable, cushioned chair sat the dark-haired man I had seen earlier. I made an obeisance to the commander and bowed to his guest and then stood waiting for Scipio to speak.

"My lord Baudoin, this is the young cleric of Mainz of whom I told you," he addressed the stranger in Latin.

Lord Baudoin, judging by his name a Frank, stood up and crossed the room to stand an arm's length away from me, looking directly into my eyes. As he studied me, I in turn studied him, not looking away from him or down at my feet as some do in the presence of their betters. He is a very tall man, standing a head above the commander and half that above my own height. He is thin, though not gaunt, and very pale of skin. I suspect that he has spent much time indoors in study and not out on the hunt or on military campaigning like most men of his noble status. His eyes seem to bear this out for they plainly display great intelligence in their grey-green depths. He looked upon me not unkindly with a slight smile bending his lips. This mutual assessment lasted but a few moments.

"You may sit," he said with a casual flip of his hand toward the stool upon which I customarily sat when meeting with Lord Scipio.

Then he crossed back to his chair and seated himself. Scipio of course, as is his habit, paced about the room restlessly.

I sat, expectant.

"Do you know who I am?" asked Baudoin, addressing me.

"No, my lord, I'm sorry." I knew his name, that was all.

"No matter. I am brother to my lord Duke Godfroi de Bouillon, who leads the army of Lower Lorraine to Constantinople, there to meet the other armies of the West for the re-conquest of the Holy Land."

Duke Godfroi I have heard of. He is an ally, indeed a vassal, of the Alemaigne Emperor, from whom he holds his lands. One of his main holdings, Antwerp, is a day's journey or so immediately west of Bruges where I studied at the clerical school of my father's cousin, Fromond, for several years before moving to Mainz. I remember that the Duke once passed through Bruges, riding with the Comte of Flanders and his son, both named Robert, and I did have a glimpse of him from afar though I do not think I would know him if I saw him again today.

Baudoin's pronouncement of yet another armed pilgrimage bound for the Greek capital did not surprise me. There are many armies on the move lately.

"I am honoured, my lord," I told Baudoin earnestly.

That flicker of amusement returned to his face.

He waved my small courtesy away.

"My lord Scipio tells me that you are here under some interesting and unique circumstances and not entirely of your own wishes. What are your plans, now?"

I gaped at that. The notion surprised me. My plans? I had had no reason, for some time, to think that I would be allowed to make my own plans and I certainly was not empowered to choose my own destiny at this point, captive of the Hungarians as I was. Was I now to be given my freedom, freedom to return to Mainz or Aengelond or to go on to the East? I hesitated, unsure of his meaning.

"I have no plans, my lord," I answered, I hoped equivocally.

"Well, let me then tell you what has occurred with me and of my plans, and perhaps we shall find that our designs may coincide. Hmm?"

"I have travelled with the Duke, my brother, from our family lands in the mountains bordering on the Empire of the Alemaigni and with many of our noble cousins. We arrived at the frontier of the Hungarian country at the crossing of the River Leyta to the south of this fortress and sent some of our number to meet with the representatives of King Coloman at his court to petition for the right to cross through Hungary. A week later the delegation returned with the message that the King would meet with the Duke at a castle called Oedenburg to discuss the matter. There, I met the commander of this garrison and he told me that some siege machines had been left behind by Emicho and he suggested that we might be interested in them for use in the Holy Land, an idea I wholeheartedly embraced since these things are not readily available on such short notice and who knows what we will face in the East? So I have come with some few men and carts and beasts to dismantle these machines and carry them back to Oedenburg for my Lord Duke. As we rode here, Lord Scipio related the tale of the attack on Wiesselburg by the Alemaigne lord, Emicho, and of your own circumstances. I was, of course, curious to see what manner of man you might be, though I did not realise that you would be so young."

"At any rate, I have a proposition for you, young cleric. I find that I am in need of someone with some clerical skills and those skills are not easy to find in the ranks of those men who accompany the armed pilgrimage, at least it is not easy to find a man so skilled who is not already employed by someone else. I suppose I should have arranged for another clerk before ever we left Lorraine but I had thought to fulfil the duties and offices myself and have since found that my other responsibilities constrain my time and I continually fall behind on correspondence, record-keeping and other such trifles as are necessitated by the obligations of a man in my position."

"Now, as Lord Scipio has related to me, you have few choices. You can remain here, for he is happy for your company although as he has pointed out to me you do not speak his people's tongue and will have some difficulty making a place for yourself here; or you can try to make your way back to Mainz by your own means, and the commander has assured me that you are free to do that although you must know the difficulties and the dangers involved in such a fool-hardy attempt; or you may accompany me to the East as my personal clerk."

My mind whirled at this suggestion. I had been in such a hopeless state until then, supposing that I waited for death at the hands of the Hungarians whenever they chanced to tire of my presence, that I had stopped contemplating the possibility of ever regaining my freedom or of having a fu-ture to plan for. How could it be, suddenly, that I was to accompany the Franks to the East in the service of one of its army's great lords, the brother of the Duke of Lower Lorraine himself? I strove to remain calm and not betray my almost boundless happiness at this good fortune.

"Very well, my lord. I accept," I replied as calmly and quietly as I could, though perhaps a trifle too quickly. I am not sure if Lord Baudoin detected the haste for he smiled his enigmatic smile once more and nodded.

"Good. We leave tomorrow at prime. Meet me in the courtyard then with your belongings."

I was dismissed. I fairly danced back to this room, this tiny cubicle, my onetime prison, now simply a place to await a wondrous future. How shall I sleep tonight? Anticipation, impatience to be gone from here, thoughts of new-won free-dom, will make sleep impossible. The Holy Land. I savour the words, roll them on my tongue like precious gems in hand. I am going to the Holy Land.

I am a little bit surprised at my reaction to Baudoin's proposition, the ease of my acceptance of it. I suppose that by now I should feel so displaced that I should want nothing more than to return to Mainz, to the peace and security I knew there before the coming of Emicho; but his devastating arrival has served only to blunt my ambitions at the cathedral. This, I think, for several reasons.

One is that I cannot see myself returning to a place with such foul memories, memories of the deaths of so many friends, Ruth and Yaakob, Ulfrid the stable-master, and probably Brother Piccolo and Brother Ambrose, memories that now sully the good recollections of the times that preceded the coming of Emicho. And I cannot forgive the Archbishop for abandoning us all in the time of our need when he should have remained behind to protect us from Emicho, stayed the slaughter of innocents, for it was in his power to do so. How could I ever again serve such a master? No, Rothard is no longer my lord. He cannot provide any security of life there, that illusion that I trusted in before Emicho came. I will not return to Mainz.

Nor can I return to Aengelond to my father and my family. I have determined to make my own way in the world and I shall do so. In a sense, I have risen far in an instant to serve the brother of a Duke, no less. My father would be proud of this I think. I shall write him a letter and tell him of the events that have befallen me, for by now, surely, he has heard of the events in The Alemaigne lands and I should set his mind at ease that I am still alive and well. But that must wait, unfortunately. Tomorrow, I begin my journey to the Holy Land.

Idus Octobris MXCVI

Much has occurred since I last had occasion to write. I think keeping a regular record of these things now an important endeavour and I am growing into the habit of trying to do so although this does not seem possible for me to do on a daily basis. Still, remembrance serves to give perspective and a distancing from the events as they happened and perhaps a more sober reflection of such things as occur in the interim. I will strive to be accurate at any account.

I met my new lord in the courtyard of the fortress at the time prescribed on a bright, sunny, though cool, October morning. From there we were to ride south to rendezvous with his brother, the Duke. Baudoin's eyes rested for a moment on the sword-shaped bundle slung over my back but he said nothing.

He had provided for a horse for me, a grey dappled mare. By now, after the third such equestrian experience, I have become somewhat accustomed to the beasts although certainly not an expert rider. I mounted proficiently, quickly, and without incident after first bidding my host, Scipio, farewell and thanking him for his most excellent treatment of me.

I did not know then but as is usual with these things Lord Baudoin had in fact purchased my freedom from the commander along with the *onagers* and siege towers and battering rams. He told me so later. I learned that I am worth considerably less than even one *onager*. So, exchanging one kind of captivity for another, though to me it felt like freedom, I rode out with Baudoin and a dozen of his armed men, bound for Oedenburg.

I found the Lord Baudoin a most garrulous and intelligent companion. We discussed many things, not least of which was the armed pilgrimage itself. He asked me to describe to him in detail what I had experienced at Mainz and afterward. I told him what I thought appropriate although leaving out any details of my friendship with the Jews, Yaakob and Ruth, since I could not be certain how my new master would perceive such a friendship and I did not wish him immediately to think me wanting in some aspect of my personality or morals. I knew that I only protected my own interests and safety by doing this but still something itched in the back of my mind reminding me that I was in some way doing a disservice to the memory of my friends, as if through no fault of theirs their lives were something less than my own or they were in some way unworthy of my friendship, though I do not truly, deep in my heart, believe that at all. About Emicho I was most vehement in my vilification of his actions and person.

Then Baudoin surprised me with his next question for I realised he must have sensed something in the manner in which I told my tale.

"Do you think Emicho was wrong to attack the Jews?"

The ground over which we now rode was fairly marshy, following the river as it did. The track was narrow here and difficult for two horses to ride abreast so that one or the other of the two often walked in squishy ground that sucked at its hoofs and threatened to mire the animal in the black muck alongside the path. But the trail led us a shorter route to our destination than if we had stayed on the main way, the road by which the carts and horses carrying the war machines from Wiesselburg would follow.

I answered him cautiously, peering down at the ground to my left so that I might look away from him with the excuse that I watched the track carefully so my mare would not falter. Indeed, I pulled her head back slightly with the reins, slowing her, and falling a little behind Baudoin. I feared for him to see my face or look into my eyes lest my true feelings on the subject be evident, though perhaps they were already obvious to him. I considered my reply for a moment, collecting myself, and then answered as cautiously and emotionlessly as I could.

"Well, my lord, at Mainz I heard Archbishop Rothard read the Holy Father's decree concerning the armed pilgrimage to the East and I remember hearing nothing in the letter of persecution of the Jews of Mainz, or anywhere else for that matter."

By now, I was looking up again and I saw that he had turned to face me directly. He smiled.

"Yes, that is true; there was nothing of the kind in Urban's pronouncement but that isn't what I asked you, was it? What do you yourself think of the attacks?"

Baudoin has a way of looking into your eyes with a deep penetration as though he can read your heart through them, a penetrating manner that forces you to tell him the truth no matter how painful or damning that might be. Seemingly, I could not avoid the truth.

"I think it was wrong. Some of them were my friends."

"Jews? Your friends?" He questioned, incredulously. I do not think he had anticipated my answer nor believed that such a thing, friendship between Christian and Jew, could be possible. "Jews are friends to none but themselves. Money is the only friend a Jew needs."

I said nothing, chewing on my lip thinking that my foolish beliefs had got me into trouble again and not wishing to offend my new lord by contradicting him. Certainly, I disagreed with him. My friends, Ruth and Yaakob were not as he described.

"My Lord Brother, the Duke, used that to good advantage in assembling his army. He promised them protection if they would turn over their gold to him. He also threatened to look the other way should anyone attack them if they did not pay him the money he demanded. A neat bit of blackmail, neh?" He laughed heartily.

I said nothing. I thought little good of his brother's policy because it was just another example of the strong taking advantage of the weak; a practise I had begun to see defined the deeds of nobles in many lands, exploiting those too weak to defend themselves, those people the nobles should be protecting not abusing. Instead, I dared asked a question of my own, mainly just to change a subject of conversation that disheartened me.

"Is the Duke's army large, my lord?"

"With the help of Jewish money, very large, indeed," laughed Baudoin. "Of course, my brother also sold two of his holdings, Stenay and Rosay, both on the River Meuse, to raise more money for the enlargement and supply of his army, our army. As a result, thousands of *equites, milites* and *pedites* tarry at the border of the Hungarian lands awaiting word from the King and then we shall cross to the land of the Greeks and on to Constantinople."

I was impressed by this news. Surely the Lord Godfroi's army was as large, if not larger than, that of the Black Lord, Emicho. I had brief visions of the wealth and rank of my new master and of how my own fortunes might be advanced in his service but those daydreams quickly vanished like a wisp of fog in bright sunshine since I have examined more closely the truth of my position. What right do I have to expect anything grand? I am merely a lowly clerk, bought for the purpose of undertaking the tasks too drudging for Baudoin himself to perform. Still, I hope that something good will come of this new association. Certainly one good, and of great import, is that I will get to see the Holy Places. Hopefully, I will return to tell the tale.

"May I beg another question, my lord," I asked him deferentially.

"Please," he responded politely.

"Well, Lord, I am wondering how far it is to Jerusalem. And also, why it is, well, I understand that the quest to liberate the Holy Lands is an important one, but as I recall, the Holy Father Urban did not specify that particular goal in his letter to the ecclesiastics and nobility last year, so why are we going there if the Pope has not required it of us?"

"Those are two questions," he stated dryly and I immediately wondered if I had offended him but he continued with a nod and his vague smile. "And both fair queries. As to the first, Jerusalem is a very long way off indeed although I have never been there. You have heard of Peter? The holy man called the Hermit?" I nodded and he continued. "He stopped at the Duke's castle at Bouillon, which is near Liege, and told my brother of his own pilgrimage to the Holy City years ago and I think his enthusiasm for the notion of returning actually inspired Lord Godfroi to go himself. At any rate, while Peter journeyed in the East he was badly treated by the Saracens, and it is partly in order to revenge that insult that we make this journey, for my brother so vowed to the Hermit. But to answer your question, he, Peter, says that the journey to the Holy Land takes many months and the route is difficult and dangerous. So I expect that we shall be at least half a year getting there, if not longer, given the size of the army and the determination of the enemy in our path to keep us from our goal."

I pondered that statement ruefully as he continued. Would we have to fight our way all the way to Jerusalem?

"As for your second question, the why of this armed pilgrimage, I am not altogether certain of its genesis but I have seen that many men have as many different reasons for going there and my brother is but one example. I know you are right when you say that the Pope asked only for soldiers to assist the Greek emperor in his fight against the opprobrious attacks by the ungodly Saracens but something sparked the idea in the minds of pious men everywhere that the liberation of Jerusalem should be the *raison d'être* of this expedition. I think I agree that that goal is valid. Perhaps some other time we might discuss the varied motivations behind the massing of armies for this purpose but for now I think we should simply see this movement of the armed multitude as just and approved by God."

I thanked him for his answers and we rode on in silence, each lost in our own thoughts. I do not know what Lord Baudoin was thinking but my thoughts were of the Holy Land and the enemy in our path. My stomach did not feel well just then for some reason, perhaps owing to the noxious vapours rising from the swamps on our flank and upsetting the delicate balance of humours in my body.

We rode into Oedenburg at last and Baudoin immediately sought out his brother.

We were detained at the gate for a short space of time by its Hungarian guard and then escorted within the walls of the fortress by a contingent of about two dozen foot soldiers sent from inside, half of them preceding us and the other guarding our rear as if we might try to bolt through the castle and capture it. The escort seemed a bit much to me but I suppose that the Hungarians had reasons enough to distrust Westerners after the exploits of leaders like Gottschalk, Volkmar and Emicho.

Baudoin dismounted, indicating that I should do the same. He dismissed our Frankish escort who disappeared down an alleyway with half the Hungarians. The other half of our native guard led the way into the main hall.

Inside, the building was dark and my eyes immediately smarted from the thick smoke from the huge fireplace at one end of the open hall and by the sooty fumes of countless torches stuck in sconces on the wall in an attempt to bring light to the dismal windowless interior. We hardly paused in the main hall but made our way immediately to a flight of steps that led to a separate wing of the building, where, I learned, the Duke's temporary apartments were. Outside the door to Godfroi's apartments, the Hungarian escort left us and two Frankish *milites* that stood as honour guard opened the doors for Lord Baudoin. I thought I detected a slight sneer in their faces at the sight of me tagging along behind him, for my appearance was shabby and uninspiring, but I might be mistaken in that. Might they have been half-smiles of greeting?

I grew increasingly nervous with the thought that momentarily I might be introduced to a Duke, surely the loftiest secular personage I had ever met in my entire lifetime. I hardly had time to consider the consequences as Baudoin burst into Godfroi's private rooms with me in tow.

He bowed quickly to a tall, blonde-haired man standing by a table on the far side of the room.

"My lord," he greeted Godfroi, Duke of Lower Lorraine, sometime lord of Stenay and Rosay, Comte of Antwerp, his brother. Then to me he whispered, "Kneel, fool. You are in the presence of your betters."

Stung, I complied. Never had Lord Baudoin made me feel so humble in my origins since I had made his acquaintance. Humiliated, my face surely glowing red as embers with embarrassment, I knelt down quickly on bended knees with my head down and stayed that way.

"Welcome back, Brother," I heard the Duke greet Baudoin in a deep, melodious voice. "And was your mission successful? Did you find the war machines?"

"I did, my lord, and they are in exceptional condition. I left some men to dismantle and transport them to our armies."

"Excellent. You have done well. And who is this you bring with you, someone from our following petitioning for favour or redress of some wrong?"

"No, Brother, a young cleric I found held captive by the Hungarians at Wiesselburg. I paid a choice ransom for him and the war machines left behind by Emicho, who lately besieged that castle and left wanting victory."

"Indeed. We have heard of that unfortunate affair. What need have you of another cleric?"

"Well, there are certain mundane tasks he might perform for me. And further, he speaks the Greek tongue."

"Stand, boy. Let me look at you."

I raised my head, though not daring to look into the Duke's eyes lest he find me lacking in manners with such effrontery, and then slowly raised myself to a standing position. I must admit I was still somewhat sore from the time spent in the saddle on the journey here.

"Look up. Look at me. Here."

I looked up and saw him pointing with two fingers of his right hand at his own eyes. I did as bidden and looked him in the eyes without blinking or looking away.

There must be something in the family constitution that makes them judge people by what they see in their eyes for his request reminded me of my first meeting with Lord Baudoin; on that occasion, too, my face and eyes were closely scrutinised by the Duke's brother. Of course, as before with Baudoin, this allowed me the opportunity of examining Duke Godfroi.

The brothers are a study in contrasts. Godfroi is a tall man though not as tall as Baudoin who stands a few fingers taller again. Where Baudoin is dark of hair and pale of skin, his elder brother is fair and ruddy of complexion, obviously from much time spent out of doors probably in lordly pursuits such as hunting in the forests of his *demesne* or warring on his neighbours. Godfroi is quick to smile and laugh out loud while his younger sibling, though often smiling an enigmatic, emotionless smile, rarely laughs. Baudoin is secretive and private. Godfroi seems frank and open and generous of spirit where his brother is stingy with his emotions. Truly, I could hardly believe they were born of the same womb. Of course, that need not be the reality either, though that is not for me to say. They are both great lords who I am sure know well their own family history and I am only a lowly clerk whose opinion counts not in the least.

Godfroi finished his examination of me and stepped back a pace.

"How is it that you come to speak the Greek tongue, then?" he asked, his voice soft and deep and calmly resonant. "Have you been to the Eastern Empire?"

"No, Lord Duke, I have never been to the Greek lands. I learned to speak it when I was a student in Mainz. My *magister* there, a Benedictine monk and physician, thought Greek a valuable language for the study of medicine since there are several ancient, venerable texts on the subject in that language and of course, the founder of medicine, Hippocrates of Cos, was himself a Greek. My magister thought that all physicians should know the tongue."

"You are a physician, too? You *are* a versatile young man," he commented with surprise in his voice.

"Well, your pardon but no, lord. I was only a medical student at the time of Emicho of Leisingen's assault on the cathedral and my teaching master was killed, as I believe, during the attack. Had that not happened I would still be under his tutelage there; but, no, I am no doctor, though I did learn some valuable skills from the Benedictine."

"You are a doubly useful young man even so. Even without full training in the *ars medicinae* you will have more knowledge of such things than many in our army. Have you had any field experience dressing wounds and such?"

"Yes, lord. While Emicho's prisoner I assisted a *medicus* named Waldebert in caring for the wounded during the siege of Wiesselburg castle; pulling arrows, setting broken bones, dressing wounds and the like."

He nodded solemnly. "Yes. An unfortunate event that. It, and several like it, has made our journey the more difficult and time-consuming because of the distrust created among the Hungarians with regard to the Western armies. But I am glad to hear that you have some medical field experience for we shall need your services eventually, I am certain of it. And your knowing Greek should prove useful when we arrive in the Emperor's lands."

"And now, I would like to discuss some things with my brother, Lord Baudoin, privately. You are dismissed."

I stood there for a long moment, confused. I did not know to where I was being dismissed. I looked askance at my new master.

"The boy and I have just arrived, Brother. As yet we have not determined where our quarters are. Perhaps you might..." He let the question hang in the air waiting for Godfroi to make a suggestion as to where we might be disposed to make our rest. The Duke looked slightly annoyed but replied politely enough.

"Ah. My apologies. If you find Geoffroi he will find quarters for you and then, Brother, return here."

"Thank you, Brother. I shall do as you say."

We found the Geoffroi in question; Geoffroi of Esch as it turned out, the Duke's vassal from Stenay, one of the holdings sold by Godfroi to help finance the raising and supply of his army. Geoffroi introduced us to a Hungarian steward who then found quarters for us.

Amazingly, Lord Baudoin insisted that I be lodged near his own quarters, in the event, as he said, that my services should be required at short notice or late at night. He would rather not have to wait while I was being summoned from the stables out in the courtyard or some other such distant and humble lodging. I had little to do in order to settle into my quarters since I had no worldly belongings other than the clothes on my back, filthy from the ride from Wiesselburg, and my bundled sword. I thanked the steward, who looked blankly at me, apparently not apprehending my meaning, and then departed.

I had left Baudoin's company earlier at his own chambers and I assumed he would be by now in the meeting with his brother. Thankfully, he did not summon me that night. I wanted nothing more than to sleep and could not even concern myself with musing about the substance of that meeting as I laid down my head on the lumpy straw mattress of the bed.

Next day, very early in the morning, barely sunrise in fact, Lord Baudoin arrived at my room. I struggled to my feet, still in my dirty clothes, bleary-eyed and trying desperately to summon my brain to service.

"We are leaving to rejoin the army. Immediately."

He seemed unaccountably angry and curt but I simply nodded, for my place was not to question my lord, and told him I was ready. I followed him out to the courtyard, where the twelve *equites* who had accompanied us from Wiesselburg waited with our horses. We mounted and rode out of Oedenburg, in the chill of the October morning. We travelled quickly, almost, it seemed to me, as if Baudoin feared pursuit; though none followed us. Before the sun had reached the zenith to warm the day somewhat we were at the River Leyta on the western boundary of the Hungarian lands where the main body of Godfroi's army awaited his return.

I have seen large armies before. Peter the Hermit's following was huge, probably numbering more than twenty thousand although that included its common members, too, who comprised at least half or more of the gathering, and Emicho's army, while smaller, consisted of a more strictly military force of about five thousand. Godfroi's army was somewhere between the two in size, perhaps about ten thousand. Nonetheless, it was far superior to either of the other armies I had seen in terms of its organisation and discipline and in terms of its apparent prosperity. It looked better equipped and less bedraggled than Peter's following or Emicho's troops, probably because Godfroi's people consisted of more reputable lords and their *equites* and *pedites*—their immediate and loyal vassals—than those others, who consisted mainly of peasants, opportunists and mercenaries. The Duke and his lords had more resources with which to assemble such a puissant armigerous assemblage.

I rode into the encampment directly behind Lord Baudoin with the *equites* trailing us two abreast. The camp, far more organised than Emicho's had been, was set up much like an old Roman *castrum* with a wide central avenue running north and south and another running east and west, rather like the *cardo* and the *decumanus*. The camp was thus divided into four major blocks and these large areas were further subdivided into smaller blocks where each lord, with his retainers, had his compound. The camp looked like a large town except that tents stood in the stead of buildings.

Baudoin's compound was located on the southeast corner of the intersection of the two main streets. The most important lords were located nearer the centre with the lesser folk located outward according to rank so that on the outskirts of the camp were the common soldiers and the poorer non-combatants. This made sense militarily, for if the camp was attacked the outer sections would act as a buffer through which the attackers would have to negotiate, giving the *cnichts* at the centre time to arm themselves for a counterattack. Still, it seemed rather heartless in another way since those on the outskirts were least capable of defending themselves from such an attack. Yet, if given that little extra space of moments for mounting the counter-thrust, the *equites* might in the end save those people as the mounted soldiers would have a clear, swift route up the broad main streets to charge the attackers.

The entrances to each of the main avenues themselves were heavily guarded even now with no sign of an enemy nearby. We were not stopped by the guards, however, since Lord Baudoin was recognised immediately. The guards merely saluted him and his *cnichts* as we rode past.

Before long, after Baudoin and I had dismounted and the *equites* took our horses away, I found myself being given a small tent of my own nestled against the huge house-like tent belonging to my lord. Again, this proximity was explained in terms of my being available readily should Baudoin require me. The present occupant, a cleric in minor orders, was ordered to move out. Grumbling his protest, he gathered his belongings. But I did not wait around to see him off and move in myself. Instead, Lord Baudoin ordered me to follow him to his own tent.

Inside his lodgings, Baudoin introduced me to his chamberlain, Henry of Esch, brother to Geoffroi who was the

Duke's chamberlain, and outlined for his benefit and mine my new duties. These consisted mainly of copying letters for him and writing down words he dictated to me as well as some accounts-keeping; all things familiar to me.

Then he ordered Henry to find for me a new wardrobe since I could not be seen any longer in the shabby, filthy garments I now wore. For this I was grateful and expressed my gratitude to Baudoin. He waved me away and I followed Henry out of the main tent to a supply tent where we rummaged through a number of crates and bales before we found some garments fitting to my station and profession and physical person; several tunics and leggings and a new cloak and boots. I thought this incredible finery indeed and thanked the chamberlain. He merely grunted and left me.

I retired to my own little tent and stored my new belongings there, except for those I decided to wear, laying everything atop the bundled sword. I stripped off the grimy, torn robe I had been wearing ever since Mainz and balled it up in one corner, thinking that one of these days I should perhaps have a bath, but there was no hurry for that for it is a dangerous enough practice. Then I dressed myself in one of the tunics, green with some simple embroidery in white around the collar and cuffs, and a pair of brown leggings. Over the footed leggings I slipped the calf-high boots. They were a bit large for my feet but not uncomfortably so. I clomped around outside for a few moments getting used to them. I had just bent to duck back into the tent when I heard a call behind me.

"Very fine clothing. And what have you done with Albert that you are so familiar with his tent?"

I turned to see a short, shorter than me even, Frank with laughing eyes and a round face smiling at me. His clothes were elegant and richly stylish and worn without pretension. His tunic lay open, unlaced to the sternum despite the coolness of the day, and his cloak he had carelessly slung over one shoulder. He was thick-set and powerful looking. One of the Duke's noblemen I guessed.

"I'm sorry, my lord. This is the tent to which Lord Baudoin assigned me. I know nothing of this Albert."

"Albert is a pain in the ass, anyway, can't decide whether he wants to be a priest or a clerk, and even so, always complaining at doing the slightest clerical work; or anything else for that matter except sitting in his tent reading. Don't

worry about it. I was joking. Who are you?"

"I am Lord Baudoin's new clerk, recently come from Mainz."

"'Recently come from...'," he paused. "I don't remember Lord Baudoin being in Mainz recently." He sounded puzzled and somewhat suspicious. "Well, he didn't find me in Mainz. He found me a prisoner in Wiesselburg Castle and ransomed me in exchange for my services."

"Just you?"

I agreed that this was so.

"Ah, I see. They threw you in as part of the deal for the new war machines, did they?"

I nodded reluctantly, sheepish. "Something like that."

He threw back his head and laughed uproariously and continued laughing while tears formed in his eyes.

"The look on your face! Well, don't feel too badly about it," he said, through his mirth. "If worse comes to worst we can always throw you under our arms and use you for a battering ram against the Saracen gates if we don't get any use out of you as a clerk in the Holy Land."

That idea appealed to me not at all and I thought of the sword I had taken from the dead Odo, Drogo's man, on the road to Wiesselburg, now stored in the tent with my other belongings. I wondered if sweordsman was an occupation I should consider taking up before we arrived in enemy territories.

"Do you have a name?" he asked me.

I told him and asked his in return.

"I am yet another Baudoin, I'm afraid. There seem to be far too many of us on this expedition. I am Baudoin of Stavelot, recently come from the Frankish lands." Then he bowed grandly, in a mocking, courtly fashion.

This embarrassed me and I looked around hastily to see if anyone had seen. No one had.

"Please, my lord, this is unseemly. I am only a clerk," I protested.

"Well, I am only a vassal, and not a very important one at that, to Duke Godfroi. Perhaps we are both a little out of place in this grand company we keep, hmmm?" His eyes sparkled with mirth still.

Baudoin of Stavelot was a hard man not to like. His familiarity led me to ask a direct question of him, something I would not have done under normal circumstances, under more formal circumstances.

"My lord, is there somewhere I might find something to eat? I have fasted since yesterday. We left Oedenburg early this morning and had no time for breakfast."

"You must be starved, my friend. Of course. Follow me."

And I found myself following where Baudoin of Stavelot led.

◆

On the next day, after sext, Duke Godfroi arrived at the camp from Oedenburg. He was furious.

He burst into Comte Baudoin's tent where I sat at a low table copying out some correspondence for the Duke's brother, the dust of the road still heavy on his clothing. His face flamed with his anger and his fury excluded all other emotion. He passed right by me and seemed not to notice that I was there.

Baudoin, who had been poring over some letters I had written for him earlier in the day, rose quickly to his feet and casually greeted Godfroi.

The Duke ignored all formality and good manners and began to hack at his brother with a sword of bitter words.

"What the hell did you think you were doing leaving Oedenburg without my permission?"

"Brother...," began Baudoin but Godfroi would not be cajoled.

"No. Not a word else it is to answer my question. You know what is at stake here. We need you in Oedenburg with King Coloman."

"Am I a common criminal that I should be held prisoner by the Hungarians?"

"No. You are a nobleman and my vassal and you have vassals of your own to whom you owe some responsibility. Their fates, all our fates, are in your hand."

I was unsure what they argued about but certainly I forbore to ask. Instead, I lowered my head and worked diligently at my task. I had neither been asked for an opinion nor given leave to go so I pretended not to listen, though in fact I paid close attention. Anyway, they both ignored me or were unmindful of my presence, which is probably the same thing.

Now, Baudoin spoke again, deadly quiet. I glanced up and saw the fury mounting in his visage.

"My place is with my vassals, with this army. You, gentle brother, would give everything away to placate the Hungarian king. I am your brother! How can you sell me over like this? Like Judas?"

"There are no thirty pieces of silver involved here. You know that. Your presence with the king serves only to guarantee the good behaviour of our people as we cross the Hungarian domain."

"Then why not Baudoin Le Bourg or one of the other lords?"

"One who is not you, you mean? This is too obvious for me to explain but I will." He sighed and I could see the anger had receded in him.

I could see the rage in Baudoin's face renewed, though, at this patronising attitude adopted by his brother.

"You must go because you *are* my brother. I lead the army, so I cannot be the one. You are closest to me in authority and rank and Coloman knows I would not see any harm done to you, my closest kinsman. With you at his side, the king knows that all will pass peacefully until you are returned to us after we cross the River Sava into the Greek lands."

"Yes, but why must he also have Godivere and the children?"

"Wouldn't you rather have your wife and children at your side and know that they were safe? Better they should go. Their presence will guarantee your good behaviour while you are with the Hungarians and preclude the possibility that you will try to escape."

Baudoin seemed to be wearing down before his brother's argument. Some of the high colour left his face as he became less choleric. He paused a long moment before he finally answered.

"Damn you, Godfroi. I have never been able to refuse you anything."

The Duke embraced him, one arm over his brother's shoulder. "I would be deeply grateful to you if you would do this for me, for all of us. It is a very selfless thing to do and a difficult thing for me to ask. I don't like the idea of you a prisoner of the Hungarians any more than you do, you know."

He smiled a warm, loving smile and Baudoin's anger melted away.

Baudoin smiled ruefully and nodded his acquiescence. "Very well. We will go."

"Splendid," his brother said seriously. "I am in your debt."

"Yes," Baudoin said thoughtfully, so quietly that I could barely hear. "You are."

And so we rode back to Oedenburg to meet the king.

◆

Several days passed before we reached Oedenburg once again, since now the entire Frankish army was on the move, which considerably slowed the journey. We travelled not at all as I thought an army on the march would travel. I had presumed that most of the military men would lead the columns and the ladies and their families would form their own contingent with the supply wagons following, and a substantial guard bringing up the extreme rear. Instead, the wide column straddled the entire road and it was divided into contingents of lords and those who travelled with them, families and vassals. Godfroi's contingent, of course, travelled at the head of the army with the contingents of the other lords and their *thegns* trailing behind, strung out over several leagues.

I rode in Baudoin's group though far to its rear. My lord himself and his most important retainers rode with Godfroi far ahead of us but his contingent within the main force was led by Baudoin of Stavelot in the place of the Lord Baudoin. Near me, on a battered old mule, rode Albert, the clerk whom I had displaced from his tent. He glared over at me occasionally although I pretended not to notice and avoided his glance if I happened to look over in his direction and found him glaring at me in his unfriendly fashion.

What had I to do with his fall from position, if such it had been? So what if I rode a spirited mare and he only an old mule? That did not mean that I felt myself any more deserving of the gifts and position given me by Lord Baudoin. I decided Albert was a fool and strove to ignore him completely, and once we reached Oedenburg I did not see him again, anyway.

As we approached Oedenburg the army halted. After waiting for about a quarter hour in the warm sun, something I did not mind in the least for I intensely enjoyed riding in the fresh air and open sunshine after my long confinement first with Drogo and then with the commander Scipio in Wiesselburg, Baudoin of Stavelot made his way through the milling crowd, seeking me. I followed him to the very head of the army where waited the Duke and Lord Baudoin with his family and an escort of a dozen *equites*.

As far as I could see I was the only serving member of Baudoin's household other than Baudoin of Stavelot and the several women who attended Baudoin's wife and children. The women and children sat unseen inside a curtained wagon drawn by two large horses rather than a team of oxen as was usual. A small, withered old man drove the team. Momentarily, the group formed up with the Duke and his brother leading, followed by the wagon and then myself and Baudoin of Stavelot and, finally, the *equites* bringing up the rear. We left the army and rode to the gates of Oedenburg.

At that town, King Coloman awaited us in full state with a large retinue attending him and I saw him for the first time. He was not at all as I had imagined him to be. In my mind, I suppose I had built him up to be a prepossessing greater-than-man, for that is how kings are supposed to appear to ordinary folk, are they not? I had imagined him something like the Lord Archbishop Rothard who was tall and white-haired and dignified.

The king is the exact opposite from my mental image of him. He is dark and somewhat unattractive as people usually judge physical beauty. He sat atop his horse and even from where I sat on my own mare I could see how short he was. Partly, his stunted physical stature is a result of a twist and a hump in his back though he sat his steed in such a way as to try to hide it and indeed, at the time, I was not aware of the deformity since he wore a long, flowing rich cape that also helped to conceal it. But later, I had occasion to see him without the devices he used to minimise his disfigurement.

He smiled and greeted Duke Godfroi in Latin, calling him 'cousin' and welcoming him back to Oedenburg. The Duke responded in kind, thanking the king for his good grace and exceeding generosity and reintroducing his brother, whom the king had met a few days before.

I could see that Coloman, through his smile, eyed Baudoin warily. I knew the two had already met but I sensed that the king was taking the measure of the Duke's brother and trying to assess some lurking danger within him. I realised at once that Coloman did not trust Baudoin. But why did he feel this way about my lord?

I thought about that as one of the king's officials read aloud a letter proclaiming friendship between the Duke and his Franks and the King and the Hungarian people. He further went on to say that the Lord Baudoin would remain with the King as his guest and as Godfroi's emissary so that with him the King might discuss matters of import to both peoples, but concerning what he did not say, while the Duke himself moved the army forward without delay across the Hungarian lands to the Greek frontier. I knew better. Baudoin and those who remained with him, including me, were hostages to the good behaviour of the Frankish army and guarantors of its peaceful conduct. Further, for some reason, King Coloman was afraid to have Baudoin loose in his country. Why?

I could only ponder this puzzle while, after thanking the King for his generosity, the Duke and his escort wheeled their horses and spurred them back toward the army quietly waiting in the distance. Then there was no time to wonder more for the King decided the time had arrived to usher his guests into the town. I followed my lord into what I hoped would be his temporary captivity.

Caput Donus

My Lord Baudoin is angry. He has sent everyone away from his tent, including his wife, Godivere, and her children and me. This does not bother me since I am always uncomfortable in the face of his rage anyway; and I now have the opportunity to continue my journal. However, I could see in the Comtesse Godivere's face her own anger at this summary dismissal as she, with her maid, led the children from the tent. I left immediately behind them with head bowed in humility to make for my own tent. Then after a moment, walking through the chill late autumn air, I thought better of that intention. I caught up to the Comtesse Godivere and her little troupe.

"My lady," I called, hesitantly, for this was a great presumption on my part to ask speech of her and I had never before so presumed.

She slowed and turned to me, diffident. "Yes?"

"I only wanted to offer you my tent as shelter, my lady, for these winds are brittle, until such time as Lord Baudoin's anger has passed and you may return to your own. It is small but perhaps it will do?" I spat out the words quickly, in staccato, so my nerve would not waiver.

She motioned to her maid to take the children on ahead. Then she stopped, facing me, her grey-blue eyes curtained by long, delicate, black eyelashes.

"That is very kind of you," she said and I saw her eyes rim with tears, suddenly, which neither of us acknowledged. "My lord's anger is like the wind; it comes in gusts but then returns soon to a gentle breeze. He needs some peace and quiet for a while and then he will send for me and the children. You need not concern yourself."

She sighed and her face looked very tired indeed. I wondered what kind of trial this wandering across the continent was for her, how cut-off from her comfortable life in northern Francia she must feel, how difficult to raise her little family of girls in such a situation, never knowing what the next day might bring, tragedy always but a moment away. A great burden indeed. I felt pity for her but, of course, that was the last thing she would accept of me, another lowly servant in her husband's retinue.

"Well, the offer stands, my lady," I said and bowed to her in deep respect. She was a very gentle woman, I could see.

"Thank you. We will walk for a while. That will do the children good, to breathe some fresh air and to exercise their limbs. You are kind, but my lord's anger will pass and we shall all be in his favour once more." And with that she swept away, the long braid down the centre of her back swaying, her blue velvet skirts gathered in one tiny fist that they might be kept up out of the dirt, our moment of intimacy done. I shrugged and sought my own tent where I would rest until Lord Baudoin's ire settled.

The occasion of my lord's anger is that the Frankish army has stopped at a nearby town and has not moved since yesterday. Since we are nearing the Hungarian border crossing at the River Sava Baudoin feels that the army should cross immediately and effect our release from the Hungarians. That he has not done this, my lord feels, indicates that Duke Godfroi has given little thought to our care or comfort. I certainly did not have the temerity to disagree with him but in my humble view the hiatus makes perfect sense if the Duke is using this opportunity to re-victual and rest the army in friendly territory rather than waiting until he crosses into what could be potentially hostile country over the border in the Greek lands.

We await, therefore, the crossing of the Sava by the Frankish host several leagues to the south of the Hungarian army. I was something surprised that, as hostages, we did not remain at Oedenburg. I had assumed that we would wait in that town until the Duke's forces had left Hungary as had been agreed by Godfroi and King Coloman. The King, however, sent us with a large force of Hungarians to shadow the Franks, watching and ready for any trouble that might develop should the visitors forget themselves and start to pillage or otherwise to inconvenience the local populace. We rode along on the opposite bank of the River Danuvius for several weeks until we neared Semlin at the Greek border and then crossed over so that we were behind the Franks. Once they had crossed, we were told, we would be released to join our countrymen but then Godfroi's advance came to a halt short of the border crossing.

And now Baudoin fumes.

Sudden volatile anger is very much a part of my lord's character. He is very quick to flame into a rage but then just as quickly, as the Comtesse Godivere observed, the flames of passion die in him and he is calm and collected, even affable, once more. Though this affability is his usual state of being, there is always something coldly calculating about him as well. He seems always to study the people and the unfolding events around him in a direct, deliberate way as if he is weighing constantly the advantages or disadvantages of this or that person or happening. I believe he means ever to reap the greatest rewards for himself in this fashion. Even so, in all things he is fair and unequivocal in his judgement. In the main, so far, I have found him to be a most agreeable lord under whom to serve, which is more than I can say about some.

My thoughts turn in this regard to my former master, Archbishop Rothard. Well, no matter. My allegiance to that sometime lord is done and my loyalty to my present lord has been, until recently, unquestioned in my mind.

Now, doubts have been raised in me, not enough to make me disloyal to him, but enough to make me wonder at what exactly motivates him and to wonder if these motivations are always, in a Christian context, morally sound. A strange occurrence at Oedenburg Castle has led to these new musings.

The journey here from Oedenburg took several weeks, as I have noted, but we were delayed for the space of two days from leaving the castle by King Coloman's reluctance to release us from his immediate custody for whatever reason. And there, a strange event occurred about which I am compelled to write.

On the second evening of our stay at Oedenburg Castle in the company of King Coloman, I sat on a stool at the small table provided me, reading by the light of a hissing, sputtering, tallow candle, when I heard the door to my *cubiculum* open.

Before I could turn to see who had entered I heard a voice say, "Your wine, my lord."

Startled, I began to turn, saying, "There's a mistake. I'm not..."

And then I stopped, dumbfounded. For, facing me, wine flask and goblets in hand, stood none other than King Coloman himself. All power of speech fled from me at this apparition and I could only sit in mute amazement until after several moments I thought to kneel before him and bow my head.

"My King..." I managed to murmur.

The King grunted and, pulling up the wooden armchair—the only other piece of furniture in the room besides my sleeping pallet—to the table, plunked the wine and glasses down. Then he poured each goblet full and gestured to me.

"Come, drink with me," he invited in a smooth, velvety, almost lisping voice, speaking Latin.

Dumb as if I were wood I complied. One does not refuse a king's offer, no matter what it is or how insignificant. With a trembling hand I reached out to take the wine proffered by the King of Hungary. He sat back in the chair and with a thin smile looked me up and down. For my part, I realised suddenly that every time I had met someone of importance lately I had been subjected to this kind of uncomfortable scrutiny. Perhaps I am just sensitive to this since I have not experienced it before. However, as in those other instances, I was able to make my own examination of the King as he observed me.

He is of a height with me, though I suspect that he would have been taller had his spine not been twisted. This imperfection tended to force his body to lean generally toward the left side. He has a rather pronounced hump visible over the right shoulder, which makes his left shoulder seem to dip downward giving him an altogether awkward and unbalanced appearance. He is, otherwise, fair enough to look upon, not truly ugly or repellent, although his skin is dark and his brows are very heavy, not handsome but with a deep intelligence in his eyes and a refined manner. I wondered with dread what this unkingly-looking monarch could possibly want with a lowly, insignificant clerk utterly without refinement. I knew, though, that it must have something to do with Lord Baudoin. I prayed God that I would say nothing that might be construed as disloyal to my master.

"I understand that you are Lord Baudoin's clerk?" He began, taking a sip of wine immediately he had said this. Not really a question. He already knew I was.

"That is true, great king," I replied, hoping to sound suitably humble and not terrified as I truly felt.

"You are a loyal and faithful servant to him?"

"I try to be, lord." I felt distinctly uncomfortable in his presence and my words I forced out with difficulty. I took a great swallow of wine, hoping to free my voice from its fear-induced constraints and not sound the croaking fool.

"Good. That is very good. A lord needs loyal servants."

Then he took me completely by surprise by switching from the Latin he had begun with to the language of the Franks.

"*Vous le connaissez bien Baudoin?*" He asked.

After a moment of hesitation owing to my surprise, I answered his question, also in the Frankish tongue, "No, lord, I don't know him that well. I have only been in his service for some short weeks now."

He nodded slowly, considering this.

"Still, you have had time enough to examine his character and make your own judgements about what kind of man he is, have you not? I have watched you and you are a young man who keenly observes what passes around him. To my mind, there is little that you miss."

Somewhat taken aback at this unexpected compliment from so august a person I nonetheless maintained enough composure to consider carefully how I answered the question even though my mind whirled in confusion like a rain-swollen river.

"He seems a fair master. I am fed well and treated well. Beyond that, I can say little, great king." What had the monarch expected I would reveal?

I had hoped this answer would suffice. But no. Coloman's face clouded over with disapproval and I knew he anticipated more information than I had provided.

"Well, perhaps I can enlighten you beyond what you have said," his voice taking on a menacing tone. He bent forward and poured himself more wine then leaned back in his chair with a smug look on his face.

"Did you know, young cleric, that your lord conspired to assassinate his own uncle when he was but fourteen years of age? Yes! So that his brother might bring a claim of title to the family lands in the Lorraine thus putting he himself in a position of power and influence alongside Godfroi. So it was rumoured in the court of the Emperor, Henry; a tender age to be so bloody-minded, no? And during the contest between the Emperor and Pope Gregory a decade later, scarce twelve years gone, when Godfroi was with the army of the Emperor marching on Rome itself, Baudoin allied himself with the Comte of Namur to attack Godfroi's marquisate of Antwerp, covertly sending some of his own men to assist in the siege. But Godfroi obtained permission from the Emperor to return with his army to beat off the attack and prevailed over his enemy. Godfroi, of course, too generous of heart for his own health, suspects nothing of his brother's complicity in these events. But it is real. My agents are very reliable in that."

I sat stunned and grievously wounded in my heart by these revelations. From what I had seen of Lord Baudoin's interactions with the Duke, his brother, I had thought him ever eager to do his sibling's bidding. How could he so betray his own flesh and blood? How? And how had the King of Hungary learned of these things? I knew that my hunger to know the answers to these questions would lead me to boldness in asking more of the King.

But Coloman continued.

"So you see my dilemma? How do I know that Baudoin will not turn on Godfroi once more, perhaps *assassinate* his own brother, take control of the army and attack me? He is more than capable of such perfidy, I assure you."

This seemed excessively paranoid to me but then I am not a king. I suppose there was a dim chance that such a thing might come to pass though I rather doubted it. I knew Baudoin keenly wished to reach the Holy Land, how dedicated he was to the Holy Father Urban's purpose, outwardly at least. Surely his ambitions lay in Outremer not here in Hungary? I needed to know more.

"Lord King, forgive me, but how do you come to know these things about my Lord Baudoin?"

I thought he would be angry at my impertinence, at my daring to question him and I awaited his wrath to come down upon me. Again he surprised me. His face became serious for a moment then a small smile flickered across his mouth and a sad look came into his eyes.

"You see, I myself was married once to one of those fiery Frankish princesses. With her help and counsel I established a network of agents throughout the empire and the Frankish lands so that I might be better informed of those events in the west whose outcomes might affect the state of my own kingdom. Through those agents I learned of Baudoin's awful duplicity."

And that is why he spoke the Frankish tongue, no doubt.

Well, I could hardly oppugn his knowledge of events that occurred before my birth or when I was but a child. Certainly, I had little understanding of the political affairs and deeds of the great ones from my lowly vantage point in life.

But then, these events about which he spoke occurred before he was yet ruler— for he had only recently taken the crown of Hungary himself—when the succession to the kingship of Hungary was yet uncertain so why need he be so concerned over affairs among the Franks in those days? Or perhaps he spoke of a network of agents formed more recently when he was more certain that he would wear the crown? These agents, then—I noted he did not call them spies, which is what they really were—apparently were given to spewing unconfirmed hearsay from the past so their reliability, to my mind at least, was questionable.

Still, the greatest evidence that bespoke the truth of the matter, or at least what the King believed to be the truth, was his own fear of Baudoin and of what Baudoin might be capable. So even if his knowledge of these affairs came long after the fact and was uncorroborated there might indeed be a grain of truth to it. And yet, if these things were mere rumour I was bound to protect and defend my lord's honour. Whatever else the King believed about Baudoin in the past I knew that he must be wrong about any such intent on my lord's part now.

"My King," I ventured, "I believe sincerely that you, and Duke Godfroi I presume too, have little to fear from my Lord Baudoin. I am certain that he is committed to a nobler purpose, to the dictates of the Holy Father in Rome. He is bound and pledged to seek Jerusalem and to free it from its present unclean rulers. I believe this with all my heart, great king."

He snorted, an unpleasant, guttural sound. Then he stood up.

"Best pray that you are correct then, young cleric. For if you are not and he betrays me or his brother, then he and all who attend him as my hostages, shall die."

With that he was gone, as quickly and quietly as he had come. An awful noise began to roar in my ears in his wake. I realised after a moment that it was the rush of blood through the veins in my head.

The candle sputtered, near its end, and threatened to give up its light. I cursed it and killed its glow myself then sought my bed although I knew I would have little rest that night. How I longed to be away from Oedenburg and from the Kingdom of Hungary and gone from the company of its paranoid ruler. He sorely wounded me in my soul that night.

Thus did I personally meet and speak with King Coloman and thus did my first doubts about the brilliance of my Lord Baudoin's character begin to cast their shadows over his image in my heart.

X Kalendis Novembris, MXCVI

Today was a day for celebration for today Lord Baudoin's company, including me, rejoined the army of Duke Godfroi across the Sava. The Duke and the army had crossed into the Greek lands from Hungary on the last day of November, and then word that he had done so had arrived late the next day in the Hungarian camp where we waited. On the following day, we set out to cross the river ourselves, the Hungarians leaving us at last, remaining behind on their side of the river. Of course, Godfroi had left a troop of mounted soldiers behind, led by Baudoin of Stavelot, to escort us to the new encampment. I sighed with relief when we were out of the Hungarian lands for all of its king's suspicion had been proved groundless and we had survived our captivity.

We former hostages rode with Baudoin of Stavelot's company a few leagues to a town at the mixing of the waters of the Danuvius and the Sava called Alba Graeca by our Franks. The Franks greeted us as if we were returning heroes. We were all glad to see each other and our reunion with the Frankish army was like a homecoming, which, in a way, I suppose, it was.

IX Kalendis Novembris, MXCVI

I spent a rather pleasant day with Baudoin of Stavelot, today, although it ended less happily than it began. Duke Godfroi declared that we would rest here a few days at Alba Graeca while he sent messengers ahead, as a courtesy, to announce to the Byzantine authorities that we had arrived in the Emperor's territory. None of us knew quite how far ahead they would have to ride to meet the Byzantines, of course, although our Hungarian escorts had suggested that the governor at Nish, a city several days' ride from Alba Graeca, would be the nearest official representative of the Emperor. We would pause here and rest for a day or two and then follow our emissaries further into the Emperor's lands. While we waited, Baudoin of Stavelot invited me to join him on a tour of the town and fortress of Alba Graeca.

The town itself had been deserted when our army had arrived. Nonetheless, since Duke Godfroi had ordered it so, our people camped without its walls. He wanted to have as little impact on the place and its environs as possible because he did not wish to offend the local authorities, not that there were any of these anywhere around to be offended. Still, he allowed foragers to roam the empty streets though they found little of worth. In any case, the army had taken on supplies several days earlier and lacked little in the way of everyday necessities.

Clouds hung low over the plain, threatening snow perhaps, although so far we had been spared that particular burden. A chill wind blew from the northwest, making me glad of the woollen cloak I had thrown on, as the lesser Baudoin and I strode through the camp on our way to visit the fortress on the hilltop above the town. This hill jutted up like a blunt tooth from the surrounding flat lands, bounded on two sides by the Rivers Danuvius and Sava, while the town itself wrapped around the base of the hill behind its own fortification walls. We passed through the southernmost of the town's gates and began the ascent to the fortress along a winding narrow path.

I brought with me the sword I had taken from Drogo's dead lieutenant, Odo, at Wiesselburg. This was the first time I had dared openly to wear it. As a hostage in the Hungarian lands I could not carry any weapon without raising suspicion among our hosts and indeed I had left the *langsweord* behind as a part of my baggage conveyed by Lord Baudoin's train in the Duke's main van. Now, thrust into my belt, the weapon thumped uncomfortably against my thigh as I walked and it stuck up foolishly half an arm's length in front. I was not used to its weight or how it generally encumbered my walk. Despite the fact that I had seen soldiers wearing swords at their hips surely this could not be how they wore such weapons into battle? Baudoin answered this unuttered question momentarily.

"Have you seen much fighting?" he inquired with sceptical amusement audible in his voice and evident on his face.

I sheepishly admitted that I had not.

He stopped and pulled the weapon from my belt. He held it before me and indicated two clasps on the scabbard, pointing.

"You see, here and just here," touching each clip in turn, "are where the ends of the harness attach it to the belt at the hip. Worn in this fashion it doesn't hinder your movement according to its design. Or it may be worn slung over the back with the harness across the shoulder."

He stepped to the side, proffering the weapon to me.

"Why are you even wearing this thing today?"

Feeling silly I responded, "I thought perhaps I should start wearing it for protection now that we have reached the Greek lands. Everyone says how untrustworthy are the Greeks. Not that I know how to use it…" My words trailed off and I shrugged.

He studied me for a moment, hand to chin.

"Well, then, we shall have to remedy that. Wait here and I'll return shortly."

Before I could respond he set off at a lope back down the path toward the town. Bemused, I watched him go. I could only guess at what he intended.

While I awaited Baudoin's return I took the opportunity to admire the view from the fortress walls. As I have mentioned, Alba Graeca lies on a point of land where the River Sava to the west meets the waters of the Danuvius north and east of the town. The flat lands surrounding this junction of the two rivers affords a view for many leagues in all directions, a truly admirable vantage point that must serve well to warn the Greeks of the approach of any army from the north. I had no doubt that the sight of our vast force emerging from the hills to the north in the Hungarian lands had incited the Greeks to abandon their town and its fortress as we drew near.

As I turned to face southward in the direction of the city of Constantinople I wondered what lay ahead for us.

By now the refugees from Alba Graeca would have warned their masters that we had arrived here. Probably even now a force of Greeks advanced to meet us. What would be our reception? Would they be inclined to attack us, as had the Hungarians at first, as a result of the poor behaviour of those who had preceded us out of the West? I momentarily experienced a pang of apprehension at the thought. What would be my role in any coming conflict? I could not cower with the women and children among the baggage as I had done at Wiesselburg in effect if not fact but nor yet was I prepared to offer any proper defence as a soldier in Duke Godfroi's army; not that I had any ambitions of becoming such. Still, the ability to defend myself would be an advantage.

As I stood musing in trepidation I heard the sound of footsteps behind me and turned to see Baudoin clambering up the steps to mount the wall beside me. He carried a lengthy bundle over his shoulder that he set down immediately he came up to meet me. Unwrapping the cloth from this bundle he drew forth two objects made of wooden lathes tied together that I took to be models of the *langsweord* I carried in my own hands. Puzzled by these mock weapons I inquired as to their purpose.

"These are used in training in the art of the sword. They prevent serious injury as a result of inexperienced handling while the novice learns the correct usage of the true weapon."

He took my sword from me and replaced it with one of the mock swords.

"Now," he began, holding up the real sword, "this is the blade."

I grimaced at this assumption of my ignorance. "Yes, of course."

Baudoin smiled. "Yes. You know the sword has both blade and handle, as I'm sure nearly everyone knows. However, these parts have other elements of which you might not be aware."

He pointed the blade toward me. "The elements of the blade are the foible, the forte and the fuller."

He pointed to each in turn, the tip, the base area of the blade and the channel that bisected the steel down its length.

Continuing, he pointed out the basic elements of the handle: the guard, the grip and the pommel.

"So," he explained, "the foible is the least defensive area of the blade while the forte is the strongest area of defence. The guard is just that, the crosspiece that guards the hands from the opponent's strike. Use the pommel to control the direction and strength of your own thrust."

He demonstrated by performing a series of sharp, fast movements toward various parts of my own anatomy ending with the foible inches from my nose. I jerked backward instinctively from the sudden threat. He laughed and set down the weapon.

He picked up the other wooden sword adopting a defensive stance. I imitated him as best I could.

He frowned. "Hmmm…no, you don't grip the hilt as if you are about to hack down a tree with an axe. If you do hold it like that, before long you will be exhausted from the sheer effort of holding on to the weapon. See. Like this.

Yes. Lightly, like that. Now move your other hand over the pommel more. Yes! Good!"

Through all of his exclamations and directions I had been shifting my grip about and loosening or tightening my hands on the smooth shaft of the handle. I found that the most comfortable way was to grasp the handle itself lightly but firmly, without squeezing over hard, with the other hand resting on the pommel. The grip hand could then control the direction of the blade while the pommel hand provided the power for the thrust, giving more control and direction.

Satisfied with my grasp of the weapon, Baudoin then bade me work on my foot stance. He showed me how to lead with the foot opposite the side from which I delivered my strike, following through with the same side from which my stroke came in order to deliver a stronger blow to my opponent. He taught me a quick shuffling technique by which to speedily enter within the other's guard and by which to quickly retreat from a suspected strike. He taught me to use the pommel to pummel my opponent when the position of the blade became too awkward to slash with.

As terce faded into sext, I found myself exhausted from the repetitive efforts. Perspiring heavily, my blood running hot through my veins, panting with exhaustion, I stopped; Baudoin, on the other hand, showed little sign that he found this effort taxing. My hands had begun to blister from the unusual strain. I leaned forward with my hands on my thighs and begged to be released from the training.

My teacher laughed. "Very well, then. We'll make you a warrior another day."

I grimaced.

"I have little hope of ever becoming a warrior, my lord. But at least you've given me a start at being able to defend myself from Greeks and Saracens." I gathered up my cloak, which I had long since thrown off, and propped my *langsweord* on my shoulder, preparing to descend the hill pathway.

Baudoin clapped me on the shoulder in a comradely way and we made our way back down the track to the town below.

I do not know what I expected from Baudoin of Stavelot. I liked and admired him for his martial skills and for his generally good humour. Indeed, in most respects, he was far more congenial and worthy of compliment than my own Lord Baudoin. Still, he is a product of his station in life, as I am of mine. Such a bitter truth to learn once again.

After our training session on the summit of Alba Graeca, we made our way back to camp together. We parted near the centre of Godfroi's compound, I to my tent and he, I presume, to his. Before we went our separate ways, he asked me to join him after vespers for dinner. Of course I was delighted to be so invited and I expressed this to him as I accepted. What a wondrous opportunity, for I had never been privileged to join the great ones on such an occasion. Occasion to me at least. To them this was but another evening's meal. He told me where to meet him and I assured him I would come later and we separated.

Later, after vespers when the sun had set, I made my way to the area where I was to meet Baudoin of Stavelot. This was a large open section among the tents of Duke Godfroi's compound not far from my own tent near Lord Baudoin's own. Several large trestle tables were set up with long benches on either side within an enclosed space. Fires blazed

at either end of the area to add warmth to the chilly evening air, with torches on iron stands burning brightly to add
illumination. The nobles and *cnichts* of the various lords in
the Duke's service and some of their women, dressed in
their fine furs, gathered gaudily around these tables, already
well into their drink and food.

I looked around for Baudoin, searching the faces of the
various seated groups. Finally, I saw him seated at the farther
end of the square nearest the fire and walked to where he sat.
I stood behind him waiting for him to notice me and invite
me to sit.

Before he could do so, however, one of the *cnichts* seated
across the table from him looked up at me. He held out his
tankard to me.

"Fill this up again, boy," he slurred, drunkenly.

I only stared at him in dumb surprise at this command.
Was I a table servant that he should so command me? Had
I not been invited here by my friend, Baudoin of Stavelot,
cousin to my own Lord Baudoin and his brother, the Duke
of Lorraine, himself?

The unknown *cnicht* half-rose from his seat his words a
slushy, angry burr through his scruffy beard.

"Bring me ale, you witless fly-blown offspring of a dung
pile!"

At this outburst every head turned to look glaringly at
me. Speechless, I stood there bereft of a reply and not knowing what to do or how to react to him. I wanted to run from
there, flee to my tent and forget that my friend had ever invited me to sit among my betters.

Baudoin, who had by now seen who stood behind him rose from his seat.

"Peace, cousin, this young man is a friend to me, the Lord Baudoin's own man, and I have invited him to dine with me this evening." He gestured for me to sit on the bench beside him.

I sat there, nervously self-conscious in my shabby wool cloak, yet wishing that I had not had the temerity to accept Baudoin's invitation. After a few moments, though, the attention of the other diners wandered back to their own conversations, meals and drink. Baudoin's cousin, if such he was for this was a common enough form of courteous address among noble peers even if not related, glared at me for a while longer then he got up and staggered off into the darkness, muttering about 'sitting with peasants' or some such.

"Don't mind, Guibert," said Baudoin by way of apology. "He's just drunk. He's been surly and resentful of everyone and everything ever since his father disinherited him. That's why he came on the pilgrimage in the first place. He had a habit of riding out onto his father's demesne and making life generally unpleasant for the lesser folk there on the land. So his father decided to make his second son, Aimery, his heir. Aimery is much more sensible. He'll make a better lord of the manor than ever Guibert could be."

"Is Guibert truly your cousin, my lord?"

"Yes, he is a distant relation of my mother's kin. The Duke was somewhat reluctant to bring him but truly we need every man who is willing to make this trek to the Orient. Guibert's father made an appeal to Lord Godfroi to take him and the Duke capitulated."

That explained Guibert's behaviour but what of the rest of the company? The longer I sat with Baudoin the more I noticed that people around us stole occasional angry glances our way, at me so I believed, and I felt that Guibert was not the only one who resented my presence as an affront to their dignity, a mere cleric—if the truth be known, a clerical student, even lowlier, dining with them at table. No one offered to pass any meat or drink until Baudoin himself offered it to me. I knew it was because of my lowly stature and they felt me beneath them. Well, what did I expect, I whose life began in the rooms above a merchant's warehouse? I could befriend as many noblemen as I liked but I would never be numbered among them.

Baudoin and I passed an hour or so in pleasant conversation, nonetheless, as I tried to ignore those who shot me disapproving glances. After a time, I begged exhaustion from the day's martial instruction and the late hour and bade my host good night. Baudoin expressed disappointment that I must go, for which I was gratified, but from the relieved expressions on the faces of our neighbours, I think he was the only one sorry to see me leave. I thanked him over and again and made my way back to my tent where I slumped into my blankets, happy that the evening had ended.

I think I shall sleep now and leave off writing until another time.

V Kalendis Novembris, MXCVI

We have arrived in Nish, or Nysos as our Byzantine hosts call it, after a four-day trek. After leaving Alba Graeca, which town I have since learned is known locally as Beograd, we followed the Danuvius for half a day across a relatively flat plain then turned southward into another river valley, heavily forested, the mountains gradually crowding its sides, through which a series of narrow roads wound their way toward Nish. The snows finally came, making our journey uncomfortable and muddy, although the inclement weather lasted only the first day during which, after snowing through the beginning hours of the day, the sky propelled icy rains at us. Luckily, Baudoin of Stavelot loaned me one of his extra cloaks of oiled leather that worked wonderfully well in keeping me dry. As ever, I am grateful for his friendship and the favour that he shows me.

On the morning of the third day of our journey from Alba Graeca we travelled through a deep forest. A forbidding place, the dry, dead-looking branches shivered, clacking hollowly together in a stiff north wind, the few brittle leaves still attached rattling like dry bones. The people were strangely silent but the sound of our passage, jingling harness, sticks on the path crunching under hoof and shoe and wagon wheel, the nervous snorting and whinnying of horses, echoed through the surrounding trees.

A large part of the company riding at the head of the army's column were the Duke and his immediate retainers, including his brother the Lord Baudoin, Baudoin of Stavelot, Geoffroi of Esch and his brother, Henri, Baudoin le Bourg, and other important men with them, so I rode not far behind my own Lord Baudoin, several horses back, as was my habit now. My *langsweord* hung conspicuously heavy from the belt at my waist. I reached my hand down and loosened it somewhat in its scabbard, a nervous gesture.

Suddenly, we heard an alarming hammering of hooves coming toward us from further on up the road. Then two of the company of outriders who had preceded us in order to give advance warning of any enemy out of our sight ahead of us appeared, pounding down the narrow road, clods of mud and dead leaves flying behind them in their speed. We all pulled up short and momentarily they reached us.

One of them made an abbreviated gesture of salute to the Duke, then spoke: "My lord, a company of armed men waits ahead, two or three miles."

"And are they friend or foe?" The duke's brother asked impatiently.

"An embassage from the Emperor's governor at Nish, lord, one of whom carries a letter from the Byzantine Emperor, Alexius, himself, to Duke Godfroi."

"How many are they?"

"Perhaps half a century, lord."

By this he meant a company of about half a hundred men. The relatively small size of this force suggested friendliness since if they meant us harm they would have come in larger numbers to forestall the advance of our forces. I took the letter to be an acknowledgement from Alexius of the Duke's welcome presence. The Duke must have thought so too for he dismissed the man and we rode on at the same walking pace.

My Lord Baudoin turned around in his saddle. When he had found me in the troop of riders following along behind, he signalled for me to approach. I kicked my horse forward and a gap was made for me immediately behind him since the others there had also seen the Comte's gesture. The ranks around me closed up once more.

After a half hour or so, we came to a low rise, the forest dropping away from the road, where, at the crest of this low hill, we could see the remainder of our outriders awaiting us. The Duke signalled for the columns to halt. There was some confusion for a pace as he decided who would accompany him. Meanwhile, one of the outriders came back to meet us.

"My Lord Duke," he greeted Godfroi, and offered a brief obeisance from his saddle. "The Emperor's ambassador awaits your pleasure at the bridge below. The Greeks are on the far side of the river. None has passed to this side so there is no danger that I can see."

Most of the company at the head of the army, those surrounding Godfroi and his brother, trotted forward, myself among them, about twenty-five of us in all I would venture a guess. We rode two and three abreast down the trail to a sturdy wooden bridge spanning a swift, roiling river. On the far side, just as the outrider had said, awaited a company of Greeks in arms, seated on their horses. Though we were outnumbered twice I felt no fear since, as we have all been told, the Greeks are poor fighters, this being the reason their emperor had called on the armies of the West to defend his kingdom from the invading Saracens.

The whole company of Franks halted short of the bridge and Godfroi and Baudoin rode clattering onto the bridge. One of the Greeks came forward also and dismounted near the centre of the wooden span. He bowed deeply in obeisance and spoke rapidly in the Greek tongue. Then he rose to an upright position again.

The Duke shook his head impatiently and spoke to Lord Baudoin. Godfroi's brother then rode back to where I sat my horse and ordered me to accompany him back to the other two men. I did so without question.

I dismounted, bowed and spoke to the Greek ambassador. He was a short man, with an almost adolescent growth of beard, which was unusual for a Greek since they are more usually thicker of beard than even our Franks, though in spite of this, of course, they are not manlier. He looked most untrustworthy.

"My lord, I speak your language somewhat so my Lord Duke has ordered that you speak through me. I will in turn return his words to you. Is this satisfactory?"

"Quite, despite your abominable accent," he replied, blandly. "Tell me your lord's name." I had no time to be personally offended, and besides, I knew that I did not speak his language as well as I wrote or read it despite Brother Piccolo's best attempts to teach me.

"This is my Lord Duke Godfroi de Bouillon, Duke of Lower Lorraine, and his brother, Comte Baudoin of that same country." I indicated each lord in turn. I did not know the Greek words for 'Duke' or 'Comte' so I used the Frankish terms. "We are here by the command of the Most Holy Father and Bishop of the Holy See of Rome, Pope Urban, and wish to proceed to the Emperor's Palace at the great city of Constantinopolis."

"We are aware of why you have come," the man replied, dryly insolent. "Tell your Duke that I am Michael Cephalinios, recently appointed by the Governor of Nysos as ambassador to the bar... that is, to the Western leaders, lately come into his territory."

I glared at him for a moment, for I am sure he was about to say 'ambassador to the barbarians.' He blithely returned my look, quite unconcerned, the mannerless swine. I passed his words on to Duke Godfroi.

Before the Duke could reply Michael Cephalinios spoke again.

"I have a letter, written in the language of the Old Caesars, recently arrived in Nysos into the care of my Lord Governor there, having come directly from the hand of the Basileios, Alexios himself, to be delivered into the hands of this same Western duke, Godfroi. Your lord is to read this letter before continuing any further into our country."

He proffered the parchment to the Duke. I did not know this word 'basileios,' so I asked him. He explained, through circumlocution, that it meant 'emperor' in our tongue. I relayed his message to the Duke and his brother, toning down the arrogance, wondering at his outrageously impudent manner of speaking. These Greeks must think they own the world.

Godfroi studied the letter for a time with some obvious difficulty, and then passed it over to his more learned sibling. Baudoin quickly scanned its contents and then began laughing out loud. I saw Michael Cephalinios's face fall then cloud over at this reaction.

"It seems brother that we are making the mighty Emperor Alexius Comnenus a bit nervous. He is offering us a bribe." I noticed that the Comte gave the emperor's name the western pronunciation rather than the Greek one used by the ambassador.

A look of puzzlement on his face, the Duke asked, "What do you mean, Baudoin? What sort of bribe?"

"The Emperor would like us to know that open markets will be available all along the route to the great city, and he offers us further gifts of food and supplies, if we will only behave ourselves and not ravage the countryside on the way there." Baudoin finished with a sardonic twist of his lip and a flick of his chin directed at Michael Cephalinios.

The Duke mused for a few moments, staring at the ambassador, his eyes dark beneath his lowered brows, leaning over the high pommel of his saddle. Then he straightened and pulled up his mount's head with his reins.

"Tell the ambassador, whatever-you-say-his-name-is, that we accept his emperor's hospitality."

I transformed his words into Greek and told Michael Cephalinios what he had said. The ambassador's plump, round face had already split into a grin and he bowed to Duke Godfroi. Then he turned back to me, his face returning to its former dour expression.

"This interview is ended. Tell your lord he may follow me to Nysos at his pleasure."

"Your nose looks like a boil on a swine's ass," I told him amiably in the Frankish tongue, quietly enough so that my lords could not hear.

I saw his eyes glint in fury for just a moment before he collected himself and smiled a smile as slick as olive oil. He bowed once more toward the two lords then quickly returned to his horse and clambered into the saddle, swung his mount around, and thumped off the bridge.

I smiled to myself. As I had suspected from the beginning, he spoke the Frankish language.

I remounted my horse and Baudoin shouted for one of the Franks to go back and tell the rest of the army to catch us up. I knew this would be a difficult and time-consuming task since an army that has stopped to rest always takes some little time in resuming its former pace. As we waited, Comte Baudoin stood up in his saddle stretching his long back and neck. He looked over at me, a wry smile on his face.

"Why," he asked me, "did you tell him his nose looks like a boil on a swine's ass? Not that it doesn't, mind you," he added.

"You heard that, my lord? I thought I had said it mildly enough." Now I had fallen into the soup.

"I assume you had a good enough reason for insulting an ambassador representing his Imperial Highness, the Emperor of the Eastern Empire, Alexius?"

I swallowed, hard, and cleared my throat nervously. "Well, lord, I suspected from the beginning of our discussion that he speaks the Frankish tongue."

"Because his nose resembles an eruption on a hog's nether region? How did you reach that particular conclusion?"

I looked down in shame. Now he said it like that, it did sound rather outrageous.

"No, lord, because he understood it when I said it to him."

"How do you know he understood?"

"He became momentarily angry. And, as they say, if a look was a dagger, I'd be dead. He could say nothing about the insult unless he wanted to reveal to us that he had understood it."

Baudoin laughed until tears appeared at the corner of his eyes. And then he laughed some more.

"Well done, lad. Well done, indeed." He reached into one of his leather saddlebags. His hand came out gripping something and tossed it lightly to me.

I caught it.

"A gift," the Comte said. "So that you may have something to defend yourself from the daggers of Greek eyes."

I looked at the object he had thrown to me. It *was* a dagger, the blade about a hand long, the grip worked beautifully in silver, ivory and gold. The gift astonished me. I protested that it was far too valuable for the likes of me. But truly it was a wondrous weapon.

"No, not at all," he said. "It is little more than you deserve for you have rendered me, and your Duke, a good service here today. Now we know something that the enemy thought, and possibly still thinks, we didn't know. That can be very useful. The handle of that dagger, by the way, is made from the horn of an *oliphant*. Do you know what manner of creature that is?"

"Such as those used by Hannibal in attacking the armies of Scipio Africanus, my lord."

"You are well-read, indeed. Not many Franks have actually seen the creature in the flesh, though. Have you?"

I assured him that I had not, although I had seen a few horns from the beast at Köln long ago, or so it seems now these several years later, and expressed my wish that perhaps I might see a live *oliphant* in the Holy Land or somewhere else in the East. I hardly dared mention that I was not a Frank but Aenglisch, although, my grandfather was, of course, a Frank.

"Perhaps you might see one when we reach the great city, Constantinople; I have heard that all things under the sun eventually find their way to the Great City."

I expressed my wonder at such a notion and agreed that if this was so, then there might well be a chance to see an *oliphant* there. I think our conversation had begun to bore him then for he began looking away from me and toward the far side of the bridge. So I decided I would thank him for his gift once more and bowed low. I had to catch myself for I bowed so low that I almost fell out of the saddle. I managed with some little difficulty to straighten up again and tried to look dignified enough to be worthy of his gift. I tried but Baudoin failed to notice. When I looked up, the Comte had already moved further up the bridge.

Then, as the army began to catch us up I fell in among the riders and headed across the bridge myself.

The journey to Nish from the river crossing lasted several more days. The Greeks preceded us all the way and they kept to themselves even when we stopped at night to eat and sleep. I heard many grumbling that this insulted our leaders but others merely laughed that the Greeks wanted to be far enough away from us that they could run at the first sign of any trouble. Near the end of the third following day, by which I mean today, of course, the mountains gradually parted to reveal flat lands to the south and east. In the distance we saw many villages peppering the sides of the meandering river's floodplain. Far off, a fortress and a walled city could be seen: Nish. As the sun fell low into the mountains to the west, streaking the sky with banners of red and purple, we arrived at the city.

The ambassador, Cephalinios, surely had sent riders ahead to announce our arrival for when we came to the city a large contingent of soldiers headed by the Governor himself waited outside its gates to greet us. He met with the Duke and a number of the Frankish nobles during which conference they obviously discussed the disposition of the encampments of our people. They decided that we would camp a league or so downriver on a low rise that backed on the river, a position that assured our leaders a defensible area in which to temporarily settle.

Since a week or so had passed since our last provisioning, we needed to make use of the markets hereabouts as well and the negotiations included coming to terms for the supply of the Frankish army at reasonable prices. Further, the Governor invited the Duke and as many of his nobles who cared accompany him to a special session in the Governor's palace to discuss further matters relevant to the Franks and to the Emperor. I was honoured to attend this meeting along with my lord, Comte Baudoin.

Of course, I had no special place among those present. I merely stood behind the Comte should he require any translation from the Greek of any of those of the Emperor's contingent seated nearby him. After an hour of standing I must admit I became rather bored and fatigued by the whole thing. Certainly, the Governor seemed fluent enough in the

Latin language and also knew a smattering of the Frankish tongue, this owing to the fact that a number of Norman Franks served in his city guard. So my talents, such as they are, for the Greek language came to nought tonight, at least as far as concerned my lord, Baudoin.

I returned to my tent very tired indeed.

Tomorrow we leave for Sofia and thence to Philippopolis.

Quinque Diebus Ante Domini Nostri Natale

We are nearing Constantinople, the Great City, or Metro Polis as the Greeks say. I must admit I am very excited at seeing this wonderful place about which I have heard and read so much. We hope to reach the city before the celebrations of the Christ Mass for the birth of our Lord, five days hence. Certainly, I look forward myself to a much-needed rest, not to mention some happy festive activity during the holy days of the Nativity.

Beneath these pleasant thoughts, however, lies something blacker. I feel a deep need for purification and forgiveness, for confession and spiritual cleansing. Beyond simply atoning for the ordinary quotidian trespasses and injuries we all do to our fellows, I have need of a priest, of a shriving. For I have killed.

We had arrived at Philippopolis some time after taking leave of Nish, having first camped for a few days outside Sofia before travelling on to the further city. We camped outside Philippopolis and sent in our representatives to negotiate the resupply of our army, while at the same time, Duke Godfroi and some other eminent men also entered the city to meet with its leaders. Apparently, some of our people heard there a tale of the great lord, Hugh of Vermandois, brother of the King of Francia, passing through Philippopolis not long before as a prisoner of the Emperor.

That was poor enough news in itself but one further part of the tale chilled my blood: among those accompanying the prince was my captor of old, Drogo of Nesle. My heart leapt in to my mouth when I heard this, causing such palpitations to course through my chest that I thought the organ would burst with the emotion passing through it. Then rationality returned as I remembered my position in the entourage of Lord Baudoin. Surely, Drogo could have no further claim on me as his prisoner in the face of this attachment to my new lord's household? I have resolved to try to avoid Drogo in any case should our paths cross.

After returning to our encampment that evening, the Duke decided, after discussions with the other great men, at once to send a messenger ahead to the Emperor with a demand to release our fellow Franks. In the letter he composed, he threatened reprisals and emphasized the size of the force of Franks under his banner bearing down upon the Greeks' capital city. After Baudoin had jotted down the gist of this he ordered me to transcribe the finished version into both the Latin and the Greek languages to be sent on with the Duke's envoy.

I believe, from my reading of this letter and its subtle wording, that Godfroi wished to gain the favour of Hugh of Vermandois, who was after all the brother of the King of the Franks, by effecting his release under threat of violence against the Byzantines. Having a prince obligated to one surely is no small thing and perhaps the Frankish king himself might feel similarly obliged. Another motive surely at work within Duke Godfroi was his wish to ensure the Emperor appreciated that he should cooperate with our Franks, treating us as friends and allies rather than as invaders and so ensuring we would receive all manner of assistance as we passed through the Metro Polis on our way to the Holy Land. The Duke I think meant to be reasonable yet firm in his demands.

Baudoin on the other hand felt only contempt for the Greeks. He couched the words he dictated to me in belligerent terms meant to provoke rather than to soothe. I was sure the Emperor, if any kind of ruler at all, would be greatly offended by the venomous tone of the letter the Comte composed on his brother's behalf. However, I did my duty to my lord and wrote down all that he bade me inscribe.

On the next day's dawning, we discovered that Baudoin of Hainault and Geoffroi of Esch's brother, Henri, had ridden away before dawn to who knew where. At first we could only conjecture why they had left in such haste until, when their liege men were interrogated, we learned the truth. Eventually we discovered that the two had heard accounts contrary to the reports we had already received concerning Hugh's captivity. The rumours they had gathered indicated that the Emperor had not taken the Frankish prince as his prisoner but had instead lavished incredible gifts upon Hugh as his honoured guest at the Great City. Of course the defection of Baudoin and Henri left the Duke and his brother livid with rage especially since they gave no credence to this other tale knowing, as we all do, the perfidy of Greeks.

By the time we reached Selymbria on the southern sea coast the Duke still had received no word from the Emperor

Alexius concerning the Frankish ultimatum. Selymbria is a pretty little town a day or two's journey from Constantinople. Surrounded by low hills to the northeast and northwest, it stretches along the beach, with a fort situated on a cliff facing a long, shallow bight on the southern coast. A narrow river cascades down from the hills through a gently sloping valley, bringing fresh water to the populace there.

We spread out on either side of this waterway on the grassy rise behind the town as we set up our camp. Here we would await word from the Emperor, for Godfroi would go no farther until Alexius replied. This apparent utter disregard for the Duke's dignity and seeming nonchalance on the part of the Emperor at the looming threat of violence against his city caused Godfroi to lose all sense of propriety with respect to his earlier impeccable decorum while travelling through the Greek lands. We settled in to await a response to the Duke's letter of protest and we began to raid the countryside in search of supplies for our army. What else were we to do?

The town market left something to be desired. There was little to be had there in the way of foodstuffs or other necessities for an army on the move as large as ours. I suspect this owes to the fact of the town's proximity to the immense *urbs* of Constantinople. How can commerce at the local level thrive when such a grand marketplace is so close to hand? Not much was available that would go very far with our troops. Rather than move on to the Metro Polis, the Duke gave his leave to the folk that they might forage the countryside in search of such things as they might find desirable there. One way to gain the Emperor's attention, I suppose.

Several large parties of foragers rode out the day after we arrived on the coast to the east and west of Selymbria along the Marmoran coast in hopes of finding supplies of food with strict orders to trade only for Godfroi did not want to offend the Emperor by ransacking any villages, especially this close to the Metro Polis. I rode in one of the parties beside my friend, Baudoin of Stavelot, on his invitation. I felt no nervousness or trepidation at this, since the day was bright with cheerful sunshine, though somewhat chilly and, after all, we sought only to find a marketplace or two in order to purchase supplies, or barter for them, to replenish our people.

As the hours passed, our large group gradually split off into smaller cadres, each heading off in different directions since we had found no other towns along our route and so no markets. Some headed north, others back along the way we had come hoping for greener pastures elsewhere. Baudoin's company, of which I was part, continued to ride for several hours eastward along the bluffs above the shoreline until we came to a shelf that stretched gently down to a small, rocky inlet. Not far from the water's edge we saw an encampment strung out along the rough beach. It seemed to be in rather poor shape as there were no tents or other shelters than a few overturned boats and some lean-to's made from the scrubby wood lining the shore.

We turned our horses down the hill to investigate.

As we rode we saw people fleeing into the bushes and scrambling up the hillside trying to escape from us. This reaction was certainly understandable in the circumstances since we probably looked a fearsomely large force to the small group of refugees. They could not know our intent and must of necessity assume the worst. Baudoin ordered a halt. Then he shouted down to the people, using the Frankish tongue. This seemed somewhat pointless to me since, if they were Greeks and they probably were, they likely would not understand his words. I was astonished to find that I was wrong.

At his shouts the people, almost as one, stopped their flight and turned to face us. A dirty, bedraggled man crawled out from one of the overturned craft nearest to us and stood before us.

"My lord? You's are Franks?" he asked of Baudoin in a crude Frankish dialect that bespoke a rough, peasant up-bringing, perhaps in the Champagne.

Surprise showing on his face and in his voice, Baudoin replied, "Indeed. And you, you are a Frank as well?"

"Yes, lord. Most of us here is; some Alemaigni. Oh, I's happy to see you, lord. Can you's help us?" He asked, his voice pleading.

"What has happened? Why are you here? Where did you come from?" The questions poured out of Baudoin without giving the villein time to answer any one of them. When he stopped, finally, the other responded.

"We was followers of Peter, the Blessed Hermit, on our way to Jerusalem to be with our Saviour there."

He stopped, made the sign of the cross over himself and offered nothing further, as if the rest of his story was self-evident so Baudoin was forced, after a moment or two of waiting for the peasant to continue, to prod him for more information.

"How did you come to be here, in this bay?"

"We was ship-wrecked here." He stopped his explana-tion again. "A man gets to thirstin' what with all this talkin'.

Would you's have a splash of wine with you's a tall, lord," he asked, obsequious.

Some of our men snickered derisively at that but Baudoin obligingly uncorked his wineskin and passed it down to the other man without comment. The villein took a long swallow then smacked his lips in satisfaction.

"Hits the spot that does. Haven't had a decent swig for weeks. D'you mind if I hang on to this? My throat does get some parched when I has to talk so much."

Baudoin grinned wryly. "By all means, if it helps to keep your tongue moving. I meant, as well, why are you here in the Greek lands so far from your homeland?"

"Like I says, we was followers of Peter goin' to Jerusalem liked he asked us. There was Italians and Alemaigni with us, too. We come all the way to that big city of the Greeks, forget how it's called, big long name, but anyway, their king sent us all across to the other side of the water so's we could get on the road to Jerusalem." When he paused again, Baudoin signalled impatiently for him to continue. "Anyways, we gets to the other side and we marches down to this town called Civetot and camps out there. Peter says we got to wait for the big heads, beggin' yer pardon me lord, to come join us with their big armies 'fore we goes any farther. Well, that don't sit too well with some of the regular fighters. A bunch of 'em splits off an' some goes with the Italians an' some with the Alemaigni and they all goes off to some place to the east, another big Greek city an' we hears they takes it and're divvying up the loot 'mongt theyselves. So then we all gets off down the road to get our fair share. Not Peter, though. He's gone back to the king over in the big city. Not sure why." He paused for another long pull at the wineskin, smacking his lips loudly, then continued.

"Well, it's all just a trick. The Greeks attacks us, least we thinks they're Greeks, they looks the same as Greeks, anyways. They attacks us a mile or two down the road an' all the horse soldiers comes riding right back down the road on top of us. Ain't no way we're goin' on if the likes of them're runnin' so we all lights right back down the road after 'em the way we come up. Them Greeks're right on top of us, firin' arrows down on us from their horses an' they follows us right the way back to town. They butchers everyone they finds. A bunch of us manages to find some boats and we gets in an' heads out to sea not carin' which way we's headin' just so's we get away from those Greeks. Which we does." He stopped, looking down, and scuffed the ground with his foot.

"Anyways, we drifts for a week or so an' then we ends up here. Been here ever since. Don't know where we are but some of us're fishermen so we got that for food an' we're all too scared to go out anywhere on land 'cause we don't know where we are an' there might be more Greeks around."

"How long have you been here," asked Baudoin.

"Oh, goin' on to a couple of months, I'd guess. Nice to see you here, though." He looked abashed and again kicked the ground with his toe.

Baudoin considered for a few moments then said, "Well, get your people together and come with us. There are no Greeks about and you'll be safe enough if you stay close. We'll take you back to our camp."

The peasant lurched forward onto his knees and took Baudoin's stirruped foot in his hand, kissing it. "Thank you, lord. Praise God for sendin' you's. Thank you."

Shortly, the scruffy refugees had assembled and, after we had given them water or wine as they chose, we led off on horseback with the bedraggled little band following.

Baudoin decided that we should return to Selymbria without stopping, since he felt that the Duke and the other great lords would want to interview these people further and the sooner we got them back to the shelter of the town and our encampment the better. The ragged troupe following us on foot hindered our progress, of course, and several more hours passed before we saw the town again. With nightfall almost upon us, we rode into the Frankish camp. We left the refugees on its outskirts to find what food and accommodations they might.

Next morning, Godfroi ordered the refugees rounded up and sent to him for debriefing. My duty, as always, included recording the conversations of such meetings on behalf of my Lord Baudoin that he might have a permanent record of the event so I joined the gathering. We assembled in a large hall whose pillared facade fronted the plaza at the centre of the town of Selymbria, which the town leaders had gladly surrendered to our use on Godfroi's request.

I sat on a low bench to one side of a large polished wood table at which sat the Duke, his brother, Baudoin, another Baudoin, he of Le Bourg, yet a third Baudoin, my friend from Stavelot since he had been the one to find the Frankish survivors and, finally, Geoffroi of Esch. Other of the Frankish lords ranged around the hall nearby the table on various chairs and benches. Before long the tattered refugees, looking no cleaner though perhaps less hungry than when I had seen them yesterday, shuffled into the hall where they were herded into a clump before the table by a handful of our spearmen. Godfroi leaned toward Baudoin of Stavelot, whispering, and Baudoin pointed to the man with whom he had spoken yesterday. Nodding, Godfroi straightened and pointed to the man.

"Come forward," he ordered him.

The refugee immediately left his companions and fearfully fell to his knees, alone before the lords. Godfroi did not ask the man to stand but instead left him kneeling there and ordered him to repeat the story he had told to Baudoin of Stavelot the day before.

In a trembling voice, his eyes downcast, the villein recounted substantially the same tale he had related the previous day, although this time he did not ask for wine to keep his throat lubricated. I could tell even from where I sat that he was completely cowed.

When he had finished, Godfroi ordered him to step back and ordered another man forward from the ragged assemblage. This man spoke only Alemaigni and so the interview continued in that language. He told a story very close to that of the Frankish villein before him, adding that he had spoken with a man in the town of Civetot who had in turn spoken with a Greek merchant lately come from Nicaea. The Greek had said that Nicaea had been taken by a large Alemaigni force under their leader, a Frank named Rainald, where the Alemaigni were supposedly looting that city and dividing up its treasures. This Greek merchant, the Alemaigne refugee believed, had been a spy sent by the treacherous Greeks to gull the followers of Peter the Hermit into riding forth into an ambush with a deceitful tale of the fall of Nicaea.

In my opinion, they had been lured by their own greed at the thought of the riches waiting to be looted in the Emperor's town. Their destruction had been a result of the fact that in their greed they had rushed headlong into disaster, exercising no intelligent caution despite the fact they were in enemy and hostile territory. But no one asked me for my opinion so I did not give it.

I glanced at the Duke for a moment and I saw in his face a growing anger, although at what, I was yet unsure. Several others of the refugees came forward as bidden and each told his tale, all agreeing that they had been ambushed by Greeks. I wondered at this, since why would the Emperor send troops to destroy the very people whose help he had asked more than a year ago? Were the attackers indeed Greeks? That they were enemies of the Greeks seemed much more likely to me, though whether or not they had been Saracens was a matter for debate. Would these simple peasants know a Saracen if they met one face to face? Would I, come to that? I have no idea what a Saracen looks like although I assume since they are not followers of Our Lord, Jesus the Christ, they must be very unlike us or the Greeks since they practice an utterly foreign religion. But perhaps not.

If the attackers had been Greeks after all, conceivably some further reason had forced the Emperor to neutralize them. I had seen evidence of the kind from my experiences in Hungary with Emicho and with King Coloman. If the horde I had seen following Peter the Hermit in Mainz, now in Byzantium, had gotten out of hand or inconvenienced the Greeks in any way the Emperor might have reacted harshly in just the same way that the Hungarians had reacted to Volkmar, Gottschalk and Emicho.

Duke Godfroi believed the stories he heard, though. Adding this latest turn of events to the kidnapping of King Philippe of Francia's brother, Hugh of Vermandois, of which we had heard in Philippopolis, and the fact that the Emperor had so far failed to respond to the Duke's letter of outrage, he became completely convinced that the refugees' stories were clear evidence of the Emperor's perfidy. Thinking of it that way, I began to believe it, too.

Godfroi had also heard of our general lack of success in finding ready markets nearby. The discovery of the refugees had of course cut Baudoin of Stavelot's foraging short so that we had brought nothing else back except more hungry mouths to feed. None of the other parties had had much luck either. Everywhere they stopped they were turned away from the markets, the townspeople in the area citing that they had nothing to share and lacked substantial resources with which they could part. Although disappointed and angered, our people had reined in their resentment because of Godfroi's injunction not to engage in any unlawful actions. Now the Duke rescinded that order. He commanded the foraging parties to reform and to pursue to their maximum effort the task of bringing back supplies to the army. No restrictions.

Once again, I rode out of camp under Baudoin of Stavelot's command. This day I felt some apprehension knowing that this would be a much more dangerous mission than yesterday's. Baudoin had asked me outright if I felt any discomfort or fear in accompanying what was essentially a war party. I assured him that, though I felt some measure of fear as was only natural with this my first such foray, I would not let it overcome me to the point that it would interfere with the months of weapons training I had had at his hands or with my duty to our people. This answer seemed to satisfy him. However, though I said nothing of it to Baudoin, I also felt some measure of disquiet at the thought of deliberately raiding and pillaging from what were essentially innocent townspeople who were not directly responsible for the actions of their political leaders. Nonetheless, that burden would soon be theirs. I could only hope that whomever we encountered would comply with our demands.

We rode to the northeast this time, a troupe of some fifty horsemen, knowing that we would find nothing along the coast. Shortly after noon we arrived at a village, not as large as Selymbria but large enough to have its own humble marketplace. The doors and windows were all shut against us and the stalls empty. I had a grim feeling as our horsemen began to dismount.

The soldiers formed in to groups of five and six and then went door to door. Rather than knocking they simply kicked the doors in where they could and ripped the shutters off the windows and climbed through where they could not. At each house they entered they brought out whatever they could find of food or anything else deemed valuable. Soon, they had heaped a large pile of portable goods in the centre of the village's single street. None of the villagers offered us any resistance. They cowered in their houses and let us take what we wanted. And we did. We loaded our pack mules until we could load no more. Then we left, taking our stolen goods with us.

I hoped all such encounters would be as without incident.

Elsewhere, this was not the case. After we had returned from our raid I heard many of the Frankish *cnichts* boasting of the homes, farms and shops they had burned and of the people they had killed in the taking of plunder. I returned to my tent to rest and so that I did not have to listen to the evil tales of depravity.

On the following day, more raiding parties went out into the countryside, ranging far in all directions in the search for more plunder. More villages were sacked and burned and the evil continued for several more days. On the third day of the *chevauchee*, I accompanied a now grim-faced Baudoin of Stavelot with one hundred of our mounted warriors on a raid to the west. We rode for many hours until we came upon a low-walled town whose name I did not learn, though in size it rivalled Selymbria. The people there apparently had heard about the depredations upon the countryside by our Franks since they had blockaded the main street into the town, closing its main gate. We could see one area where the low perimeter wall had collapsed sometime in the past and the townspeople had thrown up a high wooden barricade to span the gap. The defenders clearly outnumbered us but the relatively poorly armed crowd behind their makeshift walls only elicited hoots of laughter from our soldiers. The gap with its wooden fence would be our target.

"Stay close by me," Baudoin urged me from my left.

I nodded and pulled my *langsweord* reluctantly scraping from its scabbard.

A number of our *cnichts* dismounted and began assailing the wooden wall with their battle axes. The defenders behind the barricade rained debris down on our men, some firing arrows, others hurling large stones, still others hurling refuse and offal. None of these hindered the assault, though. Before long, the wall was broken down, the people behind it fleeing back into the town, while our soldiers scrambled through the splintered gap to open the gates to the rest of us.

We spurred our horses forward. Riding into the town we could see that the streets were now deserted and I saw no one nearby. I followed Baudoin as he led the troop deeper into the town. Like Selymbria, this town had a large public building, some sort of meeting hall, stepped and porticoed like that other and fronting on a central plaza. Baudoin dismounted at the foot of the steps and I followed suit. Most of our horsemen rode on.

Half a dozen of us who had stopped with Baudoin strode up the stone-tiered plinth on which the building was built and through the white-stuccoed columns to the large wooden doors on the top level. The interior was well lit owing to a large opening in the roof in the centre of the building much like that other in Selymbria. The interior space consisted of a large open room with benches around the exterior walls set up on more tiered stone platforms. Rich, woven tapestries adorned the walls and a couple of men began to rip them down and roll them up for easier transport, although where they planned to sell them or what else they might do with them living in the field as we were doing on this armed pilgrimage, I could not imagine. At the rear of the hall I could see a large door and wondered where it led. Baudoin must have been thinking the same thing since he strode forward toward the door even as I spied it. Trying to stay true to his injunction to stay close to him I scrambled after his long-legged stride.

Baudoin opened the door cautiously, peering in. Just as he did this a force of more than a dozen armed men burst forth and he leapt back. As he jumped past me he grabbed the cowl of my woollen cloak and dragged me with him. We ran back to the centre of the hall, both of us shouting in fearful surprise to our comrades to close ranks for defence. Rather, Baudoin shouted for defence, I could only howl in alarm.

Everyone but me had round, flat shields of the type known as a *targe*, smaller than the great inverted tear-drop shield of the Frankish mounted warrior, but much more serviceable on these raiding skirmishes than the larger type. These *targes* they hurriedly slipped from their shoulders and held before them. I huddled in between Baudoin and another man, hoping I would be somewhat protected by the shield of the one and the *langsweord* of the other. We were far too few in number to form any sort of shield wall since the enemy could easily surround us but we had the advantage that our opponents seemed timid and reluctant to engage us in combat while we, excepting me of course, were all seasoned warriors. We revolved as a group about our centre, in hopes of confusing and further intimidating our assailants while slowly making our way toward one wall where we would have a more defensible position.

They seemed to recognise our tactic for several of them moved quickly between us and the wall. We stopped, waiting on their next move. It came almost immediately. The bulk of them, those away from the wall, suddenly rushed at us and we fell back a bit but were at once checked by the prospect of being forced into the other group of Greeks.

Two of our *cnichts* lunged at that group who fell back in fear while the rest of us broke off a bit and made a feint toward the others. Several of them rushed us and the dull thud of metal on wood and the bright clang of metal on metal resounded like hammers and bells through the hall as we met their rush. For my part, I could do little more than hold up my *langsweord* in both hands and fend off the blows.

I had heard that during the frenzy of battle a man sometimes becomes crazed with blood lust, impervious to his own pain, lost in a kind of berserker rage that takes away his mind, making him a dangerous fighter, fearful and mindful of nothing. I felt none of that. This, my first battle, left me terrified and sick. Every moment seemed an eternity, every motion part of a slow, measured, terrifying dance. I waited for the unseen blow from behind or from the side when a point or an edge would bite into my flesh and steal my life from me. Luckily, it never came.

The worst part for me occurred when two Greeks pressed in on Baudoin at once, bringing both of us near to death. Their blows came so fast and powerfully that the young lord fell to his knees under the assault. As he did, he lost balance somewhat and the edge of his *targe* caught me behind the knee, tripping me up. This had the effect of drawing me down and closer to Baudoin. Strangely, almost as if with another sense I was never aware I possessed, I knew what he was about to do even as he began to do it.

As the man on his right swung his sword, Baudoin threw up his shield to take the blow while almost immediately his own blade flashed out, the point biting deep into his opponent's throat. Unfortunately, this exposed his left side and the other man, he to the left of Baudoin, took advantage of the opening and swung his blade in a long, low arc which surely would have taken off Baudoin's shield arm. But I, with my new battle senses, saw this coming seemingly even before it began and lunged forward, thrusting my *langsweord* at the Greek as hard as I could, using both arms. The power of the thrust drove the man backward even as I propelled forward, my weapon lodged in his gut. As he hit the floor on his back I landed astraddle him and in the same moment regained my feet, twisting the blade out of him, and backed off.

I felt Baudoin clap me on the shoulder and fell back toward him, to regroup with the rest of our men. I hardly had time to consider that I had just killed a man.

With two of their men down the other townsmen grew more cautious. They seemed reluctant now to continue the fight. They milled together like a herd of cattle waiting to see what the wolves would do next. Then I noticed that three other Greeks had died under Frankish *sweords*. With nearly a third of their number dead, the rest thought better of staying to fight and momentarily fled to the door through which they had first rushed us and were gone.

"Are you alright, my lord," I inquired at once of Baudoin.

Panting, he let out a huff of air, "I'm fine. Thanks to you, my friend."

All of us were breathless, sweat dripping from our foreheads, shaking with the blood rush after the battle. All of the men gathered around and clapped my back and shoulders, congratulating me on my kill. I felt sick in the realization that I had taken a man's life at the same time that I felt pride for having come to the aid of my friend, Baudoin. I felt very confused.

Later in the day we had taken the town, then gathered and loaded everything we could transport on our pack animals. We left the town ransacked and broken. Baudoin had ordered his men not to set any fires, so the poor Greeks were spared that at least. We would not make the main Frankish camp before nightfall so we stopped just after sunset to rest for the night. We slept out on the ground throwing our horse blankets over us for warmth. I don't know if it was the cold or my conscience but I lay awake for most of the night thinking only of the face of the man whom I had killed. The look of surprise and pain on his face, his breath in my face as he let out his last gasp of air before dying. I must have struck something vital within him for his death came so quickly.

I lay awake trying to rationalize what I had done with the teachings of Brother Piccolo, his notion that all life was sacred, each representing in its way evidence of the hand of the Creator. Surely he would have condemned my deed as the foulest of crimes against another human being. But I had no choice in the matter. I must of necessity follow the commands of my lord, Baudoin Comte of Boulogne, and his brother Duke Godfroi, for we had made the chevauchee on their orders. I am Baudoin's sworn man and he my lord. In all things I must obey him for that is the way of the world and that is my oath. Further, I had killed only in defence. Surely, the Greek would have killed both Baudoin of Stavelot and me had he the chance.

Even so, the deed did not sit well with me and still does not. I wish that it had not happened and yet it is done and there is no taking it back. In the morning I still had not yet resolved the issue and as we made our way to Selymbria to join the Frankish host my heart was heavy and befuddled with confusion.

On the seventh day since we had begun our ravaging of the countryside, two of our rangers hurriedly returned to the camp to tell of a large party of Greeks approaching along the Constantinople road to the northeast. Our *milites* quickly armed themselves and the horsemen remaining in the camp mounted although I stayed behind, hanging back, unsure of my role. Shortly, Comte Baudoin and the Duke's party rode past and he called me to mount and accompany them.

I found my horse and joined the Comte's company, then all marched out on the road to challenge the newcomers, still a league or so from Selymbria. Surely, we thought, this must be a retaliatory force sent by that most perfidious Greek emperor, Alexius. First he kidnaps our Frankish prince, Hugh, then he denies us markets and supplies and now, finally, after we had come so far to help him and his people, he sends an army down upon us, just as he had done to the Hermit's people.

To our surprise, the Emperor's force had not advanced. Rather, they had halted and were lolling by the road, horses grazing idly in the fields and the men themselves sitting or standing in knots offering no aggression, though clearly wary with weapons at the ready, even though surely they had seen us approaching them.

A quartet of Greek horsemen rode toward us, hands well away from their weapons. Evidently, they wished to speak with us.

I assumed that my lord Baudoin had brought me along, once again, to act as his interpreter to the Greeks for certainly my fighting prowess, despite my performance on the chevauchee with the lesser Baudoin of Stavelot, had not raised me much further in the lord's esteem, although I had received a new fur-lined cloak from him as a result of my help in preventing his cousin's maiming or death at the hands of the Greek villager. Not as a soldier but as an interpreter I readied myself to ride forward to talk with the Emperor's men. Then, the forward-most rider began to speak to us in the Frankish tongue.

"I am Radulf of Peeldelau. Who leads?"

Godfroi nudged his horse forward. "I do. I am Godfroi of Bouillon, Duke of Lorraine. You are a Frank?"

Radulf inclined his head. "I am, my lord. I once served Robert Guiscard, Duke of Apulia, and his son, Bohemond, in Dyrrachium but now I serve the Emperor Alexios Comnenos, who has sent me to escort you and your people peaceably to his great city of Constantinople. He sends your people gifts of food and supplies and gold for you, their leader."

"We have food and supplies," the Duke replied. "The towns hereabout have been accommodating enough, despite their initial reluctance."

Many of the Franks within earshot laughed aloud at that. There was a murmur and more laughter as those who had heard passed along the comment to those who had not and those who had understood the joke explained it to those who had not. Radulf sat uneasily, clearly discomfited.

"Nonetheless, lord duke, the Emperor requests you move on to the great city."

"He must first release the King's brother."

"My lord?" Radulf looked puzzled.

"Hugh of Vermandois. Brother to the king of the Franks, Philippe. We know he was kidnapped; we heard of it in Philippopolis."

Radulf leaned in his saddle facing a man astride a horse behind him.

"Roger. What of this?"

The Roger addressed walked his mount forward. "My lord," he spoke deferentially to Duke Godfroi. "My lord, I have seen the Lord Hugh in the great city. I can assure you he is not a captive. Nor was he kidnapped."

"And who are you, that I should believe anything you say to me?"

"Your pardon, my lord. I am Roger, son of Dagobert. I also serve the Emperor."

Godfroi rolled his eyes impatiently. "Obviously. What of the Prince Hugh?"

"Lord, he is a guest of the Emperor Alexios. I have seen him in the palace, happy and enjoying the Emperor's hospitality. He was not kidnapped. Lord, he is a guest, nothing more."

Radulf interrupted. "Duke Godfroi, the Emperor has sent a generous gift of gold to you. To assure you of his friendship. I humbly beg to present this gift to you, now."

Godfroi nodded. With a gesture, Radulf bade one of the other horsemen ride back to the main van and shortly he returned leading a horse that carried two ornately decorated chests astrap its withers. Radulf dismounted, walked to the pack horse and then threw open one of the chests. I could see Godfroi's eyebrows rise as he saw the glistering contents of the box.

"These are the Emperor's bezants, my lord. His gift to you."

Godfroi hesitated. "A guest you say. Are you certain?"

"Yes, lord, the prince Hugh is the Emperor's guest" said Radulf. "And the Emperor would like you to be his guest at the great city as well. At your pleasure of course."

I think the Emperor's generous gift of gold and Radulf's heartfelt invitation had swayed the Duke.

"Come," Godfroi said to Radulf. "You will dine with us tonight."

He swung his horse around and spoke back over his shoulder. "And we will leave for your great city in the morning."

Caput Decimus

Duo Dies Post Domini Nostri Natale

I shall never forget my first view of the Great City of Constantinople. We had ridden out of Selymbria two days before, Radulf Peeldelau and his confrere, Robert, riding alongside Duke Godfroi and Comte Baudoin. I rode with Baudoin of Stavelot farther back in the procession, we two and others acting as chaperones to the covered *plaustrum* bearing the wife of Baudoin, Godivere, and her children and servants. Our Frankish army stretched out for many leagues along the road behind, probably the main part of it still gathering its belongings at Selymbria, preparing for the journey along the Constantinople road to the northeast.

The journey itself was rather dull and certainly uneventful. The road stretched through leagues of rolling countryside, low trees bordering the byways gradually giving way to farmland and the occasional villa as we progressed northerly and closer to the city. I found the rhythmic swaying of my horse under me somewhat hypnotic and I was soon lost in my thoughts.

The prospect of seeing and experiencing a city as large and renowned as Constantinople for me bordered on the excitement I surely would feel at visiting the Papal See at Rome or the Holy City of Jerusalem itself. I pondered the unlikelihood of my position. I could never have dreamed those many months ago when I had first heard about the Holy Father Urban's request for an armed pilgrimage to the East, and particularly after Archbishop Rothard had denied me permission to join the movement, I would one day soon ride into the greatest city of the Eastern Empire of the Greeks, the capital of its emperor, Alexius Comnenus, accompanying a comte of the Franks, Baudoin, and his brother, the Duke of Lower Lorraine, Godfroi de Bouillon, as their sworn man. However unlikely, I was here nonetheless.

For some strange, sad reason I found myself thinking about Brother Piccolo. I wondered what had become of him, if he had survived the assault on the cathedral at Mainz and if so, did he still reside there. The desertion of Rothard had enraged him and somehow I doubted that he could have rationalized the Archbishop's behaviour and reconciled with a man who had abandoned his constituency in such a heinous and cowardly fashion. I could not. Had the Brother moved on, I wondered?

I owed the Benedictine so much in terms of the knowledge he had taught me of the *ars medicinae* and generally for the compassionate worldview he had given me. He had not hesitated to come to the aid of a Jewish boy in need nor had he scoffed at my friendship with his parents, Ruth and her husband, Yaakob. He had not hesitated to offer his services to any who needed them even at the threat of death brought by the arrival of Emicho and his dark army to our city and the very doors of our home. He was a great, kind-hearted man. I know that I shall try to emulate him in everything I do for the rest of my life.

"You seem unusually quiet, my friend," Baudoin of Stavelot offered from his horse beside me.

"Sorry, lord," I responded momentarily. "I was only thinking."

"Of nothing too serious, I hope," he smiled.

"I was remembering my former *magister*, a Benedictine monk, at the cathedral school in Mainz. He was, still is I hope, a physician and a very learned man. A good man and kind."

"I believe you have mentioned him before."

"Yes. It's true. I have. It's just that I have been wondering what he would have thought about me taking the life of another man. It's not what he trained me to do. Quite the opposite, in fact." I spoke bitterly, though I had not meant to.

"Ah, that Greek. Perhaps your *magister* would have pointed out to you that in the taking of one life you saved the lives of many?"

I nodded. "Perhaps. Still, I think that when we have arrived at the capital, I will find myself a priest and ask for God's forgiveness."

"And so you should. No man should take delight or not find regret in killing others. But it is the way of the world and we have come to do the work the Holy Father commanded us to do. You are a soldier now; a soldier of Christ and of the army of Duke Godfroi and your immediate overlord, Baudoin. I'm sure all of them understand that if we are to reach Jerusalem we must eat. If the Greeks had given us free markets as they promised to do none of that would have happened. You should not trouble yourself unduly with the incident for there is no fault in the matter for you."

I knew that he was right, although I did not think of myself as a soldier. I felt no better about killing the man but I had done my duty, both to my lord Baudoin and ultimately to the Holy Father Urban and the holy mission with which he had entrusted our armies. I felt better realizing this even though I would still ask for God's forgiveness as soon as possible.

We rode on to Constantinople.

Then at last the Magnum Urbs lay before us. In all my dreams of the Emperor's capital I could never have imagined it as so tremendous a place. I had seen London, Köln and Mainz and other cities in the West but none of these compared to the breadth and size of Constantinople; each would have been lost inside its massive walls with room to spare. As we topped the last of the low hills before the land sloped down to the sea, the city came into view. Its megalithic walls draped across the land, stretching for what must be miles from one side of the immense metro polis to the other and all around it, from the Marmoran Sea on the one end to the inlet of the tapered bay called the Golden Horn on the other. From our distance it was impossible to judge the height of the those walls but it must have been prodigious for they looked huge even at our remove.

At the Emperor's request, delivered through Radulf Peeldelau, we rode not to the city itself but to the tapering upper waters of the Golden Horn. We continued along the hills, looking down over the flat plain on which the city lay, travelling northward to where the Horn curved in a long sweep like an elbow and began to widen its course as it flowed east until it emptied into the strait dividing the Black Sea, as the upper sea is called, from the Sea of Marmora.

We settled in along the hills near a rivulet that flowed into the Horn so that we would be close to a source of fresh water. From these heights we had a magnificent view of the walled city below us and the sea beyond. Over the water were the lands formerly held by the Emperor where the Infidel waited for us. Stupidly, I studied the landscape of the distant, farther shore trying in vain to spot some evidence of our enemy there. I could not even see people behind the walls of Constantinople, so far away was it; how could I see anything beyond the strait of St. George, as the watercourse separating this land from that is called?

Nearer, below, I could see the monastery near the suburb called Cosmidium and all the many smaller suburbs scattered across the plain. Smaller in contrast to the city of Constantinople that is. In their own right, these clusters of dwellings, markets and stables, taken together, represented a city nearly as large as that behind the great walls. How could the Emperor deny us sustenance now? We could simply take by violence whatever we wanted from these nearby suburbs as we had in Selymbria, if he did so. In any case, he had already sent messengers and supplies were on the way for our army.

We settled in and celebrated the Christ Mass as best we were able. A great tent had been set aside as a something of a church in which all the Duke's more important lords and their families, if such were present with their patriarchs, might celebrate the holy day. Duke Godfroi's own chaplain oversaw the mass. I for my part was able to confess my sin of homicide and received the blessing of one of the chaplain's lesser priests as a true soldier of our ultimate liege lord and spiritual master, the Christ. Afterward, I found Baudoin of Stavelot and the two of us got roaringly drunk on ale and for a time I forgot my guilty mind.

Today, two days after the celebrations of the Nativity, we had a royal visitor. By this I do not mean Alexius Comnenus, of course, but rather that prince of the Franks who had preceded us to Constantinople, Hugh of Vermandois. At first we were glad to see that the prince had escaped his Greek captors and we waited to hear how he had managed it, perhaps by ransom. As it turned out, Hugh had come at the behest of the Emperor, indeed as the latter's ambassador to Godfroi.

We saw his party advancing up the road alongside the Horn after they exited the city through the northernmost gate in the walls. This is called the Blachernae Gate, they say, owing to its proximity to a palace by the same name. Hugh and his escort rode slowly, with all the placid dignity of a royal embassage, as one would expect. They reached the outskirts of our encampment and, when the people understood that Hugh was with the party, the cheering crowds of our Franks parted to let them pass on to Godfroi's quarter.

The Duke had prepared a large open area on a hilltop for the reception. We had, of course, been forewarned of the Prince's arrival since a messenger had been sent out earlier in the day, delivering a vellum letter into the hands of Geoffroi of Esch, the Duke's chamberlain. Geoffroi had passed this to Baudoin, the Duke's brother, who read aloud to Godfroi that Hugh desired a conference with the Frankish leaders at their encampment and then the Duke gave orders immediately to prepare a meeting area where Hugh of Vermandois could be received as befitted his rank and dignity.

As personal clerk to Comte Baudoin I was ordered to attend my lord at the meeting. I waited with others of lesser rank along the sides of the impromptu courtyard in the open air of the space provided to the purpose. The day was damp and chill and earlier in the morning a light drizzle had finished, just enough to render the ground slick, with puddles gathered here and there and sticky mud adhering to everything.

I wore the oiled cloak given to me by Baudoin of Stavelot for it warmed me and kept back the chill somewhat, especially with the hood thrown over my head to prevent my body's warmth from escaping. Underneath, I wore buckskin pants with high boots of reddish leather laced to the knees, a linen shirt and over that a woollen tunic for additional warmth. Altogether, I was pleased with my appearance; so much more presentable was I now than in the shabby gown I had worn when I first arrived in the Comte's service. In the clothes my lord provided me these days, I looked nearly as well accoutred as many of the lesser Frankish lords present today.

Shortly after we had assembled, Prince Hugh arrived with his embassage. They dismounted their horses and a score or more of men entered the field-court of Godfroi. Curiously, I examined the prince. He was a man of middling height, not tall but neither was he short, in age perhaps forty years, a rather plain cast of face, a gloomy expression framed by a rather sparse wintering beard, and his head topped with limp, brownish hair tending to gray; an altogether unprepossessing individual but well-dressed in a sumptuous cloak of black fur trimmed in white ermine. A man of some wealth and dignity surely.

I was enjoying all the pomp and ceremony of Hugh's arrival when suddenly my heart leapt to my throat as I saw a man in the prince's escort whom I recognised instantly. It was Drogo of Nesle, my captor of old who had carried me from Mainz to Wiesselburg as his forced chronicler. I had heard rumour in Philippopolis that he rode with Hugh of Vermandois, now I knew it to be true. I hunched into my cloak, pulling the folds of its hood close around my face. However, I had nothing to fear for the moment as all eyes were on Duke Godfroi of Lorraine and his visitor, Prince Hugh of Vermandois.

The two lords embraced, giving each other the kiss of peace on each cheek. They finished their greeting with a hug and clap on the back then stepped away from each other. Some time passed while Hugh introduced those notables of his party whom he deemed worthy of introduction, Drogo among them, but also Guillaume Charpentier and Clarambold de Vendeuil both of whom I recognised from the army of the dread Emicho of Leisingen, and then the Duke did the same, introducing his brother, Baudoin, Geoffroi of Esch, Baudoin le Bourg, Baudoin of Stavelot and some others. Many of the women were there and were also introduced, including Comte Baudoin's wife, Godivere.

I had seen very little of Baudoin's lady in recent weeks. She spent most days in the tents set aside for her and the children and the other noble ladies of the camp, occasionally taking brief walks for fresh air and exercise with other groups of ladies and their families, always accompanied by a number of personal guards. Now, as I saw her for the first time in several weeks, she appeared drawn and tired. Still beautiful, she looked pale and sickly and she seemed to sway a bit on her feet as though exhausted. Nonetheless, she comported herself well and received an affectionate hug and kiss from the brother of the King of the Franks. She eschewed any such familiarity from any of the other of his comrades, though, immediately stepping back behind her husband, for which I was happy. I could not imagine that pig Drogo's lips profaning the delicate ivory of her cheek.

Soon the great lords retired to one of the larger tents nearby the square and the crowd around it began to disperse to whatever regular routines demanded their attentions. Geoffroi of Esch sent a boy to collect me, as I had expected since the Comte earlier had informed me that my presence as chronicler would be required at the meeting, and I was ushered quietly and discreetly into the meeting tent. I found an empty stool set aside for me, placed unobtrusively near one of the canvas walls within hearing of the meeting, and took out from under my cloak the wooden case in which I kept my parchments, inks and writing implements. The flat oaken coffer also served as an impromptu desk for these occasions where I had no access to anything more conventional.

Duke Godfroi spoke, relating the journey the Frankish army had made through the Lotharingian lands, Hungary and into the Empire of the Greeks. Hugh listened attentively, occasionally asking a question or inquiring further clarification. He seemed genuinely interested and concerned about the welfare of these countrymen settled here temporarily outside Constantinople so far from their homeland. When Godfroi had finished, Hugh cleared his throat and spoke.

Hugh must have explained to the company that he had not been a prisoner of the Emperor but rather a guest for now he spoke on the latter's behalf. "Cousin," he said to the Duke, "know you are welcome in these lands by the Emperor, Alexius Comnenus. He wishes me to tell you that he is grateful for your devotion and that of your people to God's holy work as he is grateful to the Blessed Father Urban for bringing its necessity to the attention of the lords of the West."

The Duke smiled and nodded graciously. Baudoin, his brother, merely scowled.

I furiously scribbled, trying to take down every word.

"Now that you have arrived, the Emperor wishes for you to move across the strait of St. George to the far shore as soon as you are rested and it is possible for your army to continue its journey. A place called Pelecanum has been prepared for you a few days' journey from the farther shore. There you may wait for the other armies of the West, and from there you may take the Holy Father's, and the Emperor's, war into the East. He wishes to assure you that all manner of assistance will be provided to that end."

Duke Godfroi responded in a gracious tone. "And we are most grateful for that assistance of course. When may we expect to receive the benefits of the Emperor Alexius's largesse? We need food for our people, fodder for the horses, additional weapons, guides to take us through the lands across the strait. The St. George, you say? As you have mentioned, we must also wait for the other Frankish armies to arrive here and so we must be sustained by the Greeks' generosity until such time as they do come. My messengers tell me that it may be several more months before the other counts, Raymond of St. Gilles, Robert of Flanders, Stephen of Blois and others who are making their way to the great city on the Holy Father's armed pilgrimage, reach Constantinople. Will the Emperor provide for us until then?"

Hugh bowed his head in acknowledgement of all that Godfroi had said. "Of course," he replied. "You shall have all these things and more. The Emperor recognises that you have arrived here long before the Easter Holy Week rendezvous time determined and sanctioned at Clermont one year past; but he is nonetheless grateful for your enthusiastic devotion to Urban's cause and his own. He will happily provide all that your people require until such time as the other lords arrive with their armies."

"Excellent. Then we have an accord," Godfroi said jovially. "When we have resupplied and rested we will move on."

But Hugh of Vermandois hesitated, clearing his throat. "There is just one condition. One thing the Emperor Alexius expects of you and your lords in return."

"Now we find the pickle in the wine vat," commented Comte Baudoin loudly. Hugh ignored the remark and continued to look directly at Godfroi.

"The Emperor requires of you and all your leading lords an oath of fealty to him, recognising that he is the rightful overlord and suzerain of all lands you may conquer, all the way to Jerusalem. That such lands having been conquered are held from him in fief. That he is the natural overlord of all those domains which are a part of the Roman Empire in the East. If you swear this oath then he will see to all of your needs from here to Jerusalem."

At this revelation, the Frankish lords exploded in violent protestations. The tumult continued for some time as the great men raged against this proposal brought by the prince. Godfroi spent a long period in close discussion with his brother and some other lords while the rest shouted profanities and roared their displeasure. Then, at last, the Duke stood and raised his arms, calling for silence among the gathering.

He spoke to Hugh of Vermandois, "My lord prince. We will not do this. We will not swear allegiance to the Greek emperor and violate our prior oaths."

To which the prince replied haughtily, "You must, cousin. Without the oath you will be forbidden ships with which to cross the strait and to carry on to the East and the emperor will deny you sustenance."

Godfroi was unimpressed. "The Roman Emperor Henri is my liege lord. I have no other. I cannot rescind that oath in favour of the Greek. Would you have me offend my true liege lord? How can you ask such a thing? Would you take such an oath and deny the authority over you of your brother, the King of Francia?"

Hugh cleared his throat self-consciously and shook his head. "I understand that you are oath-bound to Henri, nonetheless you must swear homage to the Emperor Alexius if you would have anything of his munificence. The Emperor also requests, as do I, your presence in the city for an interview with him that we may all discuss issues of mutual concern."

Godfroi, adamant, replied angrily, "I will not come! I most certainly will not suffer such an insult in person at the knee of Alexius. By point and edge will we reconcile before ever I give this Greek my oath." Then, considering further, as ever a man of discretion, he softened somewhat, "However, I will send a delegation to the city to hear Alexius's terms directly from him. Perhaps some compromise might be reached."

I saw Comte Baudoin smirk at his brother's concession. He would not be among the delegation I was sure.

One chosen to go to the city was Geoffroi of Esch. I believe Godfroi chose him so that the chamberlain might persuade his brother, Henri, who had abandoned our army at Philippopolis, to return to the army. Perhaps he hoped that Henri might also have information about the Emperor's plans for us and the other armies of the West.

The Duke then named Baudoin of le Bourg, Baudoin of Stavelot and Werner of Grez to accompany Prince Hugh to Constantinople to meet the Emperor. My lord Comte Baudoin leaned over to his brother and whispered something in his ear at which Godfroi nodded and then, much to my surprise, named me as well. Once again, my ability to speak the Greek tongue took me along into the paths of the great ones.

Just after sext, our illustrious company of Franks, and me accompanying them of course, travelled down the road alongside the Golden Horn and through the Blachernae Gate. Thus, I arrived, at long last, at the Metro Polis, the capital city of the Emperor Alexius, Constantinople.

Explicit Pars I. Incipit Pars II.